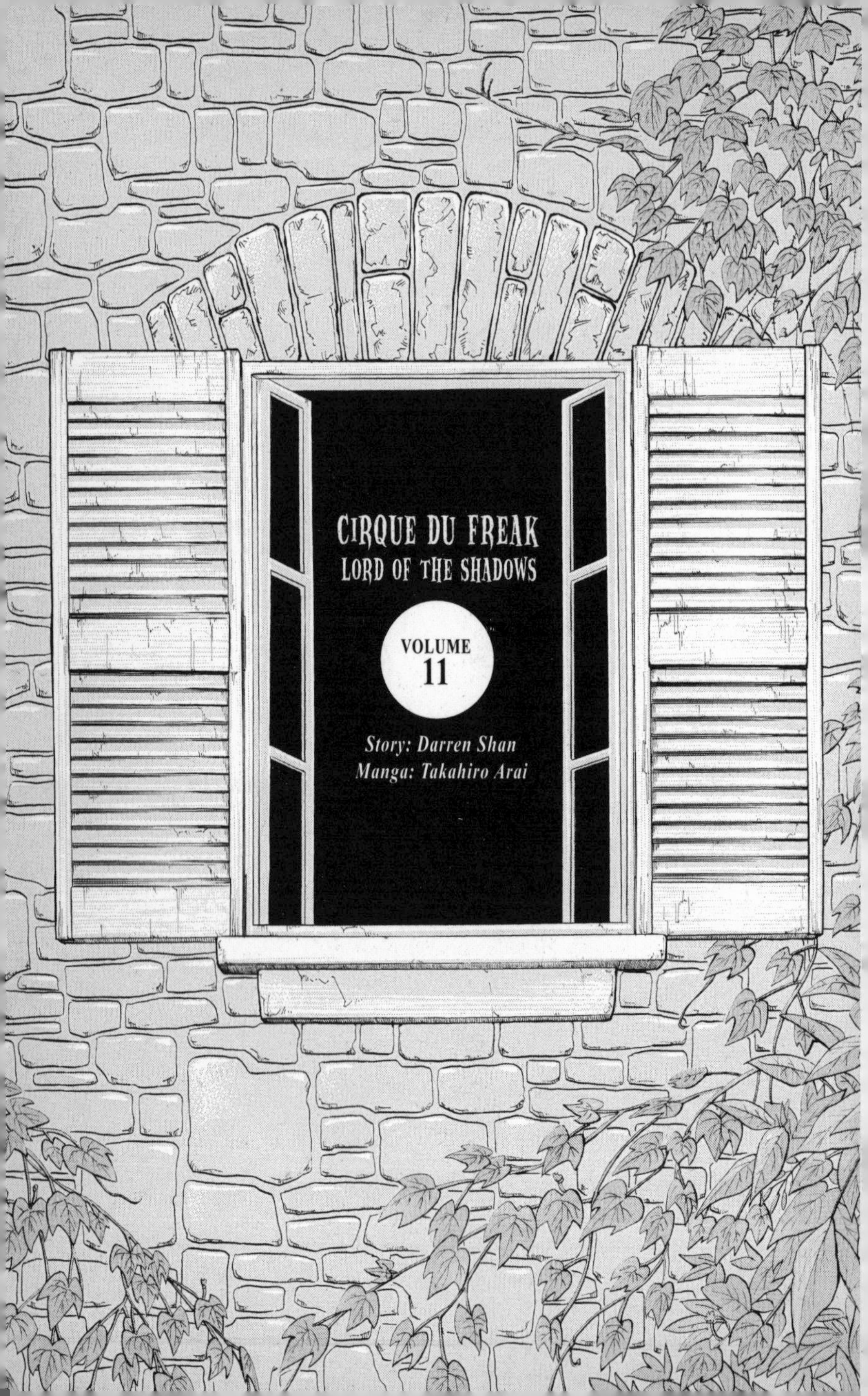
CIRQUE DU FREAK
LORD OF THE SHADOWS
VOLUME 11
Story: Darren Shan
Manga: Takahiro Arai

## A SUMMARY OF THE LAKE OF SOULS:

SEEKING TO OVERCOME THE LOSS OF HIS MENTOR, MR. CREPSLEY, DARREN JOINS HIS FRIEND HARKAT ON A TRIP TO A WORLD OF MONSTERS THROUGH MR. TINY'S MAGIC. DARREN AND HARKAT JOURNEY THROUGH THIS WORLD UNTIL THEY REACH THE LAKE OF SOULS, WHERE THEY LEARN THAT IN HIS FORMER LIFE, HARKAT WAS KURDA SMAHLT. OFFERING THEIR FAREWELLS TO KURDA, DARREN AND HARKAT RETURN HOME, WHERE THEY ARE SHOCKED TO LEARN THAT THIS ALTER-NATE WORLD WAS SIMPLY THE FUTURE, LONG AFTER THE WAR OF THE SCARS HAS CONCLUDED...

CIRQUE DU FREAK 11
# CONTENTS

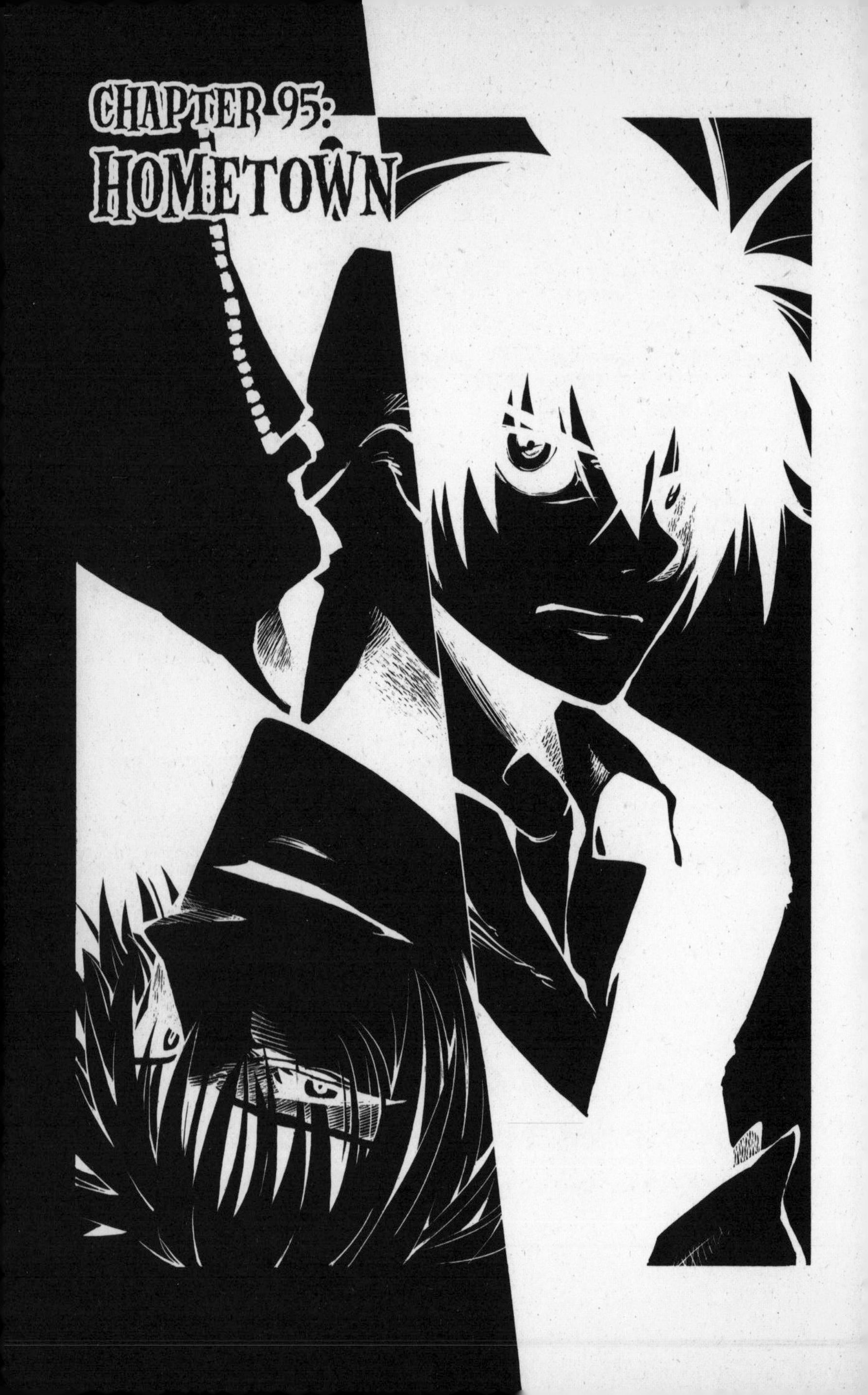
CHAPTER 95:
HOMETOWN

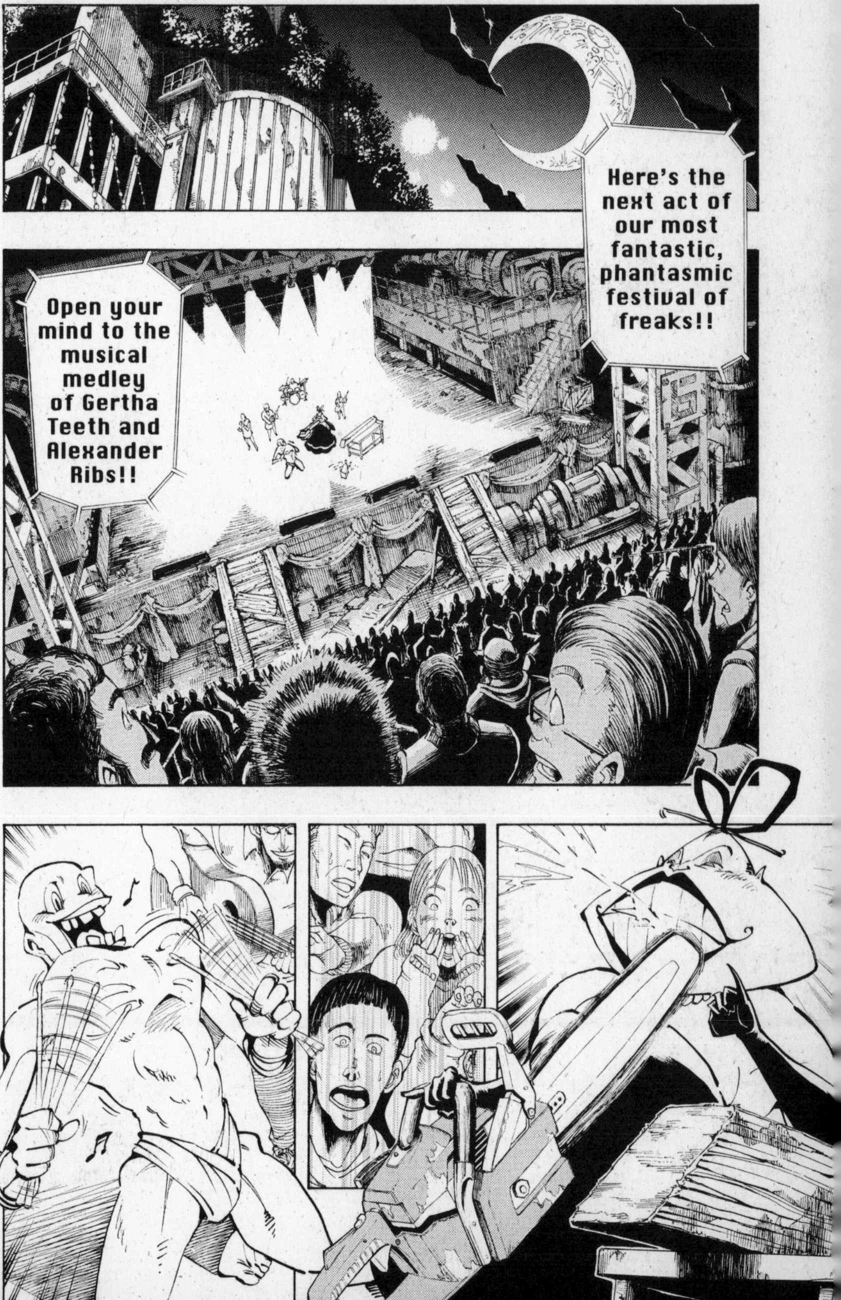
Here's the next act of our most fantastic, phantasmic festival of freaks!!
Open your mind to the musical medley of Gertha Teeth and Alexander Ribs!!

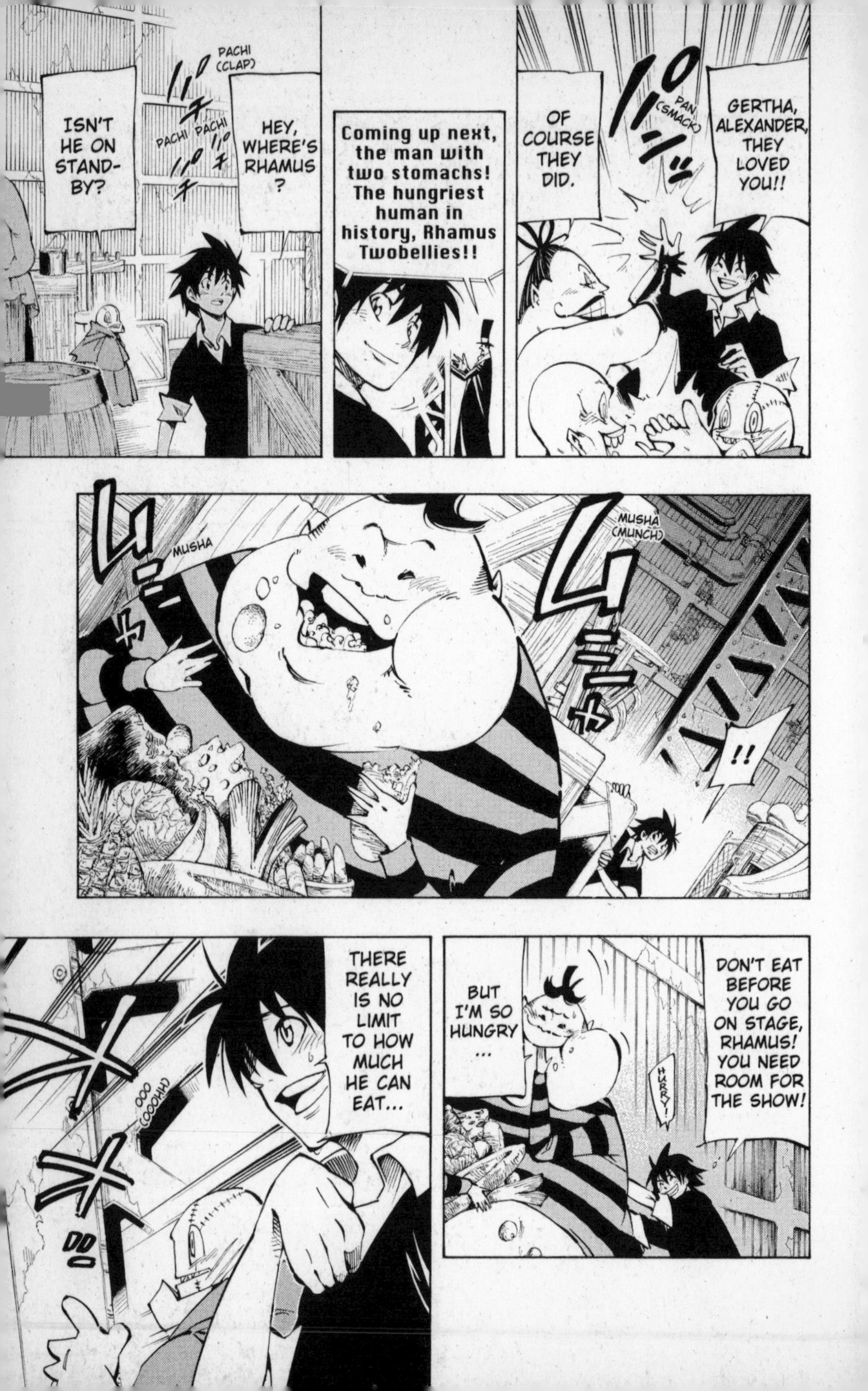
GERTHA, ALEXANDER, THEY LOVED YOU!!
PAN (SMACK)
OF COURSE THEY DID.
Coming up next, the man with two stomachs! The hungriest human in history, Rhamus Twobellies!!
HEY, WHERE'S RHAMUS?
PACHI (CLAP)
PACHI PACHI
ISN'T HE ON STANDBY?
MUSHA (MUNCH)
MUSHA
!!
DON'T EAT BEFORE YOU GO ON STAGE, RHAMUS! YOU NEED ROOM FOR THE SHOW!
HURRY!
BUT I'M SO HUNGRY ...
THERE REALLY IS NO LIMIT TO HOW MUCH HE CAN EAT...
OOO (OOOHH)

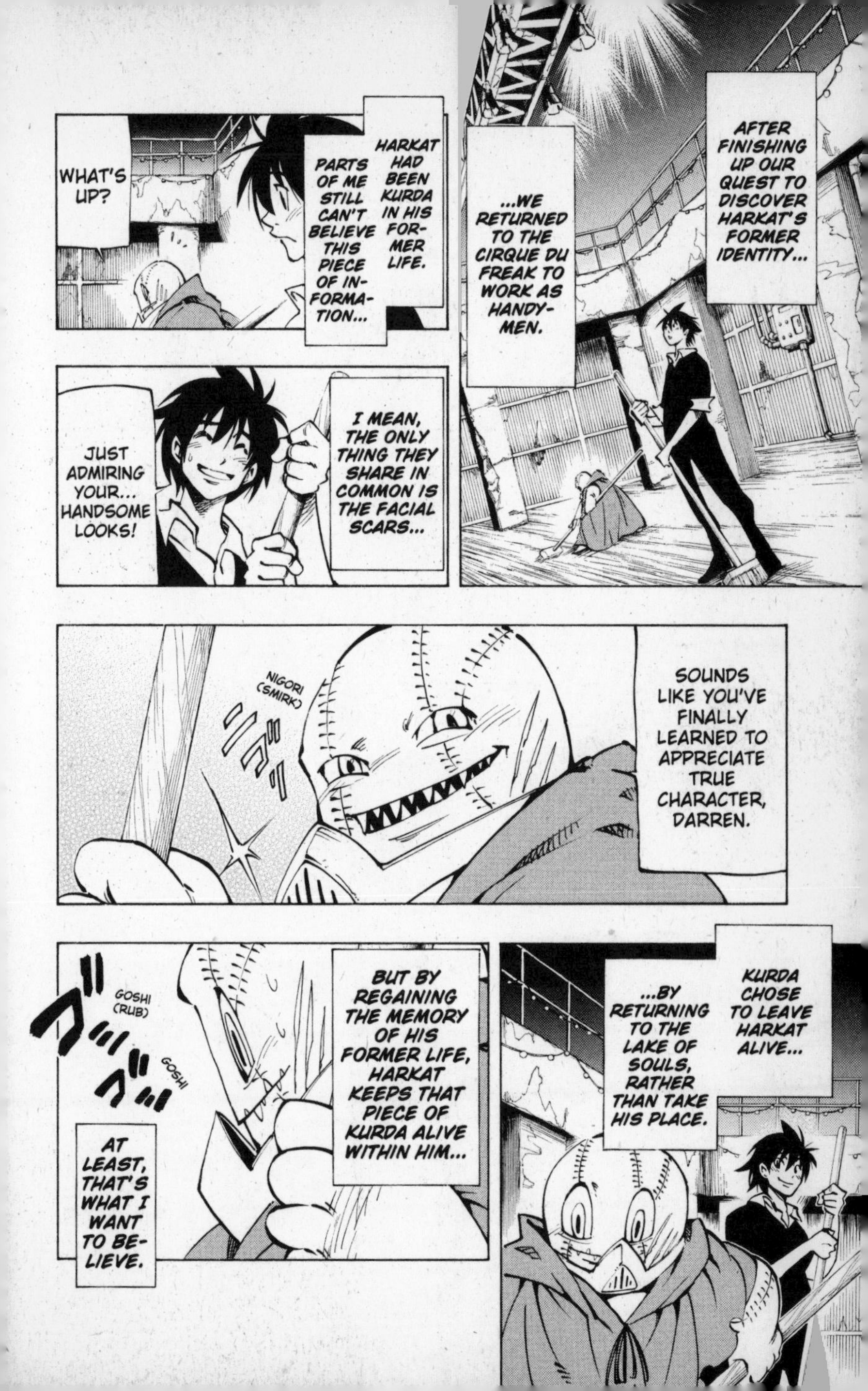
AFTER FINISHING UP OUR QUEST TO DISCOVER HARKAT'S FORMER IDENTITY...
...WE RETURNED TO THE CIRQUE DU FREAK TO WORK AS HANDYMEN.
HARKAT HAD BEEN KURDA IN HIS FORMER LIFE.
PARTS OF ME STILL CAN'T BELIEVE THIS PIECE OF INFORMATION...
WHAT'S UP?
I MEAN, THE ONLY THING THEY SHARE IN COMMON IS THE FACIAL SCARS...
JUST ADMIRING YOUR... HANDSOME LOOKS!
SOUNDS LIKE YOU'VE FINALLY LEARNED TO APPRECIATE TRUE CHARACTER, DARREN.
NIGORI (SMIRK)
KURDA CHOSE TO LEAVE HARKAT ALIVE...
...BY RETURNING TO THE LAKE OF SOULS, RATHER THAN TAKE HIS PLACE.
BUT BY REGAINING THE MEMORY OF HIS FORMER LIFE, HARKAT KEEPS THAT PIECE OF KURDA ALIVE WITHIN HIM...
GOSHI (RUB)
GOSHI
AT LEAST, THAT'S WHAT I WANT TO BELIEVE.

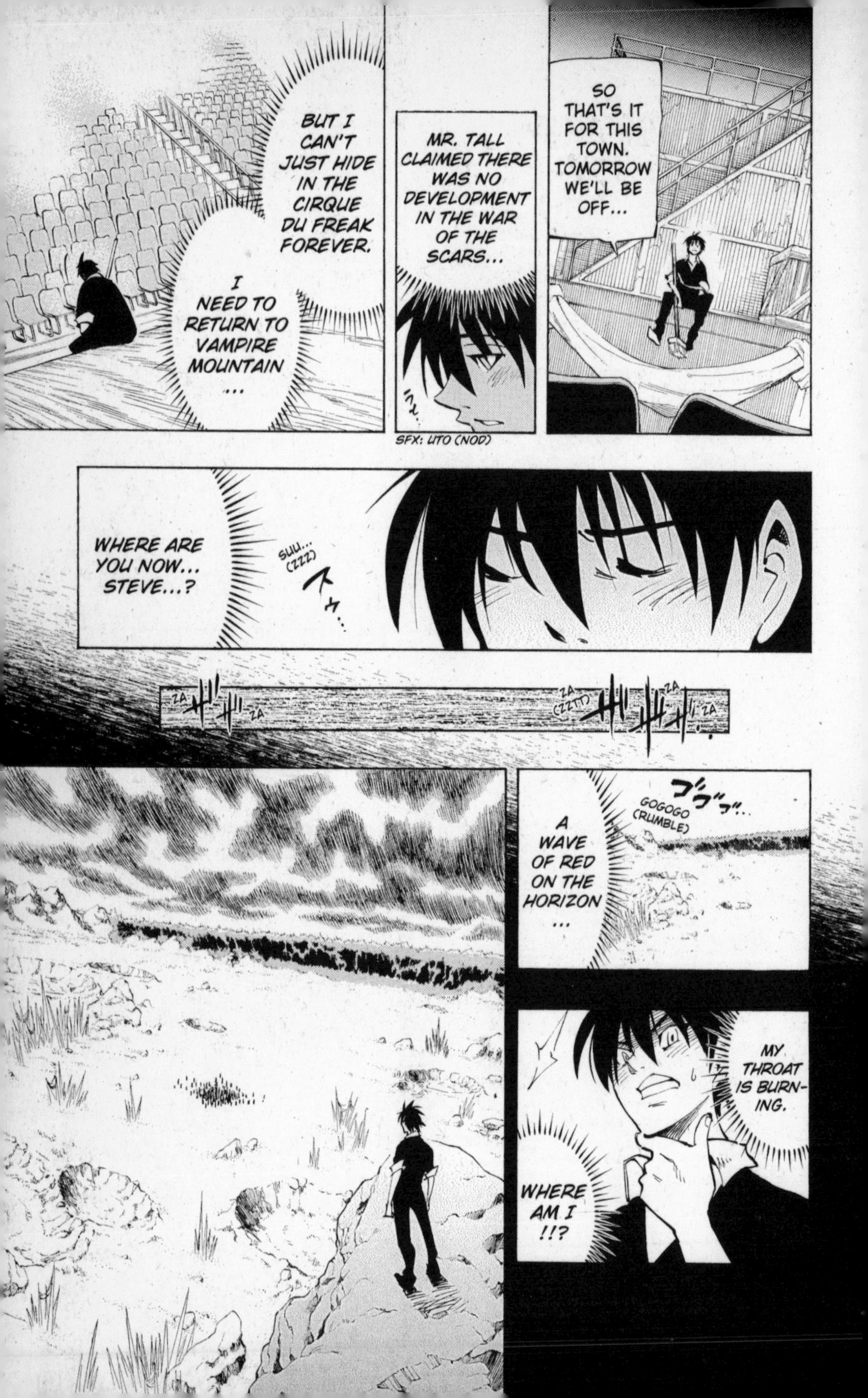
SO THAT'S IT FOR THIS TOWN. TOMORROW WE'LL BE OFF...
MR. TALL CLAIMED THERE WAS NO DEVELOPMENT IN THE WAR OF THE SCARS...
SFX: UTO (NOD)
BUT I CAN'T JUST HIDE IN THE CIRQUE DU FREAK FOREVER.
I NEED TO RETURN TO VAMPIRE MOUNTAIN...
WHERE ARE YOU NOW... STEVE...?
SUU... (ZZZ)
ZA (ZZTT)
ZA
ZA
ZA
ZA
GOGOGO (RUMBLE)
A WAVE OF RED ON THE HORIZON...
MY THROAT IS BURN-ING.
WHERE AM I !!?

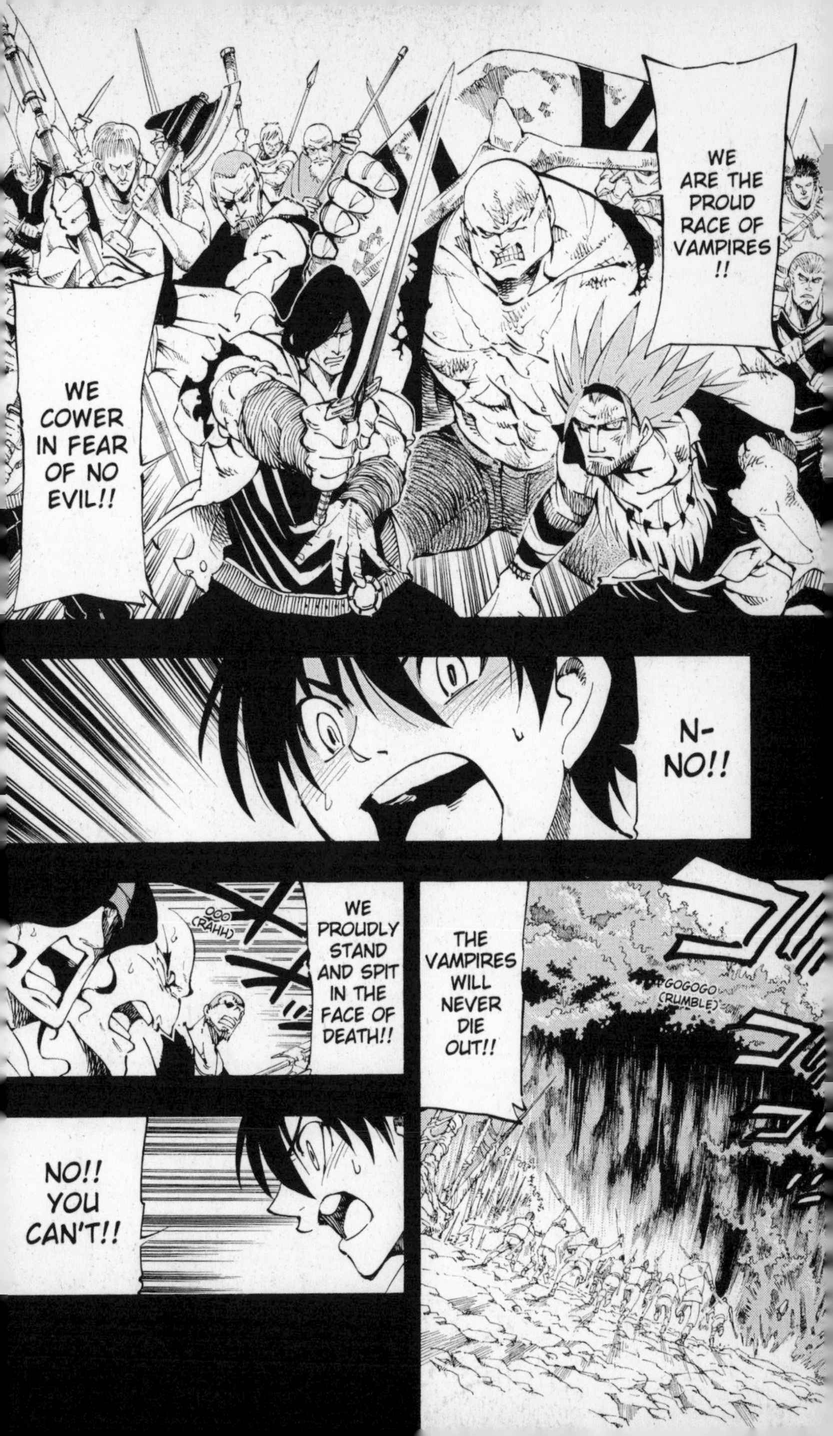
WE ARE THE PROUD RACE OF VAMPIRES!!
WE COWER IN FEAR OF NO EVIL!!
N-NO!!
THE VAMPIRES WILL NEVER DIE OUT!!
GOGOGO (RUMBLE)
WE PROUDLY STAND AND SPIT IN THE FACE OF DEATH!!
OOO (RAHH)
NO!! YOU CAN'T!!

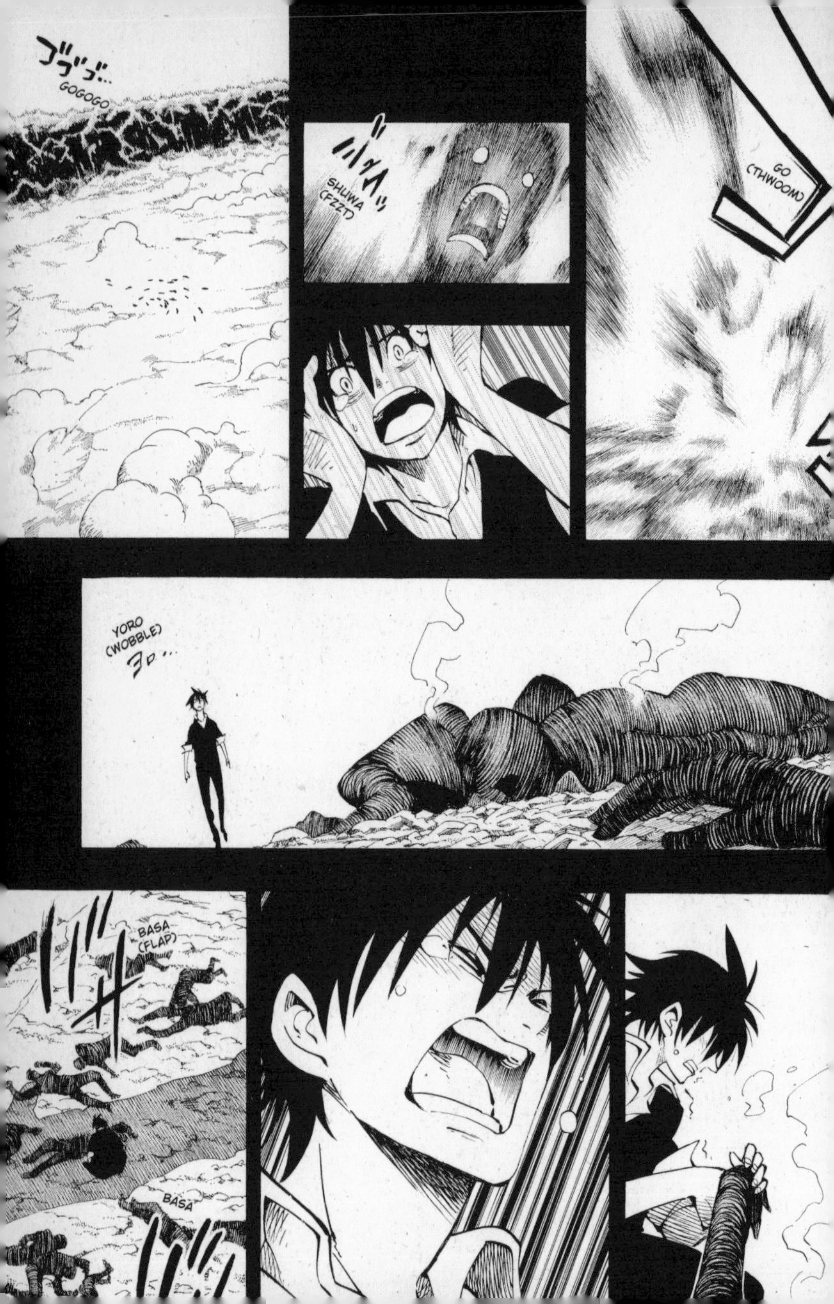

GO (THWOOM)
SHUWA (FZZT)
ゴゴゴ…
GOGOGO
YORO (WOBBLE)
ヨロ…
BASA (FLAP)
BASA

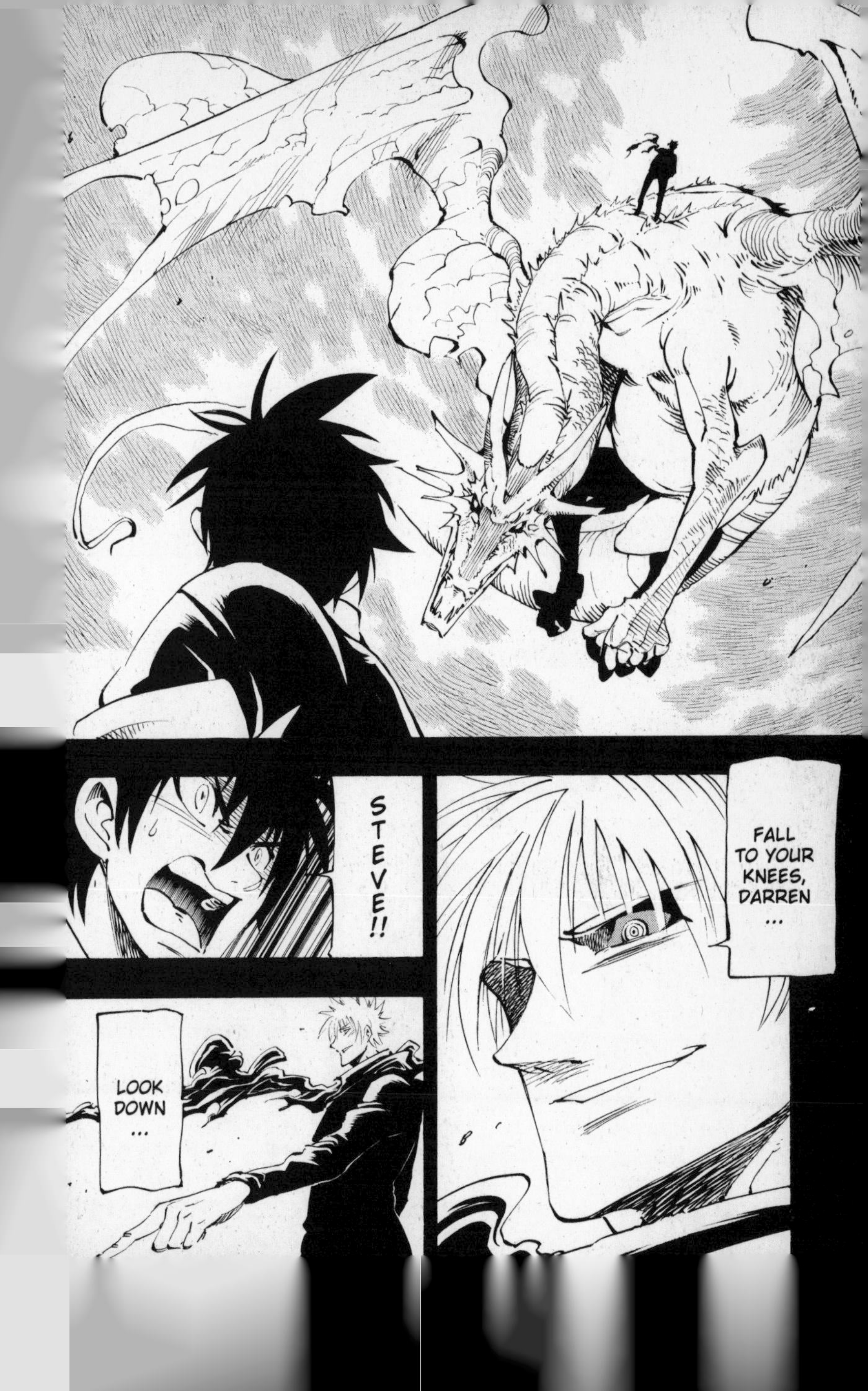
FALL TO YOUR KNEES, DARREN ...
STEVE!!
LOOK DOWN ...

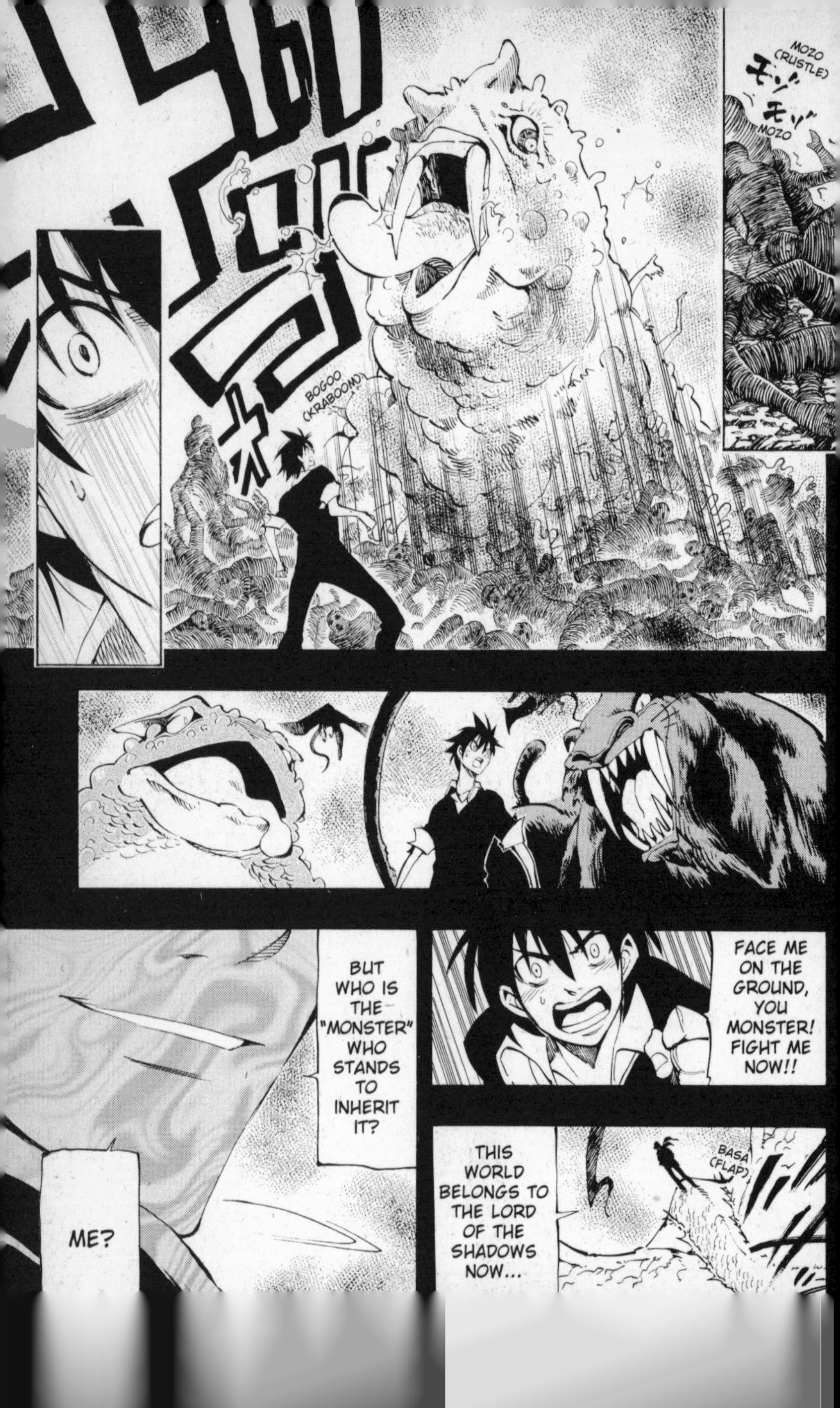
MOZO (RUSTLE)
モゾ
モゾ
MOZO
BOGOO (KRABOOM)
FACE ME ON THE GROUND, YOU MONSTER! FIGHT ME NOW!!
BASA (FLAP)
THIS WORLD BELONGS TO THE LORD OF THE SHADOWS NOW...
BUT WHO IS THE "MONSTER" WHO STANDS TO INHERIT IT?
ME?

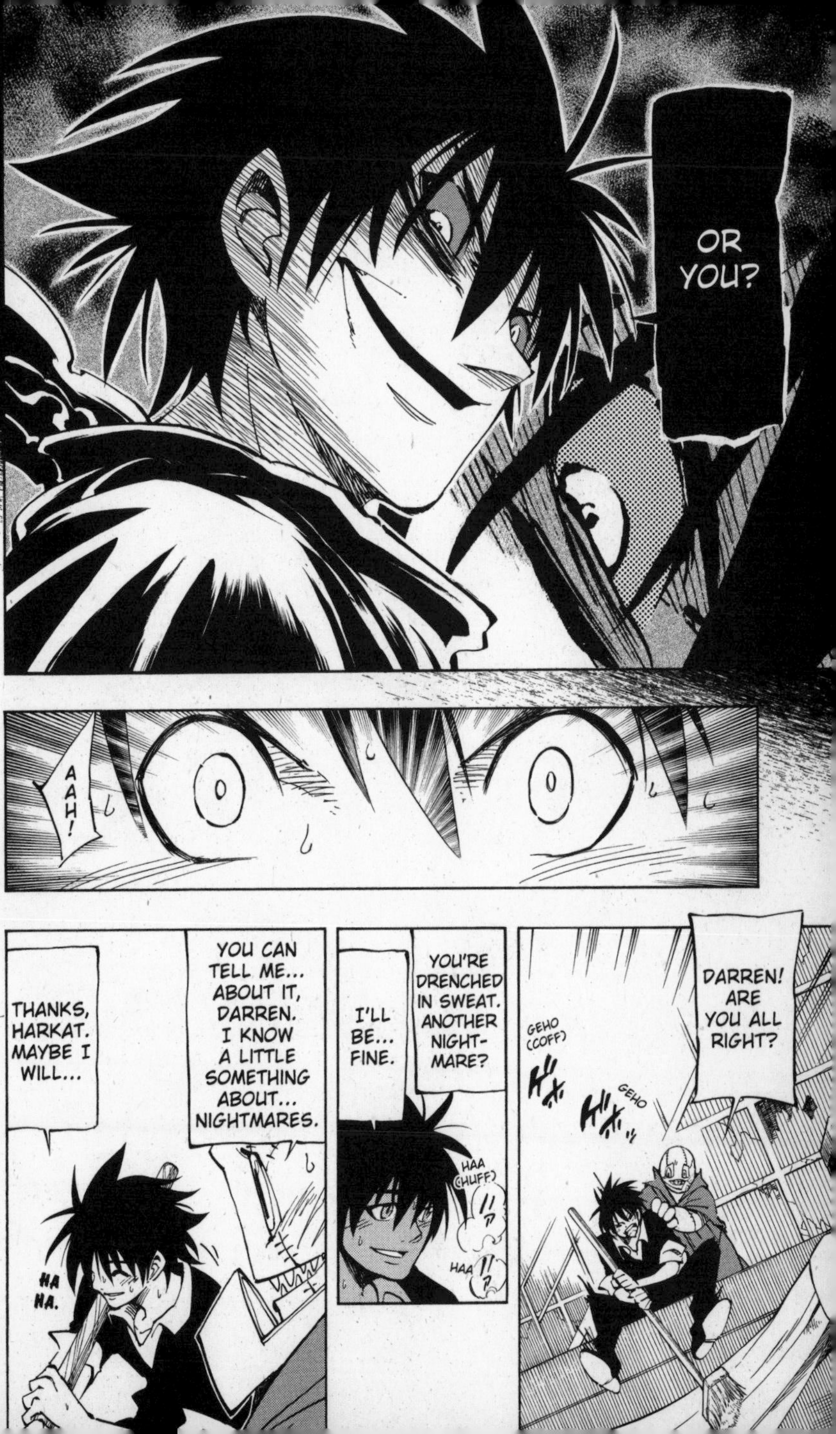
OR YOU?
AAH!
DARREN! ARE YOU ALL RIGHT?
GEHO (COFF)
GEHO
YOU'RE DRENCHED IN SWEAT. ANOTHER NIGHT-MARE?
I'LL BE... FINE.
HAA (HUFF)
HAA
YOU CAN TELL ME... ABOUT IT, DARREN. I KNOW A LITTLE SOMETHING ABOUT... NIGHTMARES.
THANKS, HARKAT. MAYBE I WILL...
HA HA.

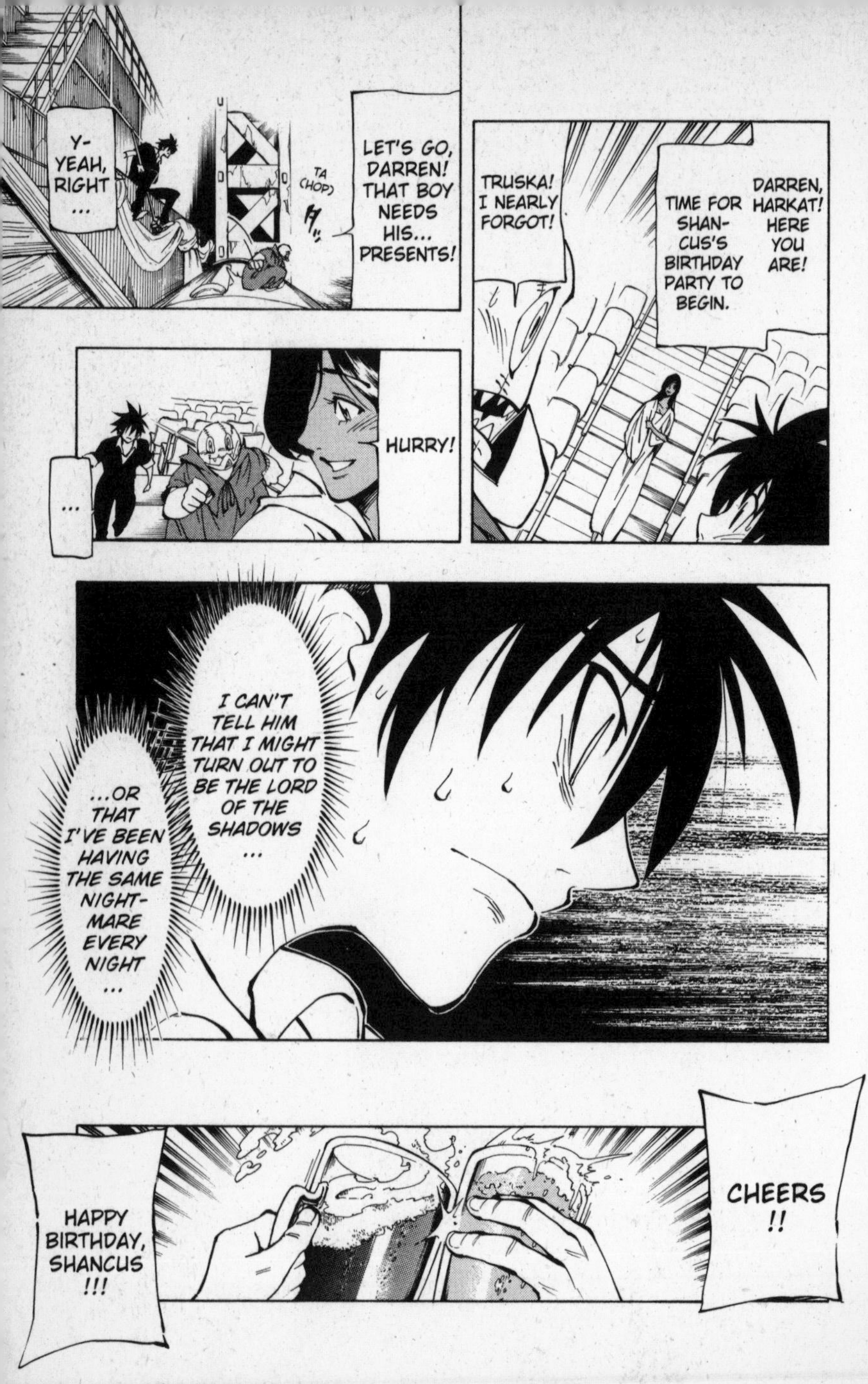
LET'S GO, DARREN! THAT BOY NEEDS HIS... PRESENTS!
TA (HOP)
Y-YEAH, RIGHT ...
DARREN, HARKAT! HERE YOU ARE! TIME FOR SHANCUS'S BIRTHDAY PARTY TO BEGIN.
TRUSKA! I NEARLY FORGOT!
HURRY!
...
I CAN'T TELL HIM THAT I MIGHT TURN OUT TO BE THE LORD OF THE SHADOWS ...
...OR THAT I'VE BEEN HAVING THE SAME NIGHTMARE EVERY NIGHT ...
CHEERS !!
HAPPY BIRTHDAY, SHANCUS !!!

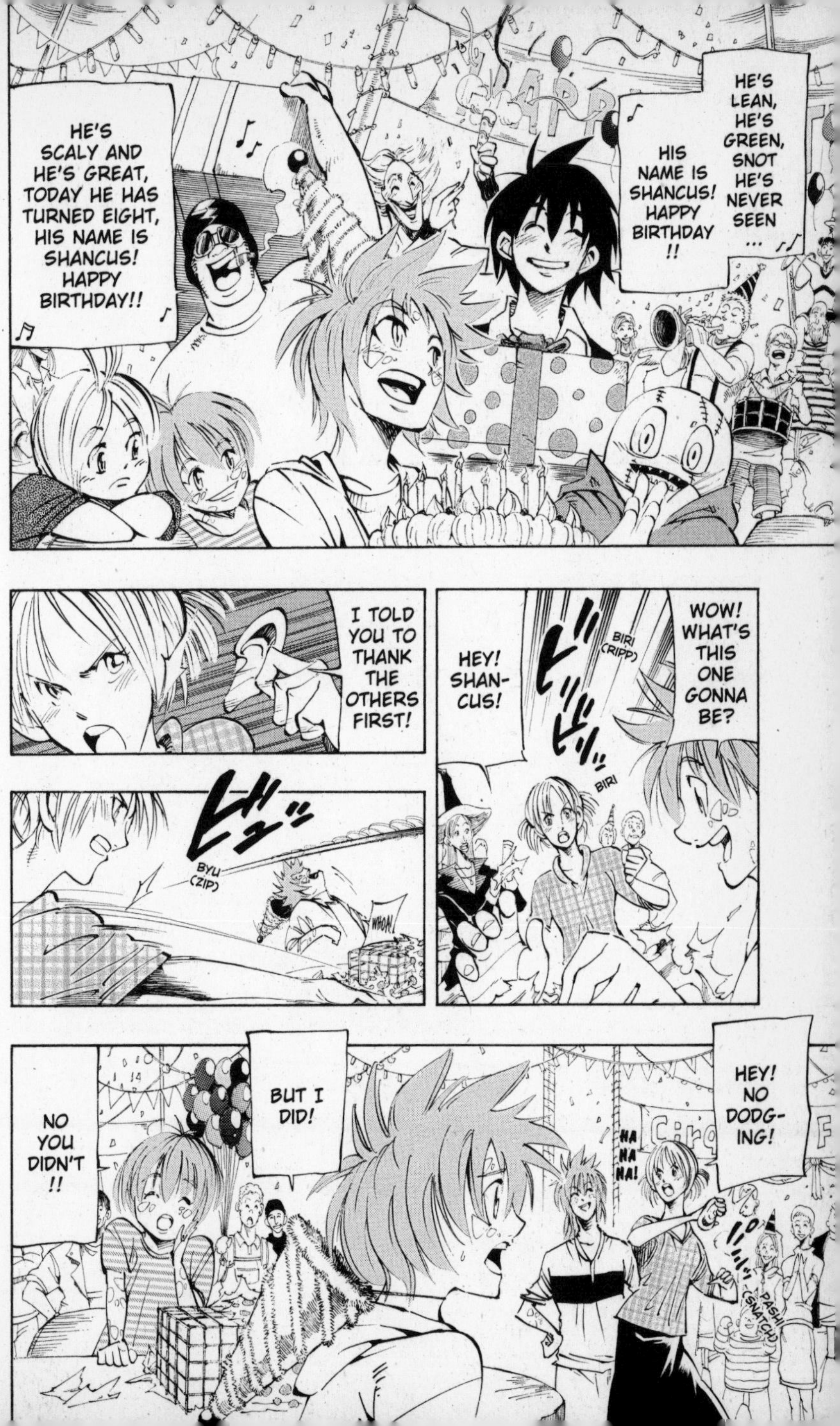
HE'S LEAN, HE'S GREEN, SNOT HE'S NEVER SEEN ...
HIS NAME IS SHANCUS! HAPPY BIRTHDAY !!
HE'S SCALY AND HE'S GREAT, TODAY HE HAS TURNED EIGHT, HIS NAME IS SHANCUS! HAPPY BIRTHDAY!!
WOW! WHAT'S THIS ONE GONNA BE?
BIRI (RIPP)
HEY! SHAN-CUS!
BIRI
I TOLD YOU TO THANK THE OTHERS FIRST!
BYU (ZIP)
WHOA!
HEY! NO DODG-ING!
PASHI (SNATCH)
HA HA HA!
BUT I DID!
NO YOU DIDN'T !!

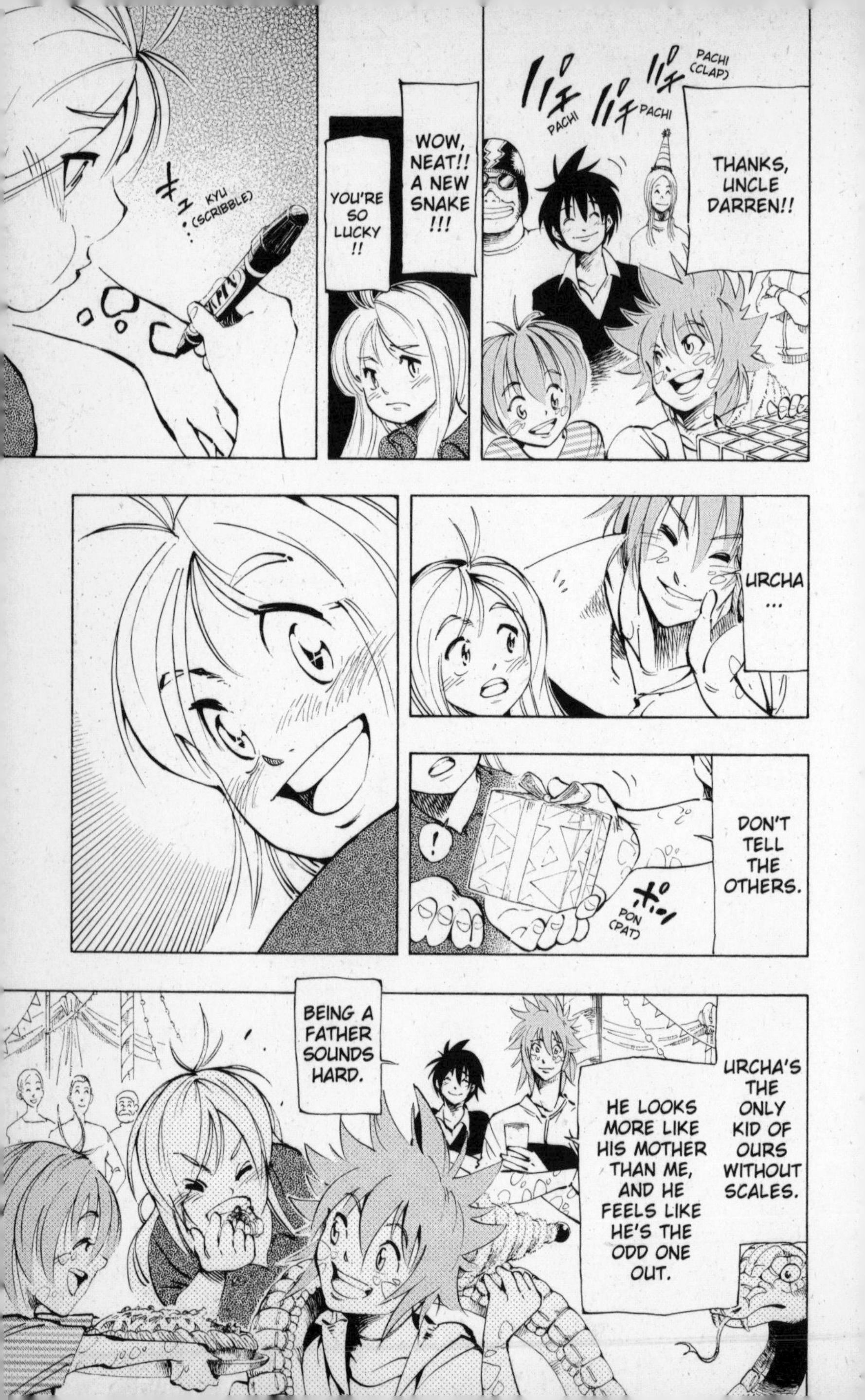
PACHI (CLAP)
PACHI
PACHI
THANKS, UNCLE DARREN!!
WOW, NEAT!! A NEW SNAKE!!!
YOU'RE SO LUCKY!!
KYU (SCRIBBLE)
URCHA...
DON'T TELL THE OTHERS.
PON (PAT)
URCHA'S THE ONLY KID OF OURS WITHOUT SCALES.
HE LOOKS MORE LIKE HIS MOTHER THAN ME, AND HE FEELS LIKE HE'S THE ODD ONE OUT.
BEING A FATHER SOUNDS HARD.

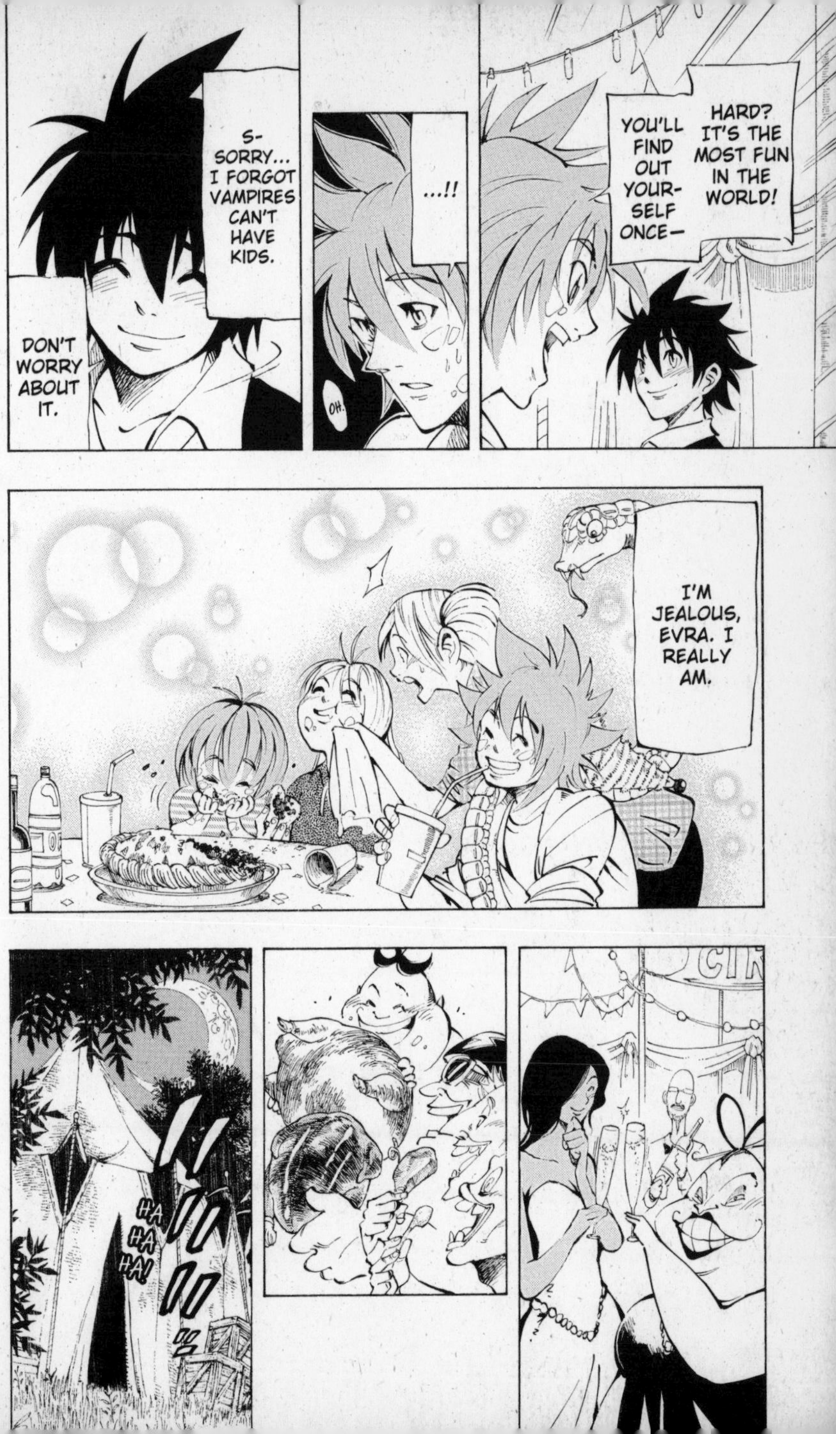
HARD? IT'S THE MOST FUN IN THE WORLD!
YOU'LL FIND OUT YOUR-SELF ONCE—
...!!
OH.
S-SORRY... I FORGOT VAMPIRES CAN'T HAVE KIDS.
DON'T WORRY ABOUT IT.
I'M JEALOUS, EVRA. I REALLY AM.
HA HA HA!

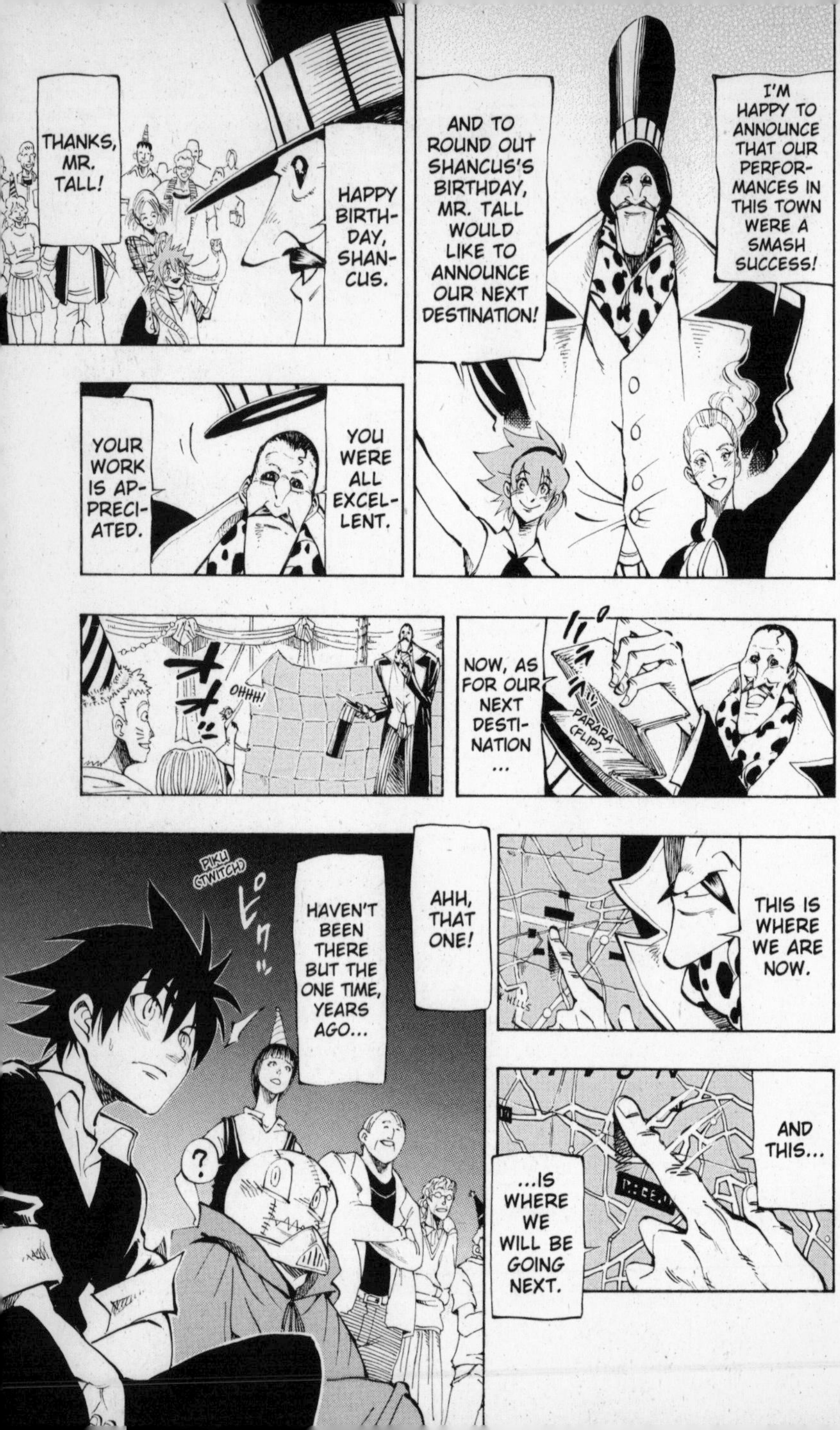
I'M HAPPY TO ANNOUNCE THAT OUR PERFORMANCES IN THIS TOWN WERE A SMASH SUCCESS!
AND TO ROUND OUT SHANCUS'S BIRTHDAY, MR. TALL WOULD LIKE TO ANNOUNCE OUR NEXT DESTINATION!
HAPPY BIRTHDAY, SHANCUS.
THANKS, MR. TALL!
YOU WERE ALL EXCELLENT.
YOUR WORK IS APPRECIATED.
NOW, AS FOR OUR NEXT DESTINATION...
PARARA (FLIP)
OHHHH!
THIS IS WHERE WE ARE NOW.
AND THIS...
...IS WHERE WE WILL BE GOING NEXT.
AHH, THAT ONE!
HAVEN'T BEEN THERE BUT THE ONE TIME, YEARS AGO...
PIKU (TWITCH)
?

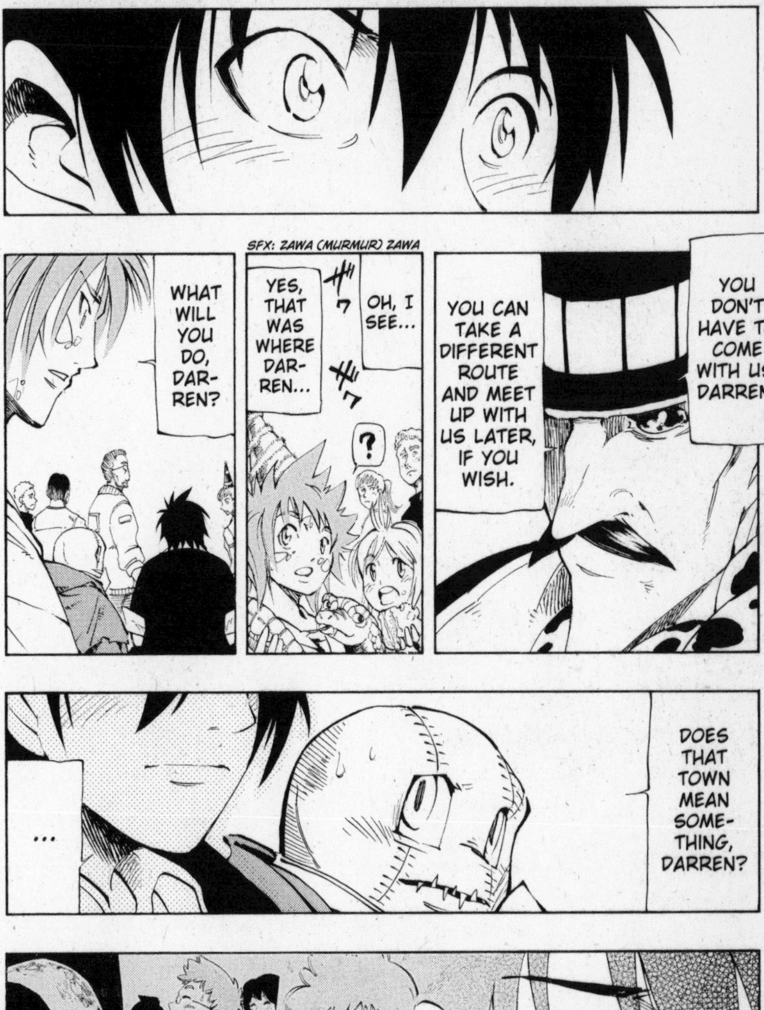
YOU DON'T HAVE TO COME WITH US, DARREN.
YOU CAN TAKE A DIFFERENT ROUTE AND MEET UP WITH US LATER, IF YOU WISH.
SFX: ZAWA (MURMUR) ZAWA
OH, I SEE...
YES, THAT WAS WHERE DAR-REN...
?
WHAT WILL YOU DO, DAR-REN?
DOES THAT TOWN MEAN SOME-THING, DARREN?
...
THAT'S THE TOWN ...

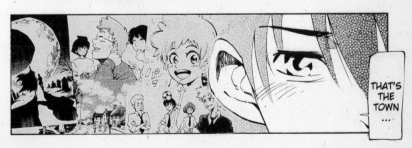

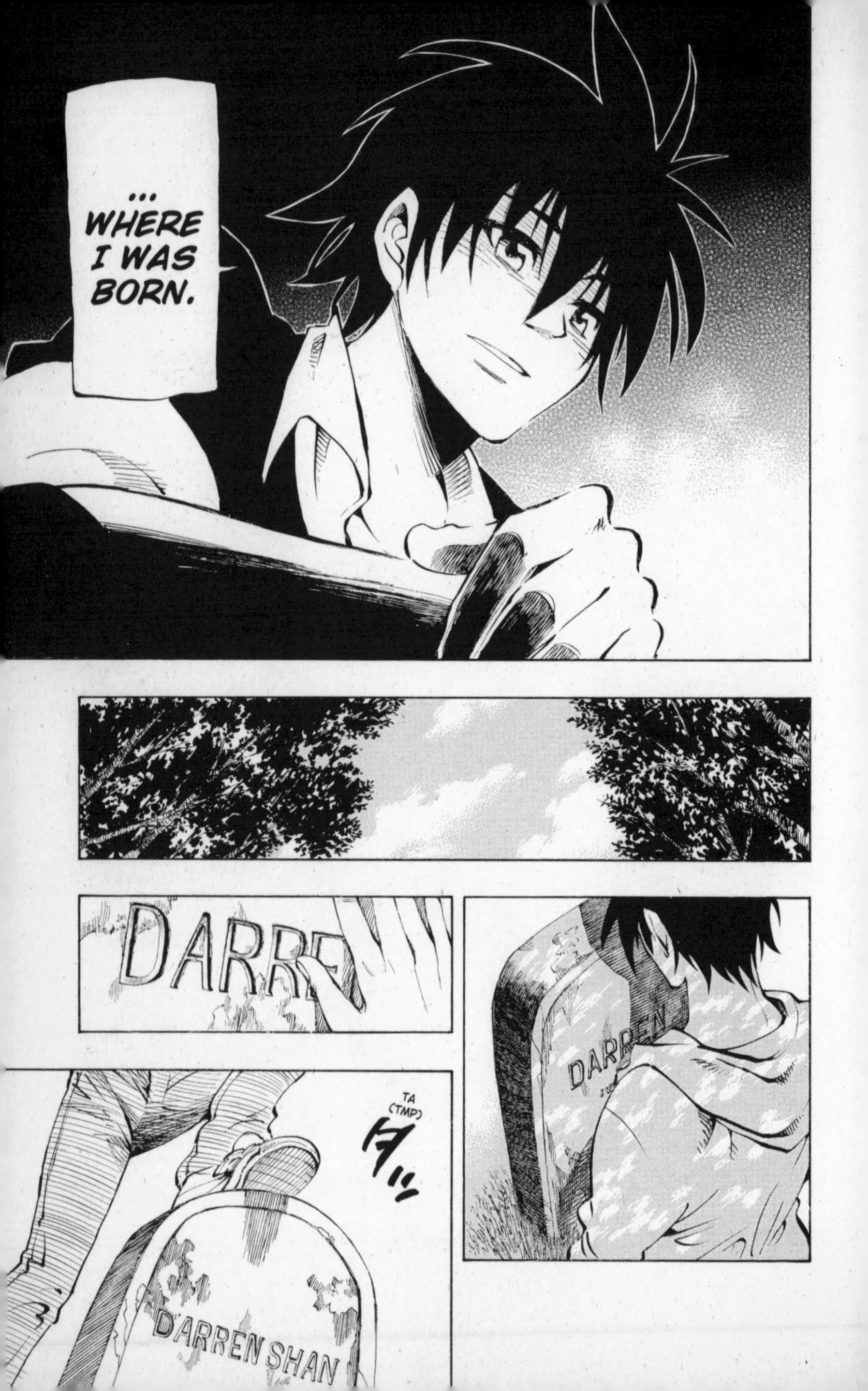

... WHERE I WAS BORN.
DARRE
DARREN
TA (TMP)
DARREN SHAN

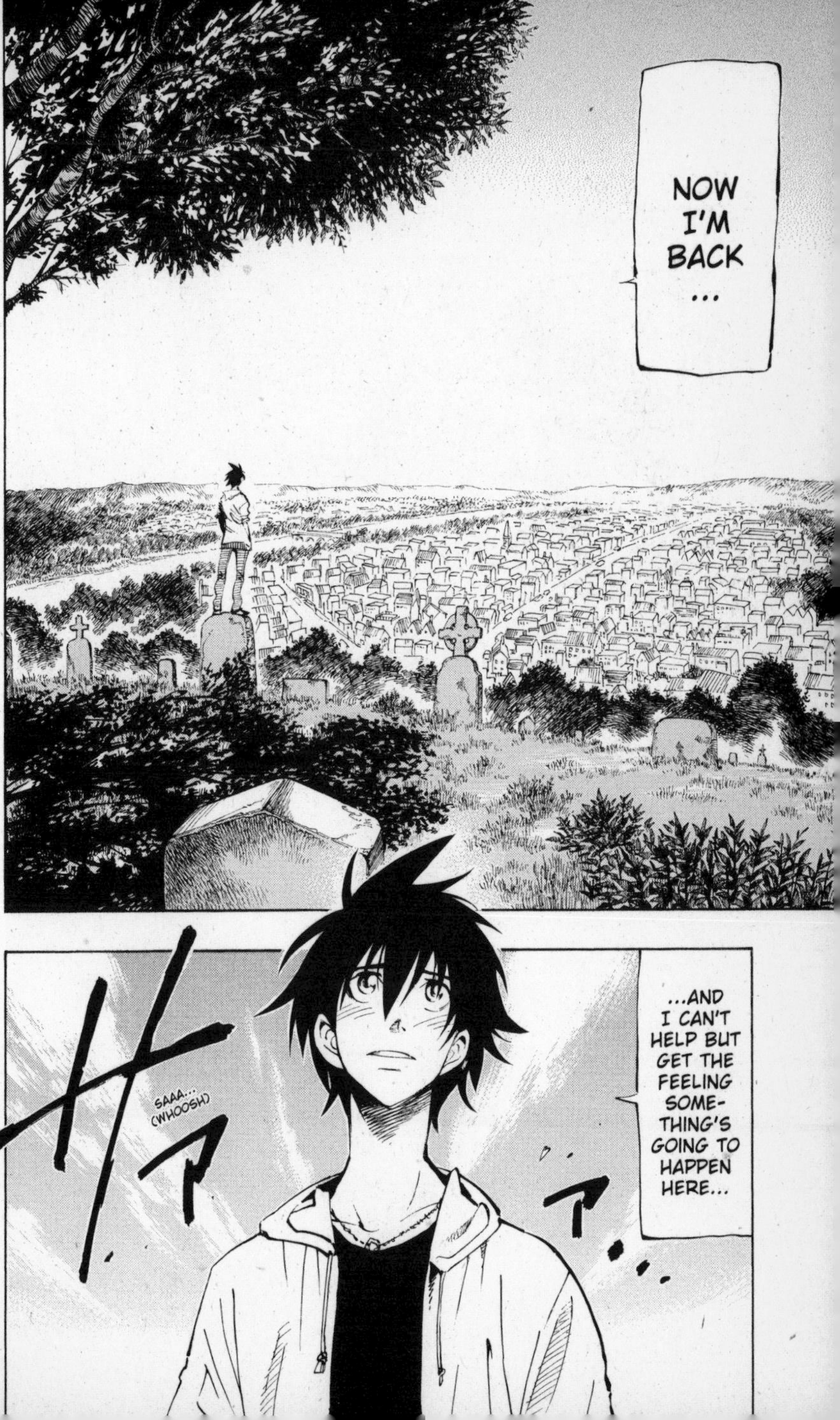
NOW I'M BACK ...
...AND I CAN'T HELP BUT GET THE FEELING SOME-THING'S GOING TO HAPPEN HERE...
SAAA... (WHOOSH)

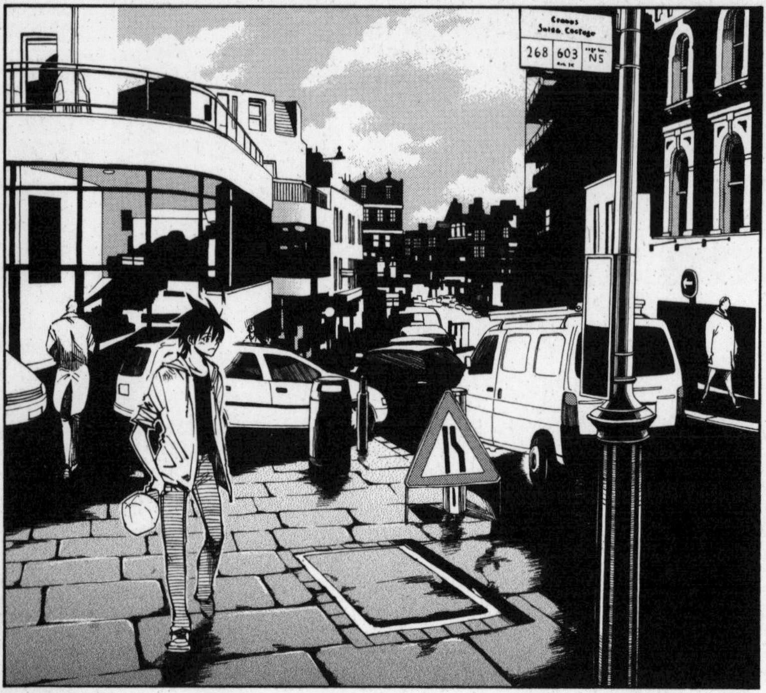
268
603
N5

# CHAPTER 96:
# FAMILY

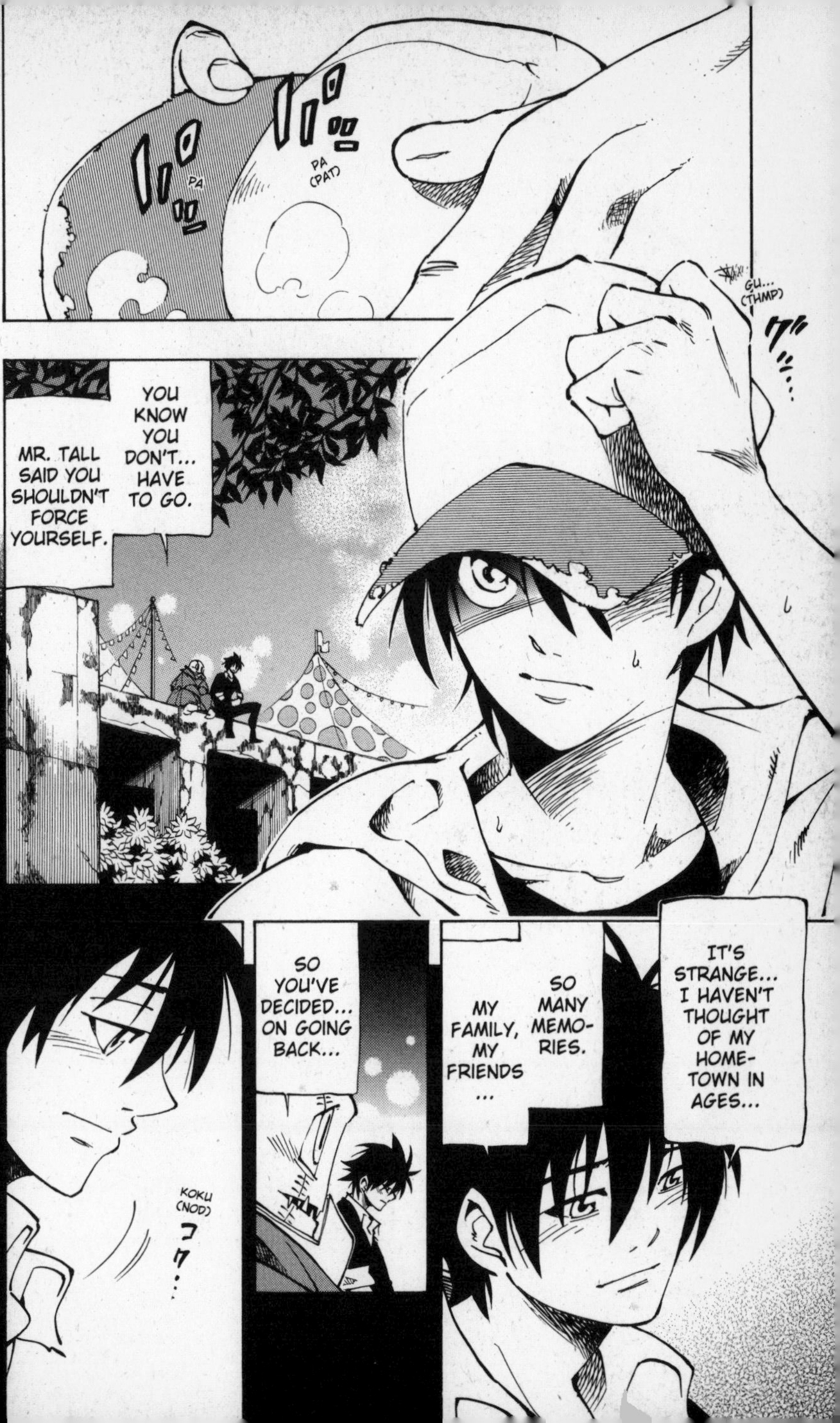
PA (PAT)
PA
GU... (THMP)
YOU KNOW YOU DON'T... HAVE TO GO.
MR. TALL SAID YOU SHOULDN'T FORCE YOURSELF.
IT'S STRANGE... I HAVEN'T THOUGHT OF MY HOME-TOWN IN AGES...
SO MANY MEMO-RIES.
MY FAMILY, MY FRIENDS...
SO YOU'VE DECIDED... ON GOING BACK...
KOKU (NOD)

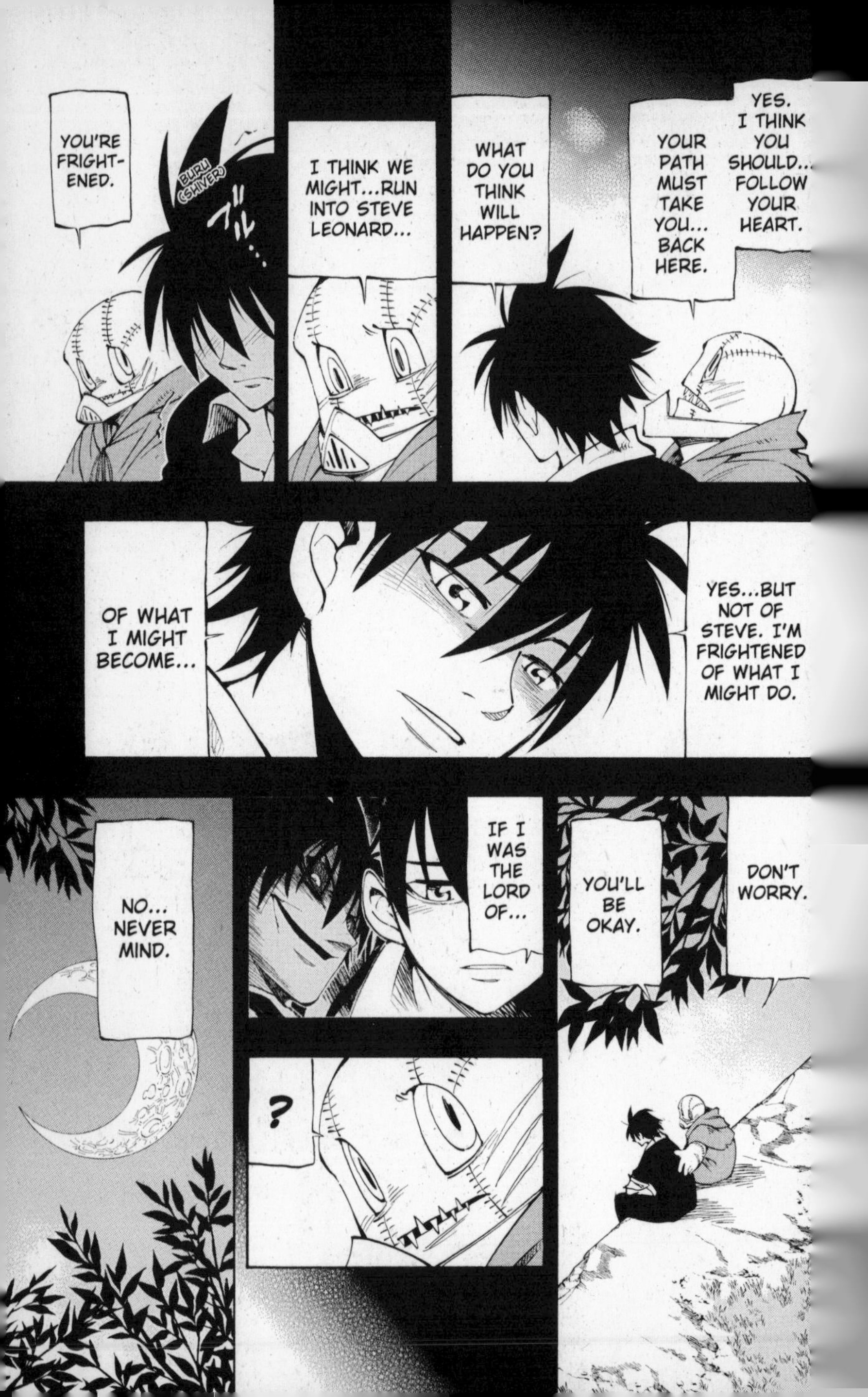
YES. I THINK YOU SHOULD... FOLLOW YOUR HEART.
YOUR PATH MUST TAKE YOU... BACK HERE.
WHAT DO YOU THINK WILL HAPPEN?
I THINK WE MIGHT...RUN INTO STEVE LEONARD...
BURU (SHIVER)
YOU'RE FRIGHT-ENED.
YES...BUT NOT OF STEVE. I'M FRIGHTENED OF WHAT I MIGHT DO.
OF WHAT I MIGHT BECOME...
DON'T WORRY.
YOU'LL BE OKAY.
IF I WAS THE LORD OF...
?
NO... NEVER MIND.

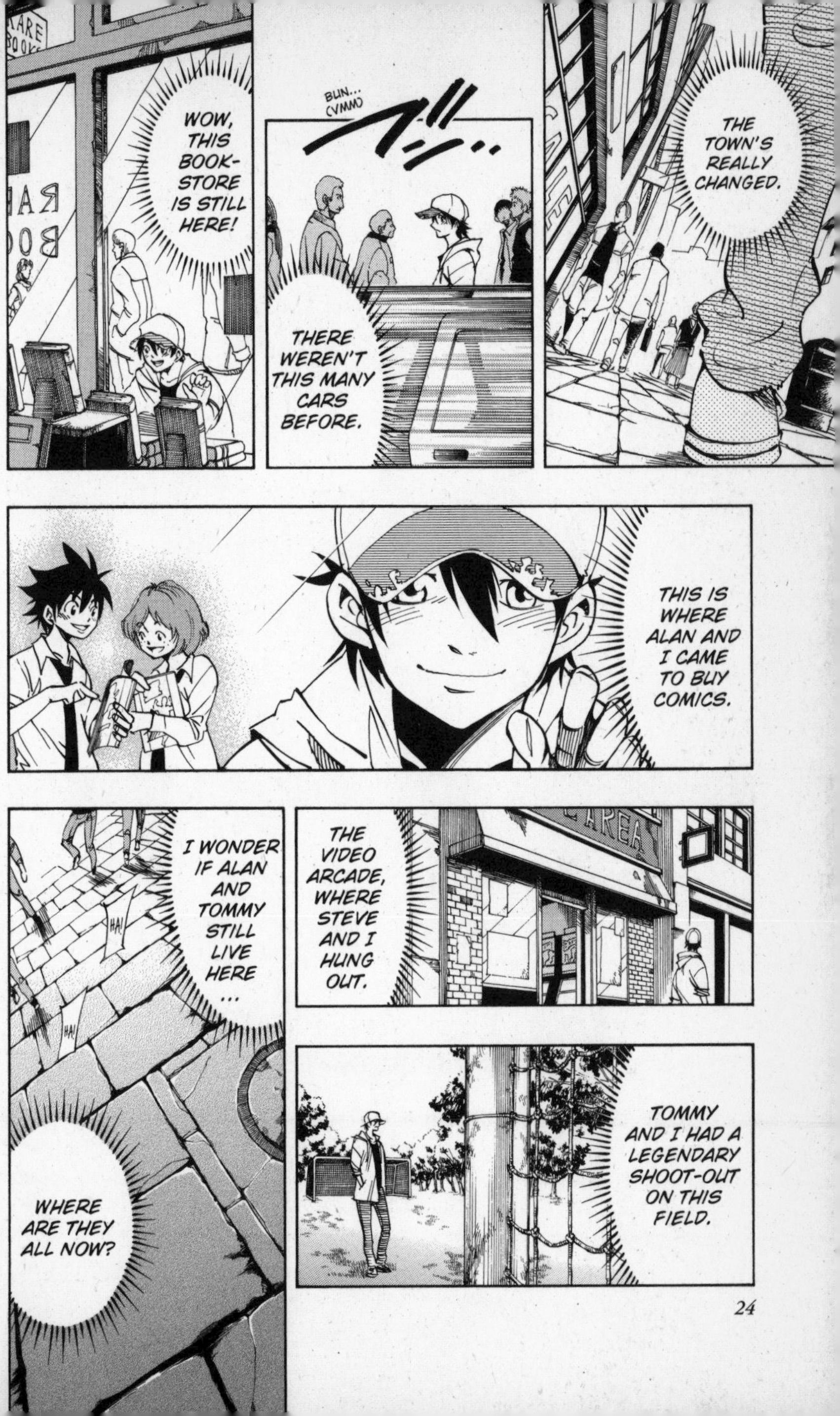
THE TOWN'S REALLY CHANGED.
BUN... (VMM)
THERE WEREN'T THIS MANY CARS BEFORE.
WOW, THIS BOOK-STORE IS STILL HERE!
THIS IS WHERE ALAN AND I CAME TO BUY COMICS.
THE VIDEO ARCADE, WHERE STEVE AND I HUNG OUT.
TOMMY AND I HAD A LEGENDARY SHOOT-OUT ON THIS FIELD.
I WONDER IF ALAN AND TOMMY STILL LIVE HERE ...
HA!
HA!
WHERE ARE THEY ALL NOW?

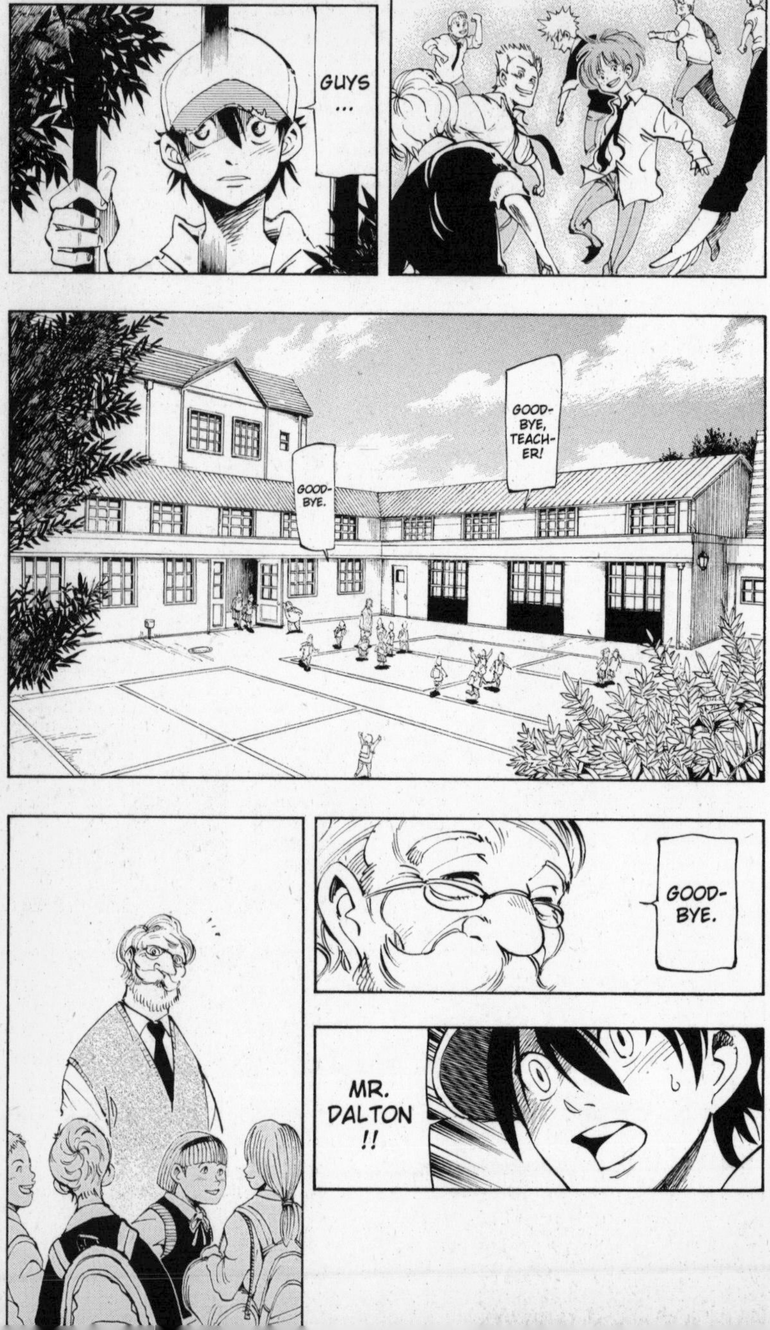
GUYS ...
GOOD-BYE, TEACHER!
GOOD-BYE.
GOOD-BYE.
MR. DALTON !!

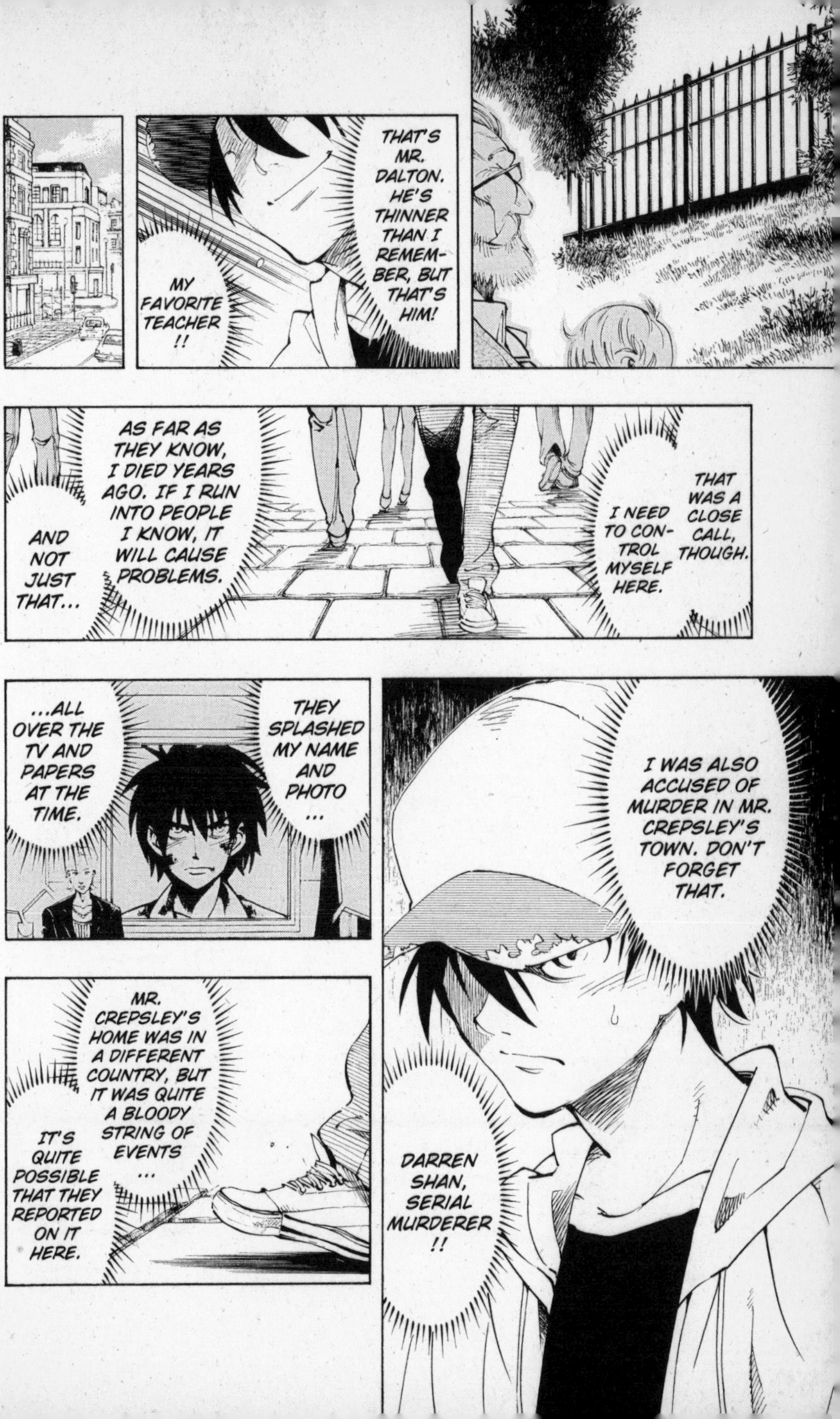
THAT'S MR. DALTON. HE'S THINNER THAN I REMEMBER, BUT THAT'S HIM!
MY FAVORITE TEACHER !!
THAT WAS A CLOSE CALL, THOUGH.
I NEED TO CONTROL MYSELF HERE.
AS FAR AS THEY KNOW, I DIED YEARS AGO. IF I RUN INTO PEOPLE I KNOW, IT WILL CAUSE PROBLEMS.
AND NOT JUST THAT...
I WAS ALSO ACCUSED OF MURDER IN MR. CREPSLEY'S TOWN. DON'T FORGET THAT.
DARREN SHAN, SERIAL MURDERER !!
THEY SPLASHED MY NAME AND PHOTO ...
...ALL OVER THE TV AND PAPERS AT THE TIME.
MR. CREPSLEY'S HOME WAS IN A DIFFERENT COUNTRY, BUT IT WAS QUITE A BLOODY STRING OF EVENTS ...
IT'S QUITE POSSIBLE THAT THEY REPORTED ON IT HERE.

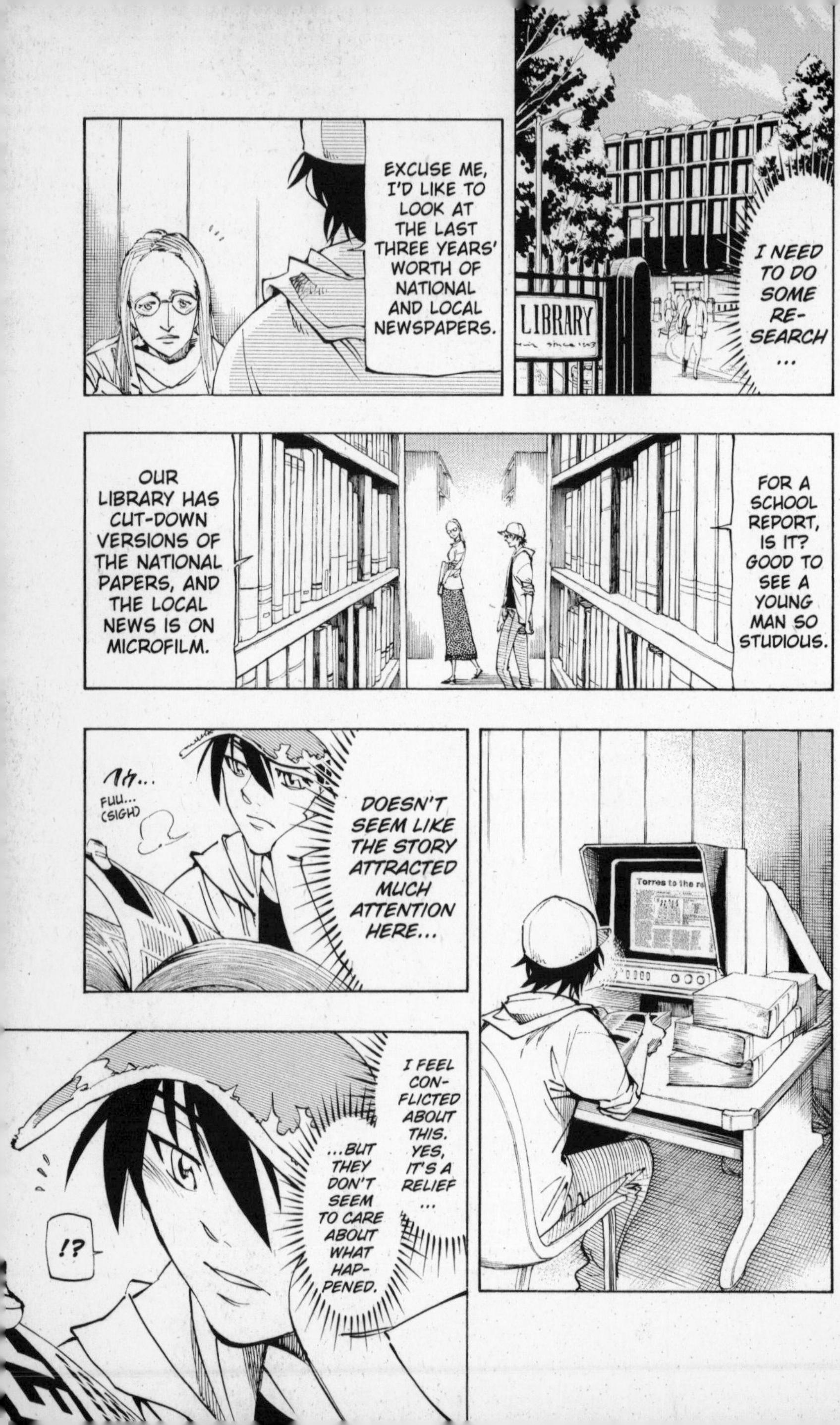
I NEED TO DO SOME RE-SEARCH...
LIBRARY
EXCUSE ME, I'D LIKE TO LOOK AT THE LAST THREE YEARS' WORTH OF NATIONAL AND LOCAL NEWSPAPERS.
FOR A SCHOOL REPORT, IS IT? GOOD TO SEE A YOUNG MAN SO STUDIOUS.
OUR LIBRARY HAS CUT-DOWN VERSIONS OF THE NATIONAL PAPERS, AND THE LOCAL NEWS IS ON MICROFILM.
DOESN'T SEEM LIKE THE STORY ATTRACTED MUCH ATTENTION HERE...
FUU... (SIGH)
I FEEL CON-FLICTED ABOUT THIS. YES, IT'S A RELIEF...
...BUT THEY DON'T SEEM TO CARE ABOUT WHAT HAP-PENED.
!?

to do

TOMMY JONES MAKES A SERIES OF UNBELIEVABLE SAVES...

WAIT, THEY DON'T MEAN... *THAT* TOMMY, DO THEY!?

S-SORRY...

Grov.
a
ps all
acing.
black
ow
ere is
y that with
e, his
e is going to
looked as if

the predictable
nelka, all £15m
on for Pizarro.
t disappoint. In
of his entry he so
d with a fine and
opportunism. Out on
er-vigorous Belletti
e centre, where
s neatly back-heeled
nelka who shot hard,
ly for Cerny to

...AND SOON SIGNED A FIVE-YEAR CONTRACT WITH A WORLD-FAMOUS FOREIGN TEAM.

HE'S NOW THE STARTING GOAL-KEEPER OF THE BEST CLUB IN THE COUNTRY.

...TOMMY JOINED A LOCAL PROFESSIONAL TEAM...

AFTER WORKING HIS WAY UP THROUGH THE AMATEUR RANKS...

TOMMY JONES, GREATEST KEEPER IN THE WORLD !!

BRILLIANT! A PRO SOCCER PLAYER !!

...AND THE MATCH IS AT THE STADIUM IN THIS TOWN!?

IT'S NEARLY UPON US!!

TOMMY'S TEAM IS IN THE SEMI-FINALS OF THIS YEAR'S TOURNAMENT...

DAY TIMES

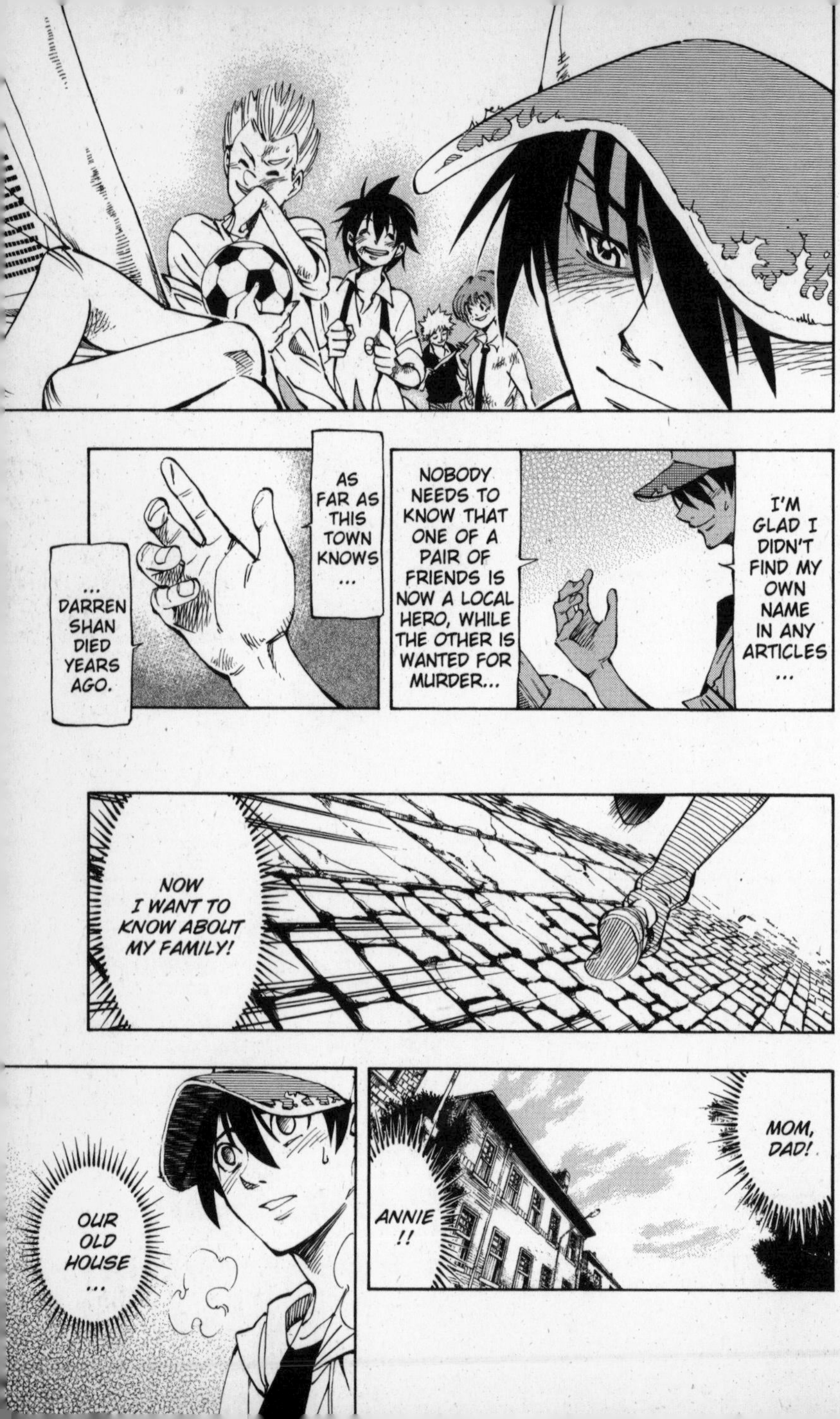
I'M GLAD I DIDN'T FIND MY OWN NAME IN ANY ARTICLES ...
NOBODY NEEDS TO KNOW THAT ONE OF A PAIR OF FRIENDS IS NOW A LOCAL HERO, WHILE THE OTHER IS WANTED FOR MURDER...
AS FAR AS THIS TOWN KNOWS ...
... DARREN SHAN DIED YEARS AGO.
NOW I WANT TO KNOW ABOUT MY FAMILY!
MOM, DAD!
ANNIE !!
OUR OLD HOUSE ...

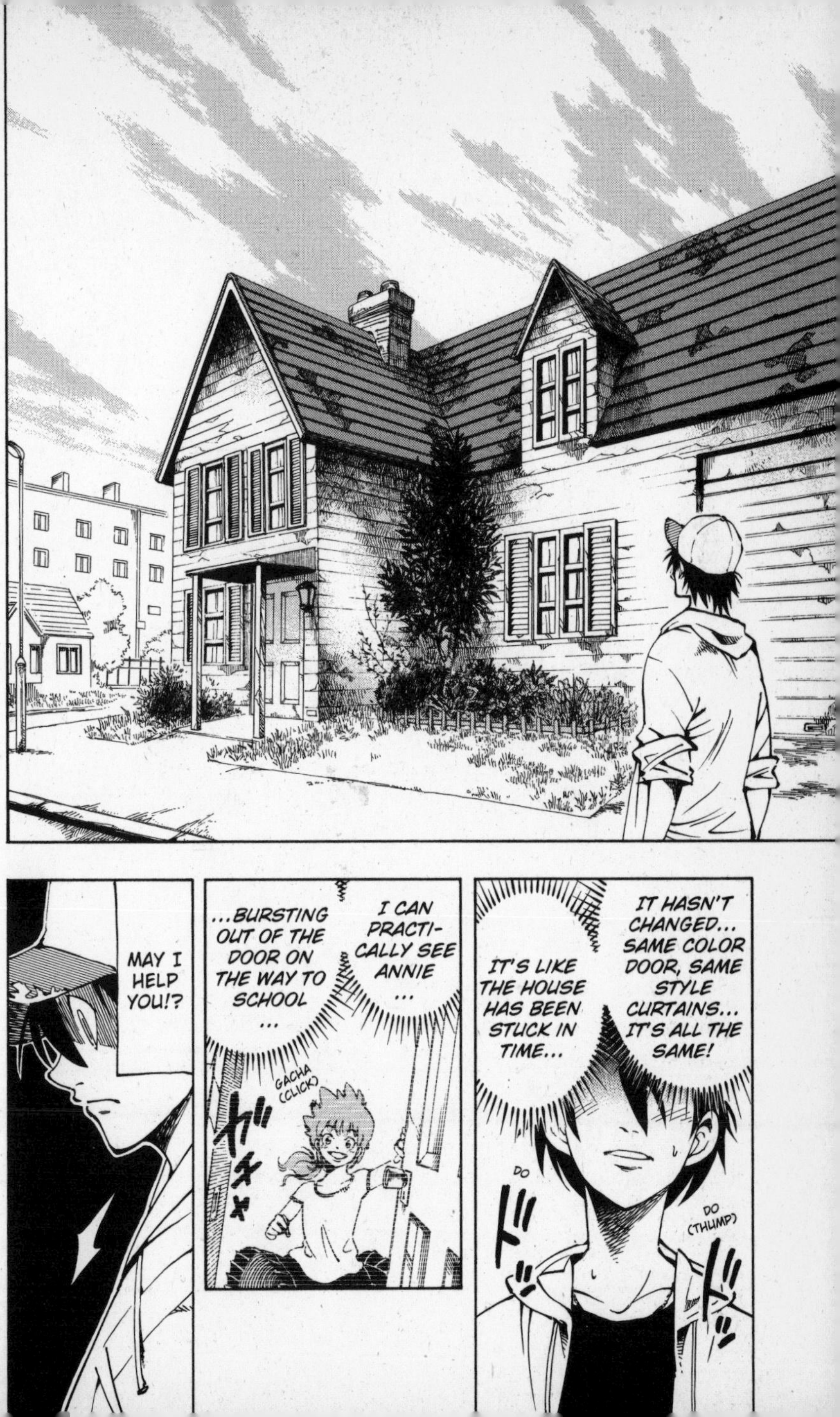
IT HASN'T CHANGED... SAME COLOR DOOR, SAME STYLE CURTAINS... IT'S ALL THE SAME!
IT'S LIKE THE HOUSE HAS BEEN STUCK IN TIME...
DO
DO (THUMP)
I CAN PRACTI-CALLY SEE ANNIE...
...BURSTING OUT OF THE DOOR ON THE WAY TO SCHOOL...
GACHA (CLICK)
MAY I HELP YOU!?

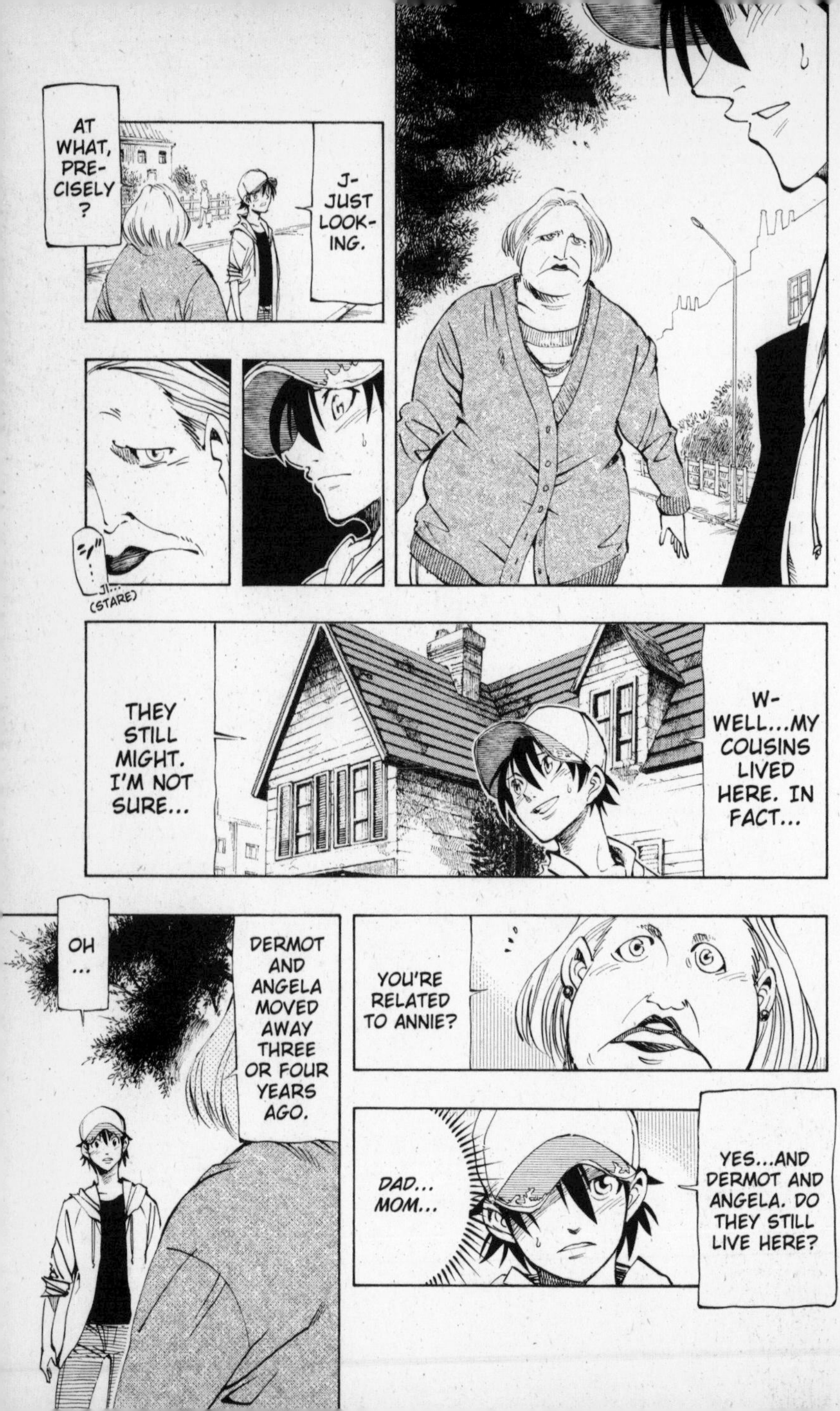
J-JUST LOOKING.
AT WHAT, PRECISELY?
JI... (STARE)
W-WELL...MY COUSINS LIVED HERE. IN FACT...
THEY STILL MIGHT. I'M NOT SURE...
YOU'RE RELATED TO ANNIE?
YES...AND DERMOT AND ANGELA. DO THEY STILL LIVE HERE?
DAD... MOM...
DERMOT AND ANGELA MOVED AWAY THREE OR FOUR YEARS AGO.
OH ...

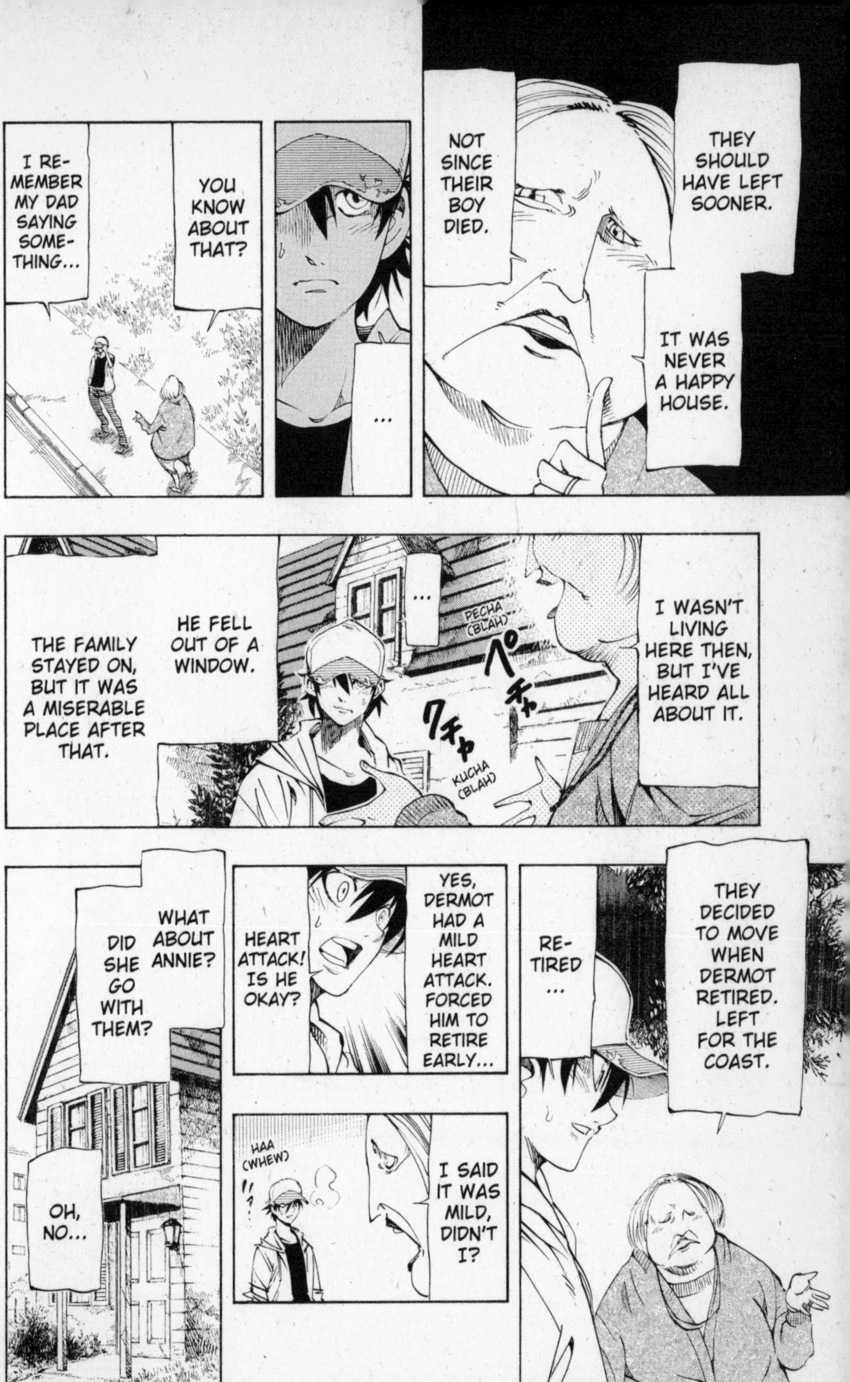
THEY SHOULD HAVE LEFT SOONER.
IT WAS NEVER A HAPPY HOUSE.
NOT SINCE THEIR BOY DIED.
...
YOU KNOW ABOUT THAT?
I RE-MEMBER MY DAD SAYING SOME-THING...
I WASN'T LIVING HERE THEN, BUT I'VE HEARD ALL ABOUT IT.
PECHA (BLAH)
KUCHA (BLAH)
...
HE FELL OUT OF A WINDOW.
THE FAMILY STAYED ON, BUT IT WAS A MISERABLE PLACE AFTER THAT.
THEY DECIDED TO MOVE WHEN DERMOT RETIRED. LEFT FOR THE COAST.
RE-TIRED ...
YES, DERMOT HAD A MILD HEART ATTACK. FORCED HIM TO RETIRE EARLY...
HEART ATTACK! IS HE OKAY?
I SAID IT WAS MILD, DIDN'T I?
HAA (WHEW)
!!?
WHAT ABOUT ANNIE?
DID SHE GO WITH THEM?
OH, NO...

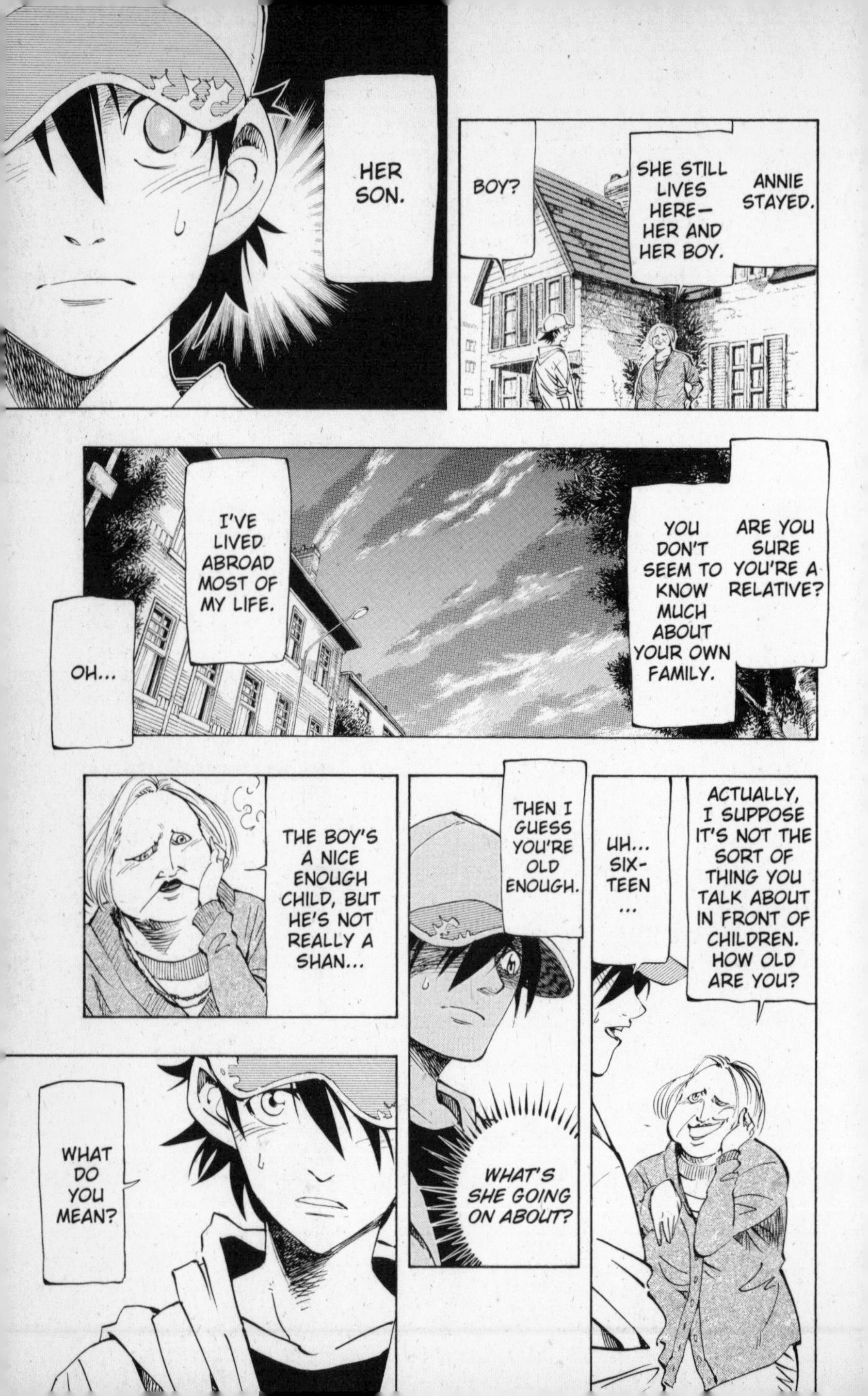
ANNIE STAYED.
SHE STILL LIVES HERE— HER AND HER BOY.
BOY?
HER SON.
ARE YOU SURE YOU'RE A RELATIVE?
YOU DON'T SEEM TO KNOW MUCH ABOUT YOUR OWN FAMILY.
I'VE LIVED ABROAD MOST OF MY LIFE.
OH...
ACTUALLY, I SUPPOSE IT'S NOT THE SORT OF THING YOU TALK ABOUT IN FRONT OF CHILDREN. HOW OLD ARE YOU?
UH... SIX-TEEN...
THEN I GUESS YOU'RE OLD ENOUGH.
WHAT'S SHE GOING ON ABOUT?
THE BOY'S A NICE ENOUGH CHILD, BUT HE'S NOT REALLY A SHAN...
WHAT DO YOU MEAN?

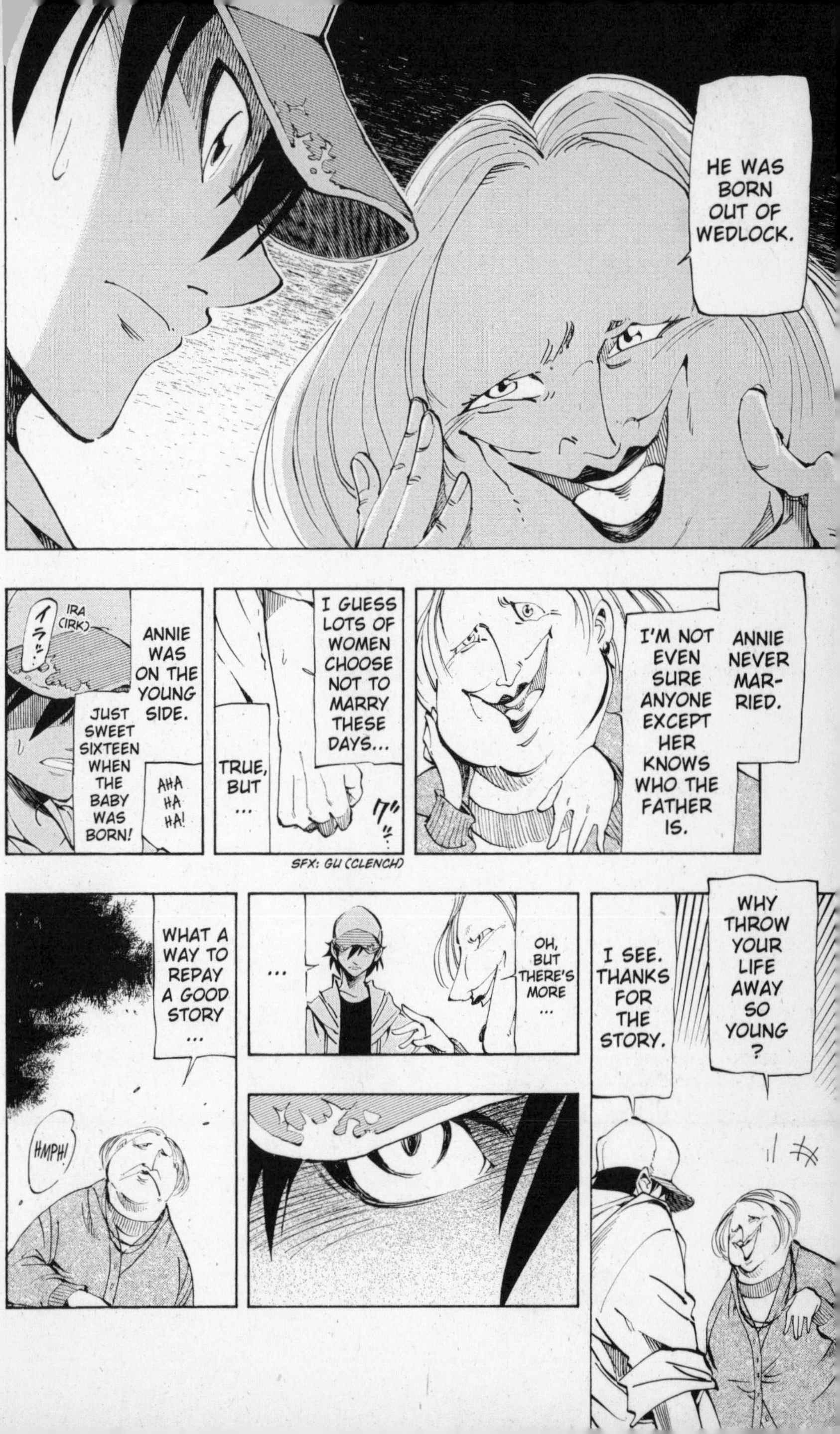
HE WAS BORN OUT OF WEDLOCK.
ANNIE NEVER MAR-RIED.
I'M NOT EVEN SURE ANYONE EXCEPT HER KNOWS WHO THE FATHER IS.
I GUESS LOTS OF WOMEN CHOOSE NOT TO MARRY THESE DAYS...
TRUE, BUT ...
SFX: GU (CLENCH)
IRA (IRK)
ANNIE WAS ON THE YOUNG SIDE.
JUST SWEET SIXTEEN WHEN THE BABY WAS BORN!
AHA HA HA!
WHY THROW YOUR LIFE AWAY SO YOUNG?
I SEE. THANKS FOR THE STORY.
OH, BUT THERE'S MORE ...
...
WHAT A WAY TO REPAY A GOOD STORY ...
HMPH!

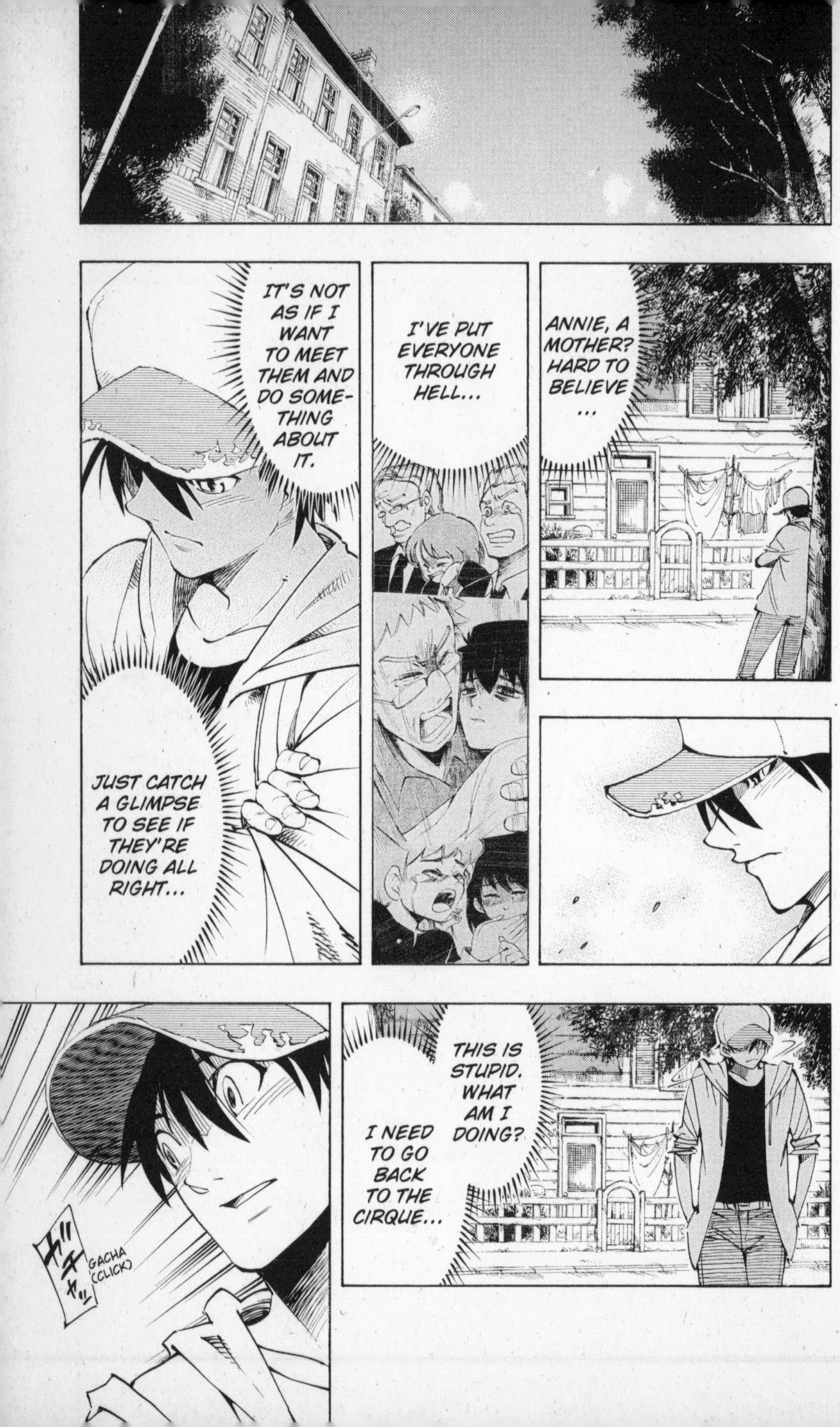
ANNIE, A MOTHER? HARD TO BELIEVE ...
I'VE PUT EVERYONE THROUGH HELL...
IT'S NOT AS IF I WANT TO MEET THEM AND DO SOMETHING ABOUT IT.
JUST CATCH A GLIMPSE TO SEE IF THEY'RE DOING ALL RIGHT...
THIS IS STUPID. WHAT AM I DOING?
I NEED TO GO BACK TO THE CIRQUE...
ガチャッ
GACHA (CLICK)

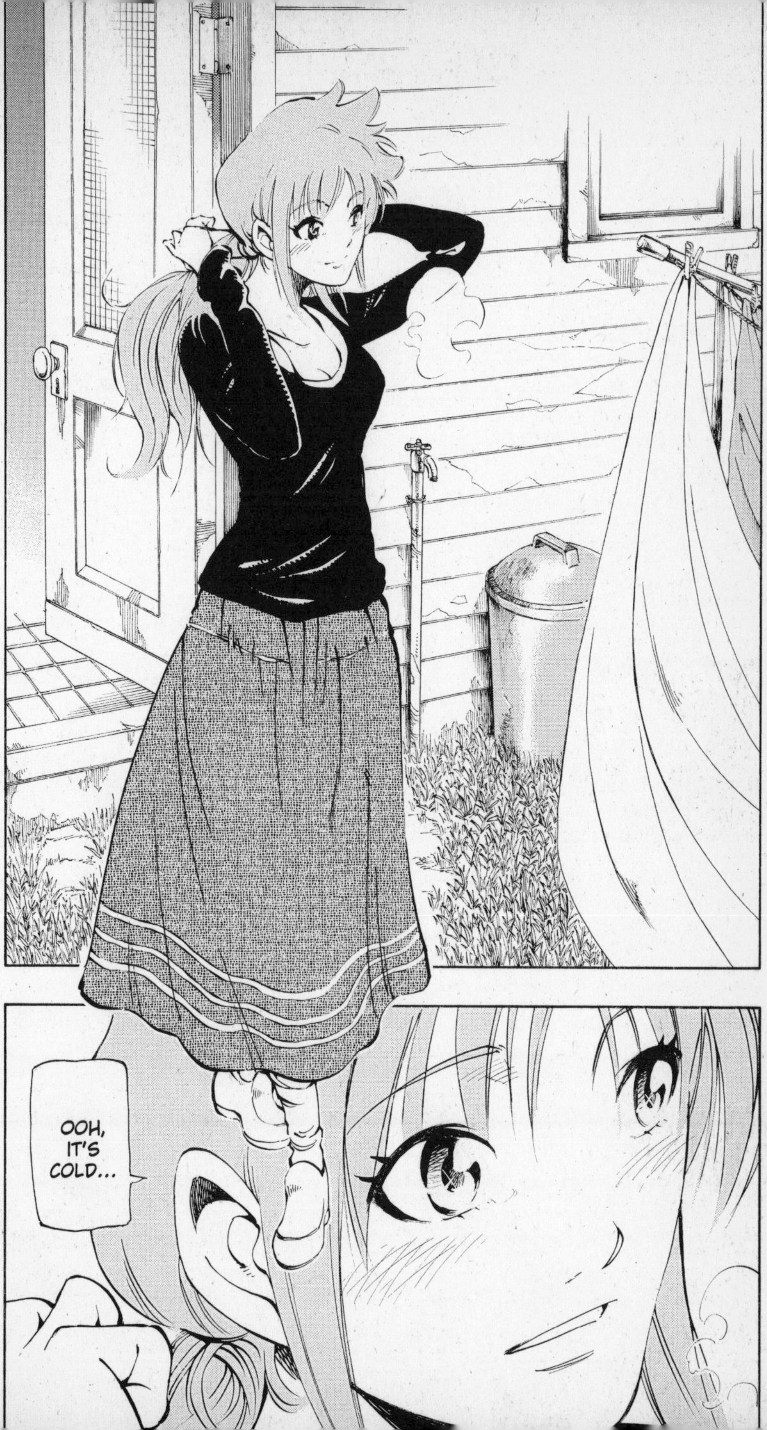
OOH, IT'S COLD...

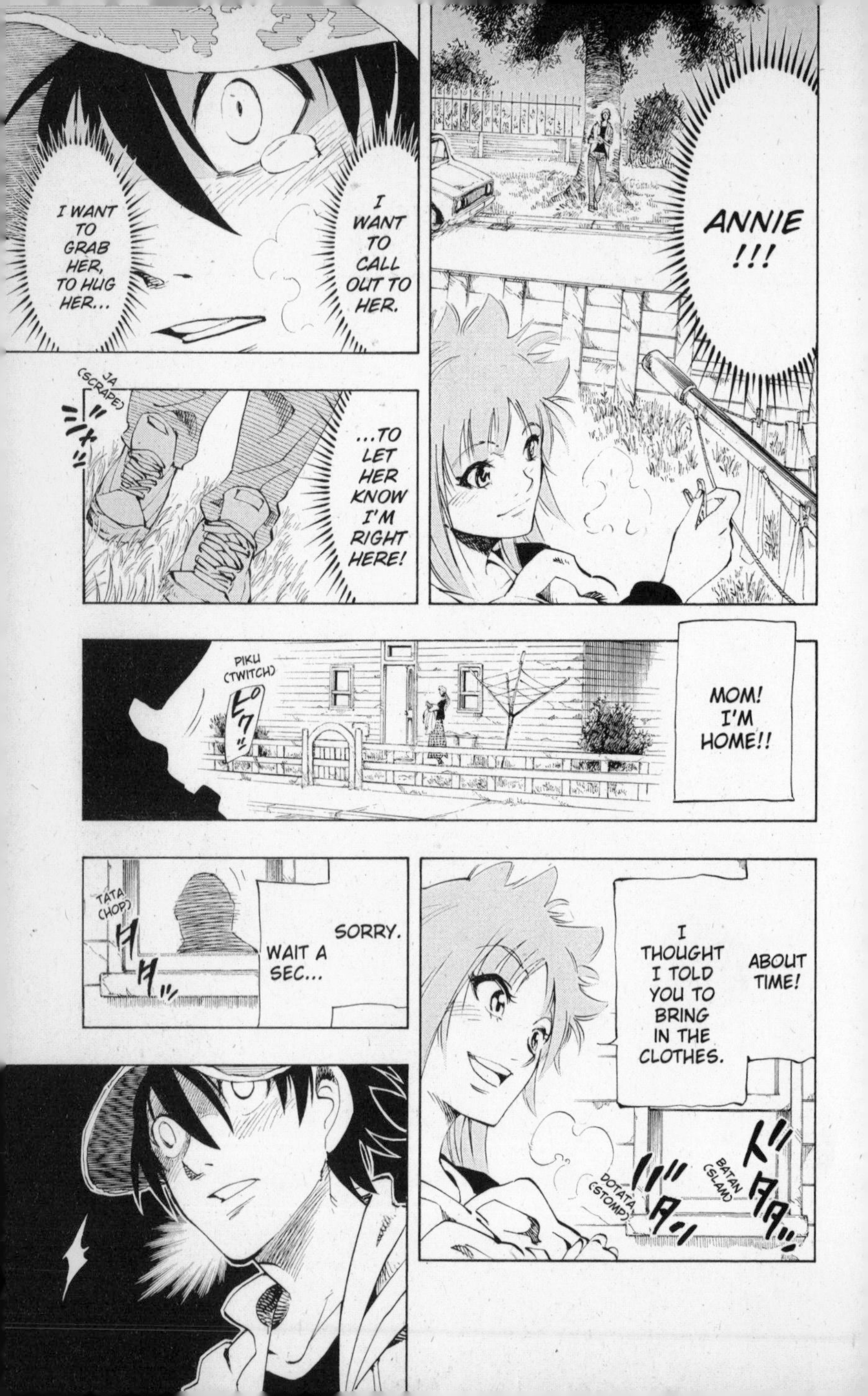
ANNIE!!!
I WANT TO CALL OUT TO HER.
I WANT TO GRAB HER, TO HUG HER...
...TO LET HER KNOW I'M RIGHT HERE!
JA (SCRAPE)
MOM! I'M HOME!!
PIKU (TWITCH)
ABOUT TIME!
I THOUGHT I TOLD YOU TO BRING IN THE CLOTHES.
BATAN (SLAM)
DOTATA (STOMP)
SORRY.
WAIT A SEC...
TATA (HOP)

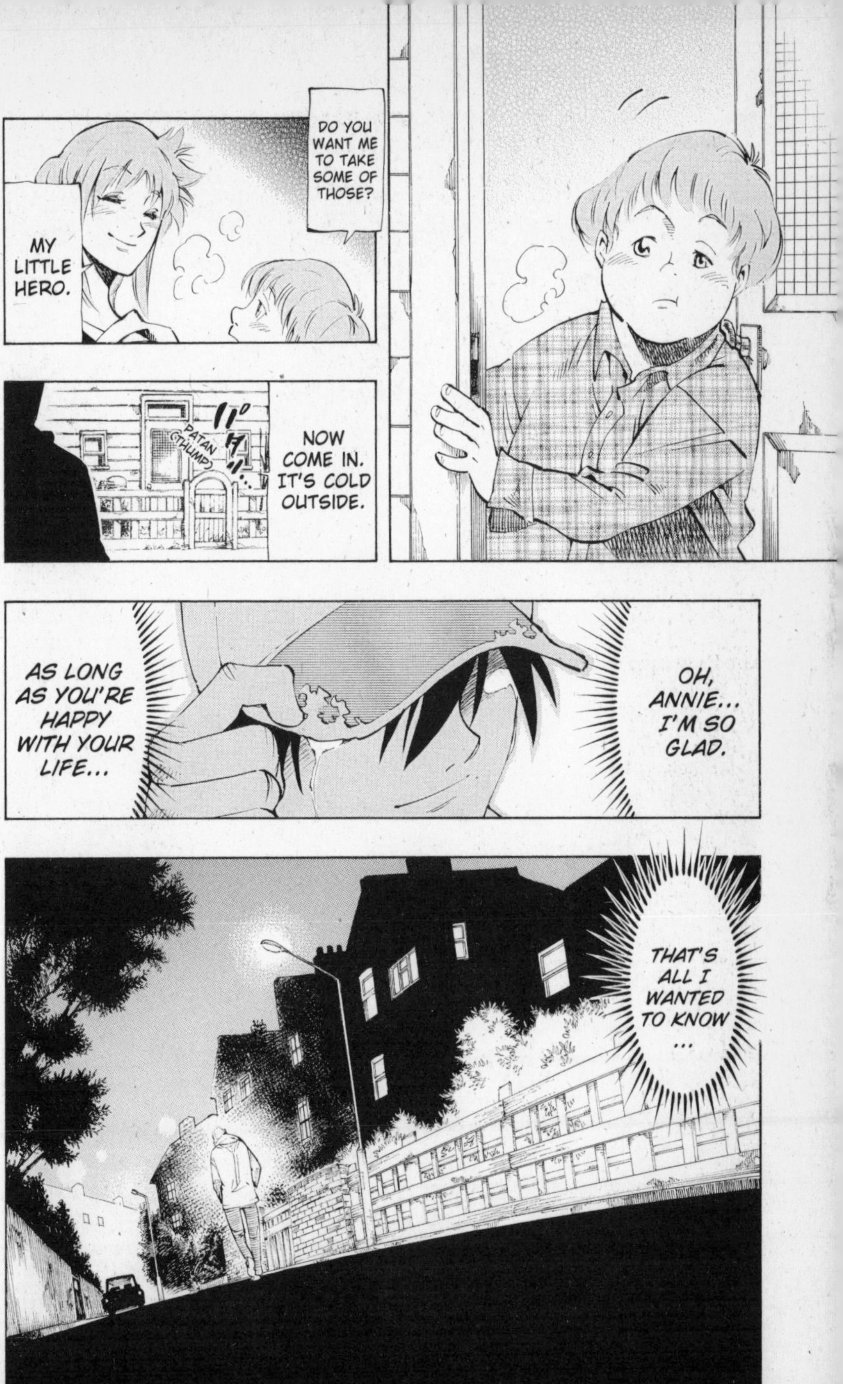
DO YOU WANT ME TO TAKE SOME OF THOSE?
MY LITTLE HERO.
NOW COME IN. IT'S COLD OUTSIDE.
PATAN (THUMP)
OH, ANNIE... I'M SO GLAD.
AS LONG AS YOU'RE HAPPY WITH YOUR LIFE...
THAT'S ALL I WANTED TO KNOW ...

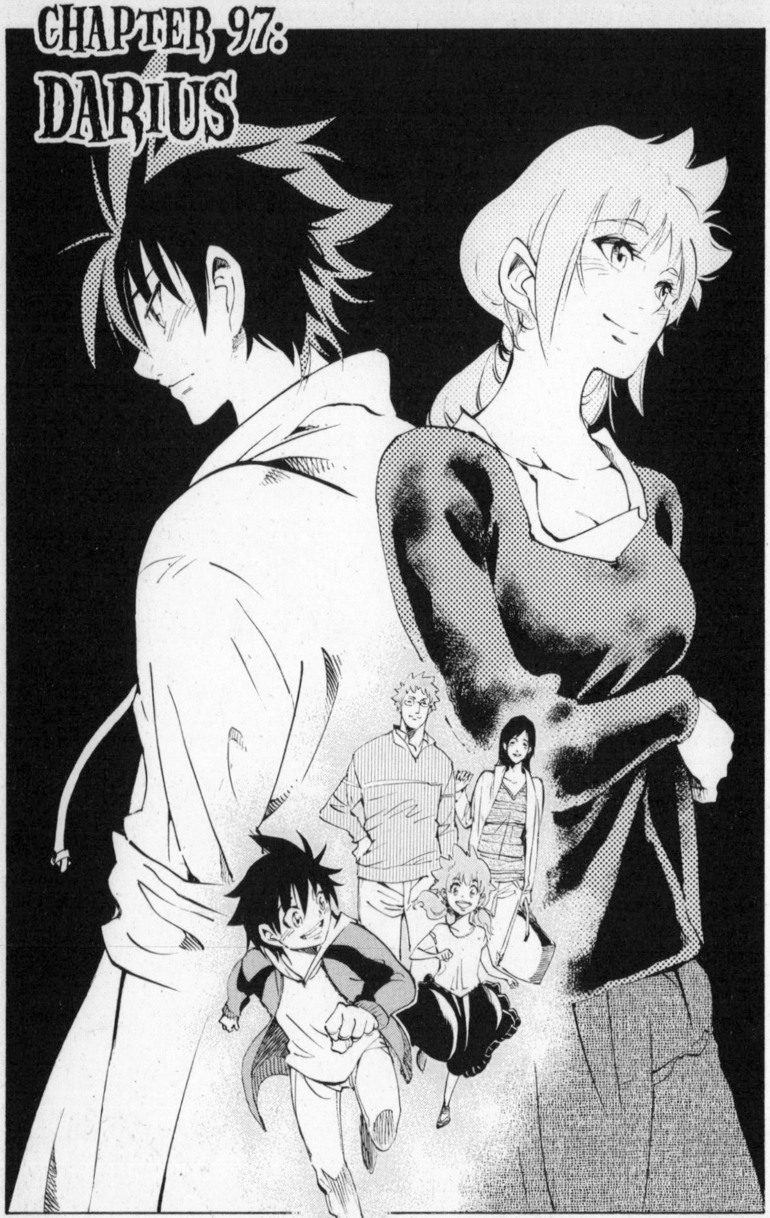
CHAPTER 97:
DARIUS

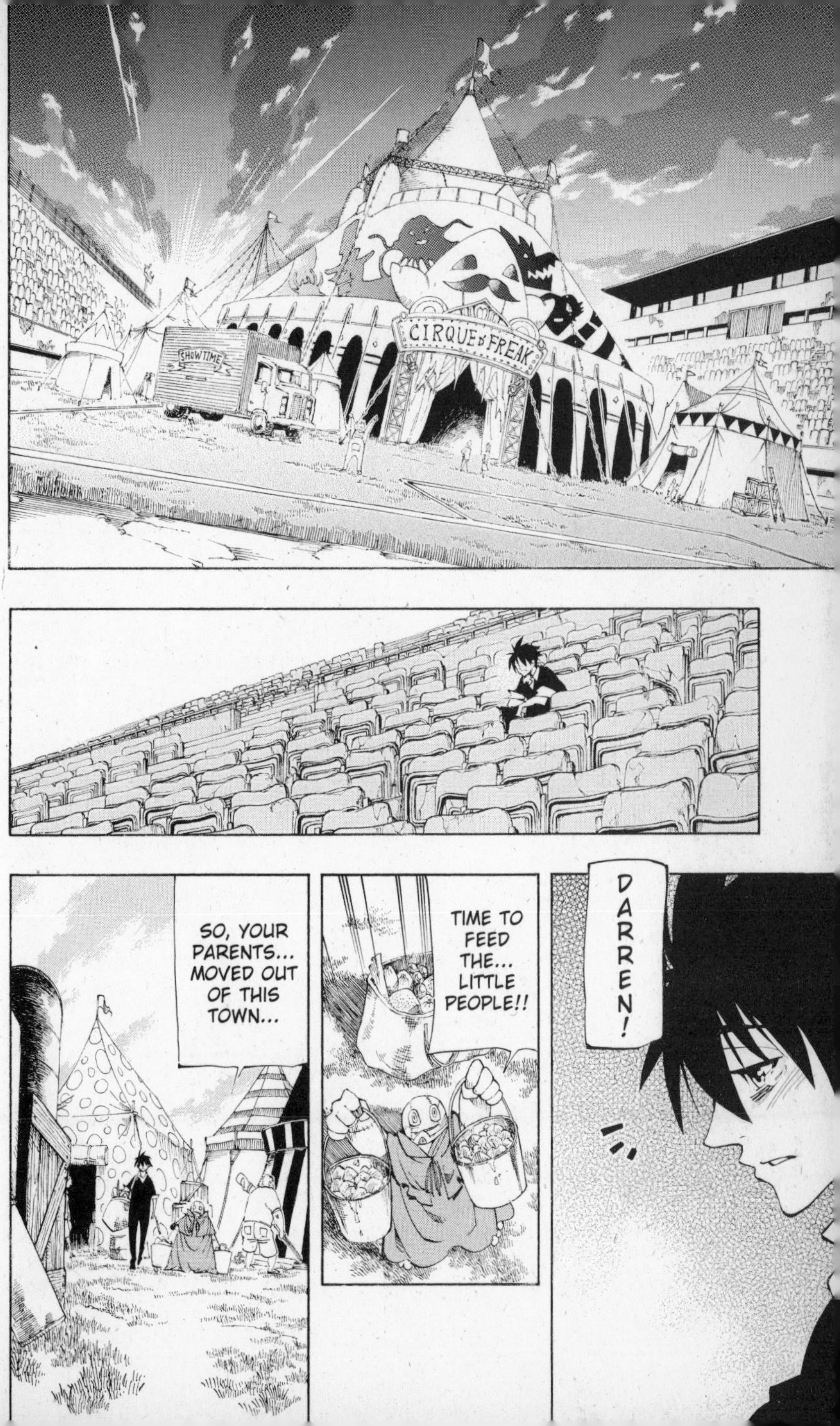
CIRQUE D' FREAK
SHOWTIME
DARREN!
TIME TO FEED THE... LITTLE PEOPLE!!
SO, YOUR PARENTS... MOVED OUT OF THIS TOWN...

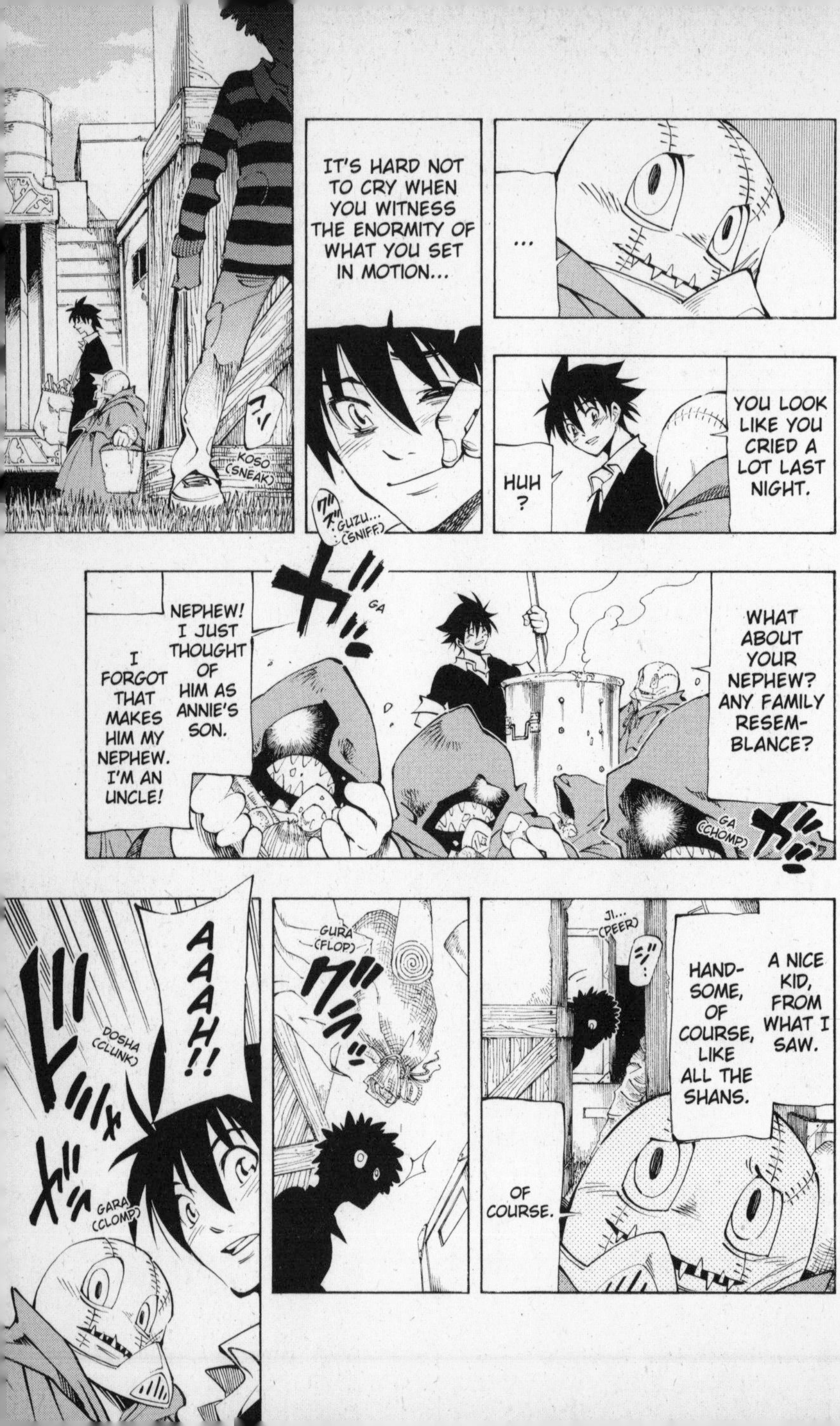
...
YOU LOOK LIKE YOU CRIED A LOT LAST NIGHT.
HUH?
IT'S HARD NOT TO CRY WHEN YOU WITNESS THE ENORMITY OF WHAT YOU SET IN MOTION...
GUZU... (SNIFF)
KOSO (SNEAK)
WHAT ABOUT YOUR NEPHEW? ANY FAMILY RESEMBLANCE?
GA (CHOMP)
NEPHEW! I JUST THOUGHT OF HIM AS ANNIE'S SON.
I FORGOT THAT MAKES HIM MY NEPHEW. I'M AN UNCLE!
GA
A NICE KID, FROM WHAT I SAW.
HANDSOME, OF COURSE, LIKE ALL THE SHANS.
OF COURSE.
JI... (PEER)
GURA (FLOP)
AAAAH!!
DOSHA (CLUNK)
GARA (CLOMP)

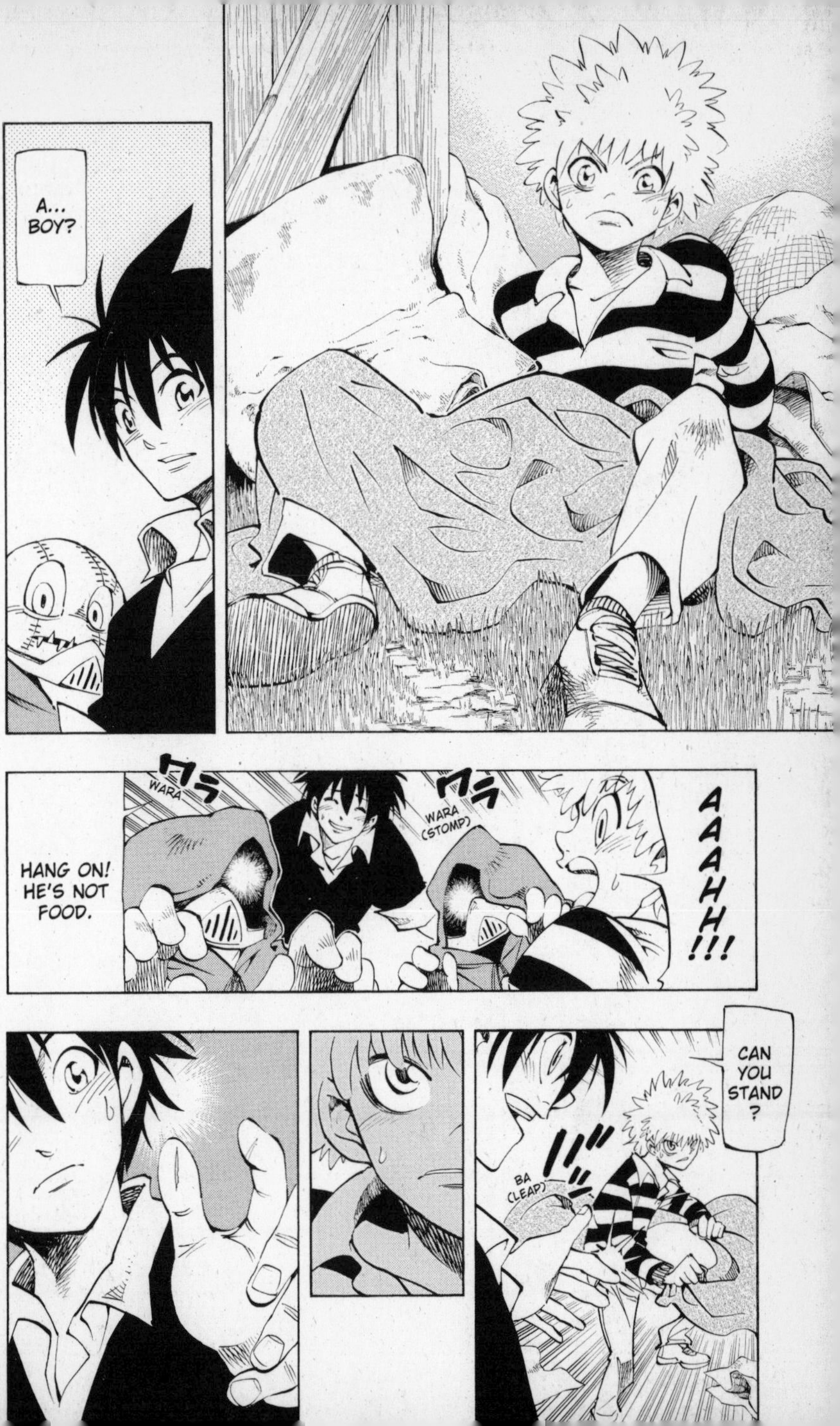
A... BOY?
AAAHH!!!
ワラ
WARA (STOMP)
ワラ
WARA
HANG ON! HE'S NOT FOOD.
CAN YOU STAND?
バッ
BA (LEAP)

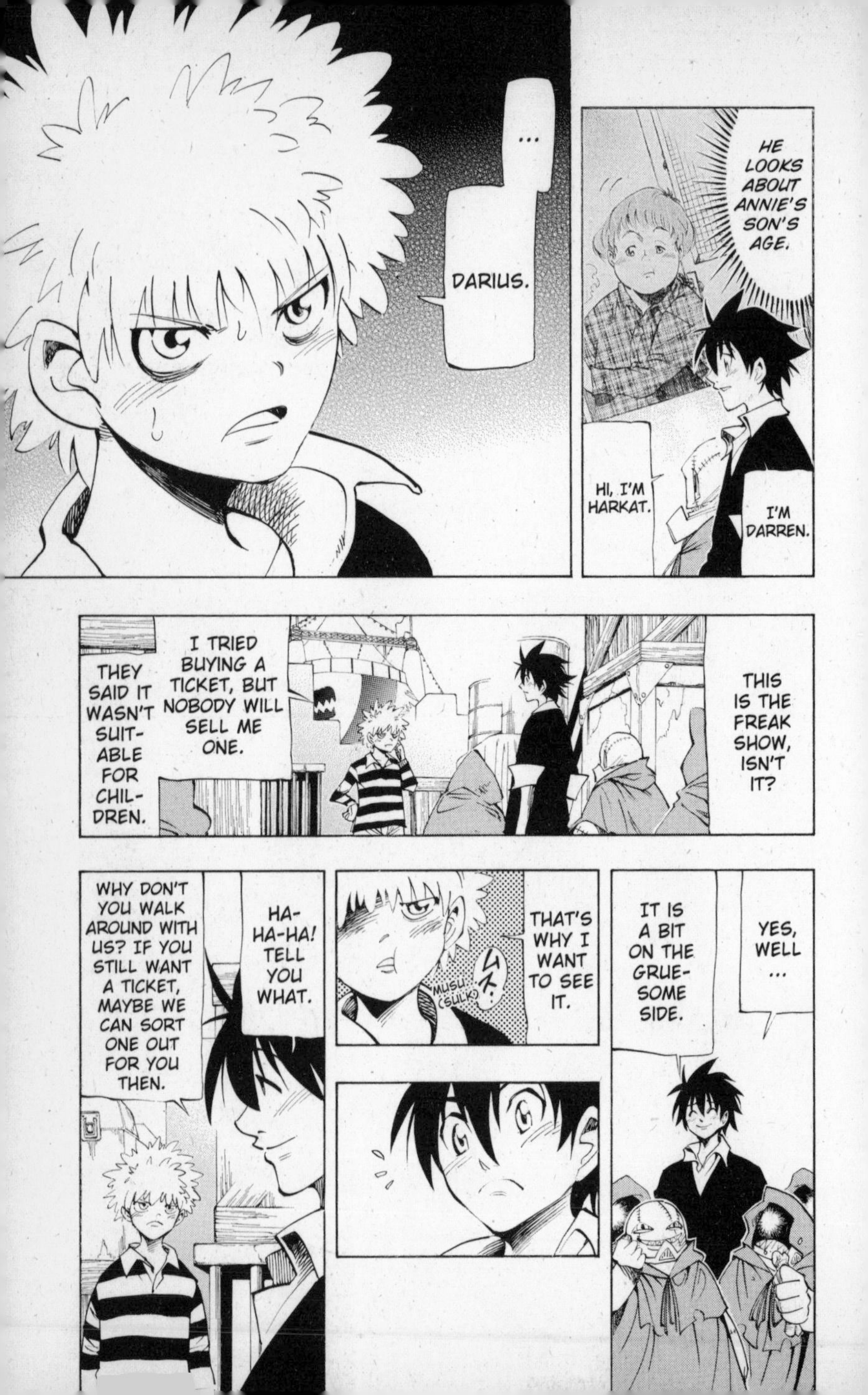
HE LOOKS ABOUT ANNIE'S SON'S AGE.
I'M DARREN.
HI, I'M HARKAT.
...
DARIUS.
THIS IS THE FREAK SHOW, ISN'T IT?
I TRIED BUYING A TICKET, BUT NOBODY WILL SELL ME ONE.
THEY SAID IT WASN'T SUITABLE FOR CHILDREN.
YES, WELL ...
IT IS A BIT ON THE GRUESOME SIDE.
THAT'S WHY I WANT TO SEE IT.
MUSU (SULK)
HA-HA-HA! TELL YOU WHAT.
WHY DON'T YOU WALK AROUND WITH US? IF YOU STILL WANT A TICKET, MAYBE WE CAN SORT ONE OUT FOR YOU THEN.

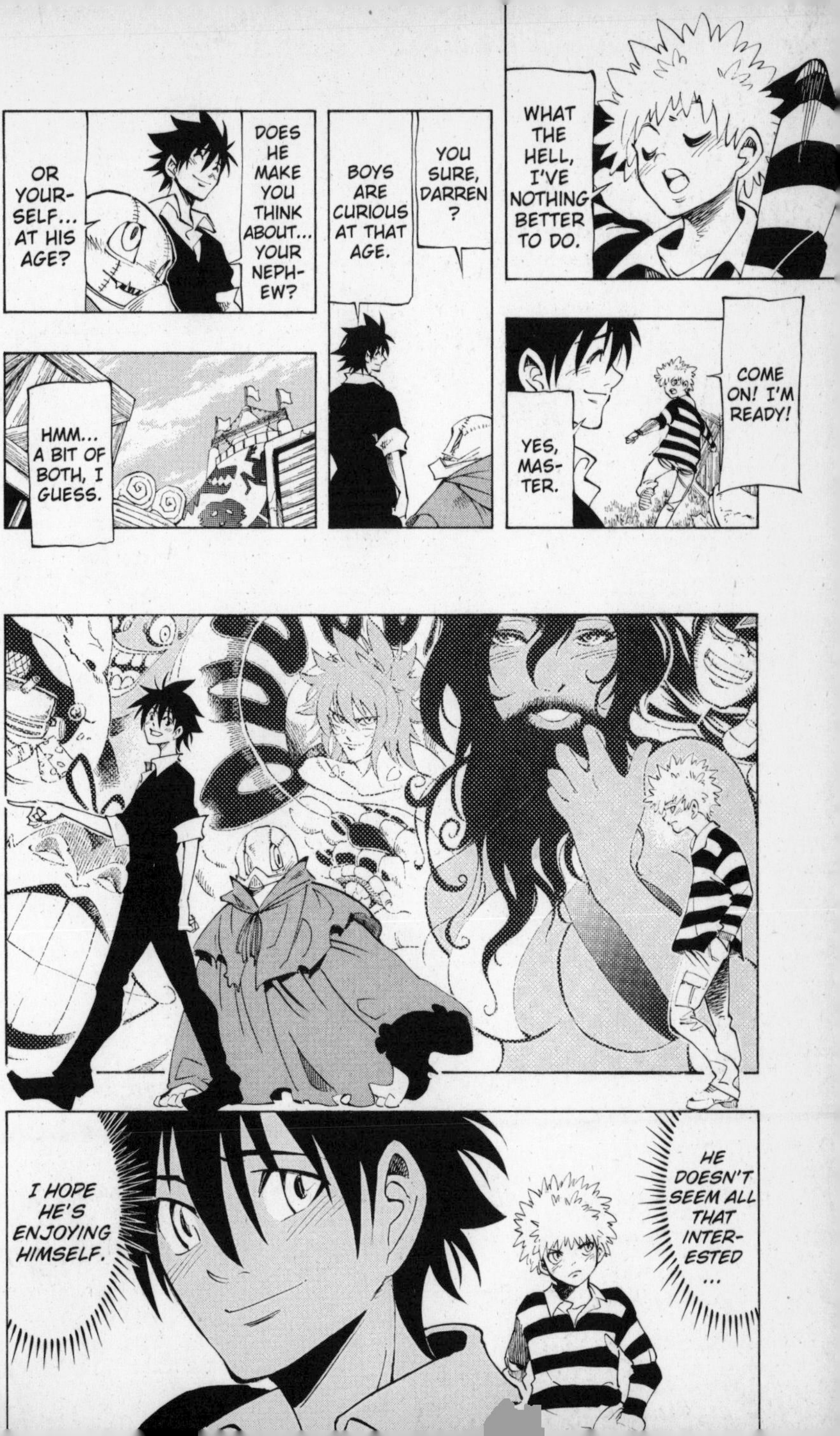

WHAT THE HELL, I'VE NOTHING BETTER TO DO.
COME ON! I'M READY!
YES, MASTER.
YOU SURE, DARREN?
BOYS ARE CURIOUS AT THAT AGE.
DOES HE MAKE YOU THINK ABOUT... YOUR NEPHEW?
OR YOURSELF... AT HIS AGE?
HMM... A BIT OF BOTH, I GUESS.
HE DOESN'T SEEM ALL THAT INTERESTED...
I HOPE HE'S ENJOYING HIMSELF.

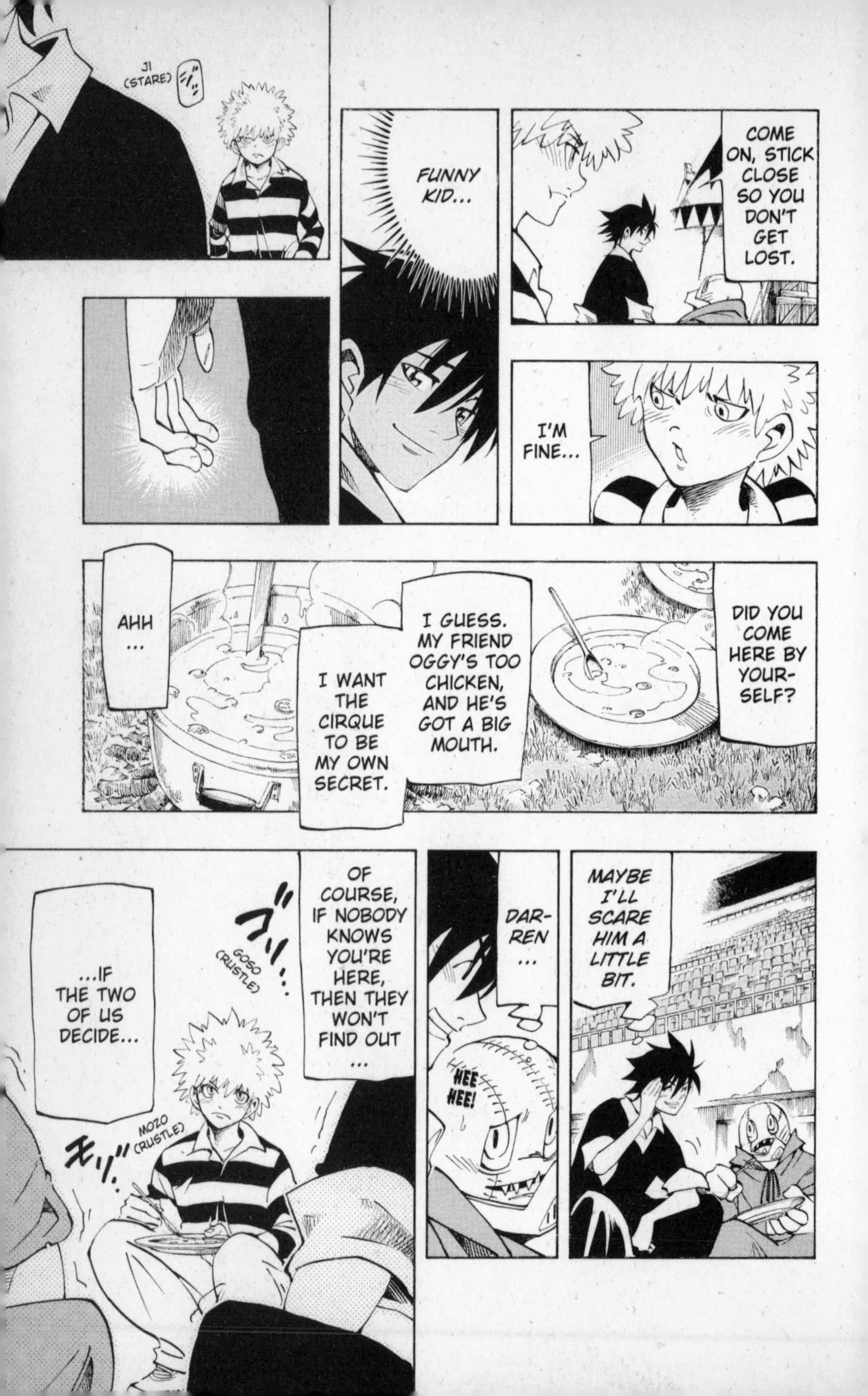
COME ON, STICK CLOSE SO YOU DON'T GET LOST.
I'M FINE...
FUNNY KID...
JI (STARE)
DID YOU COME HERE BY YOURSELF?
I GUESS. MY FRIEND OGGY'S TOO CHICKEN, AND HE'S GOT A BIG MOUTH.
I WANT THE CIRQUE TO BE MY OWN SECRET.
AHH ...
MAYBE I'LL SCARE HIM A LITTLE BIT.
DAR-REN ...
HEE HEE!
OF COURSE, IF NOBODY KNOWS YOU'RE HERE, THEN THEY WON'T FIND OUT ...
GOSO (RUSTLE)
...IF THE TWO OF US DECIDE...
MOZO (RUSTLE)

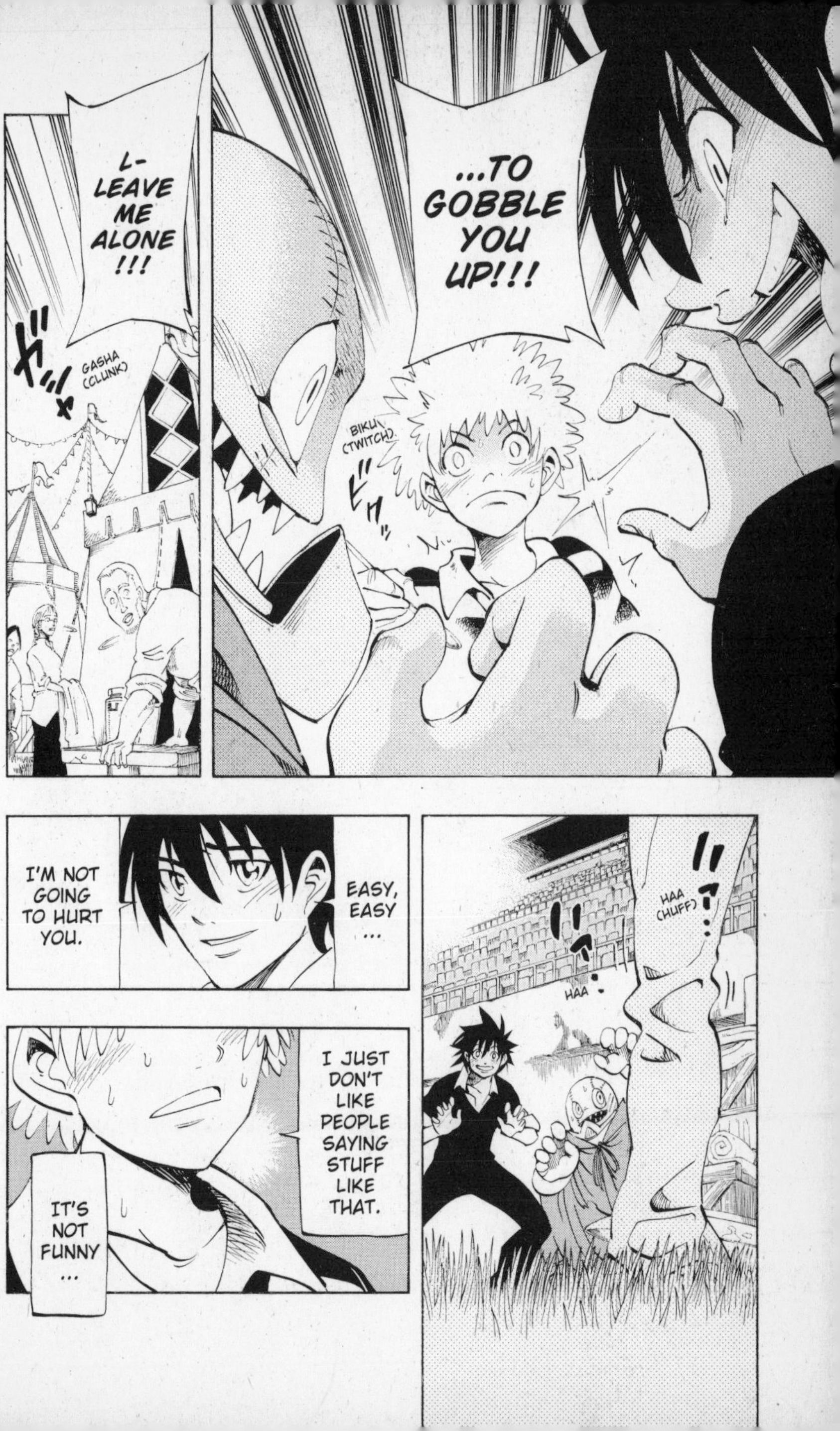
...TO GOBBLE YOU UP!!!
BIKU (TWITCH)
L-LEAVE ME ALONE!!!
GASHA (CLUNK)
HAA (HUFF)
HAA
EASY, EASY ...
I'M NOT GOING TO HURT YOU.
I JUST DON'T LIKE PEOPLE SAYING STUFF LIKE THAT.
IT'S NOT FUNNY ...

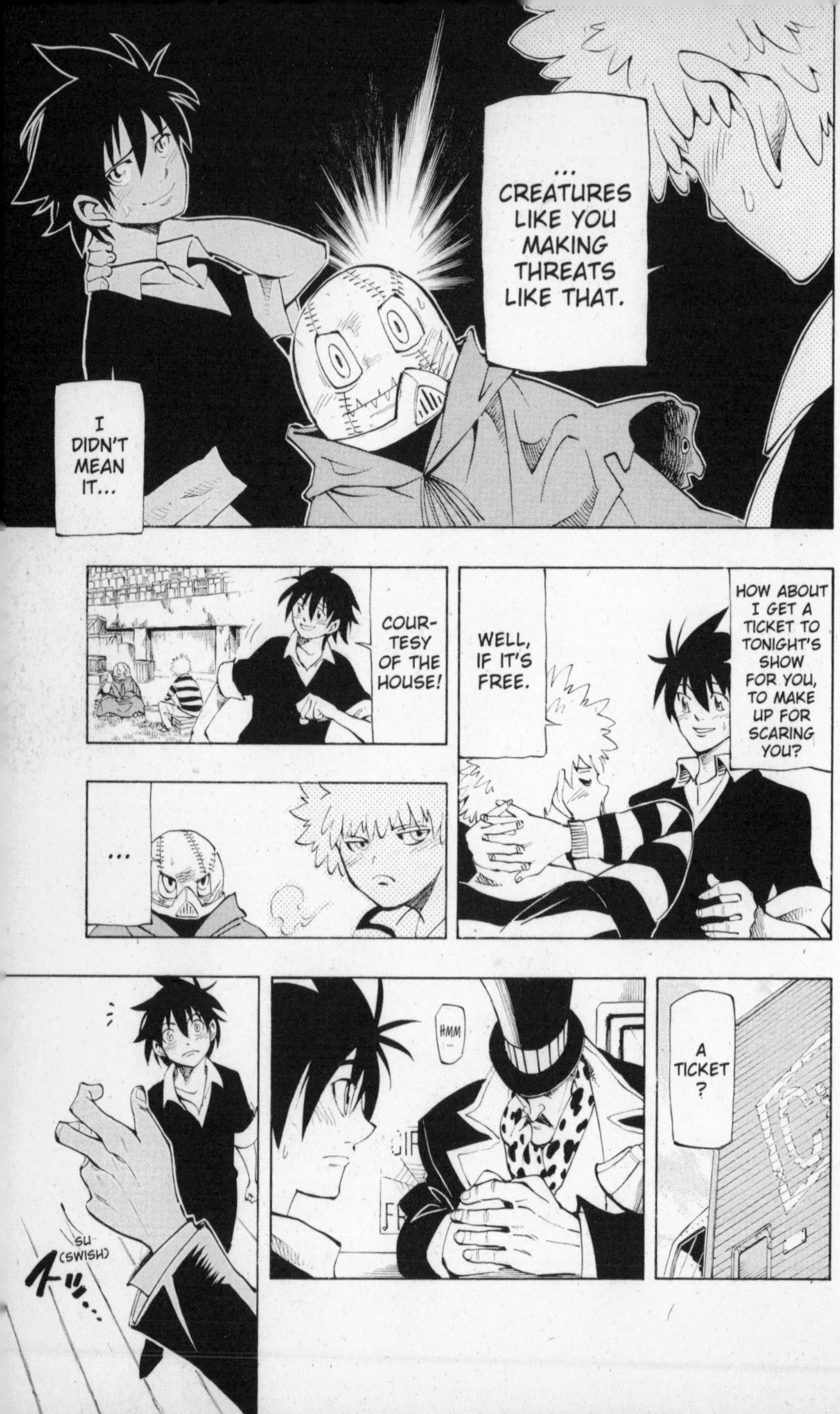
... CREATURES LIKE YOU MAKING THREATS LIKE THAT.
I DIDN'T MEAN IT...
HOW ABOUT I GET A TICKET TO TONIGHT'S SHOW FOR YOU, TO MAKE UP FOR SCARING YOU?
WELL, IF IT'S FREE.
COURTESY OF THE HOUSE!
...
A TICKET ?
HMM ...
SU (SWISH)

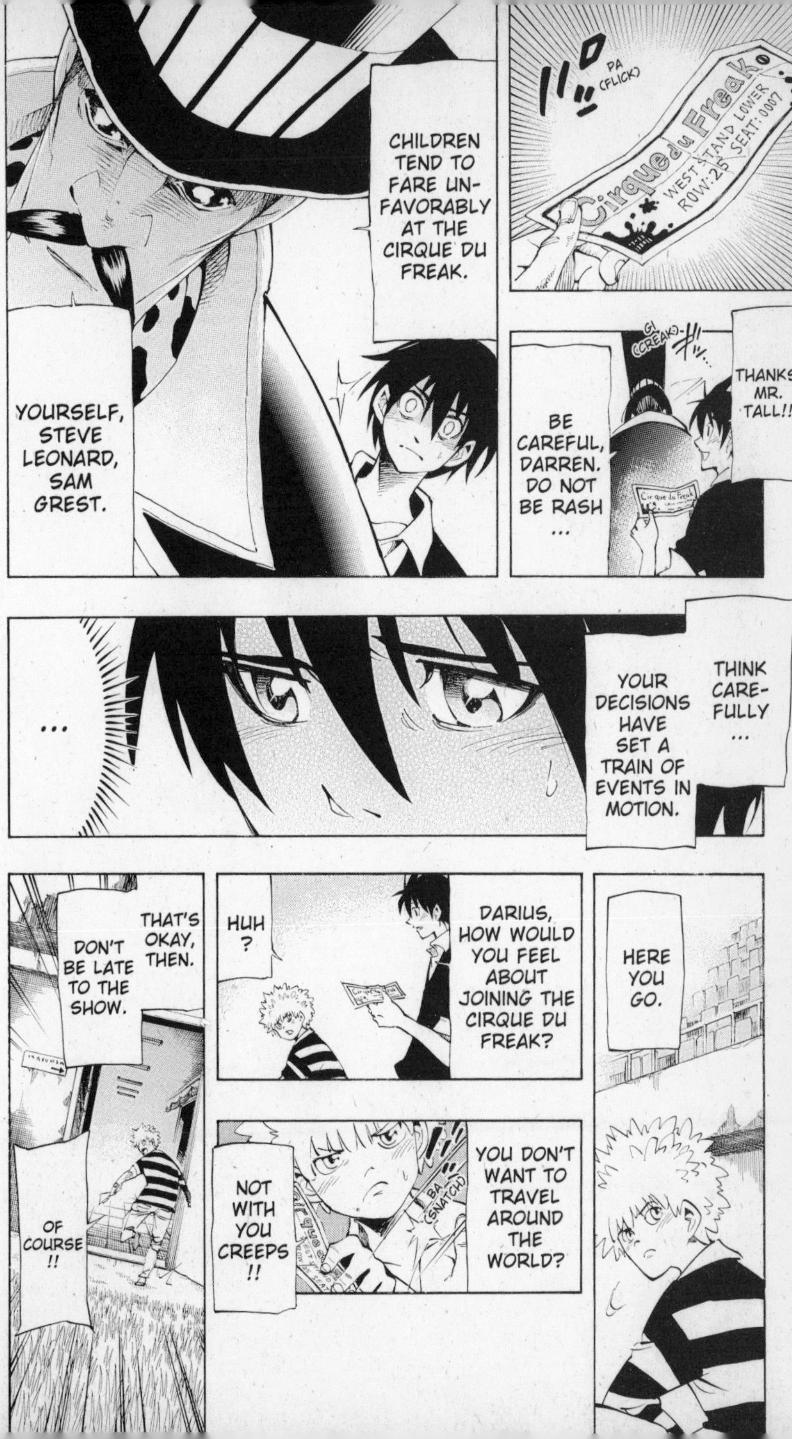
PA (FLICK)
Cirque du Freak
WEST STAND LOWER
ROW:25 SEAT:0007
GI (CREAK)
THANKS, MR. TALL!!
BE CAREFUL, DARREN. DO NOT BE RASH ...
CHILDREN TEND TO FARE UN-FAVORABLY AT THE CIRQUE DU FREAK.
YOURSELF, STEVE LEONARD, SAM GREST.
THINK CARE-FULLY ...
YOUR DECISIONS HAVE SET A TRAIN OF EVENTS IN MOTION.
...
HERE YOU GO.
DARIUS, HOW WOULD YOU FEEL ABOUT JOINING THE CIRQUE DU FREAK?
HUH ?
YOU DON'T WANT TO TRAVEL AROUND THE WORLD?
BA (SNATCH)
NOT WITH YOU CREEPS !!
THAT'S OKAY, THEN.
DON'T BE LATE TO THE SHOW.
OF COURSE !!

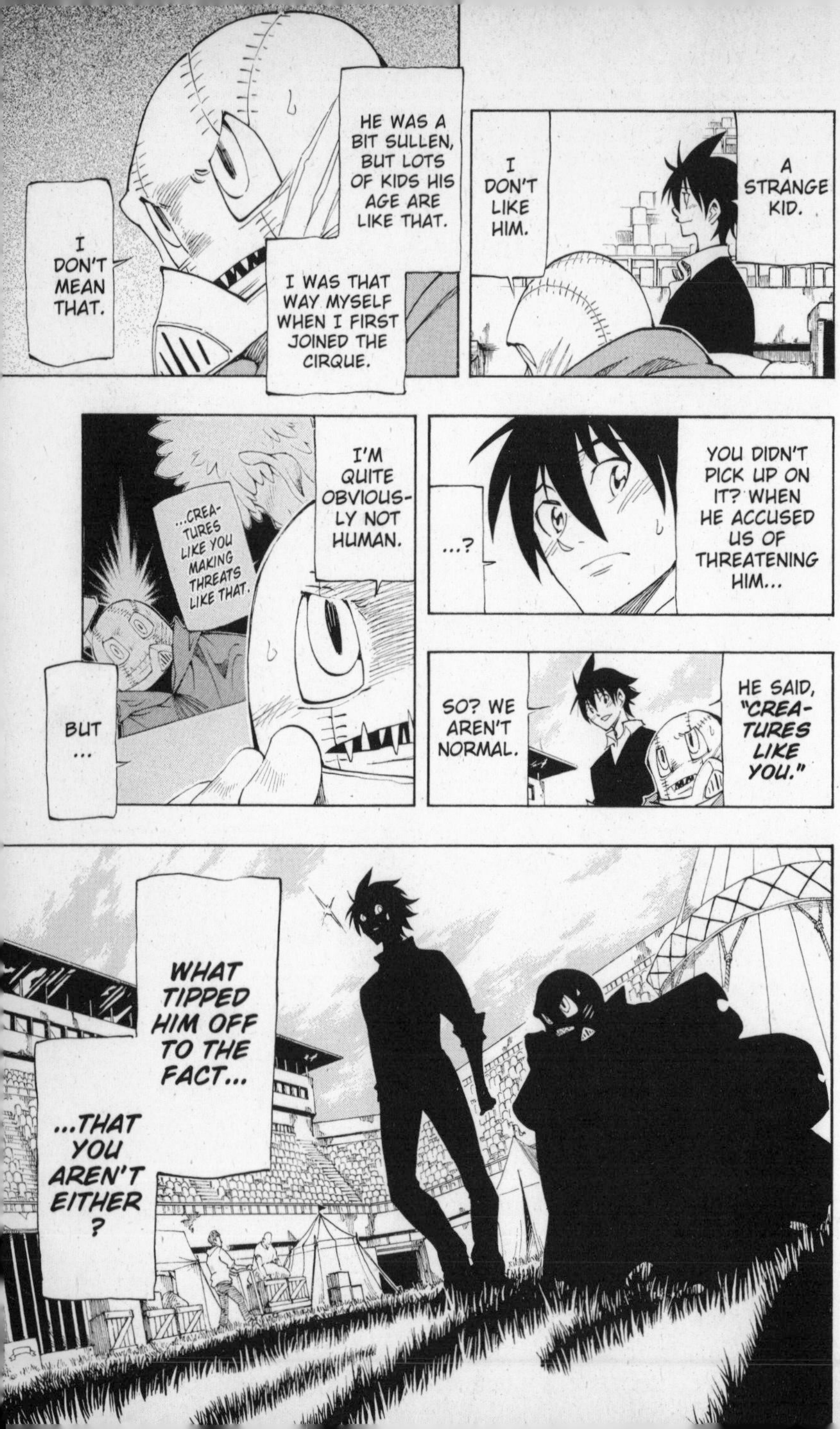
A STRANGE KID.
I DON'T LIKE HIM.
HE WAS A BIT SULLEN, BUT LOTS OF KIDS HIS AGE ARE LIKE THAT.
I WAS THAT WAY MYSELF WHEN I FIRST JOINED THE CIRQUE.
I DON'T MEAN THAT.
YOU DIDN'T PICK UP ON IT? WHEN HE ACCUSED US OF THREATENING HIM...
...?
HE SAID, "CREATURES LIKE YOU."
SO? WE AREN'T NORMAL.
I'M QUITE OBVIOUSLY NOT HUMAN.
...CREATURES LIKE YOU MAKING THREATS LIKE THAT.
BUT ...
WHAT TIPPED HIM OFF TO THE FACT...
...THAT YOU AREN'T EITHER?

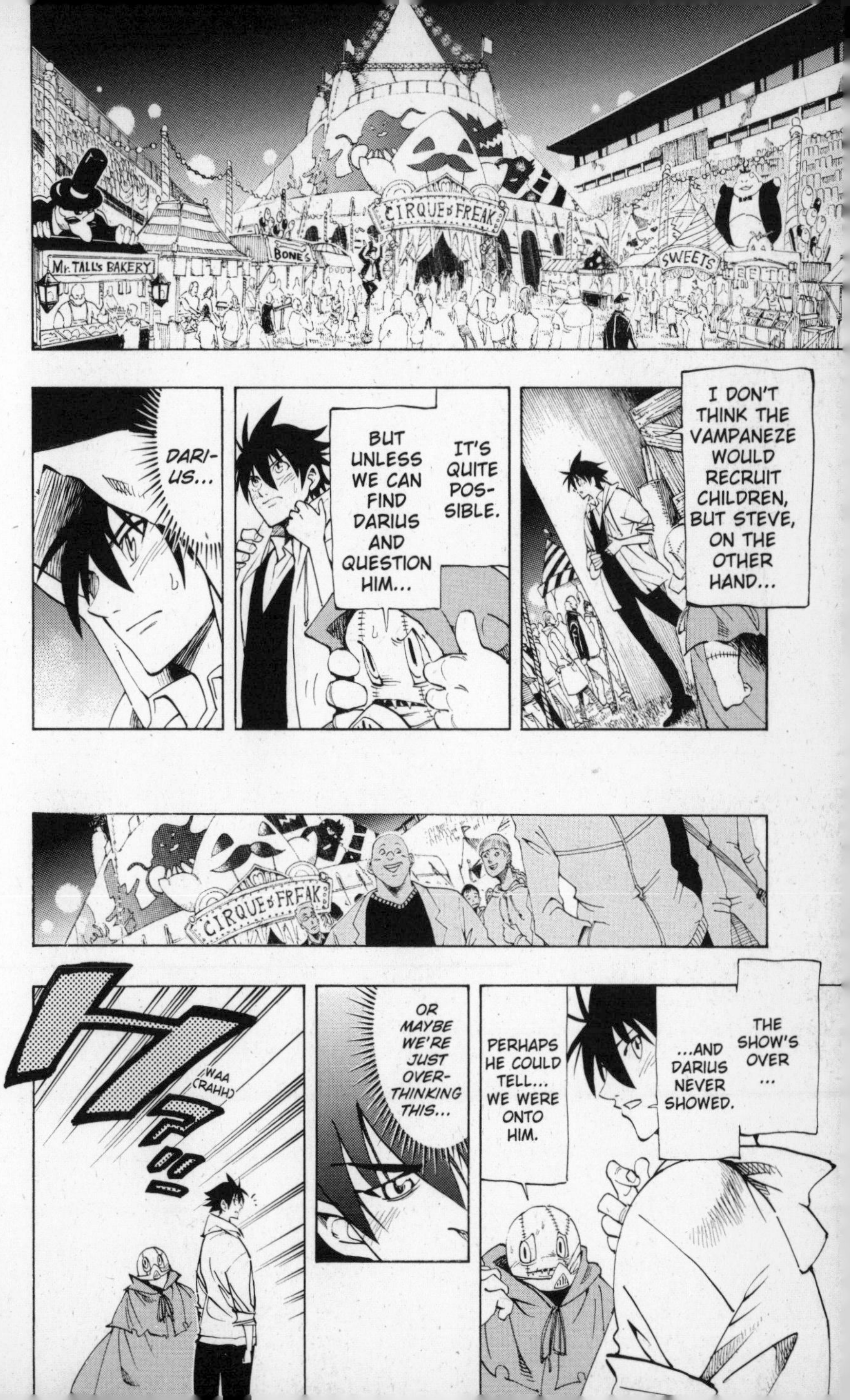
CIRQUE DU FREAK
SWEETS
BONE'S
MR. TALL'S BAKERY
I DON'T THINK THE VAMPANEZE WOULD RECRUIT CHILDREN, BUT STEVE, ON THE OTHER HAND...
IT'S QUITE POS-SIBLE.
BUT UNLESS WE CAN FIND DARIUS AND QUESTION HIM...
DARI-US...
CIRQUE DU FREAK
THE SHOW'S OVER...
...AND DARIUS NEVER SHOWED.
PERHAPS HE COULD TELL... WE WERE ONTO HIM.
OR MAYBE WE'RE JUST OVER-THINKING THIS...
WAA (RAHH)
?!

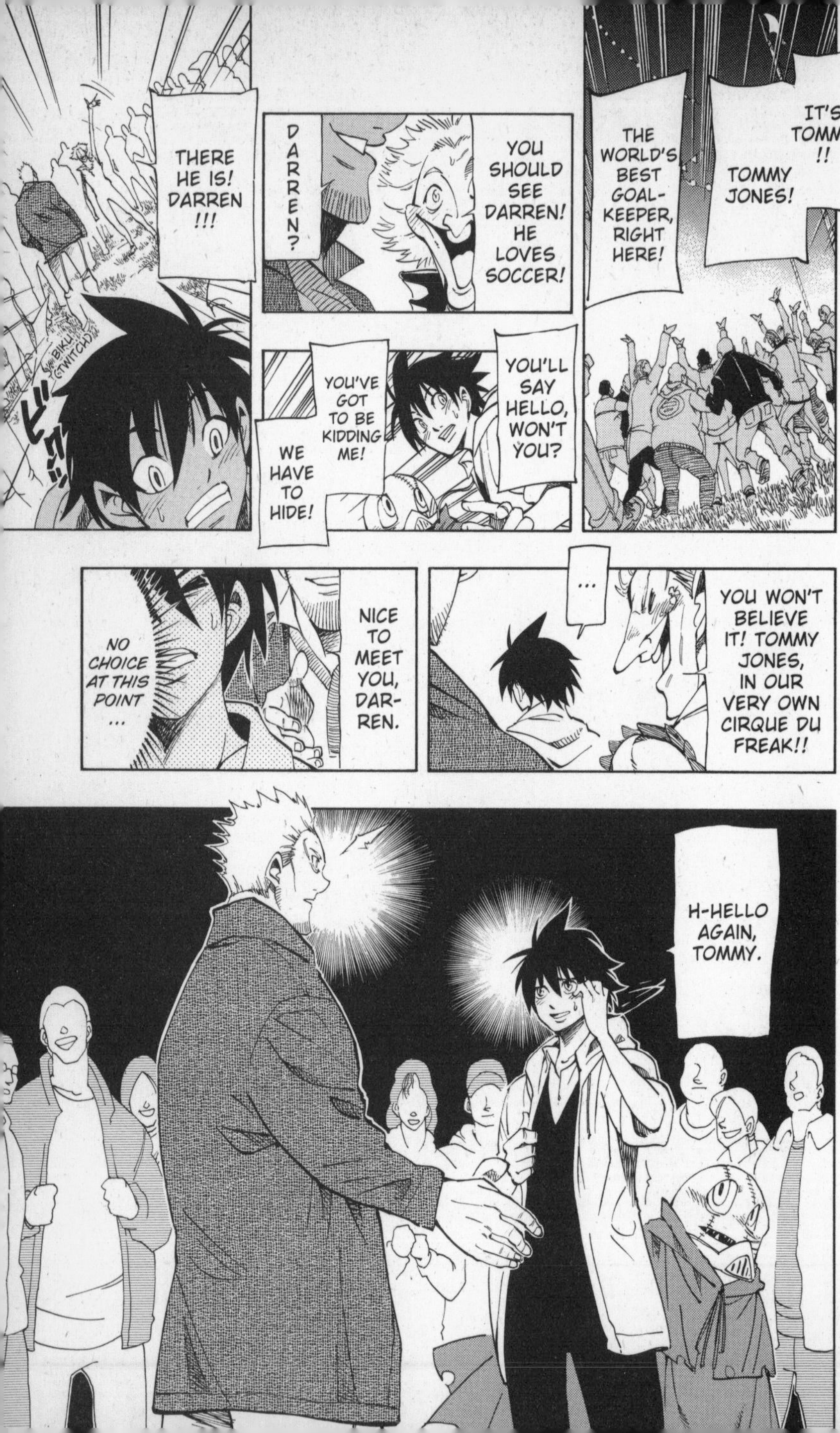
IT'S TOMMY !!
TOMMY JONES!
THE WORLD'S BEST GOAL-KEEPER, RIGHT HERE!
YOU SHOULD SEE DARREN! HE LOVES SOCCER!
DARREN?
YOU'LL SAY HELLO, WON'T YOU?
YOU'VE GOT TO BE KIDDING ME!
WE HAVE TO HIDE!
THERE HE IS! DARREN!!!
BIKU (TWITCH)
YOU WON'T BELIEVE IT! TOMMY JONES, IN OUR VERY OWN CIRQUE DU FREAK!!
...
NICE TO MEET YOU, DAR-REN.
NO CHOICE AT THIS POINT ...
H-HELLO AGAIN, TOMMY.

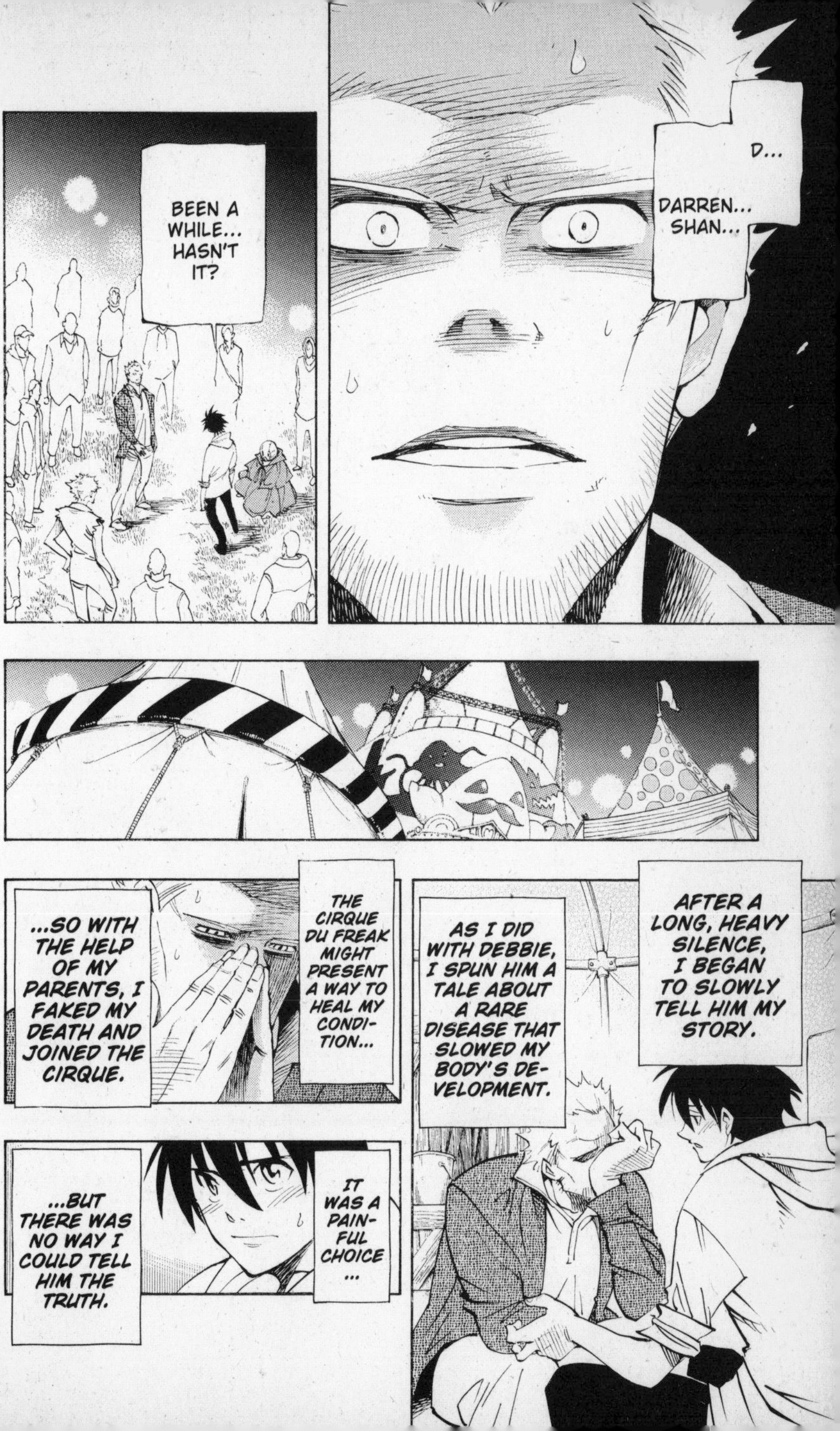
D...
DARREN... SHAN...
BEEN A WHILE... HASN'T IT?
AFTER A LONG, HEAVY SILENCE, I BEGAN TO SLOWLY TELL HIM MY STORY.
AS I DID WITH DEBBIE, I SPUN HIM A TALE ABOUT A RARE DISEASE THAT SLOWED MY BODY'S DE-VELOPMENT.
THE CIRQUE DU FREAK MIGHT PRESENT A WAY TO HEAL MY CONDI-TION...
...SO WITH THE HELP OF MY PARENTS, I FAKED MY DEATH AND JOINED THE CIRQUE.
IT WAS A PAIN-FUL CHOICE...
...BUT THERE WAS NO WAY I COULD TELL HIM THE TRUTH.

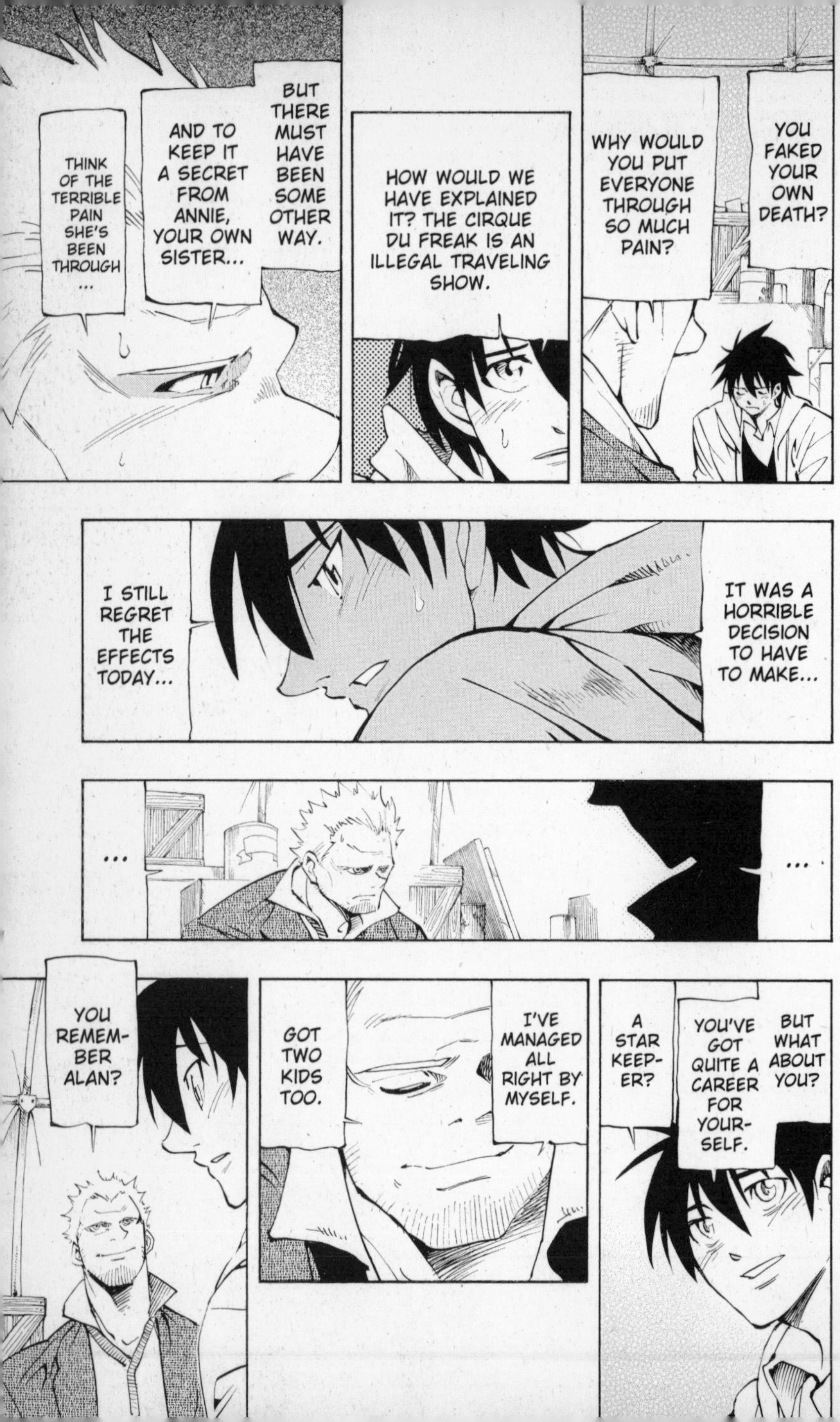

YOU FAKED YOUR OWN DEATH?
WHY WOULD YOU PUT EVERYONE THROUGH SO MUCH PAIN?
HOW WOULD WE HAVE EXPLAINED IT? THE CIRQUE DU FREAK IS AN ILLEGAL TRAVELING SHOW.
BUT THERE MUST HAVE BEEN SOME OTHER WAY.
AND TO KEEP IT A SECRET FROM ANNIE, YOUR OWN SISTER...
THINK OF THE TERRIBLE PAIN SHE'S BEEN THROUGH...
IT WAS A HORRIBLE DECISION TO HAVE TO MAKE...
I STILL REGRET THE EFFECTS TODAY...
...
...
BUT WHAT ABOUT YOU?
YOU'VE GOT QUITE A CAREER FOR YOUR-SELF.
A STAR KEEP-ER?
I'VE MANAGED ALL RIGHT BY MYSELF.
GOT TWO KIDS TOO.
YOU REMEM-BER ALAN?

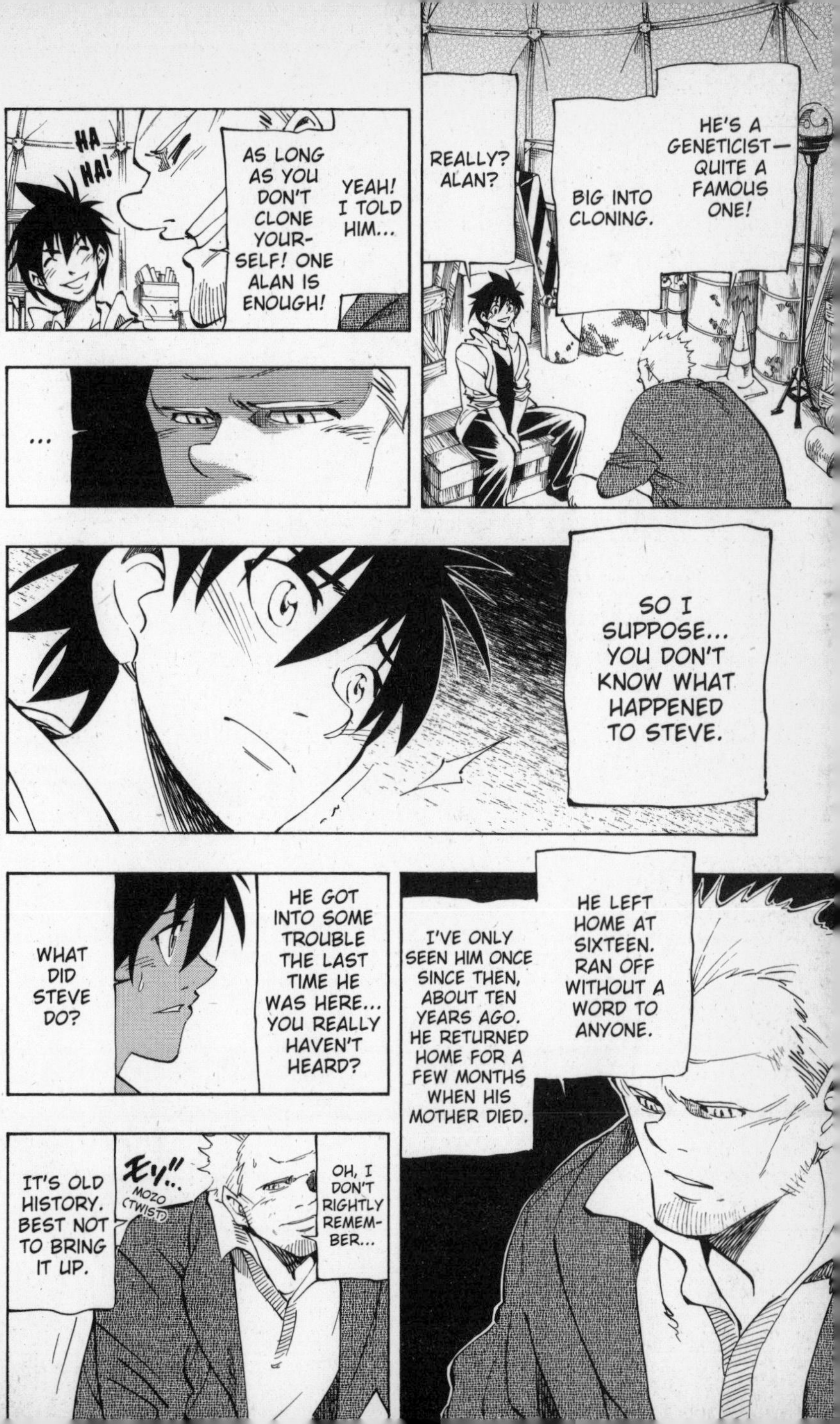
REALLY? ALAN?
HE'S A GENETICIST— QUITE A FAMOUS ONE!
BIG INTO CLONING.
YEAH! I TOLD HIM...
AS LONG AS YOU DON'T CLONE YOURSELF! ONE ALAN IS ENOUGH!
HA HA!
...
SO I SUPPOSE... YOU DON'T KNOW WHAT HAPPENED TO STEVE.
HE LEFT HOME AT SIXTEEN. RAN OFF WITHOUT A WORD TO ANYONE.
I'VE ONLY SEEN HIM ONCE SINCE THEN, ABOUT TEN YEARS AGO. HE RETURNED HOME FOR A FEW MONTHS WHEN HIS MOTHER DIED.
HE GOT INTO SOME TROUBLE THE LAST TIME HE WAS HERE... YOU REALLY HAVEN'T HEARD?
WHAT DID STEVE DO?
OH, I DON'T RIGHTLY REMEMBER...
MOZO (TWIST)
IT'S OLD HISTORY. BEST NOT TO BRING IT UP.

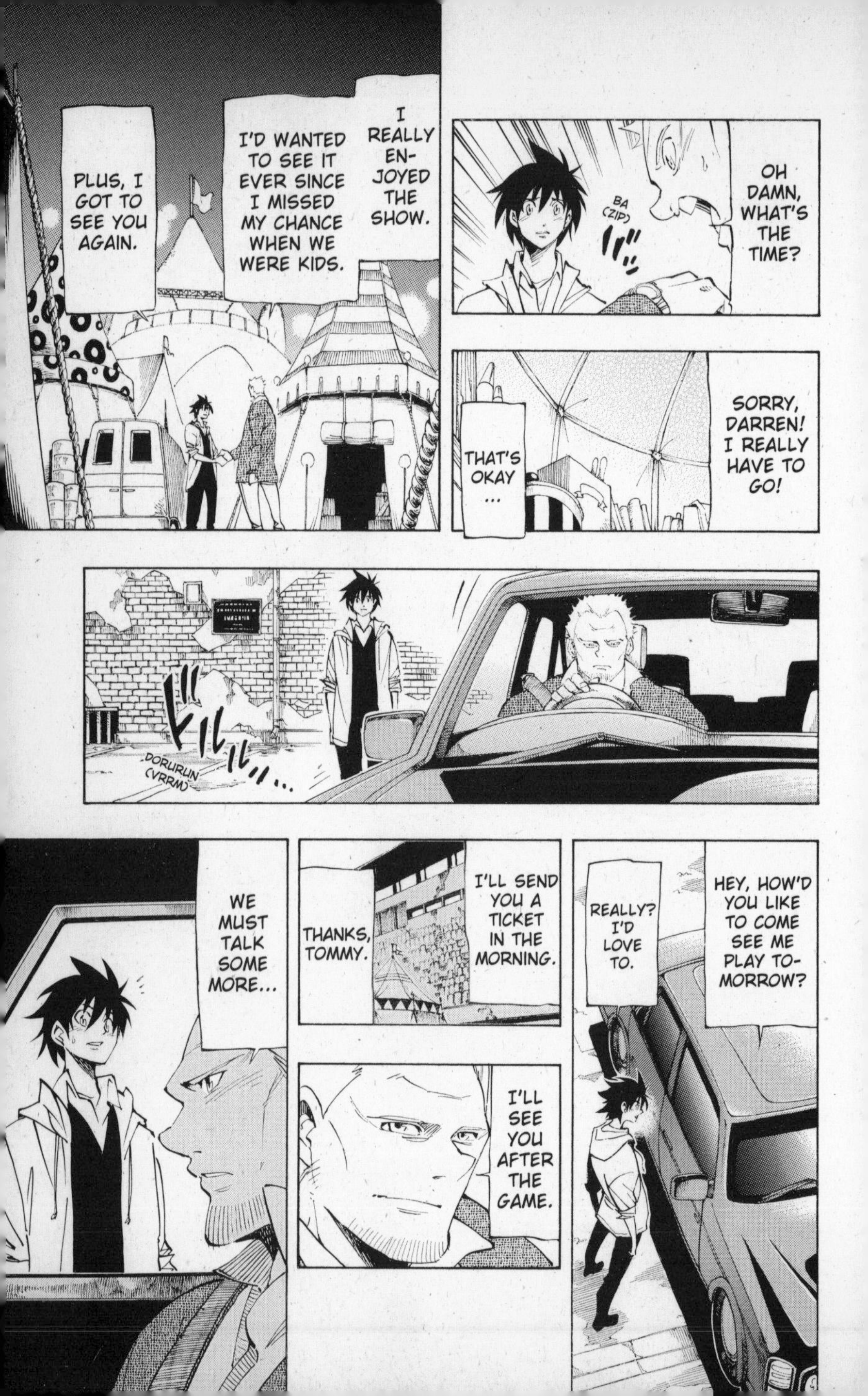
I REALLY EN-JOYED THE SHOW.
I'D WANTED TO SEE IT EVER SINCE I MISSED MY CHANCE WHEN WE WERE KIDS.
PLUS, I GOT TO SEE YOU AGAIN.
OH DAMN, WHAT'S THE TIME?
BA (ZIP)
SORRY, DARREN! I REALLY HAVE TO GO!
THAT'S OKAY ...
DORURUN (VRRM)
HEY, HOW'D YOU LIKE TO COME SEE ME PLAY TO-MORROW?
REALLY? I'D LOVE TO.
I'LL SEND YOU A TICKET IN THE MORNING.
THANKS, TOMMY.
I'LL SEE YOU AFTER THE GAME.
WE MUST TALK SOME MORE...

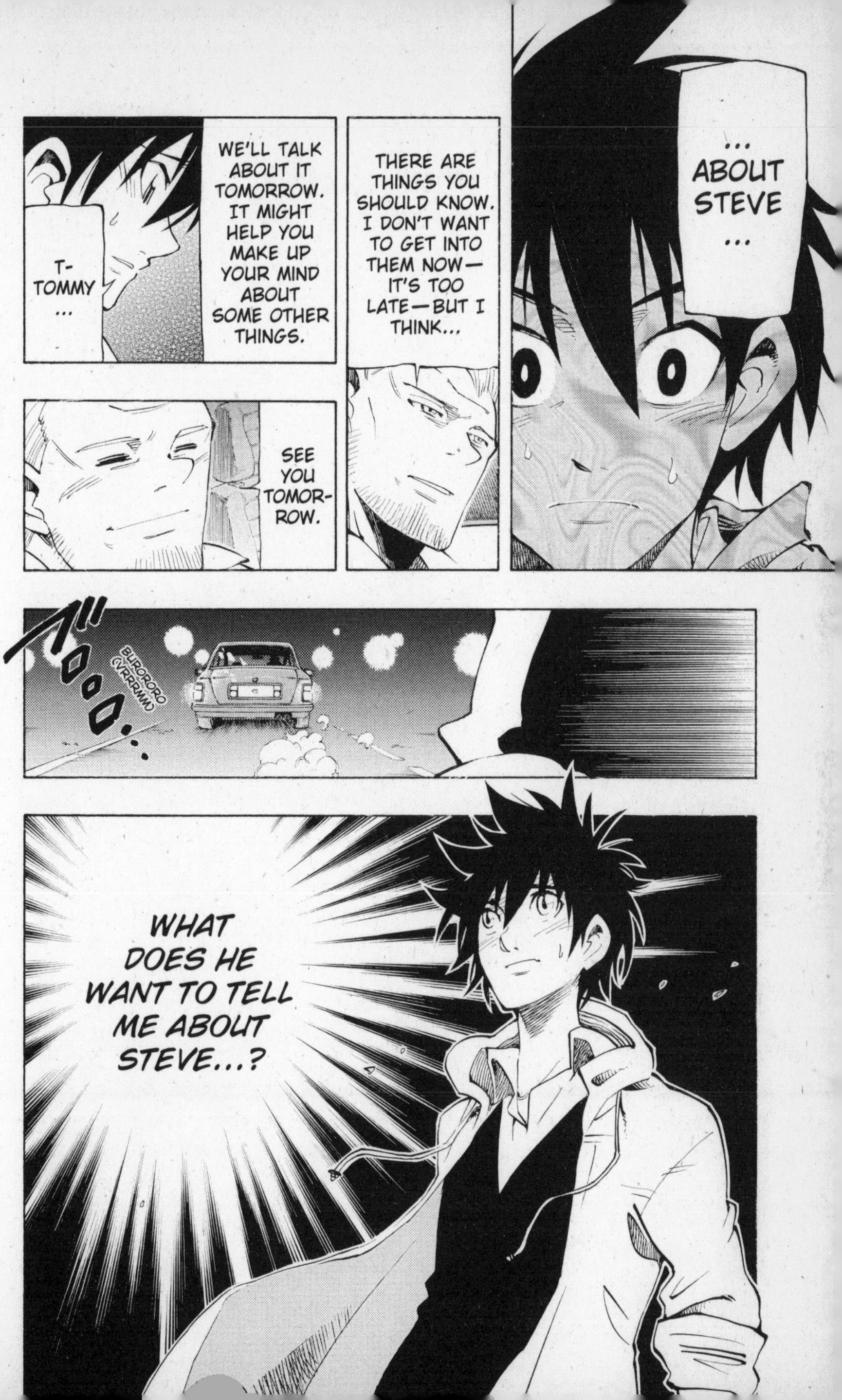
... ABOUT STEVE ...
THERE ARE THINGS YOU SHOULD KNOW. I DON'T WANT TO GET INTO THEM NOW—IT'S TOO LATE—BUT I THINK...
WE'LL TALK ABOUT IT TOMORROW. IT MIGHT HELP YOU MAKE UP YOUR MIND ABOUT SOME OTHER THINGS.
T-TOMMY ...
SEE YOU TOMORROW.
BURORORO (VRRRMM)
WHAT DOES HE WANT TO TELL ME ABOUT STEVE...?

# CHAPTER 98: THE BIG GAME

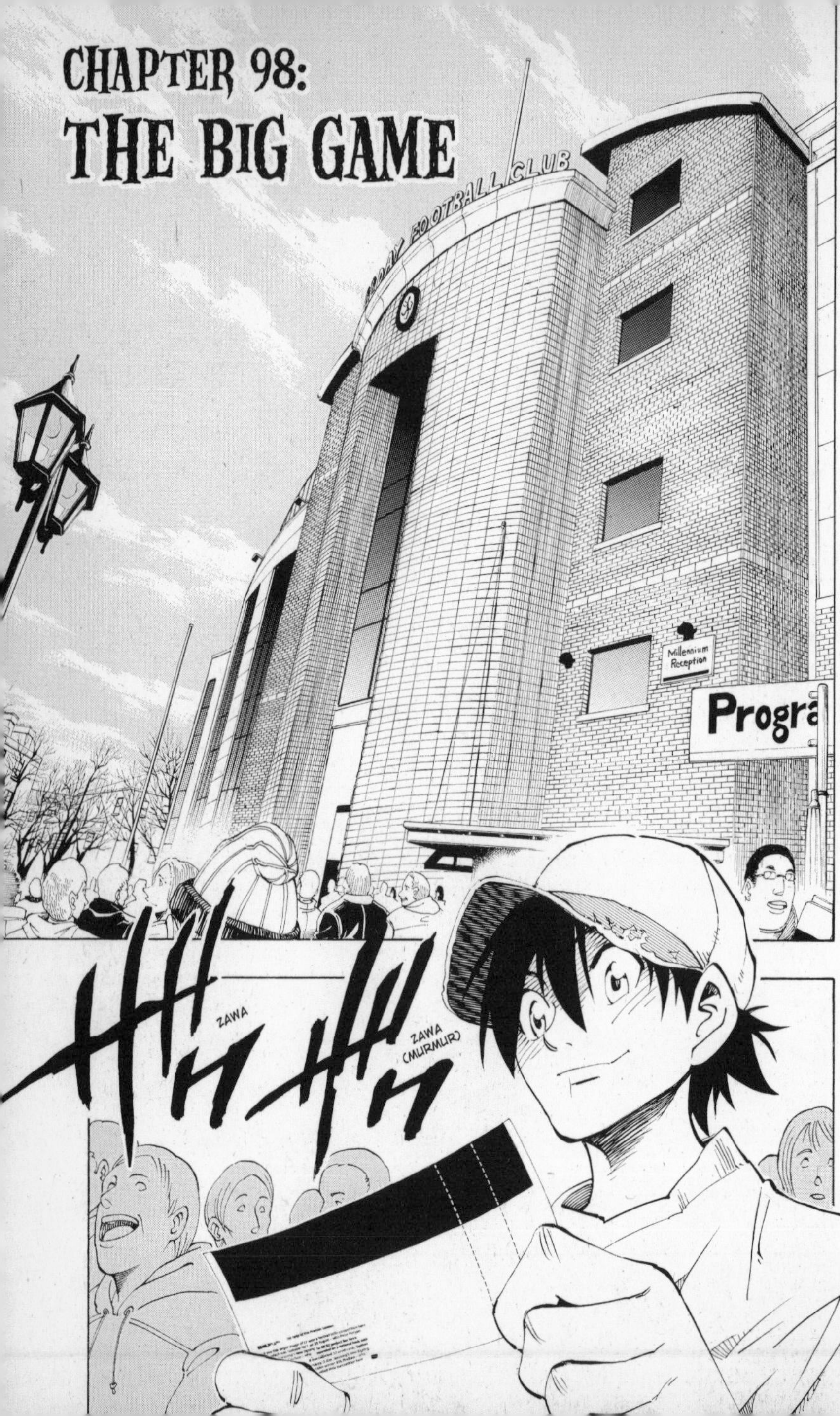
FOOTBALL CLUB
Millennium Reception
Progra
ZAWA
ZAWA (MURMUR)

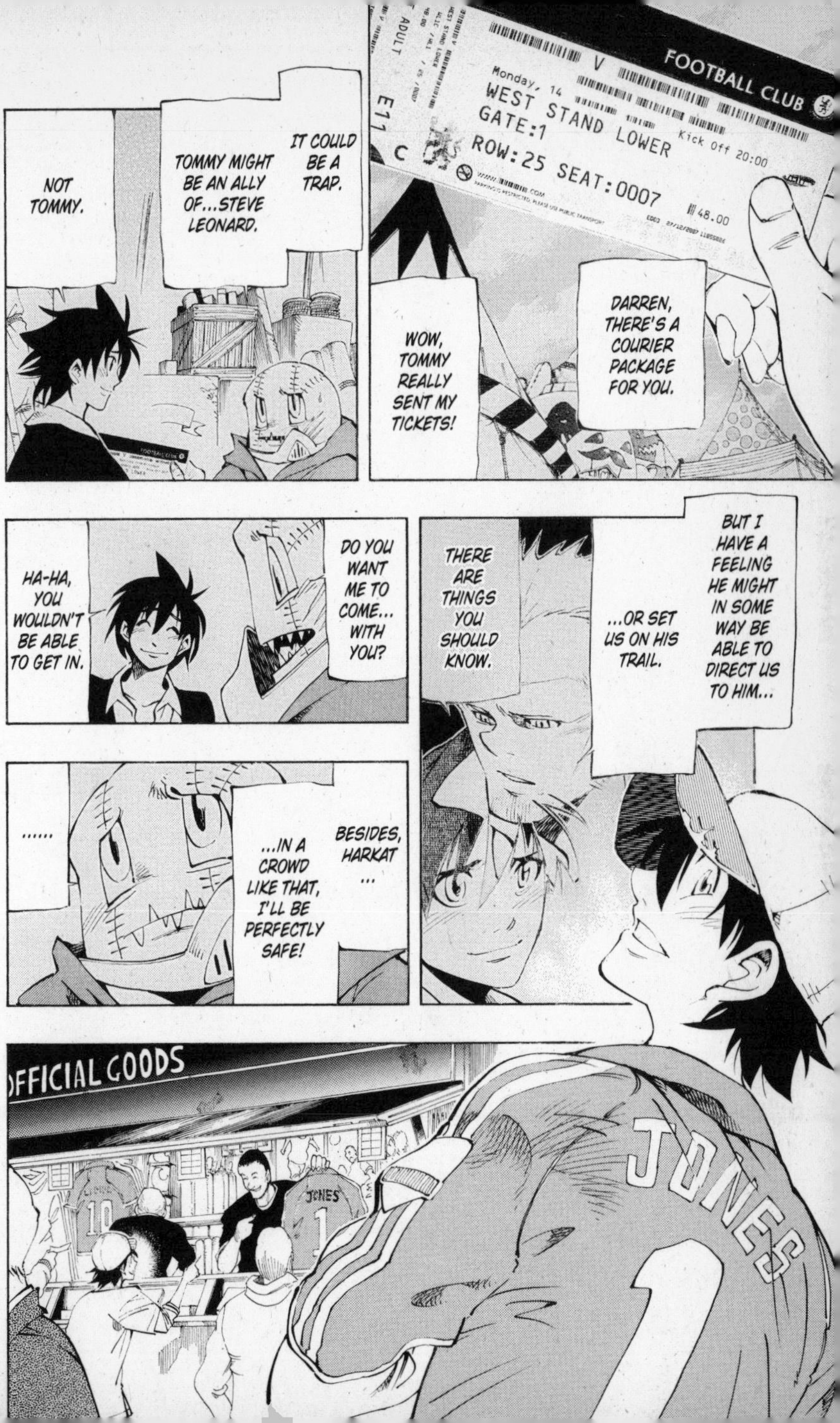
FOOTBALL CLUB
Monday, 14
WEST STAND LOWER
GATE:1
ROW:25 SEAT:0007
Kick Off 20:00
48.00
ADULT
E11
C
DARREN, THERE'S A COURIER PACKAGE FOR YOU.
WOW, TOMMY REALLY SENT MY TICKETS!
IT COULD BE A TRAP.
TOMMY MIGHT BE AN ALLY OF...STEVE LEONARD.
NOT TOMMY.
BUT I HAVE A FEELING HE MIGHT IN SOME WAY BE ABLE TO DIRECT US TO HIM...
...OR SET US ON HIS TRAIL.
THERE ARE THINGS YOU SHOULD KNOW.
DO YOU WANT ME TO COME... WITH YOU?
HA-HA, YOU WOULDN'T BE ABLE TO GET IN.
BESIDES, HARKAT ...
...IN A CROWD LIKE THAT, I'LL BE PERFECTLY SAFE!
......
FFICIAL GOODS
JONES
JONES

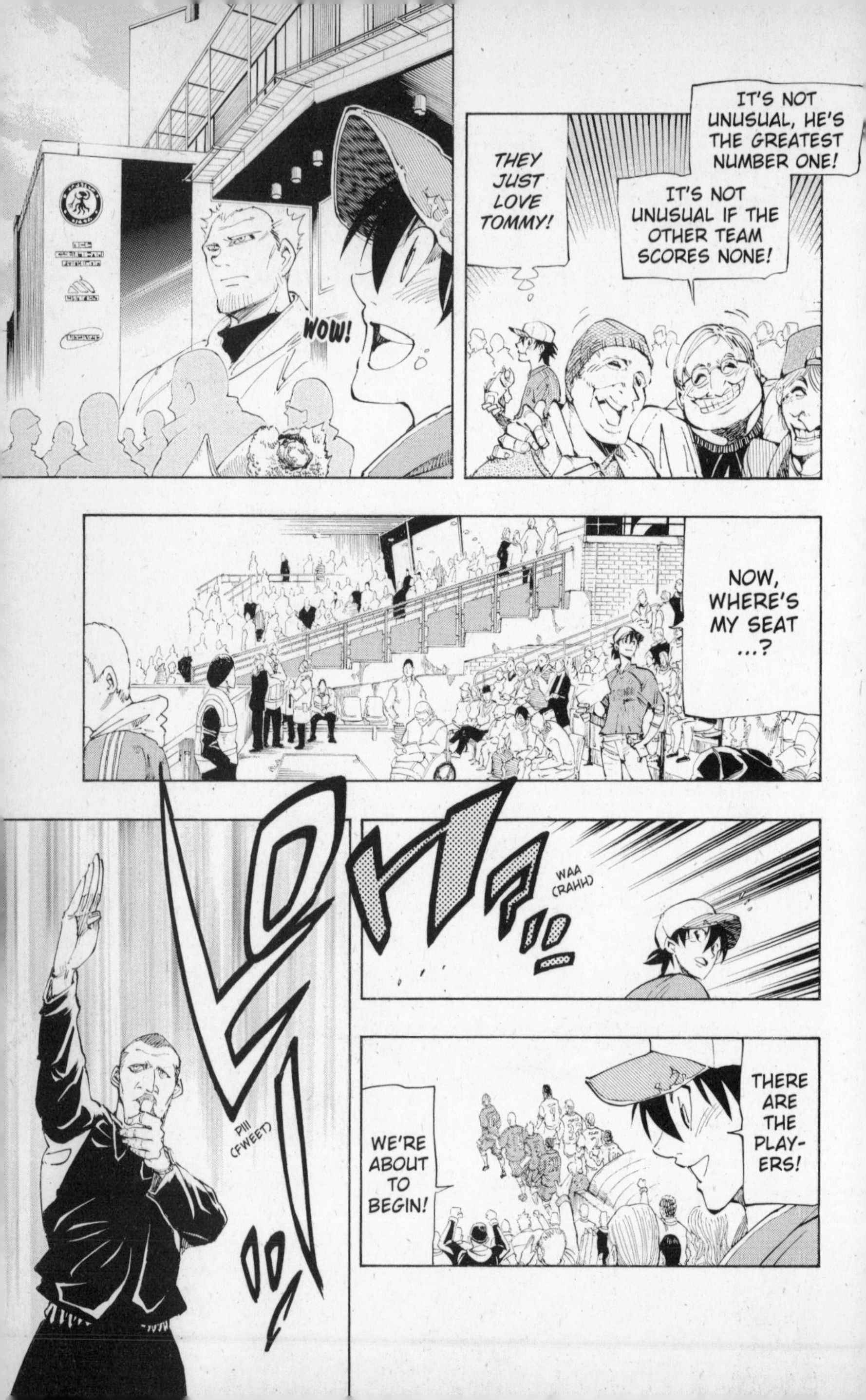
IT'S NOT UNUSUAL, HE'S THE GREATEST NUMBER ONE!
IT'S NOT UNUSUAL IF THE OTHER TEAM SCORES NONE!
THEY JUST LOVE TOMMY!
WOW!
NOW, WHERE'S MY SEAT ...?
WAA (RAHH)
THERE ARE THE PLAY-ERS!
WE'RE ABOUT TO BEGIN!
PIII (FWEET)

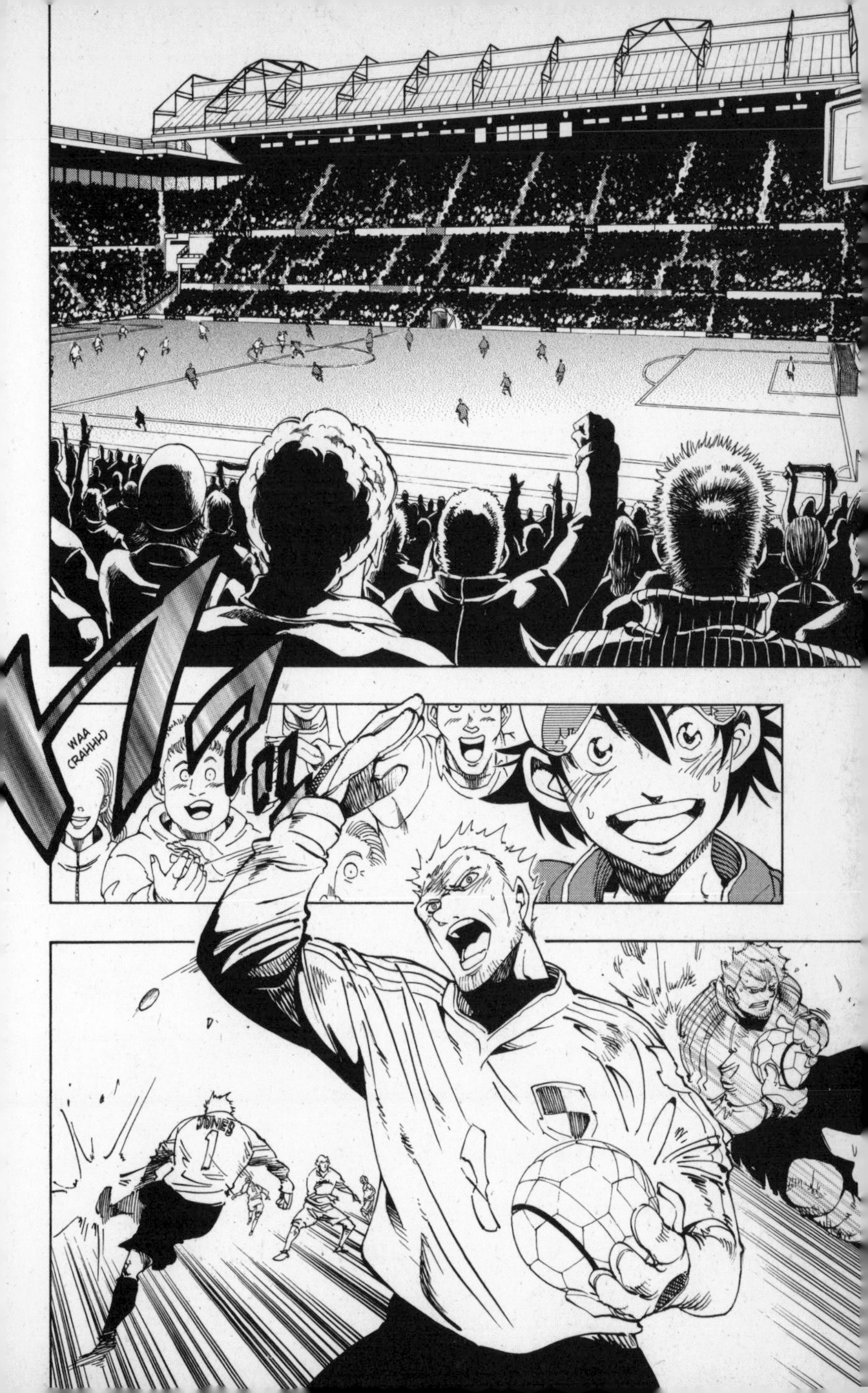
WAA (RAHHH)
JONES 1

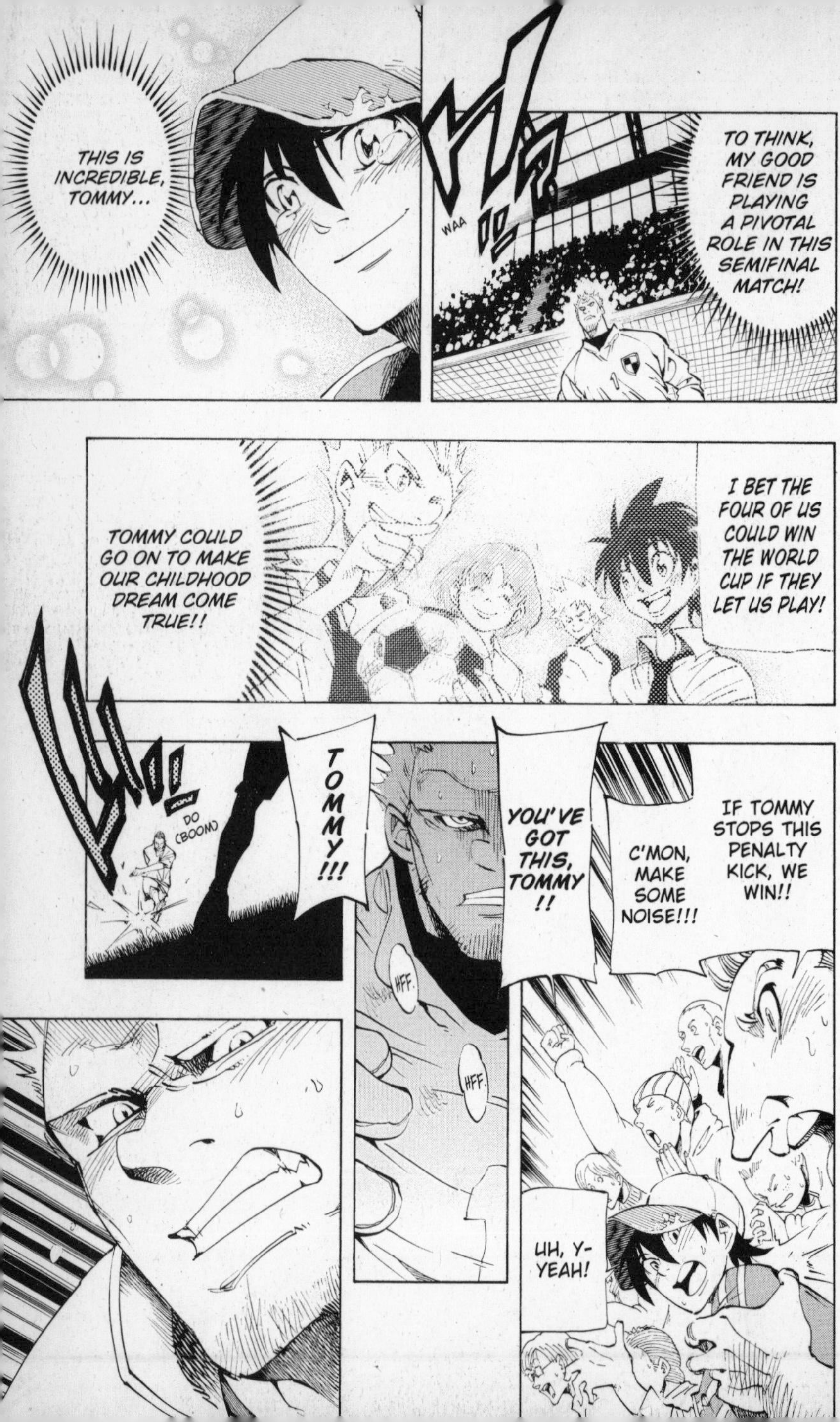
TO THINK, MY GOOD FRIEND IS PLAYING A PIVOTAL ROLE IN THIS SEMIFINAL MATCH!
WAA
THIS IS INCREDIBLE, TOMMY...
I BET THE FOUR OF US COULD WIN THE WORLD CUP IF THEY LET US PLAY!
TOMMY COULD GO ON TO MAKE OUR CHILDHOOD DREAM COME TRUE!!
IF TOMMY STOPS THIS PENALTY KICK, WE WIN!!
C'MON, MAKE SOME NOISE!!!
YOU'VE GOT THIS, TOMMY!!
UH, Y-YEAH!
TOMMY!!!
HFF.
HFF.
DO (BOOM)

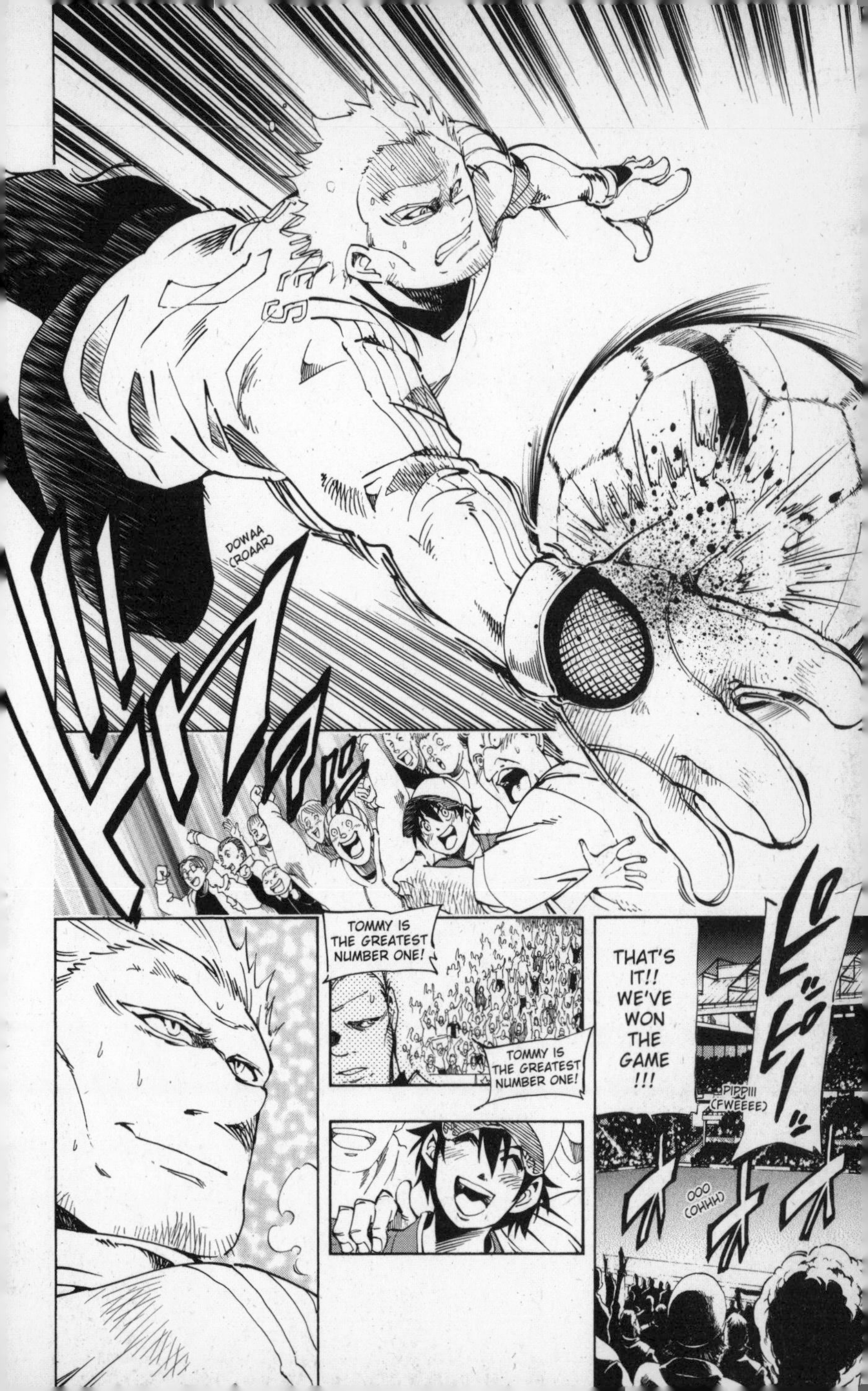
DOWAA (ROAAR)
PIPIII (FWEEEE)
THAT'S IT!! WE'VE WON THE GAME!!!
OOO (OHHH)
TOMMY IS THE GREATEST NUMBER ONE!
TOMMY IS THE GREATEST NUMBER ONE!

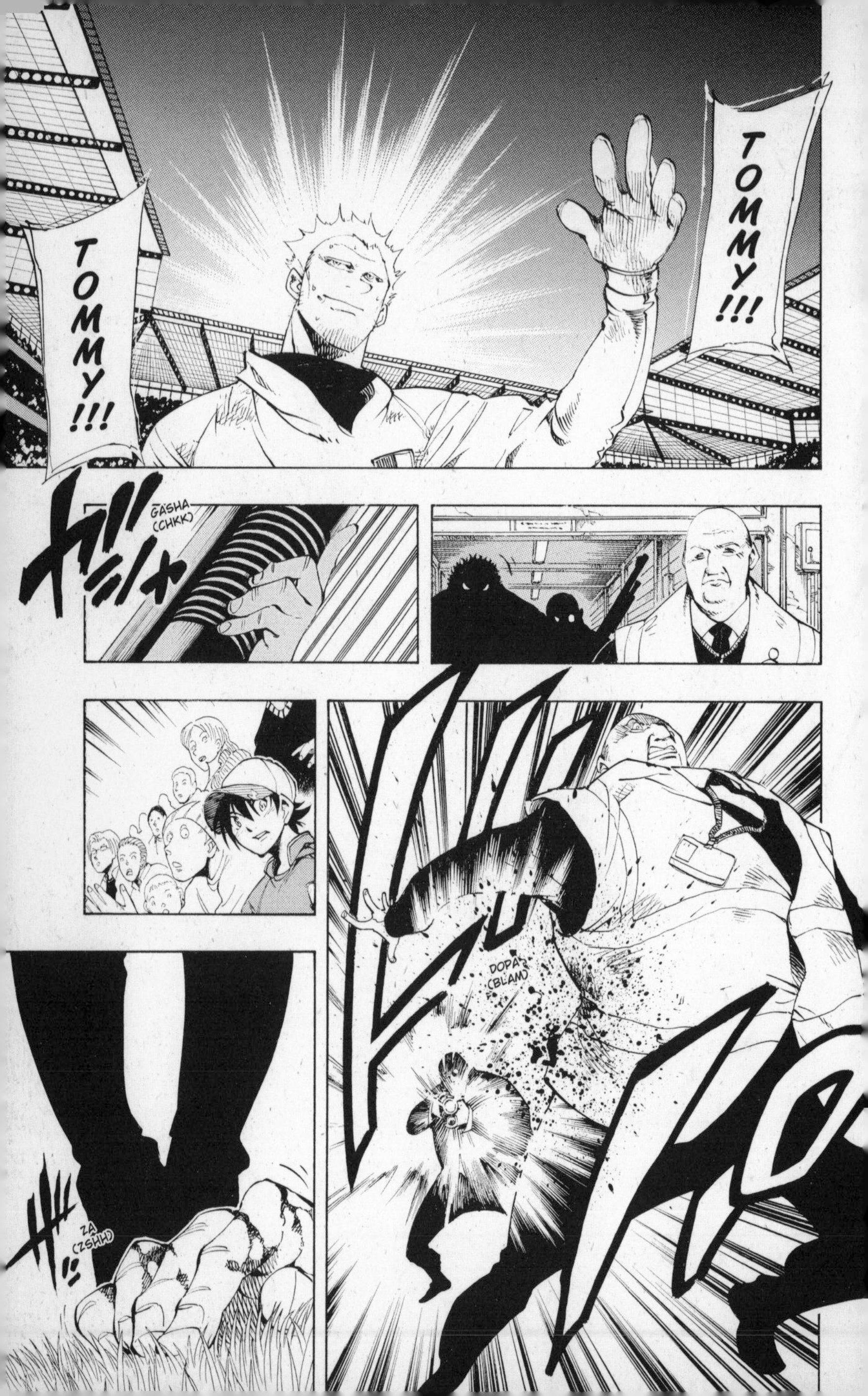
TOMMY!!!
TOMMY!!!
GASHA (CHKK)
DOPA (BLAM)
ZA (ZSHH)

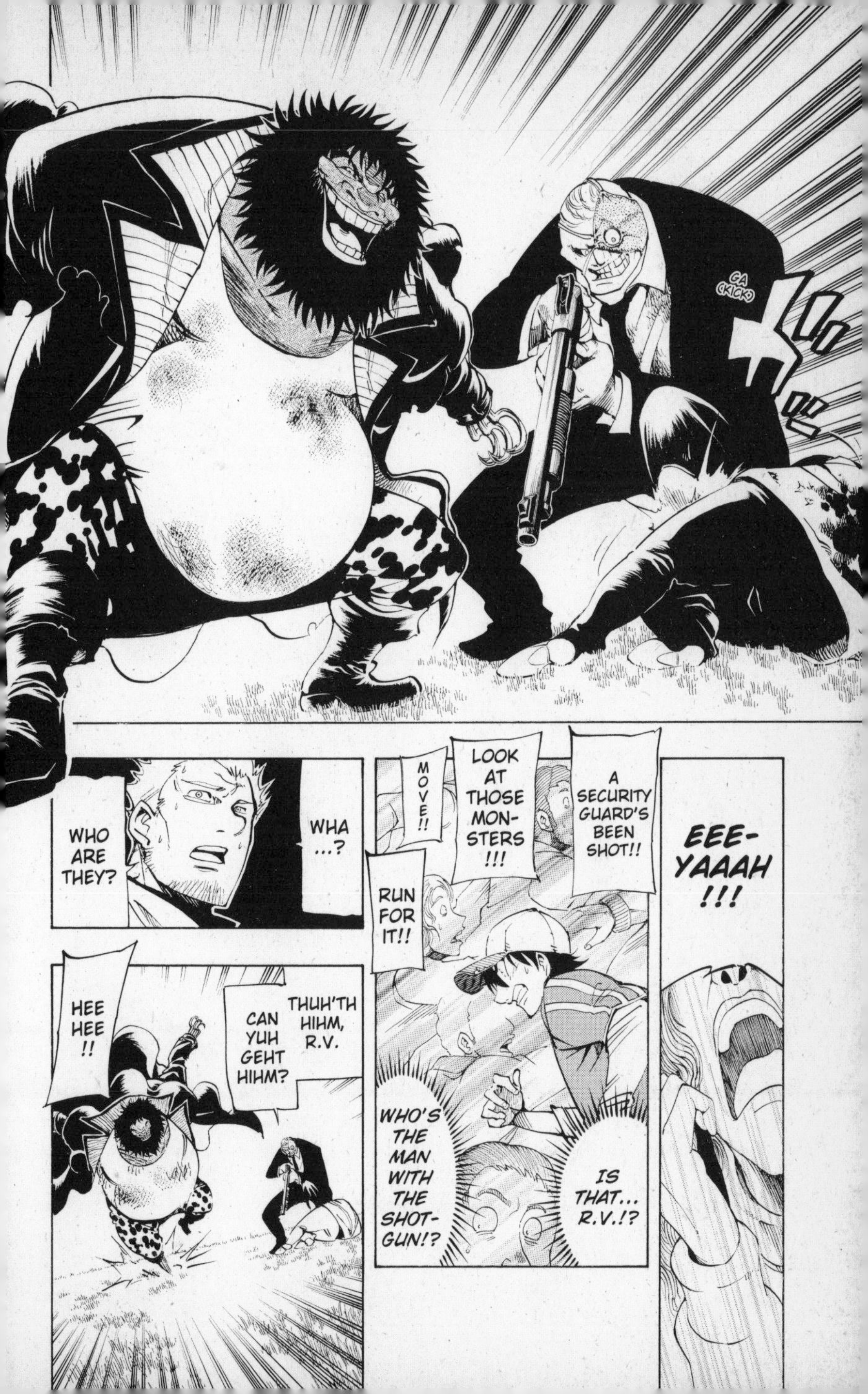
GA (KICK)
EEE-YAAAH!!!
A SECURITY GUARD'S BEEN SHOT!!
LOOK AT THOSE MON-STERS!!!
MOVE!!
RUN FOR IT!!
IS THAT... R.V.!?
WHO'S THE MAN WITH THE SHOT-GUN!?
WHA ...?
WHO ARE THEY?
THUH'TH HIHM, R.V.
CAN YUH GEHT HIHM?
HEE HEE!!

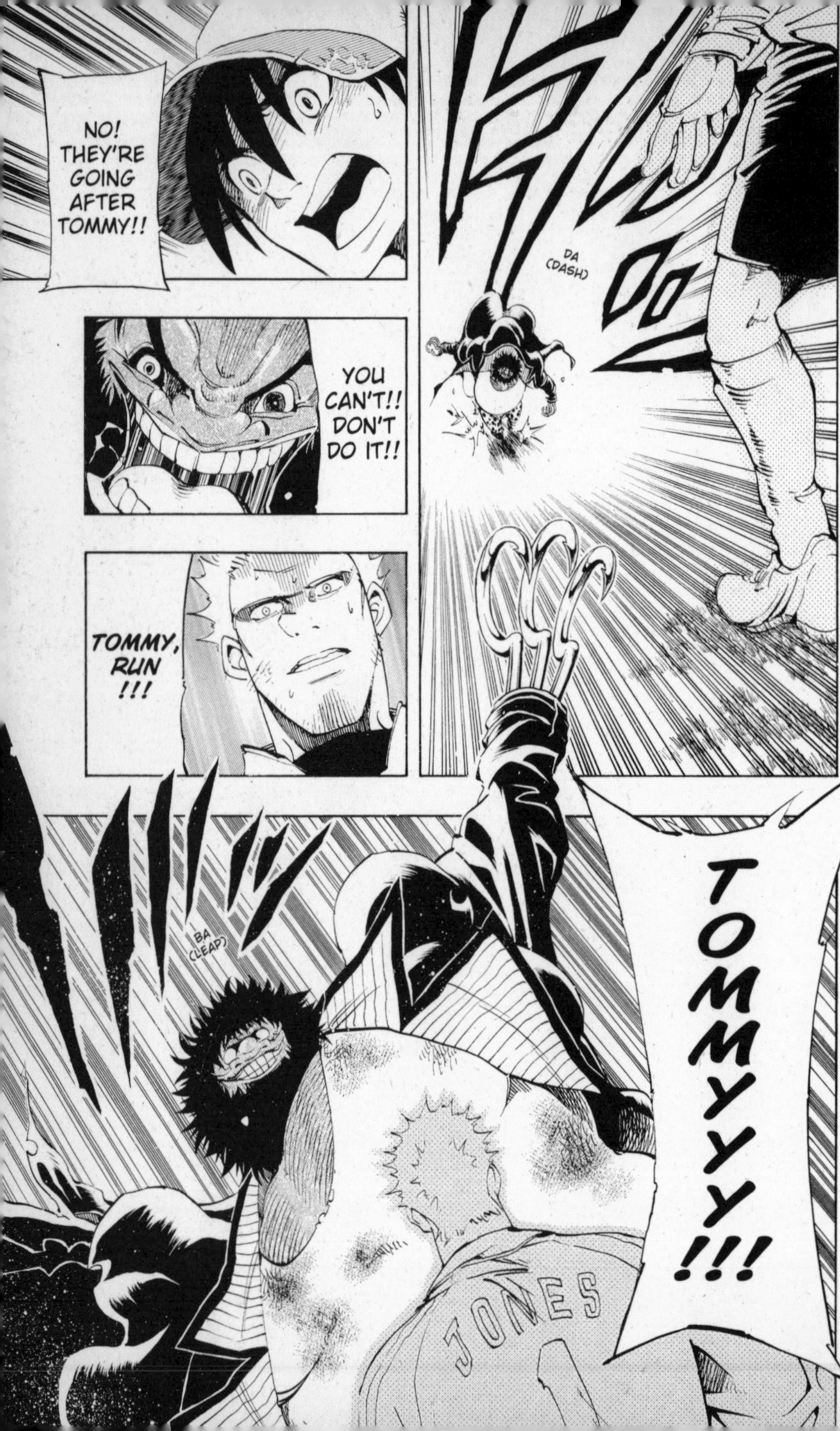
DA (DASH)
NO! THEY'RE GOING AFTER TOMMY!!
YOU CAN'T!! DON'T DO IT!!
TOMMY, RUN!!!
TOMMYYY!!!
BA (LEAP)
JONES

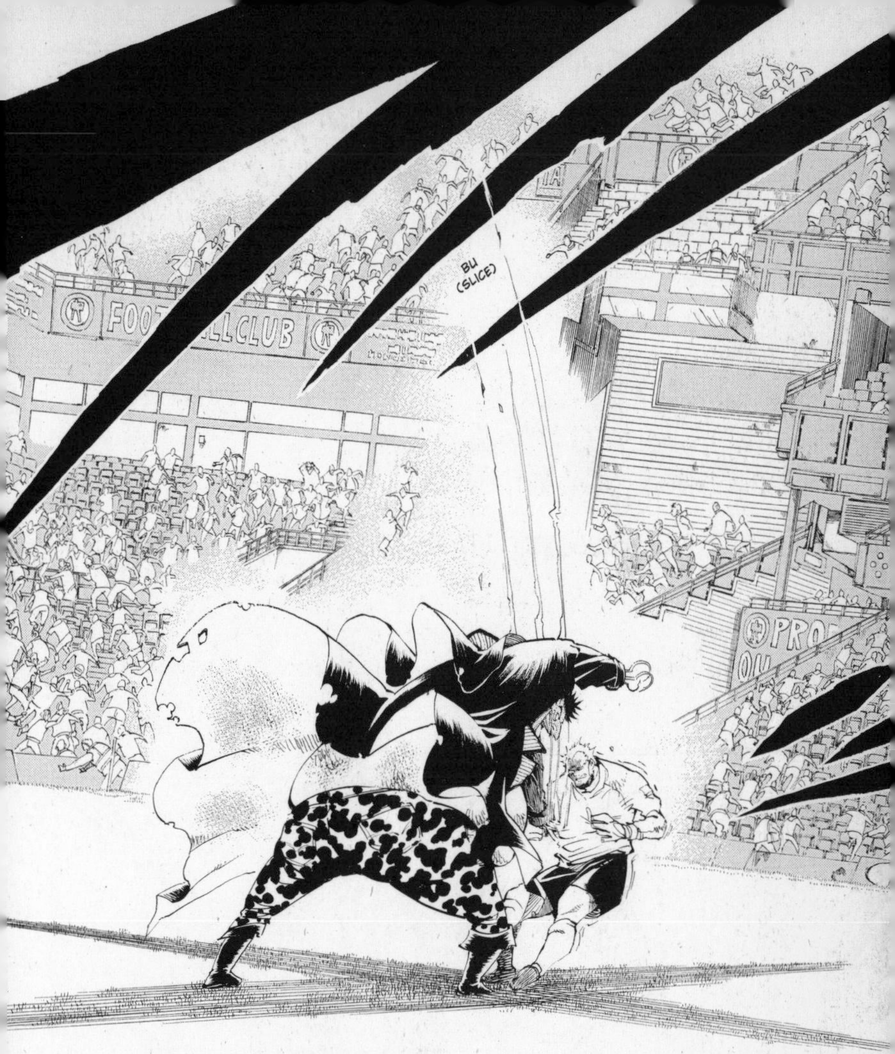

BU
(SLICE)
FOOT
LLCLUB
PRO
OU

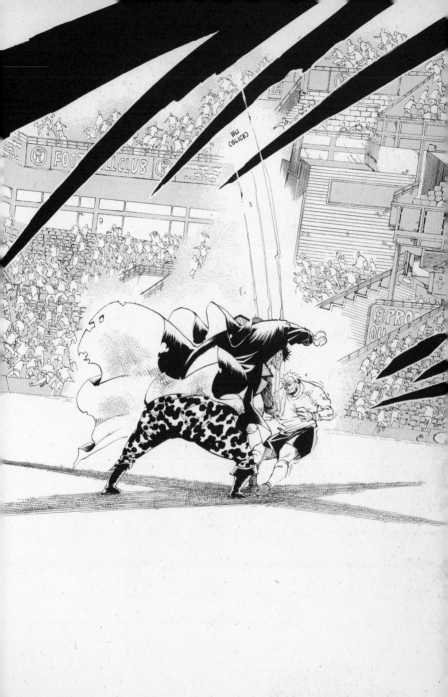

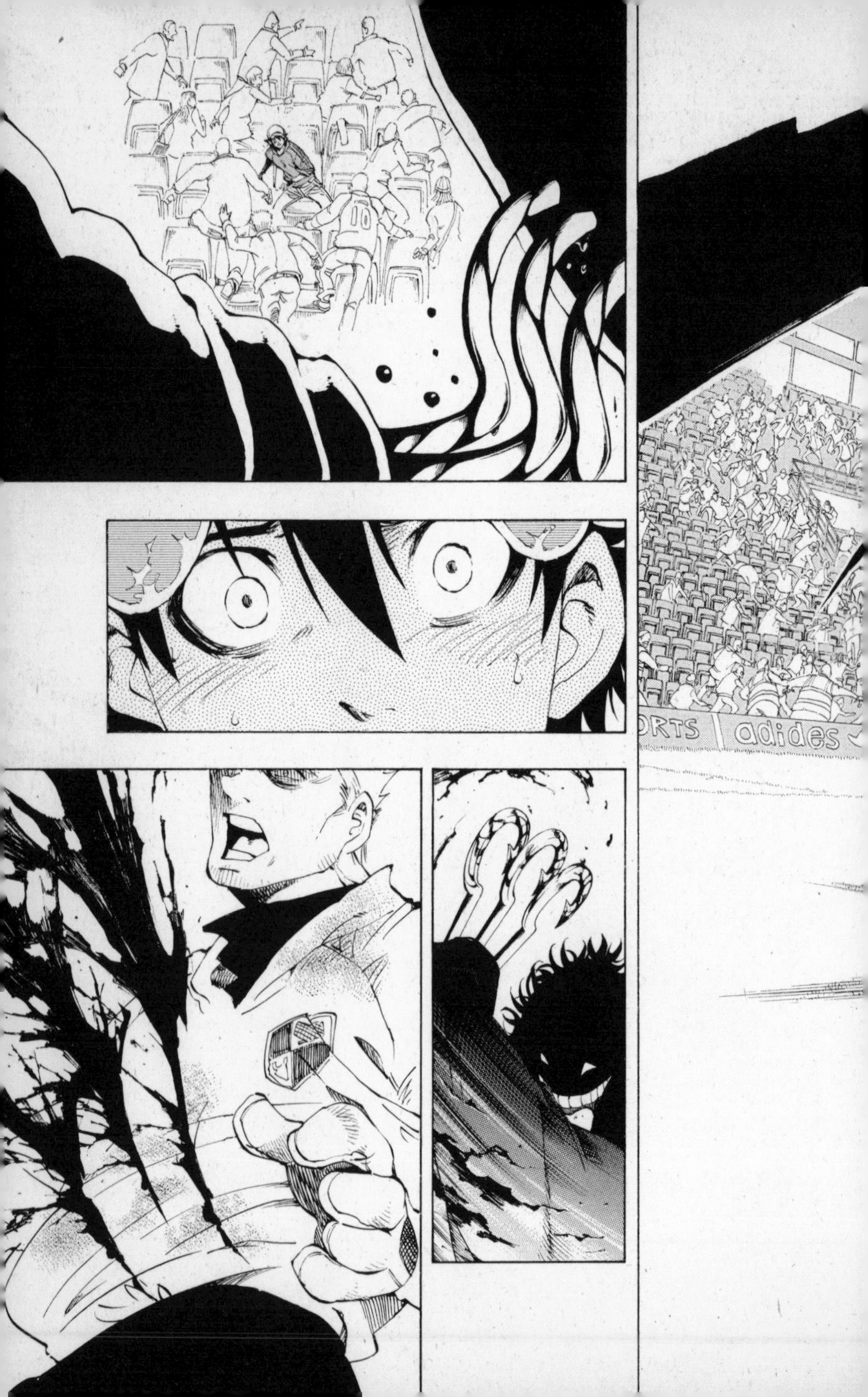

RTS
adides

SCRAM, IF YOU VALUE YOUR LIFE!!

OUTTA THE WAY!

TOMMY.

TOMMY.

TOMMY!!

TOM-MY...

KYAA (AAHHH)

WAA (AAHH)

BURU

BURU (SHIVER)

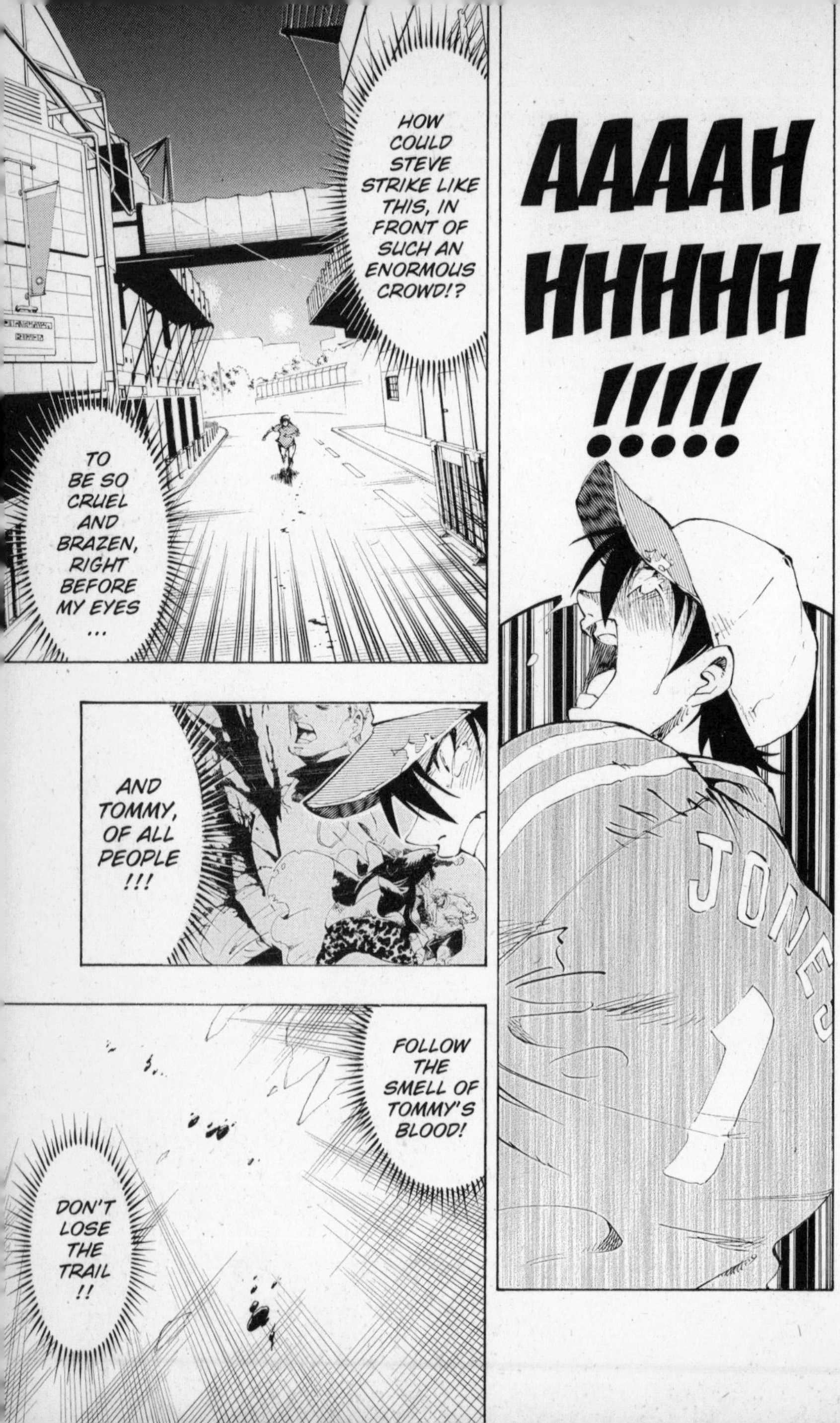
AAAAH HHHHH !!!!!
JONES
HOW COULD STEVE STRIKE LIKE THIS, IN FRONT OF SUCH AN ENORMOUS CROWD!?
TO BE SO CRUEL AND BRAZEN, RIGHT BEFORE MY EYES ...
AND TOMMY, OF ALL PEOPLE !!!
FOLLOW THE SMELL OF TOMMY'S BLOOD!
DON'T LOSE THE TRAIL !!

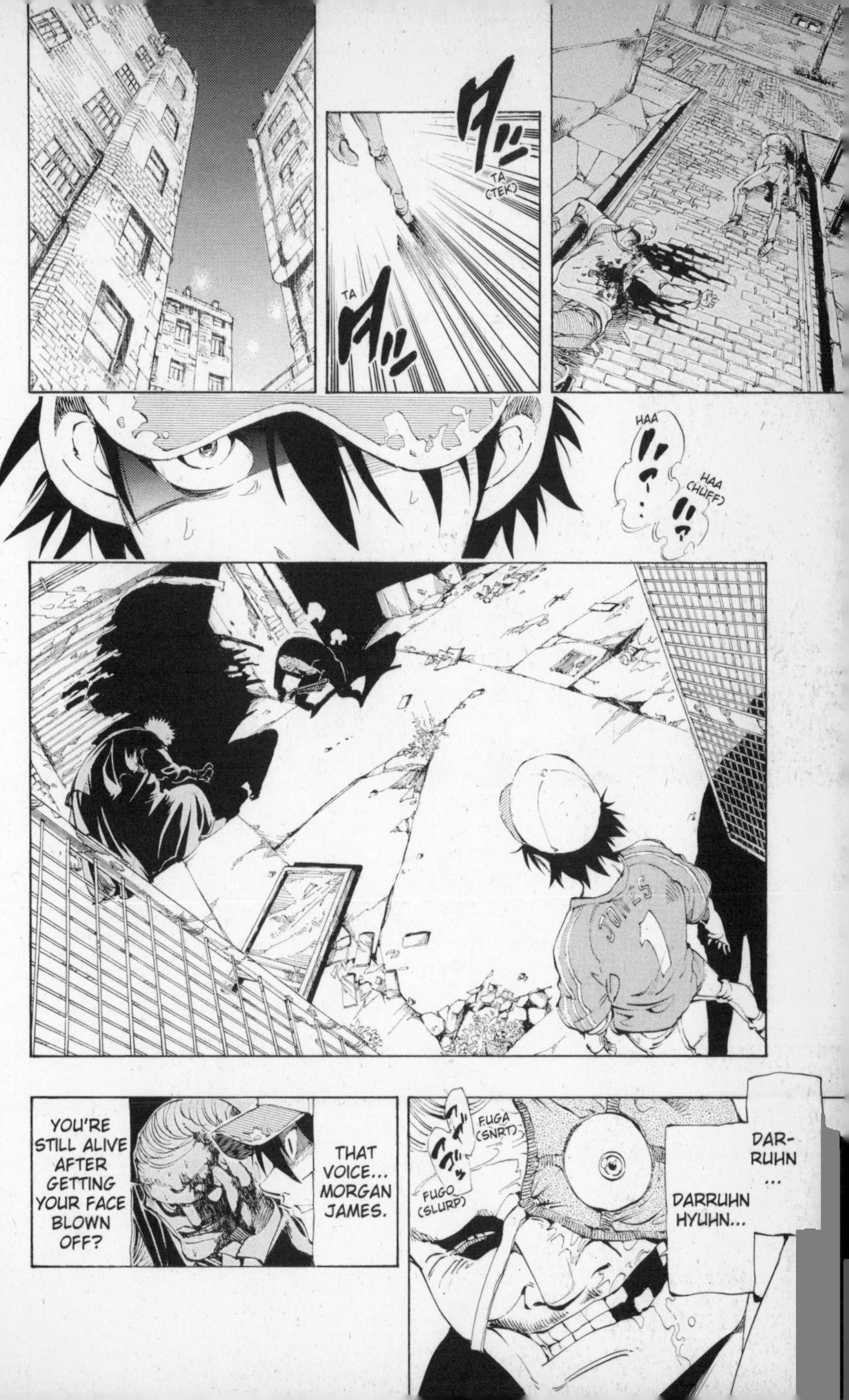
TA (TEK)
TA
HAA
HAA (HUFF)
DAR-RUHN...
FUGA (SNRT)
DARRUHN HYUHN...
FUGO (SLURP)
THAT VOICE... MORGAN JAMES.
YOU'RE STILL ALIVE AFTER GETTING YOUR FACE BLOWN OFF?

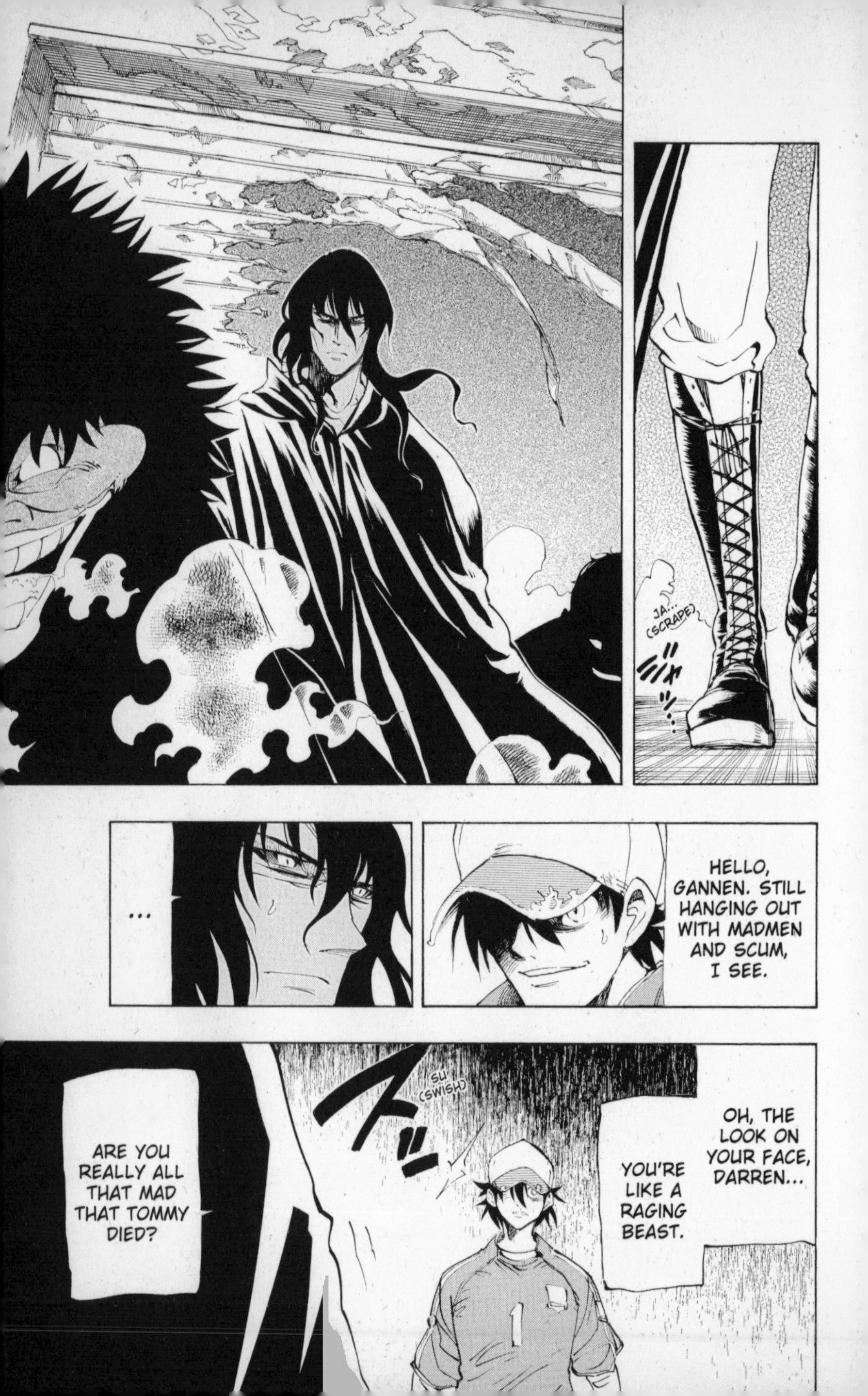
JA... (SCRAPE)
HELLO, GANNEN. STILL HANGING OUT WITH MADMEN AND SCUM, I SEE.
...
OH, THE LOOK ON YOUR FACE, DARREN...
YOU'RE LIKE A RAGING BEAST.
SU (SWISH)
ARE YOU REALLY ALL THAT MAD THAT TOMMY DIED?

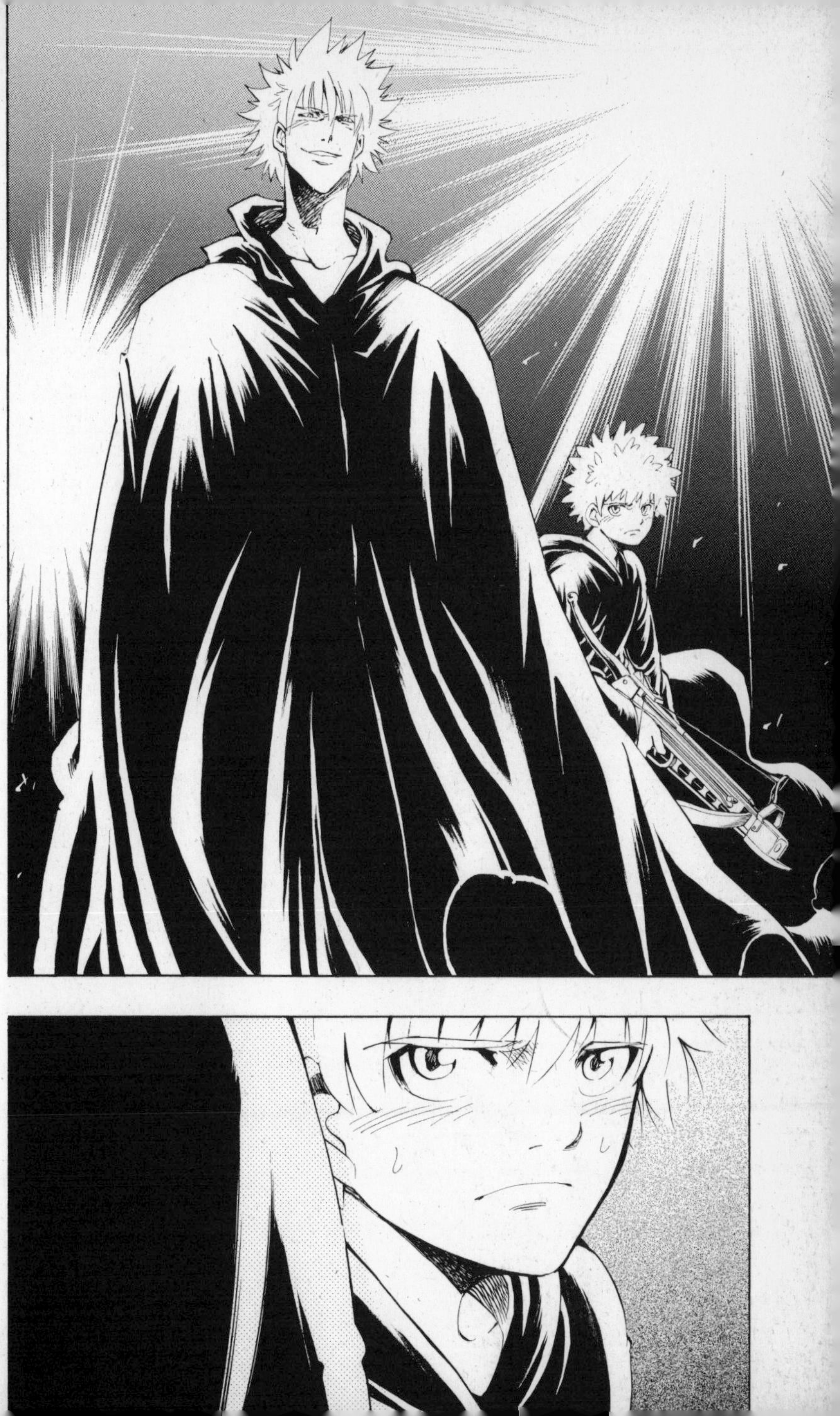

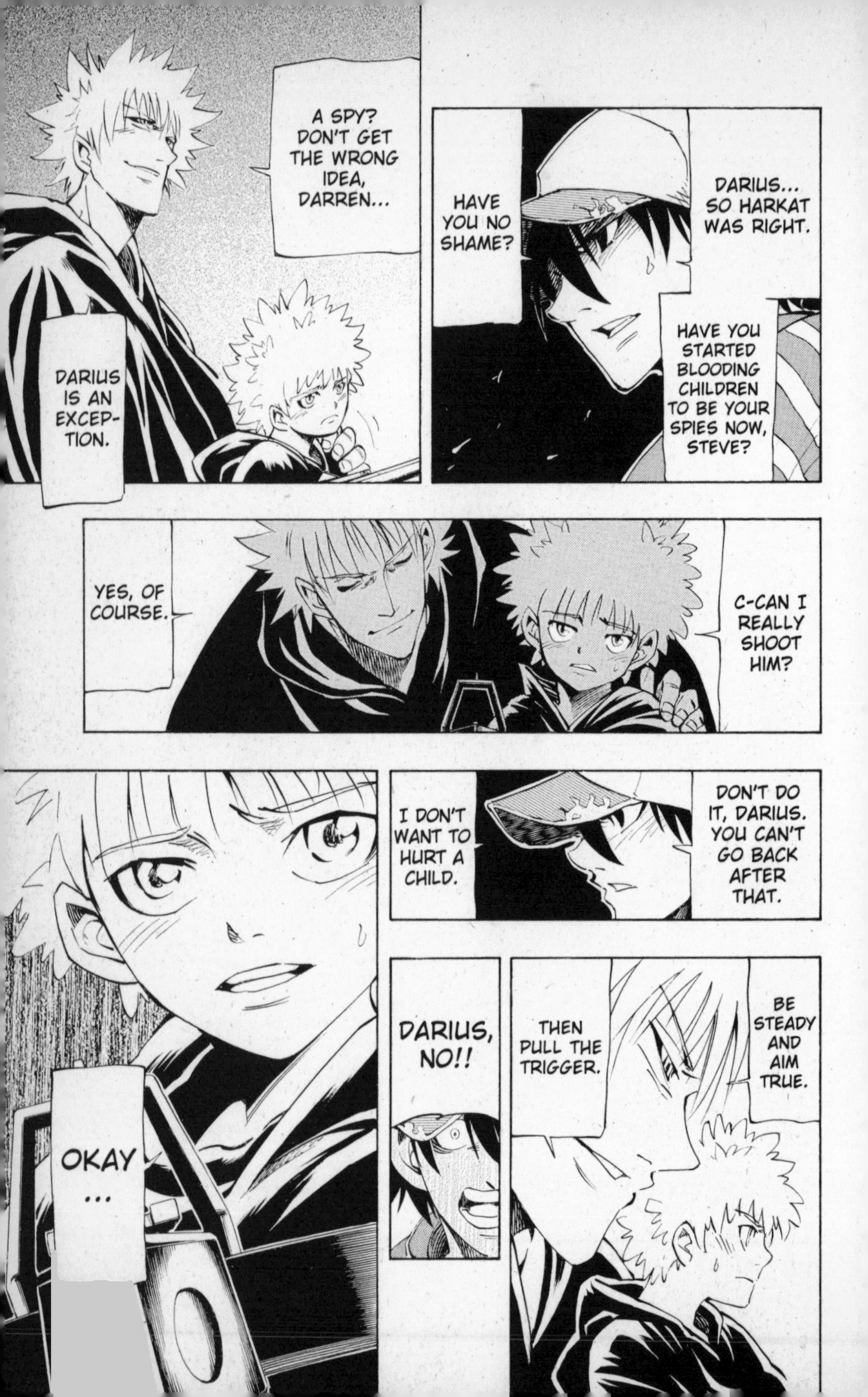

DARIUS... SO HARKAT WAS RIGHT.
HAVE YOU NO SHAME?
HAVE YOU STARTED BLOODING CHILDREN TO BE YOUR SPIES NOW, STEVE?
A SPY? DON'T GET THE WRONG IDEA, DARREN...
DARIUS IS AN EXCEP-TION.
C-CAN I REALLY SHOOT HIM?
YES, OF COURSE.
DON'T DO IT, DARIUS. YOU CAN'T GO BACK AFTER THAT.
I DON'T WANT TO HURT A CHILD.
BE STEADY AND AIM TRUE.
THEN PULL THE TRIGGER.
DARIUS, NO!!
OKAY ...

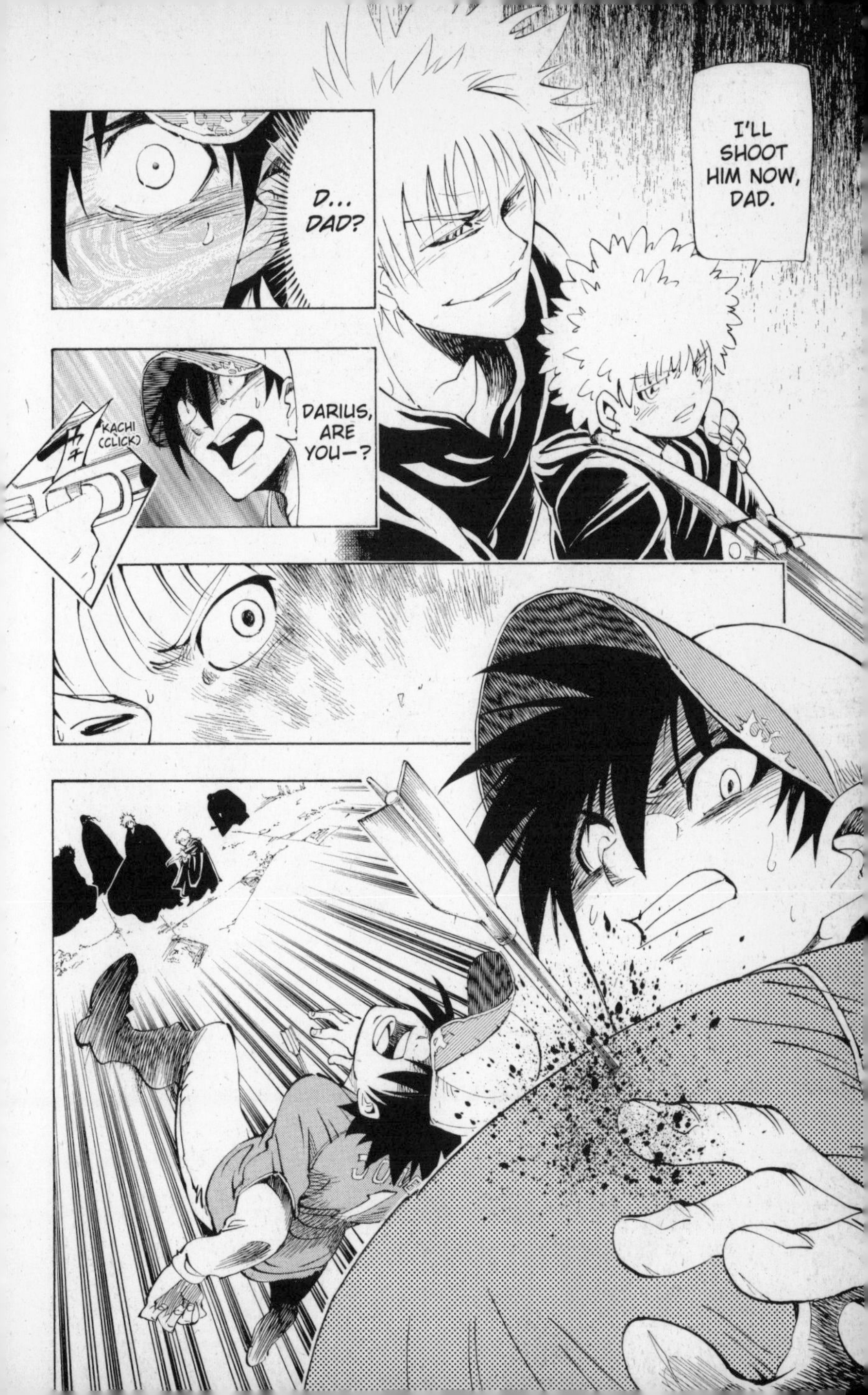
I'LL SHOOT HIM NOW, DAD.
D... DAD?
DARIUS, ARE YOU—?
KACHI (CLICK)

# CHAPTER 99: LAUGHINGSTOCK

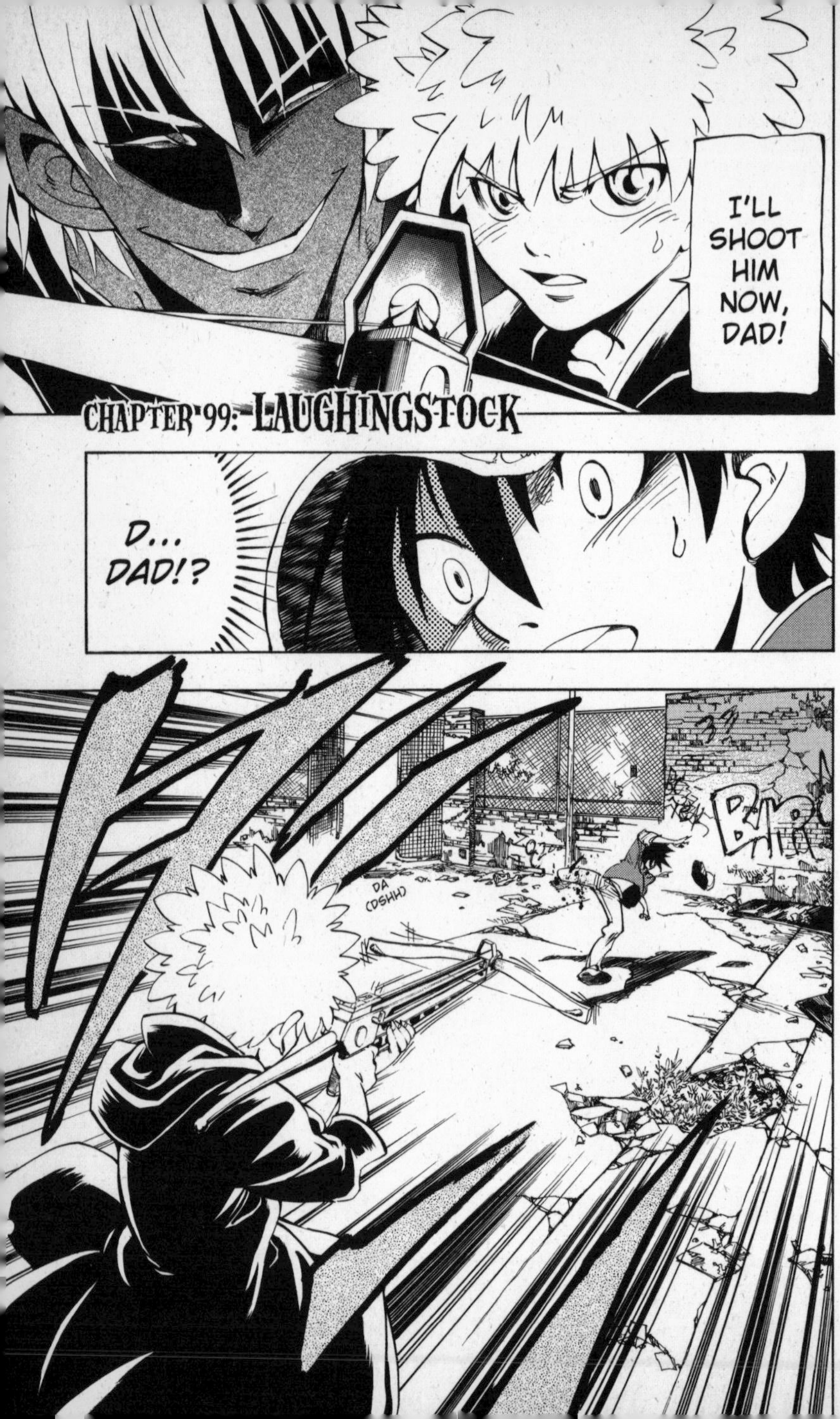
I'LL SHOOT HIM NOW, DAD!
D... DAD!?
DA (DSHH)

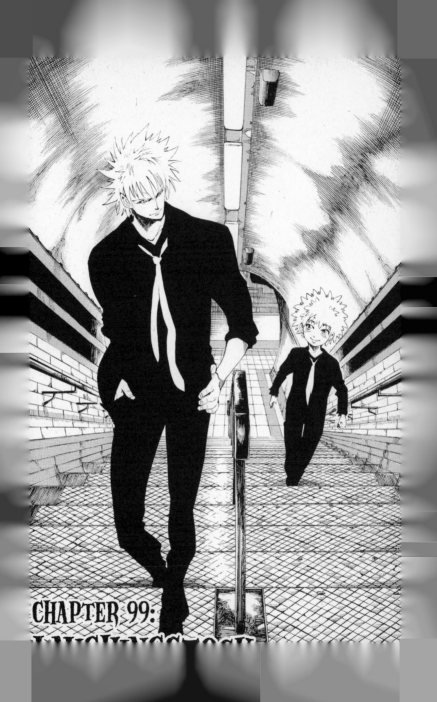

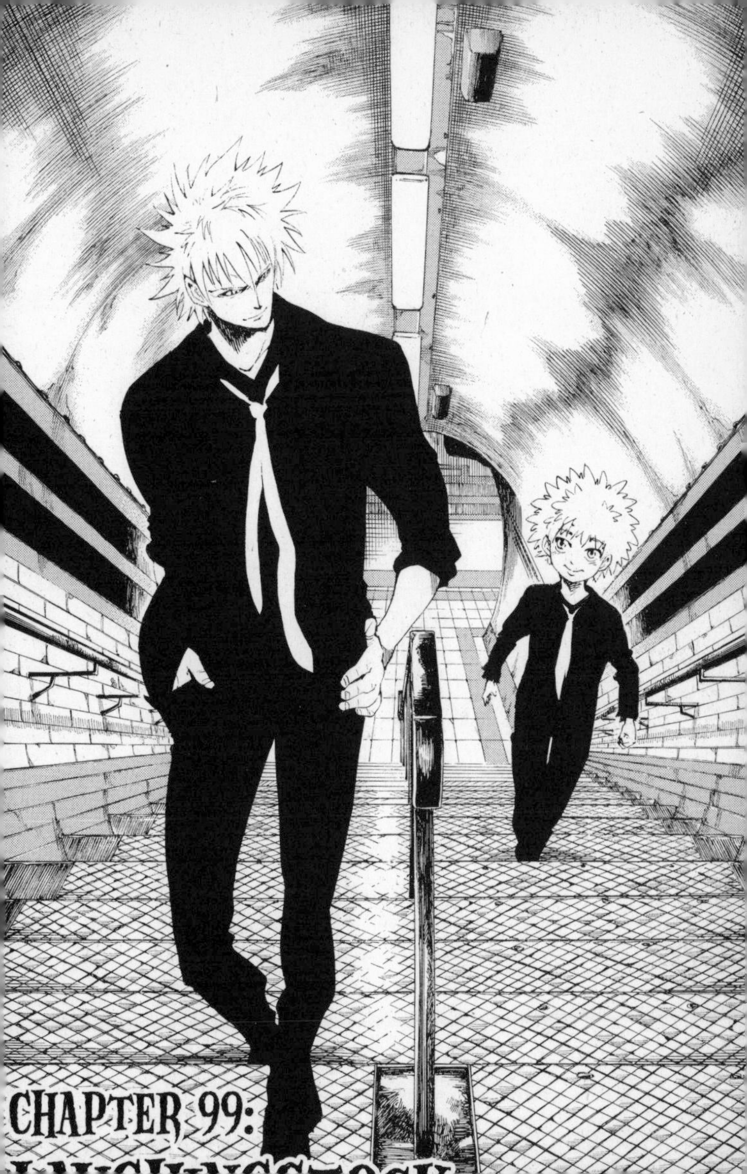
CHAPTER 99:

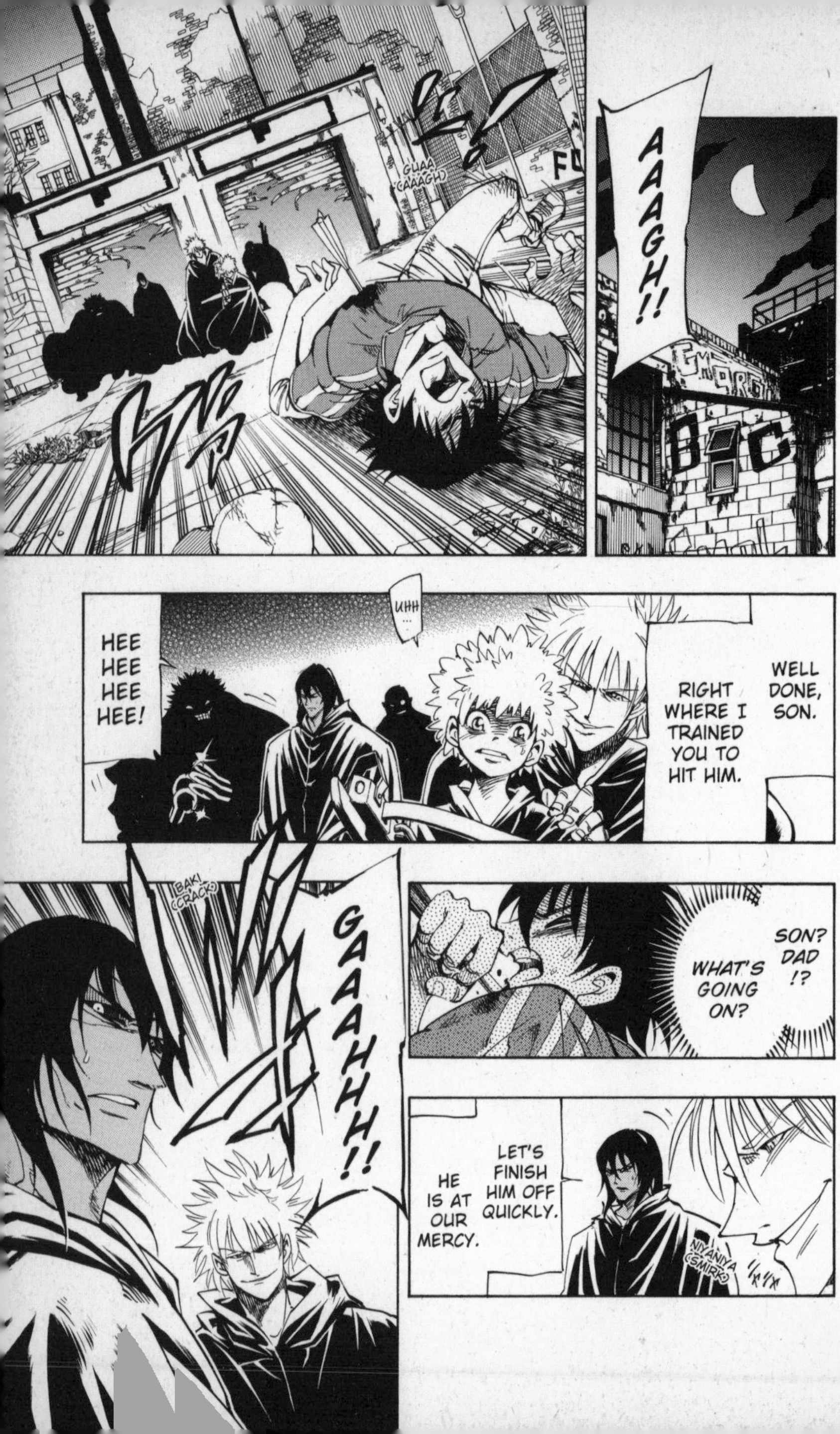
AAAAGH!!
GUAA (AAAGH)
WELL DONE, SON.
RIGHT WHERE I TRAINED YOU TO HIT HIM.
UHH ...
HEE HEE HEE HEE!
SON? DAD!?
WHAT'S GOING ON?
LET'S FINISH HIM OFF QUICKLY.
HE IS AT OUR MERCY.
NIYANIYA (SMIRK)
GAAAHHH!!
BAKI (CRACK)

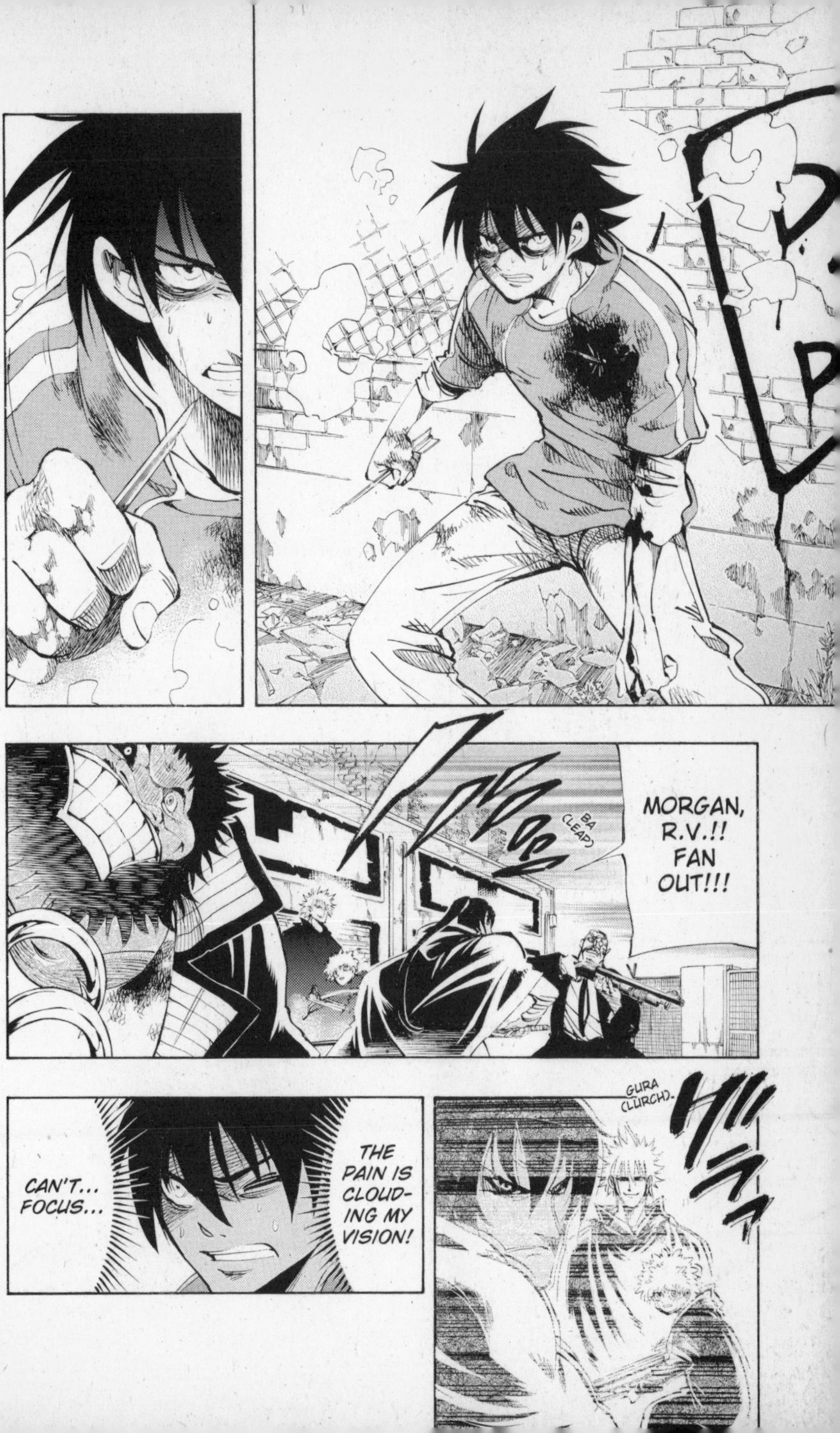
MORGAN, R.V.!! FAN OUT!!!
BA (LEAP)
GURA (LURCH)
THE PAIN IS CLOUDING MY VISION!
CAN'T... FOCUS...

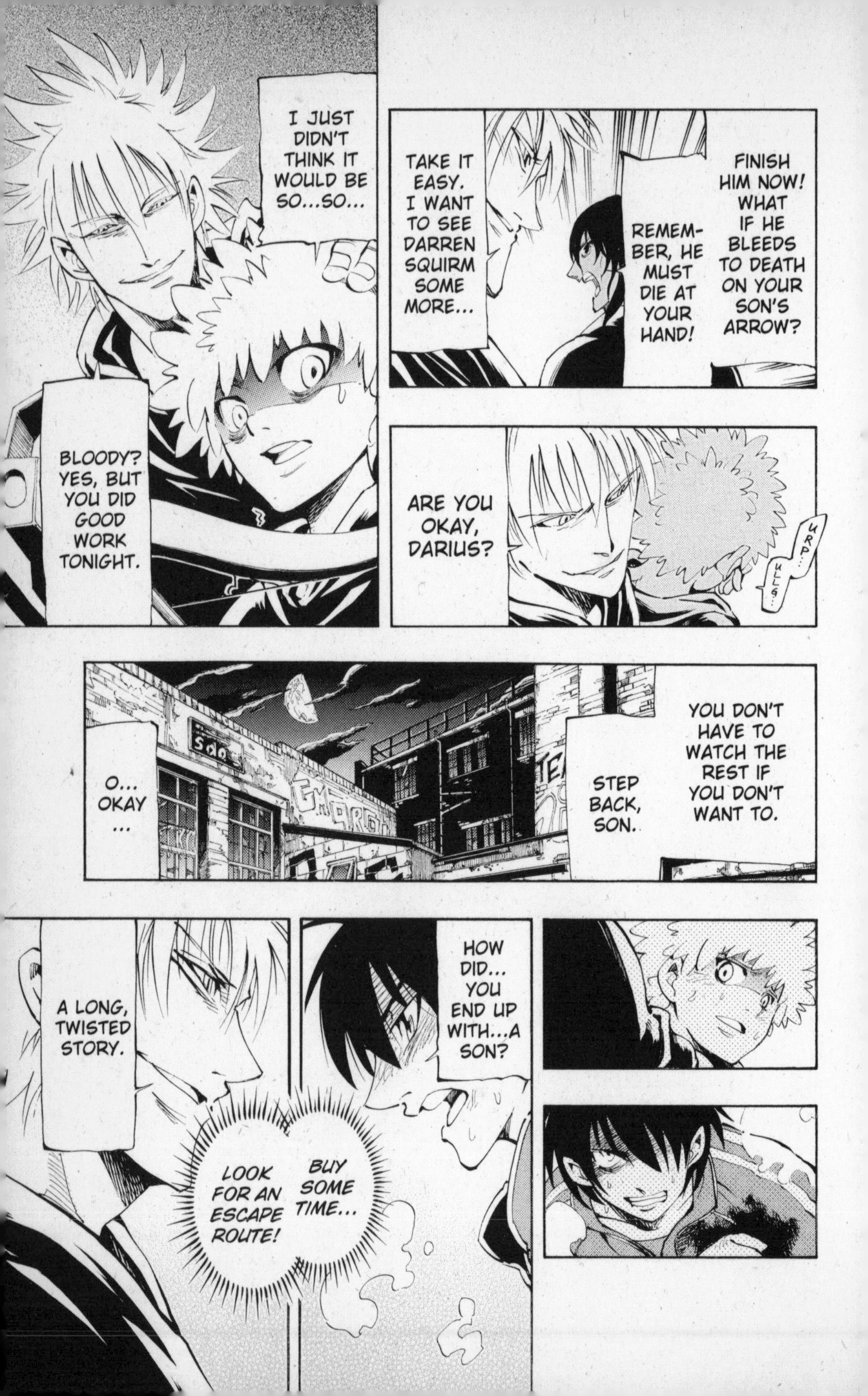
FINISH HIM NOW! WHAT IF HE BLEEDS TO DEATH ON YOUR SON'S ARROW?
REMEMBER, HE MUST DIE AT YOUR HAND!
TAKE IT EASY. I WANT TO SEE DARREN SQUIRM SOME MORE...
ARE YOU OKAY, DARIUS?
URP...
ULLG...
I JUST DIDN'T THINK IT WOULD BE SO...SO...
BLOODY? YES, BUT YOU DID GOOD WORK TONIGHT.
YOU DON'T HAVE TO WATCH THE REST IF YOU DON'T WANT TO.
STEP BACK, SON.
O... OKAY ...
HOW DID... YOU END UP WITH...A SON?
BUY SOME TIME...
LOOK FOR AN ESCAPE ROUTE!
A LONG, TWISTED STORY.

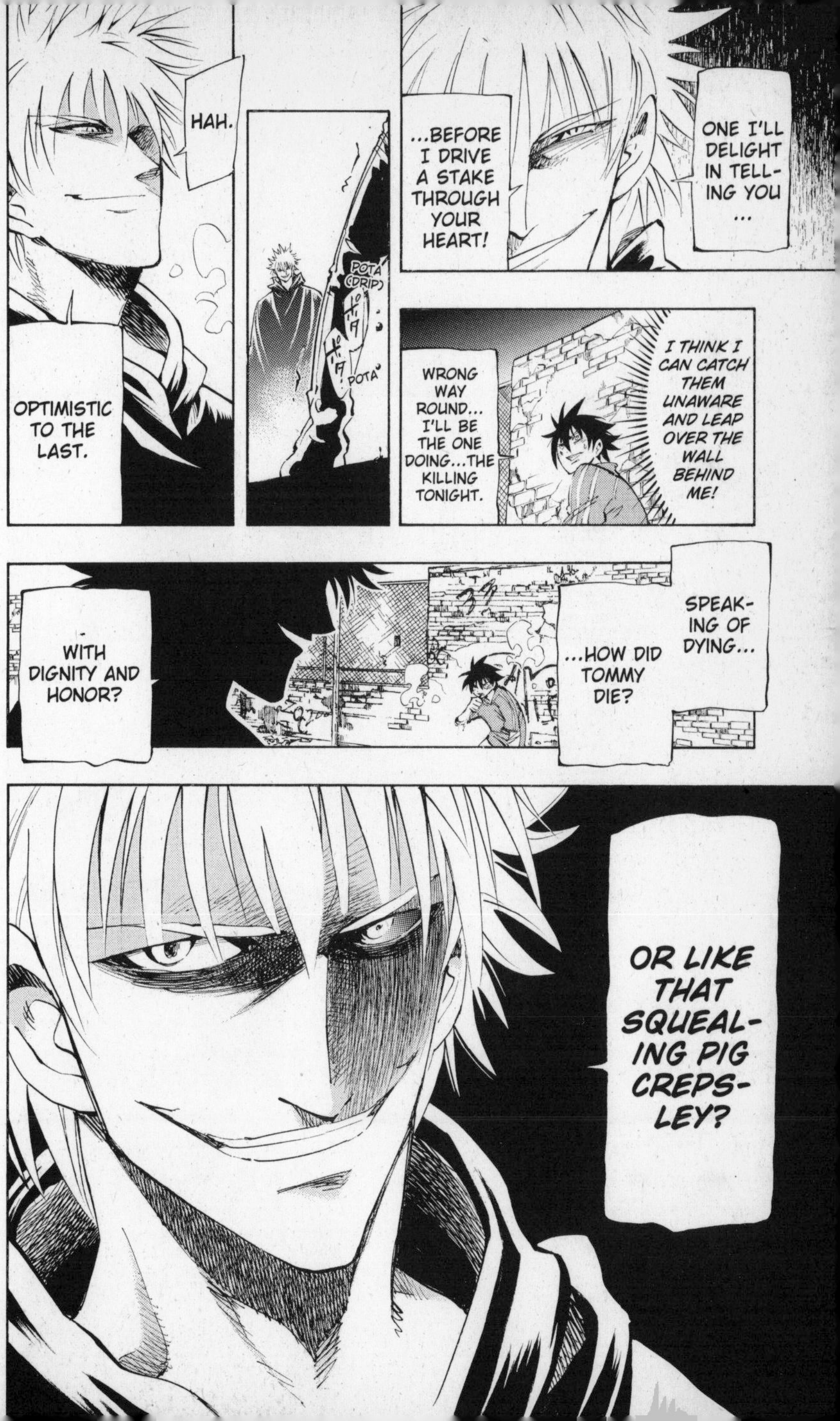
ONE I'LL DELIGHT IN TELL-ING YOU ...
...BEFORE I DRIVE A STAKE THROUGH YOUR HEART!
I THINK I CAN CATCH THEM UNAWARE AND LEAP OVER THE WALL BEHIND ME!
WRONG WAY ROUND... I'LL BE THE ONE DOING...THE KILLING TONIGHT.
POTA (DRIP)
POTA
HAH.
OPTIMISTIC TO THE LAST.
SPEAK-ING OF DYING...
...HOW DID TOMMY DIE?
WITH DIGNITY AND HONOR?
OR LIKE THAT SQUEAL-ING PIG CREPS-LEY?

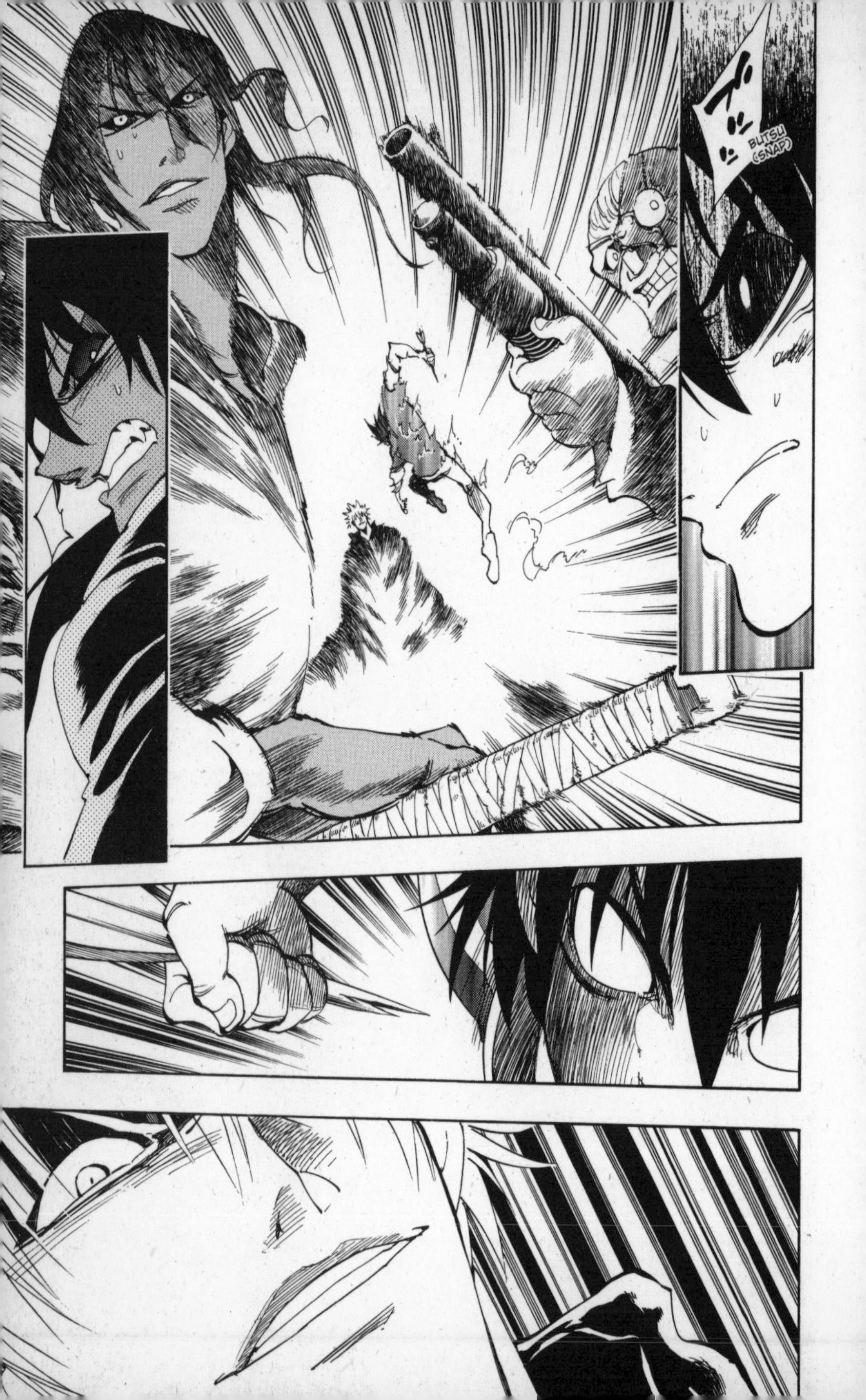
ブッ
BUTSU (SNAP)

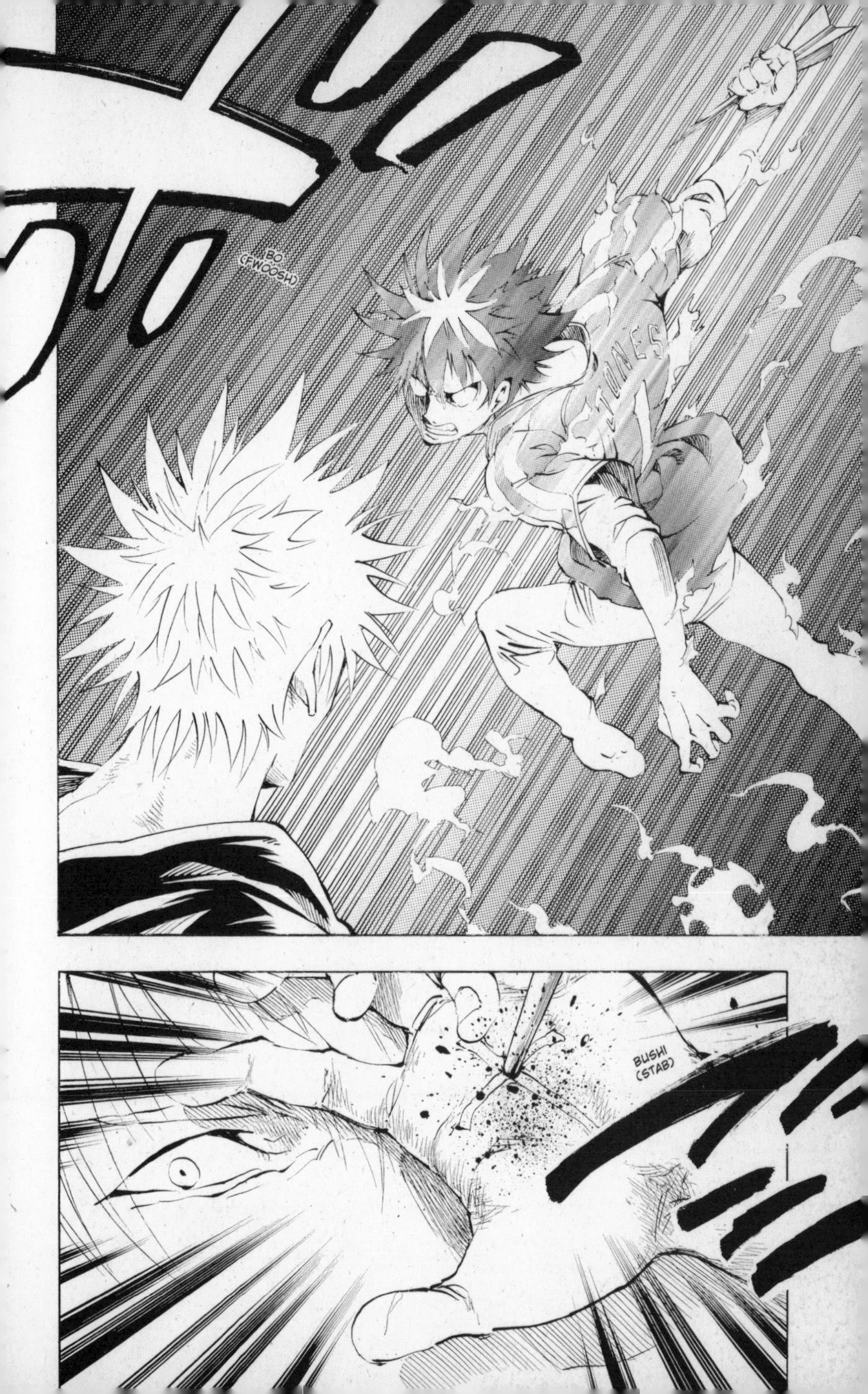
BO (FWOOSH)
BUSHI (STAB)

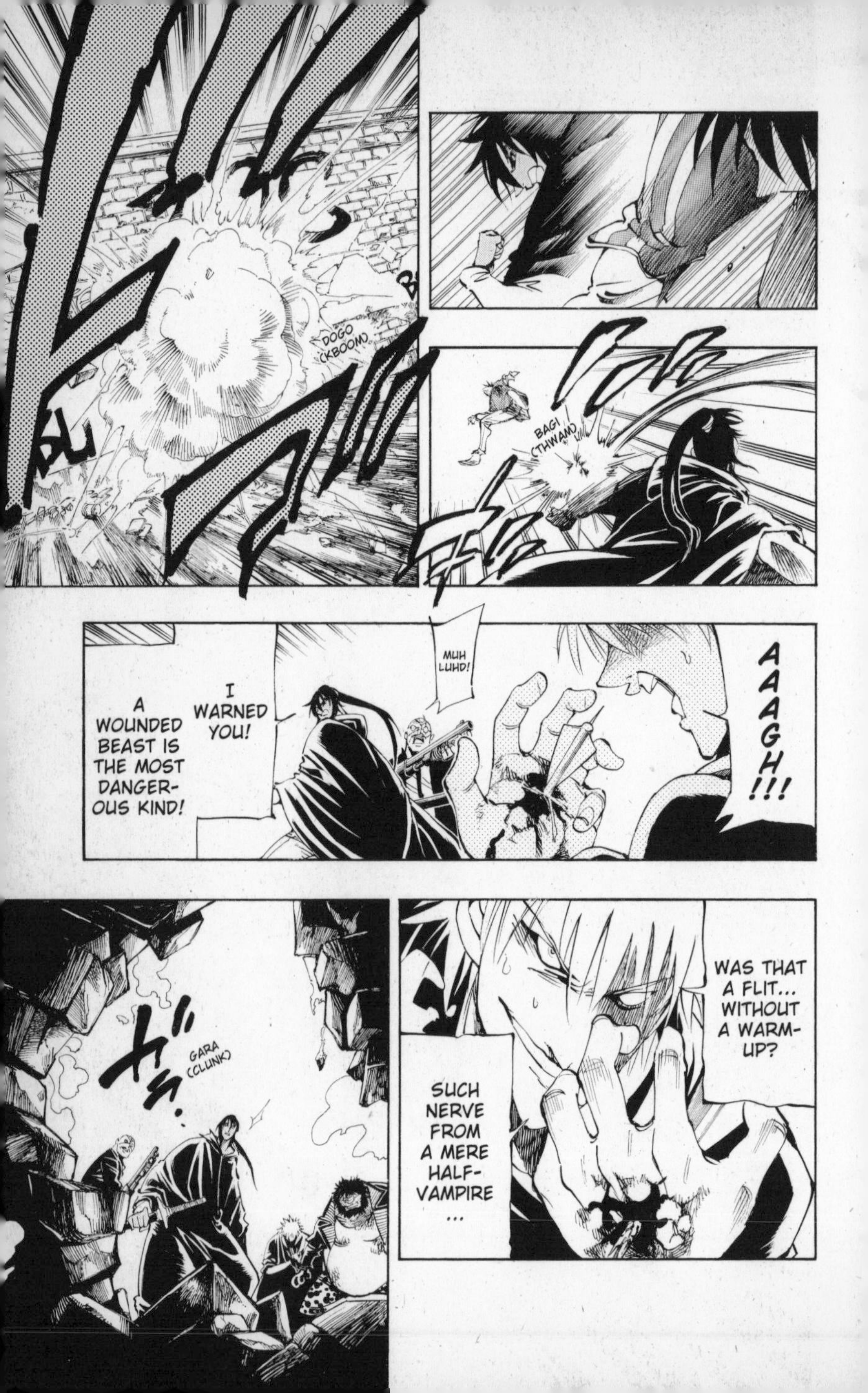
BAGI (THWAM)
DOGO (KBOOM)
AAAGH!!!
MUH LUHD!
I WARNED YOU!
A WOUNDED BEAST IS THE MOST DANGER-OUS KIND!
WAS THAT A FLIT... WITHOUT A WARM-UP?
SUCH NERVE FROM A MERE HALF-VAMPIRE ...
GARA (CLUNK)

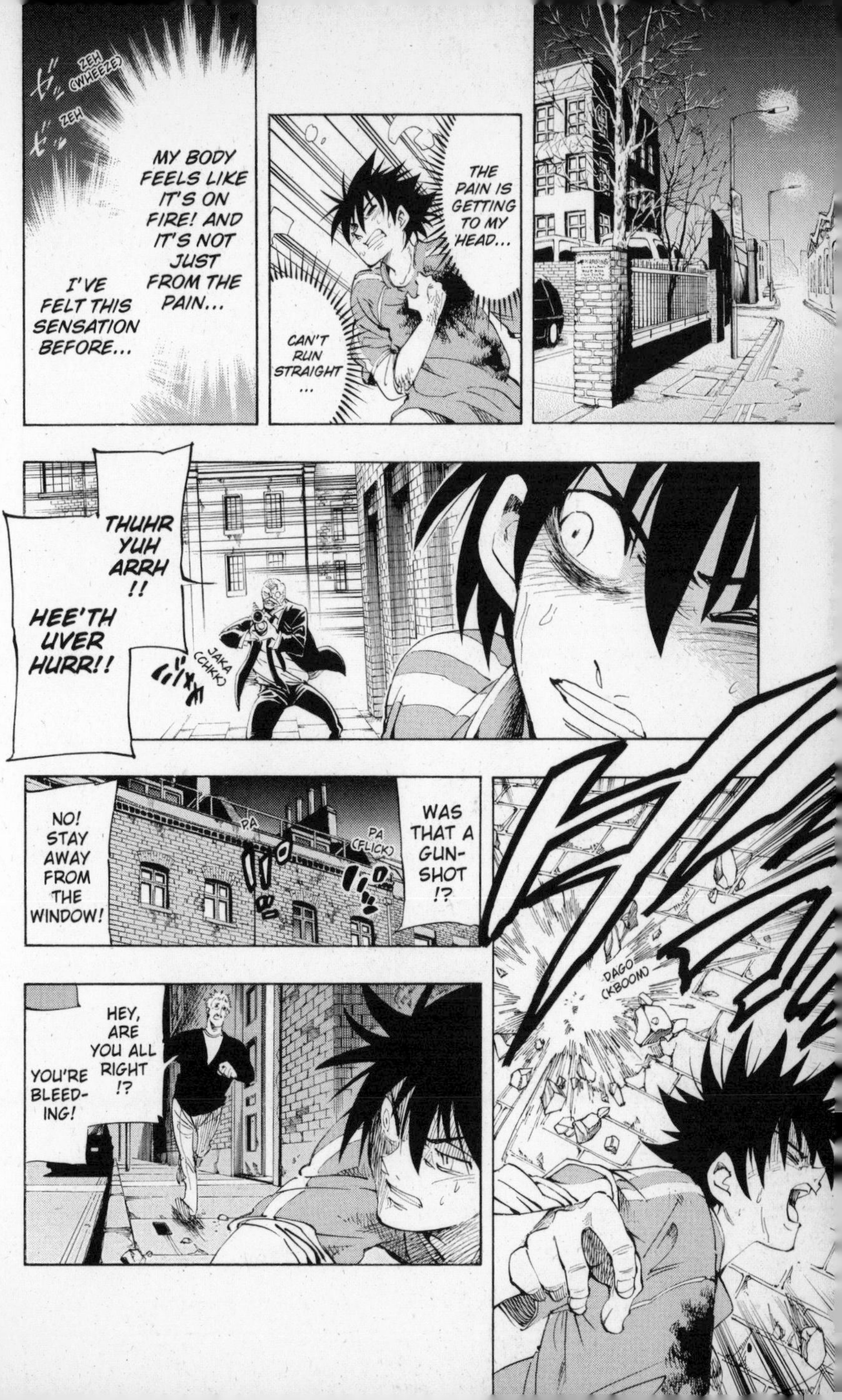
THE PAIN IS GETTING TO MY HEAD...
CAN'T RUN STRAIGHT...
ZEH (WHEEZE)
ZEH
MY BODY FEELS LIKE IT'S ON FIRE! AND IT'S NOT JUST FROM THE PAIN...
I'VE FELT THIS SENSATION BEFORE...
THUHR YUH ARRH!!
HEE'TH UVER HURR!!
JAKA (CHKK)
DAGO (KBOOM)
WAS THAT A GUN-SHOT!?
PA
PA (FLICK)
NO! STAY AWAY FROM THE WINDOW!
HEY, ARE YOU ALL RIGHT!?
YOU'RE BLEED-ING!

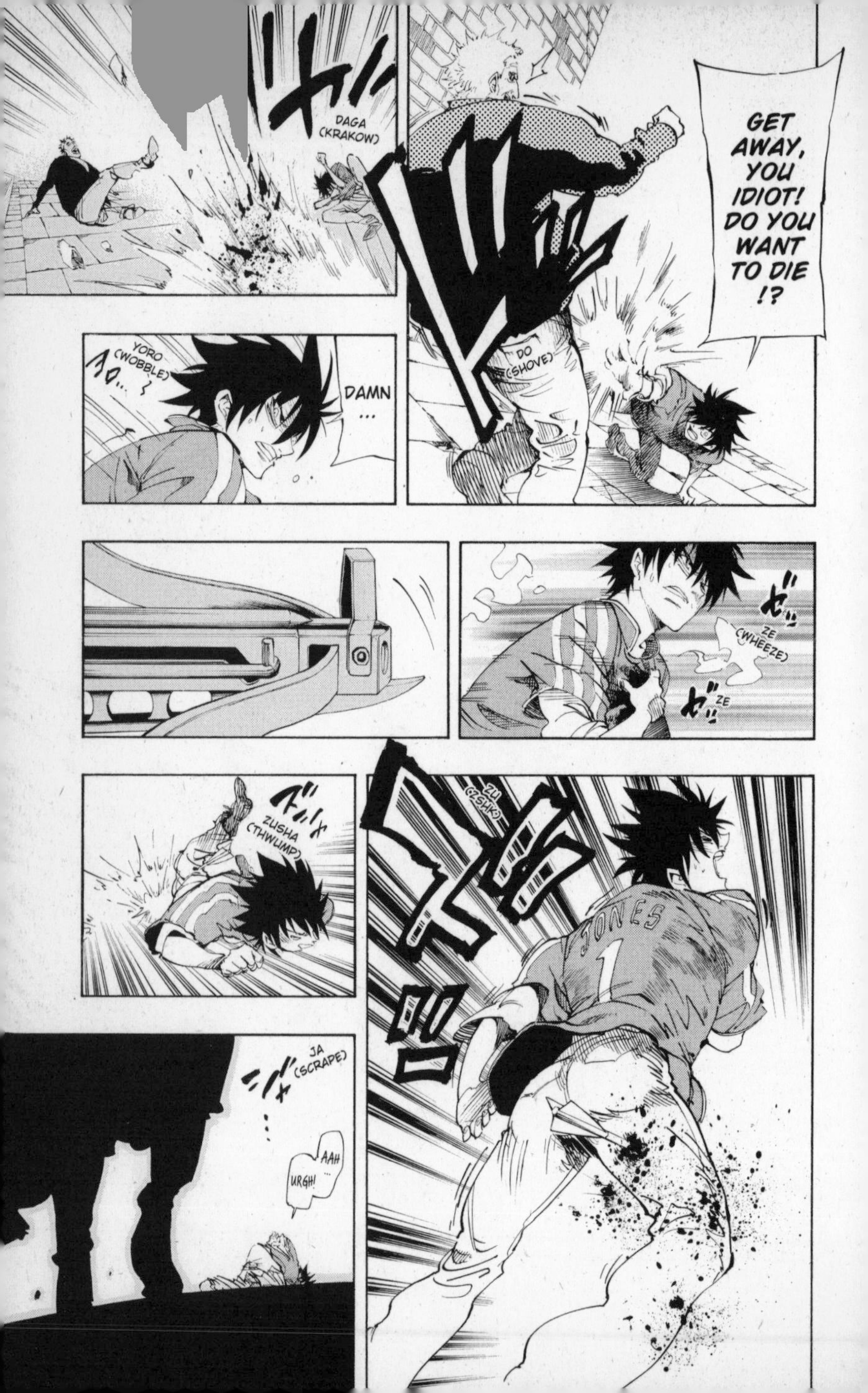

GET AWAY, YOU IDIOT! DO YOU WANT TO DIE !?
DAGA (KRAKOW)
DO (SHOVE)
DAMN ...
YORO (WOBBLE)
ZE (WHEEZE)
ZE
ZU (ZSHK)
ZUSHA (THWUMP)
JA (SCRAPE)
...
AAH ...
URGH!

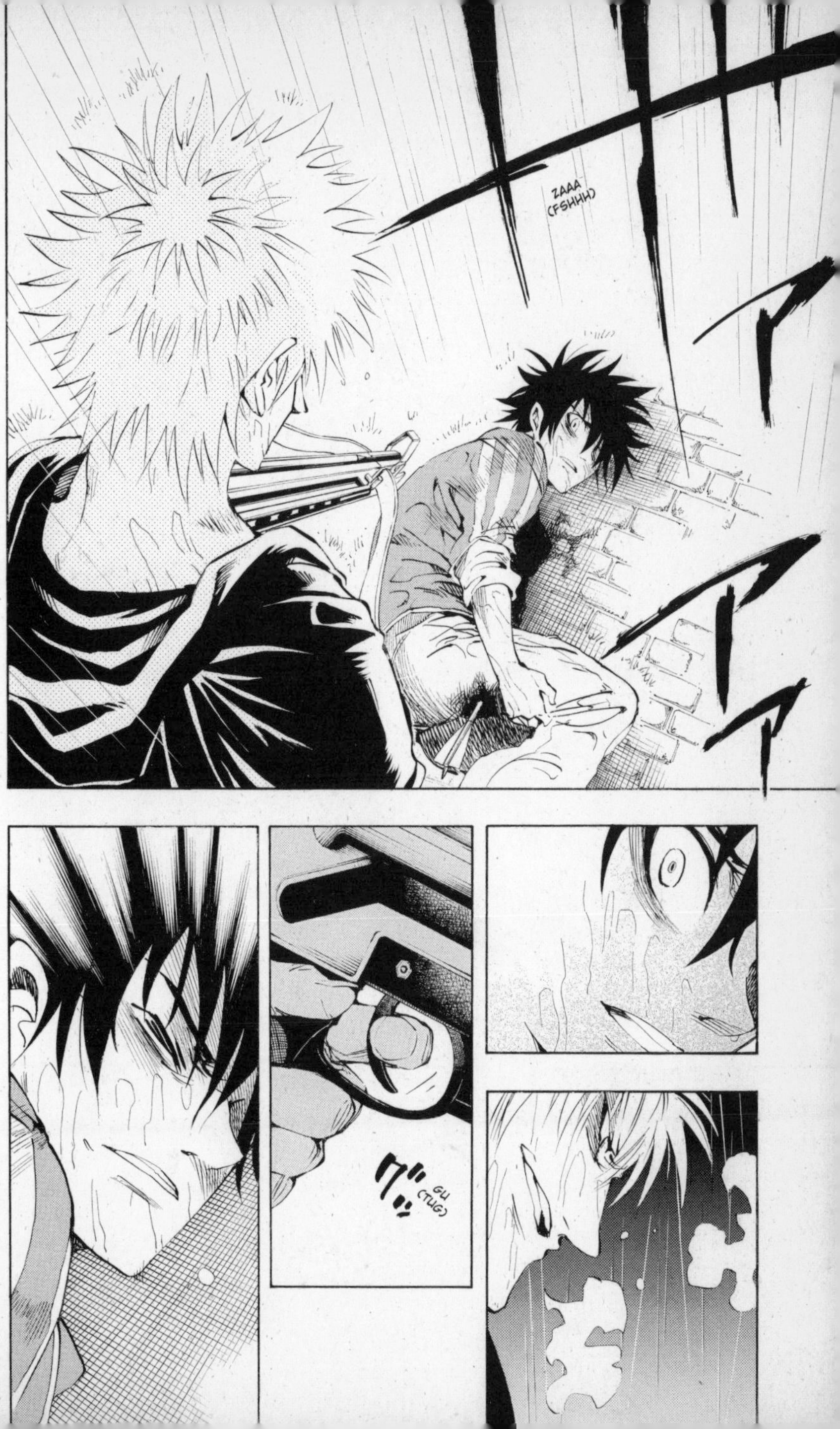
ZAAA (FSHHH)
GU (TUG)

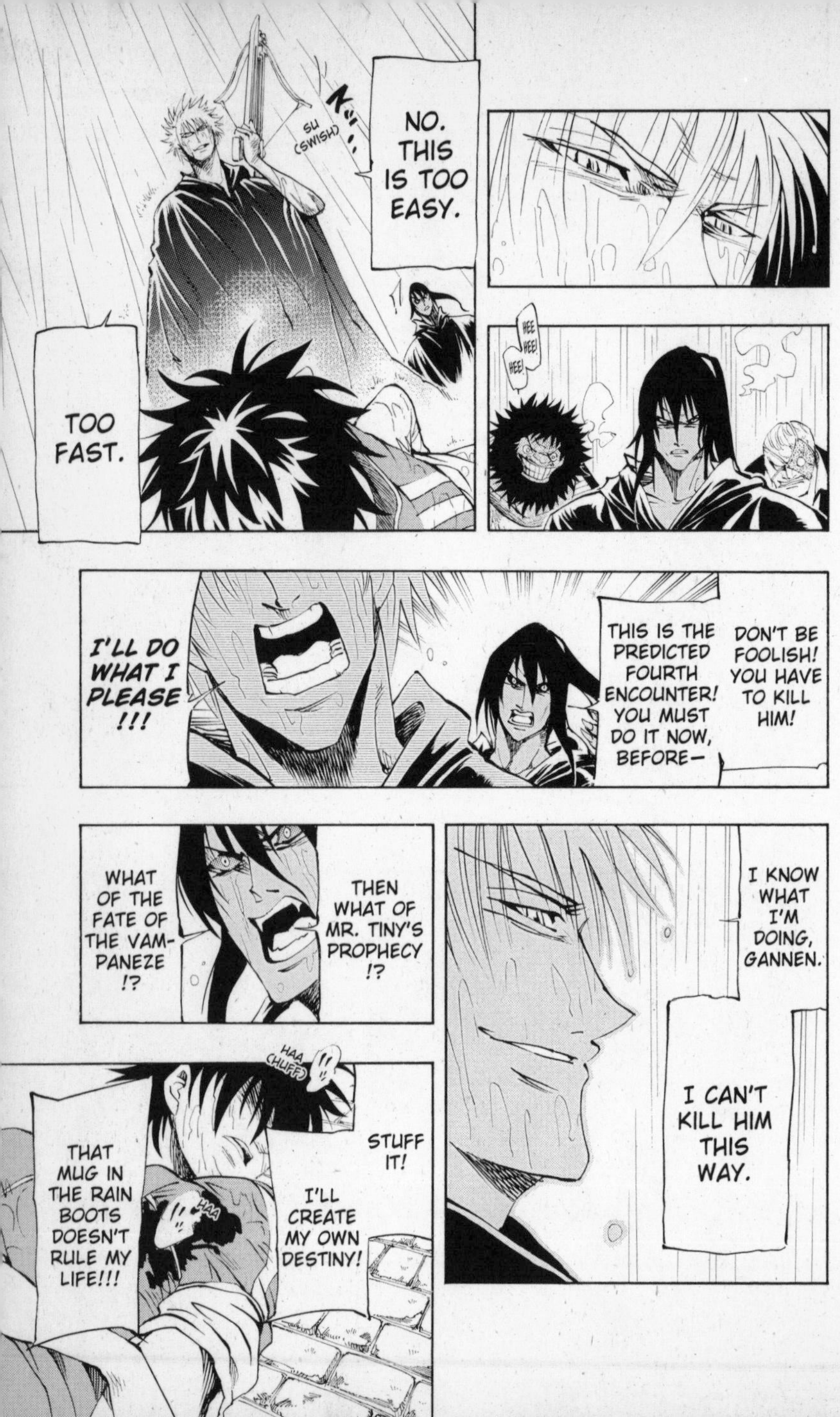
HEE HEE! HEE!
SU (SWISH)
NO. THIS IS TOO EASY.
TOO FAST.
DON'T BE FOOLISH! YOU HAVE TO KILL HIM!
THIS IS THE PREDICTED FOURTH ENCOUNTER! YOU MUST DO IT NOW, BEFORE—
*I'LL DO WHAT I PLEASE!!!*
I KNOW WHAT I'M DOING, GANNEN.
I CAN'T KILL HIM THIS WAY.
THEN WHAT OF MR. TINY'S PROPHECY!?
WHAT OF THE FATE OF THE VAMPANEZE!?
HAA (HUFF)
STUFF IT!
I'LL CREATE MY OWN DESTINY!
HAA
THAT MUG IN THE RAIN BOOTS DOESN'T RULE MY LIFE!!!

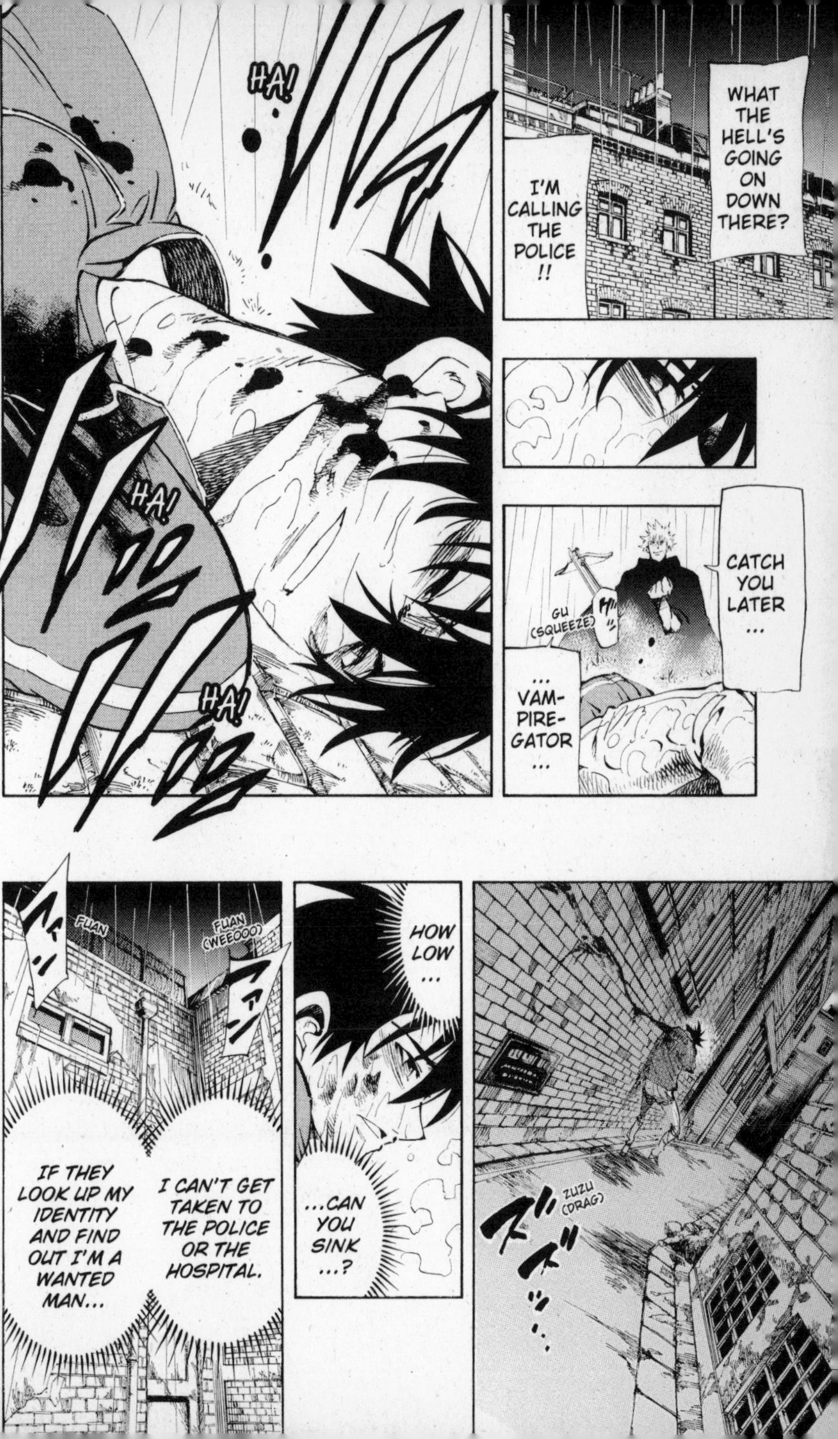
WHAT THE HELL'S GOING ON DOWN THERE?
I'M CALLING THE POLICE !!
CATCH YOU LATER ...
GU (SQUEEZE)
... VAMPIRE-GATOR ...
HA!
HA!
HA!
ZUZU (DRAG)
HOW LOW ...
...CAN YOU SINK ...?
FUAN
FUAN (WEEOOO)
I CAN'T GET TAKEN TO THE POLICE OR THE HOSPITAL.
IF THEY LOOK UP MY IDENTITY AND FIND OUT I'M A WANTED MAN...

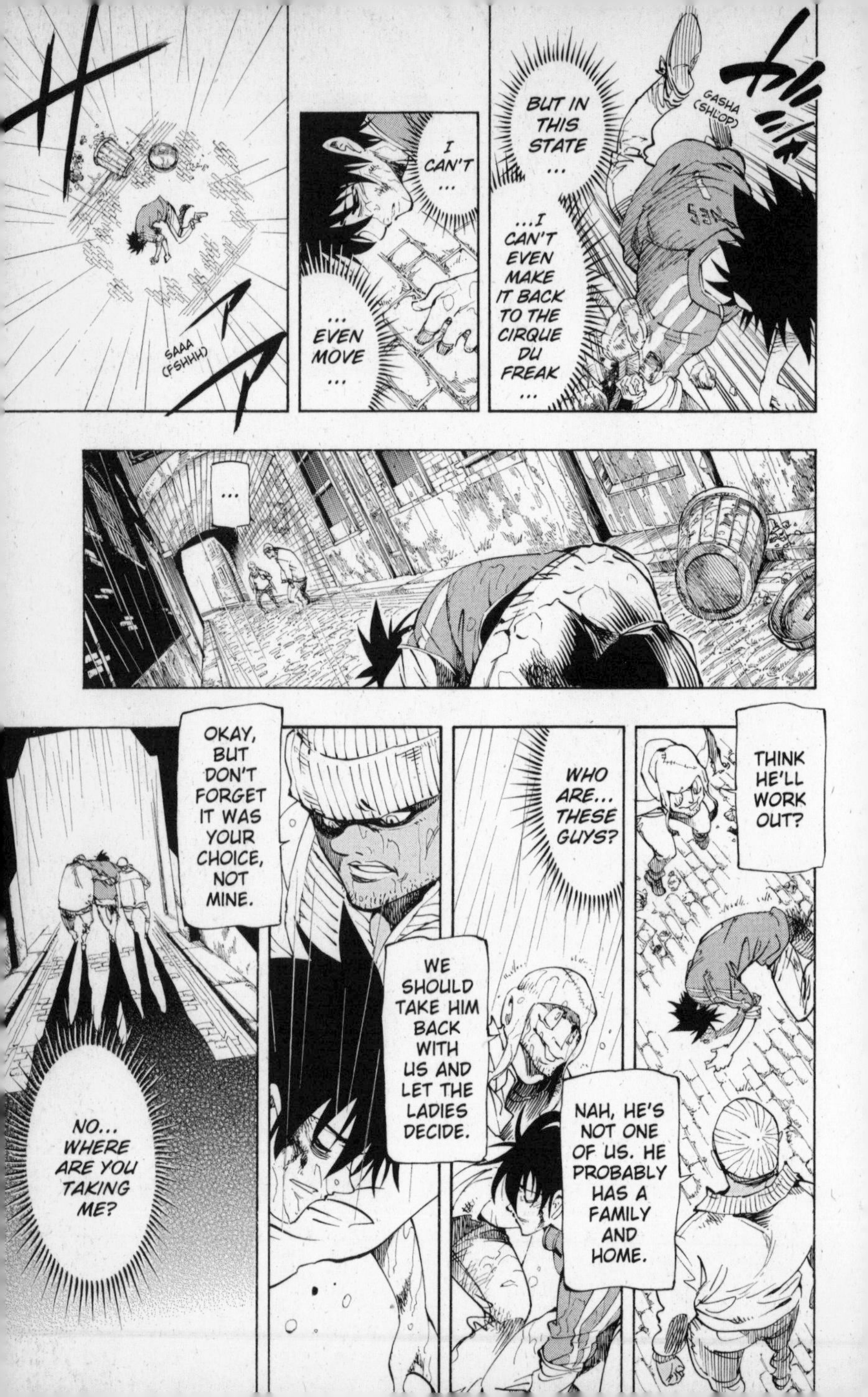
GASHA (SHLOP)
BUT IN THIS STATE ...
...I CAN'T EVEN MAKE IT BACK TO THE CIRQUE DU FREAK ...
I CAN'T ...
... EVEN MOVE ...
SAAA (FSHHH)
...
THINK HE'LL WORK OUT?
NAH, HE'S NOT ONE OF US. HE PROBABLY HAS A FAMILY AND HOME.
WHO ARE... THESE GUYS?
WE SHOULD TAKE HIM BACK WITH US AND LET THE LADIES DECIDE.
OKAY, BUT DON'T FORGET IT WAS YOUR CHOICE, NOT MINE.
NO... WHERE ARE YOU TAKING ME?

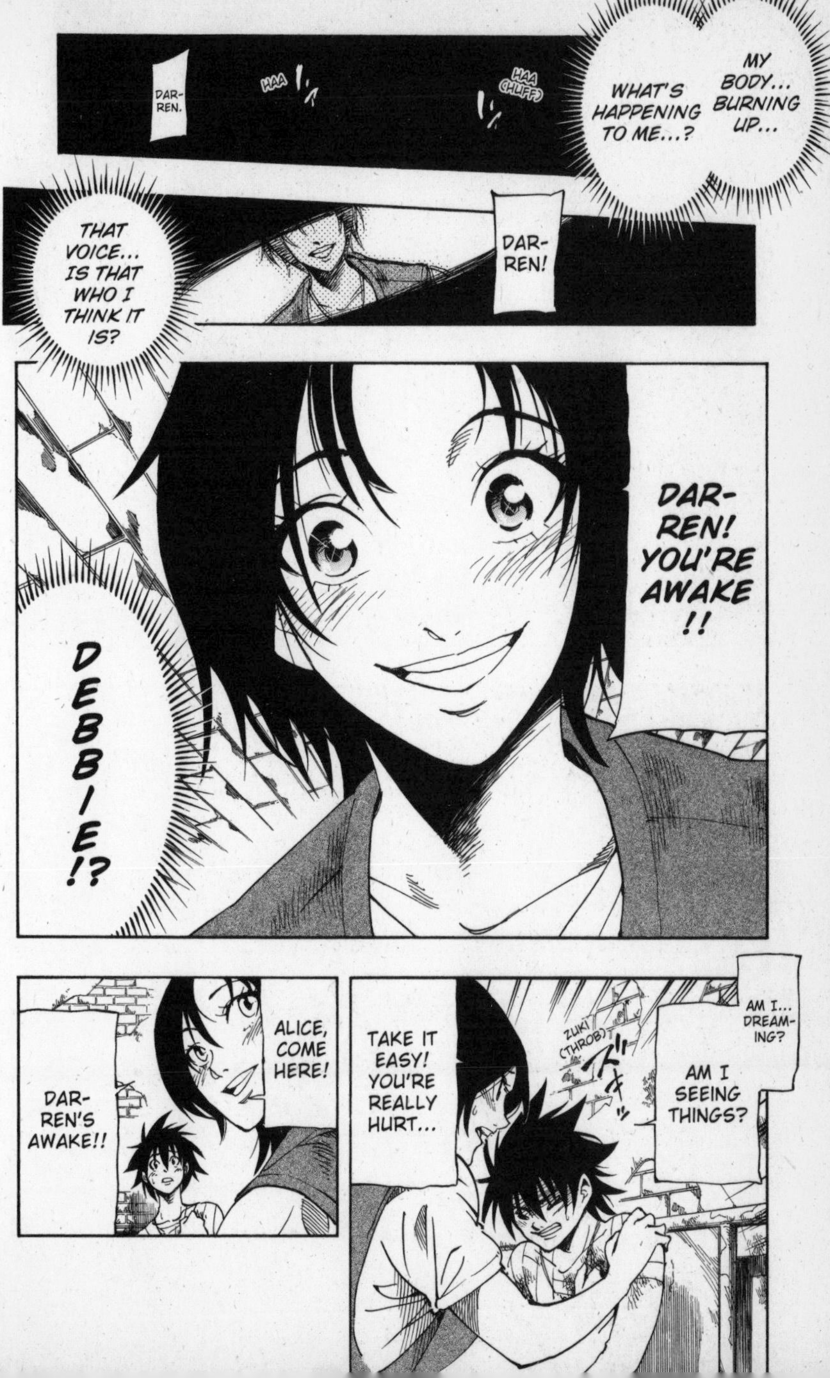
MY BODY... BURNING UP...
WHAT'S HAPPENING TO ME...?
HAA (HUFF)
HAA
DAR-REN.
DAR-REN!
THAT VOICE... IS THAT WHO I THINK IT IS?
DAR-REN! YOU'RE AWAKE!!
DEBBIE!?
AM I... DREAMING?
AM I SEEING THINGS?
ZUKI (THROB)
TAKE IT EASY! YOU'RE REALLY HURT...
ALICE, COME HERE!
DAR-REN'S AWAKE!!

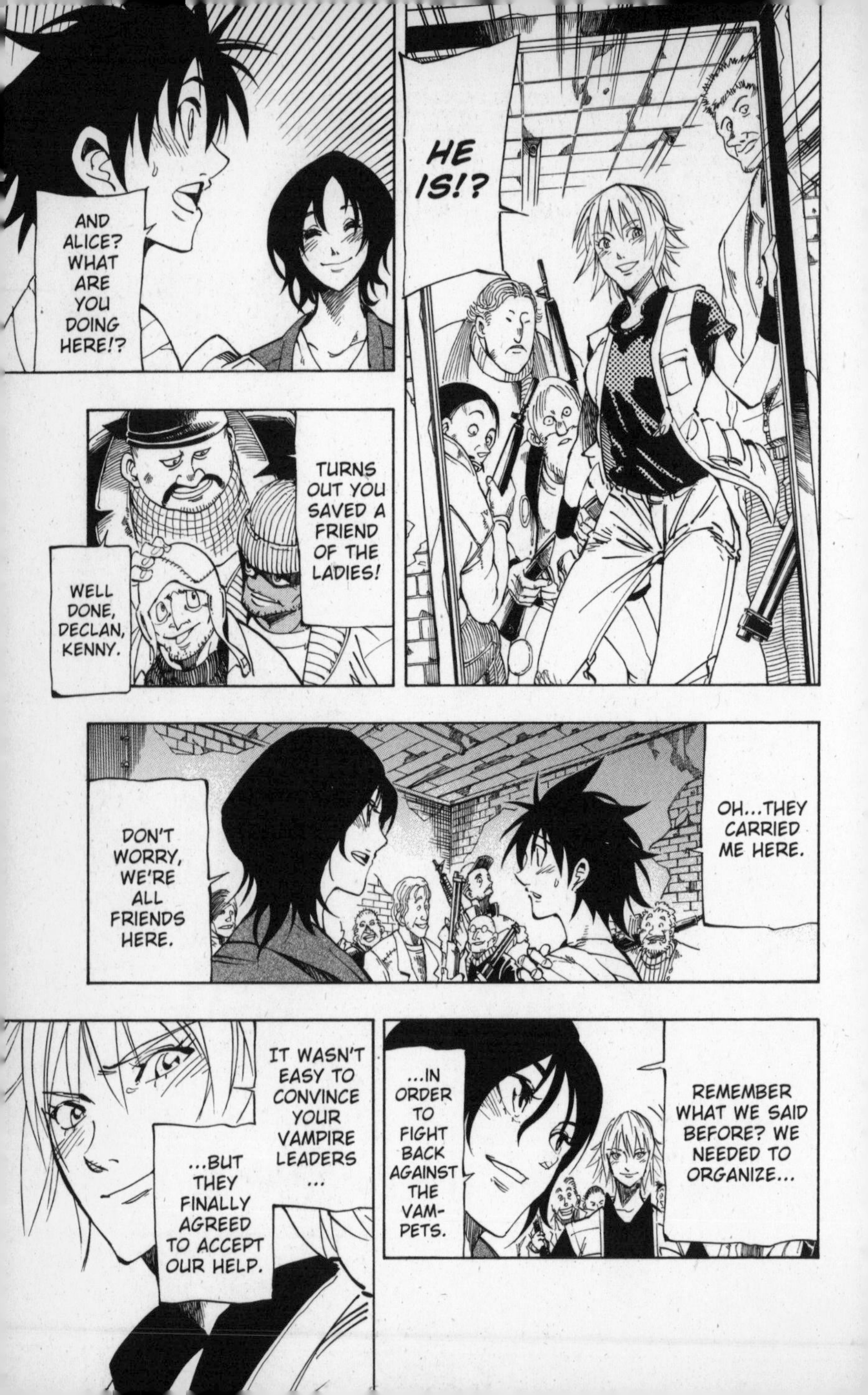
HE IS!?
AND ALICE? WHAT ARE YOU DOING HERE!?
TURNS OUT YOU SAVED A FRIEND OF THE LADIES!
WELL DONE, DECLAN, KENNY.
OH...THEY CARRIED ME HERE.
DON'T WORRY, WE'RE ALL FRIENDS HERE.
REMEMBER WHAT WE SAID BEFORE? WE NEEDED TO ORGANIZE...
...IN ORDER TO FIGHT BACK AGAINST THE VAM-PETS.
IT WASN'T EASY TO CONVINCE YOUR VAMPIRE LEADERS ...
...BUT THEY FINALLY AGREED TO ACCEPT OUR HELP.

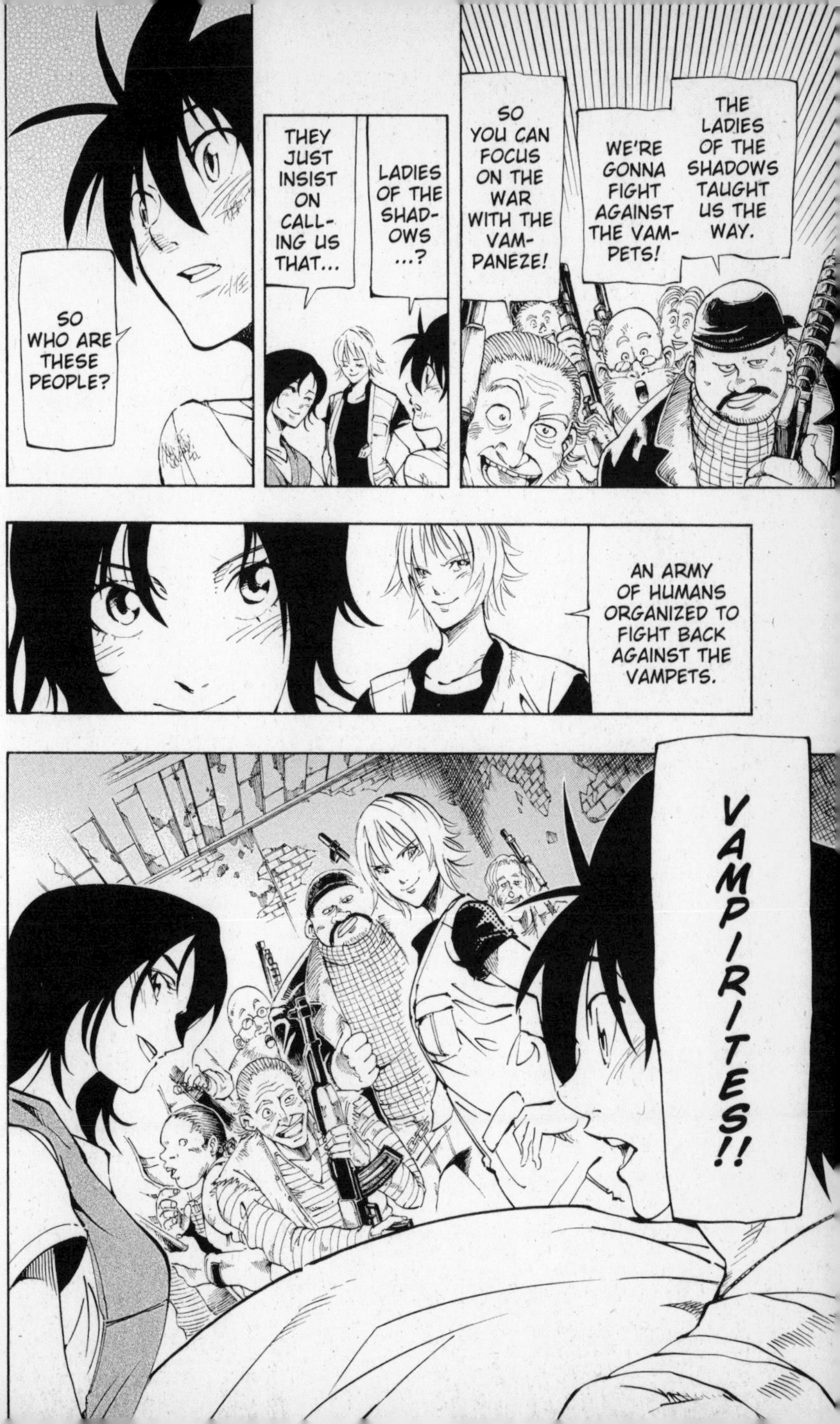
THE LADIES OF THE SHADOWS TAUGHT US THE WAY.
WE'RE GONNA FIGHT AGAINST THE VAMPETS!
SO YOU CAN FOCUS ON THE WAR WITH THE VAMPANEZE!
LADIES OF THE SHADOWS ...?
THEY JUST INSIST ON CALLING US THAT...
SO WHO ARE THESE PEOPLE?
AN ARMY OF HUMANS ORGANIZED TO FIGHT BACK AGAINST THE VAMPETS.
VAMPIRITES!!

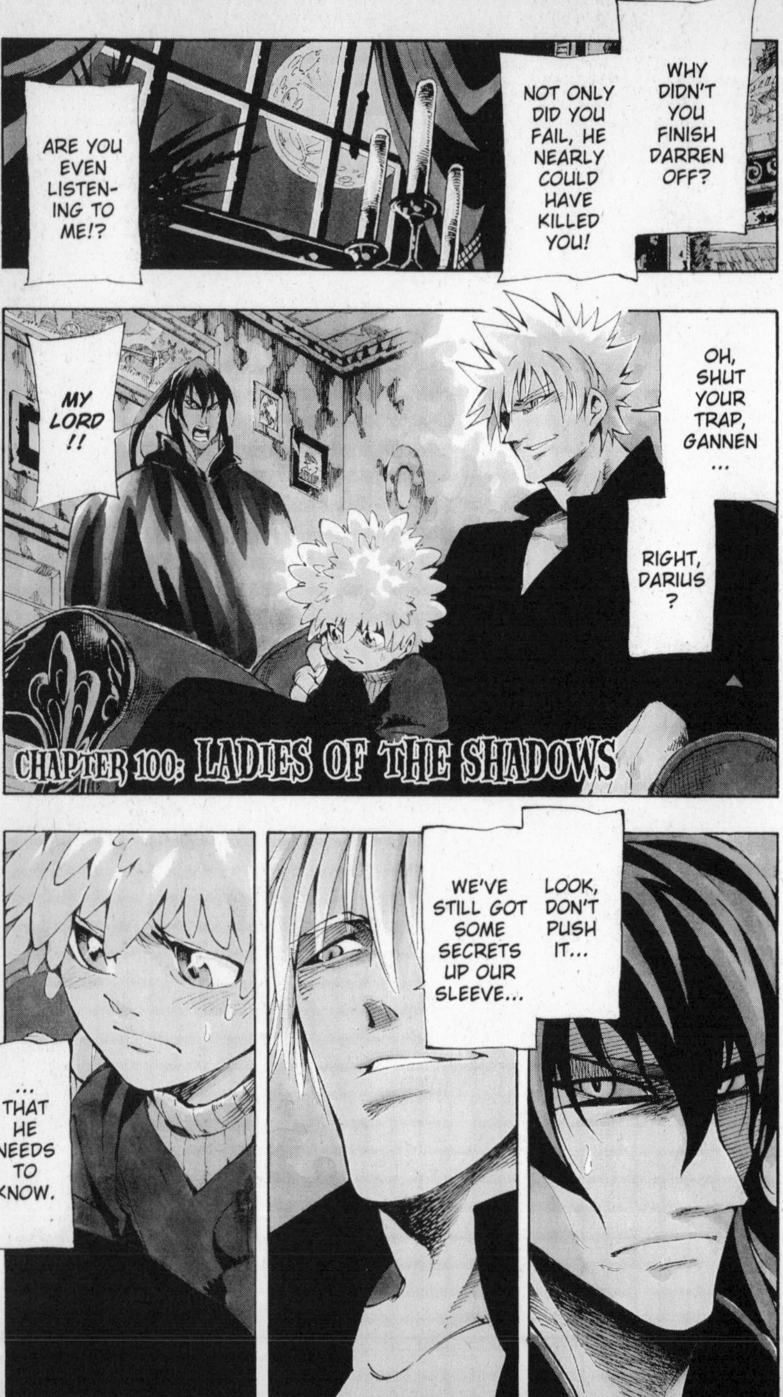
WHY DIDN'T YOU FINISH DARREN OFF?
NOT ONLY DID YOU FAIL, HE NEARLY COULD HAVE KILLED YOU!
ARE YOU EVEN LISTENING TO ME!?
OH, SHUT YOUR TRAP, GANNEN...
RIGHT, DARIUS?
MY LORD!!
CHAPTER 100: LADIES OF THE SHADOWS
LOOK, DON'T PUSH IT...
WE'VE STILL GOT SOME SECRETS UP OUR SLEEVE...
... THAT HE NEEDS TO KNOW.

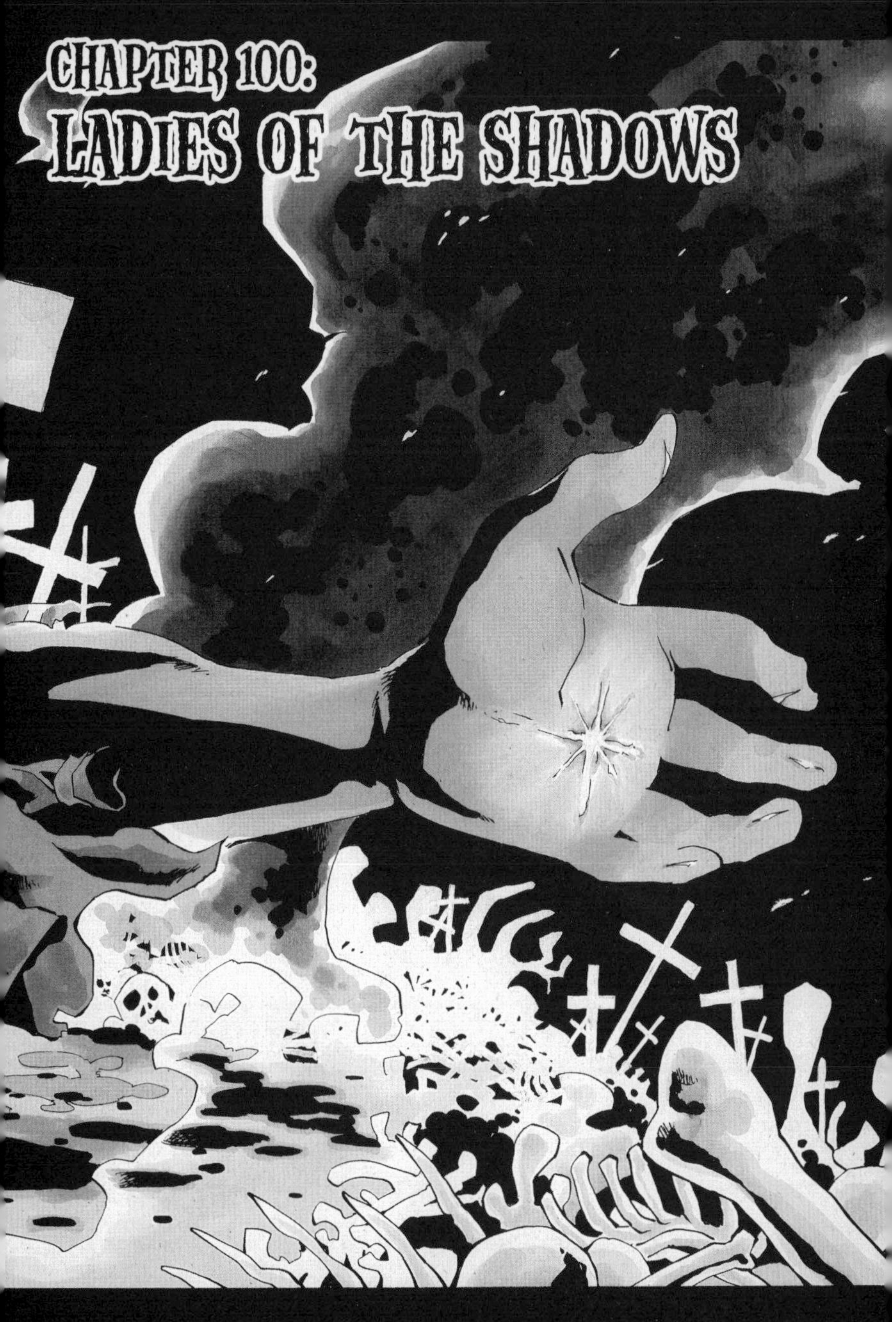
CHAPTER 100:
LADIES OF THE SHADOWS

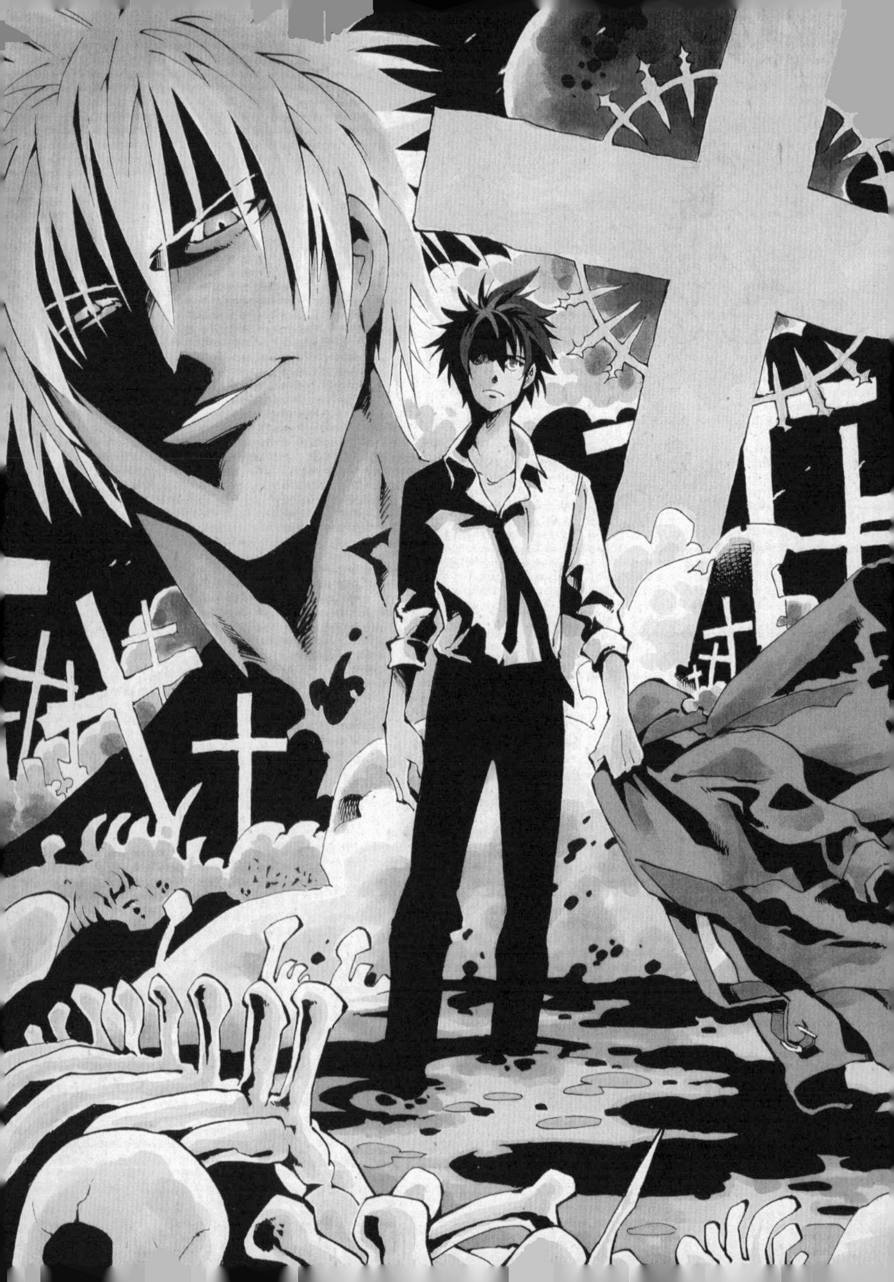

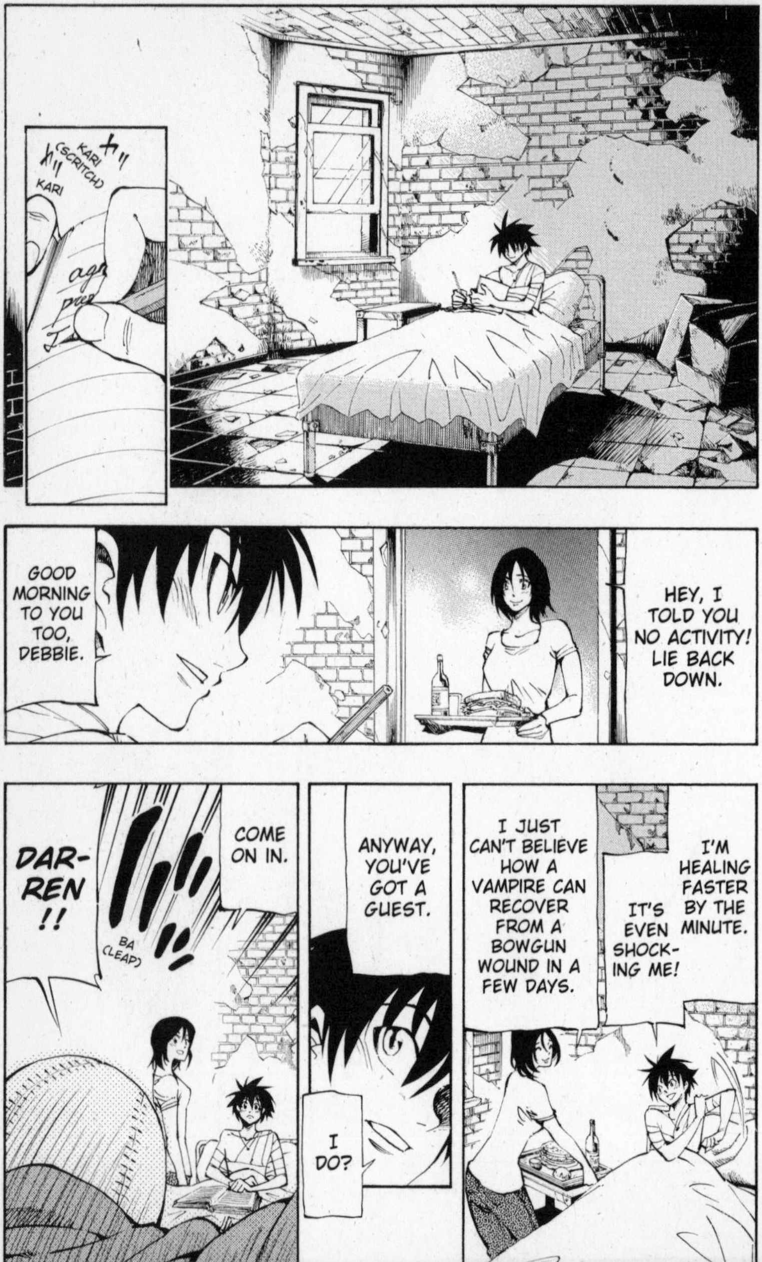
KARI (SCRITCH)
KARI
HEY, I TOLD YOU NO ACTIVITY! LIE BACK DOWN.
GOOD MORNING TO YOU TOO, DEBBIE.
I'M HEALING FASTER BY THE MINUTE.
IT'S EVEN SHOCKING ME!
I JUST CAN'T BELIEVE HOW A VAMPIRE CAN RECOVER FROM A BOWGUN WOUND IN A FEW DAYS.
ANYWAY, YOU'VE GOT A GUEST.
I DO?
COME ON IN.
DAR-REN!!
BA (LEAP)

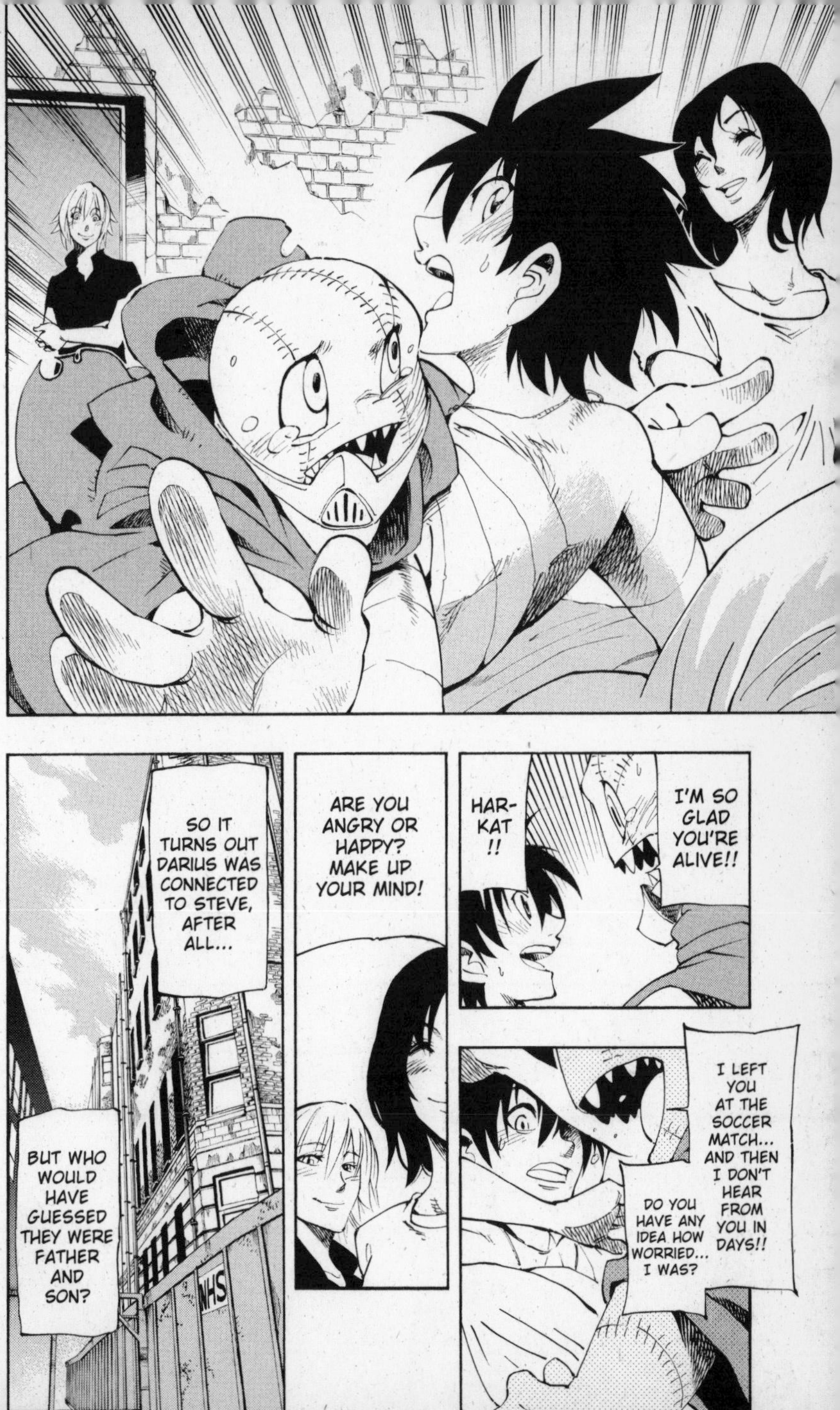
I'M SO GLAD YOU'RE ALIVE!!
HAR-KAT!!
I LEFT YOU AT THE SOCCER MATCH... AND THEN I DON'T HEAR FROM YOU IN DAYS!!
DO YOU HAVE ANY IDEA HOW WORRIED... I WAS?
ARE YOU ANGRY OR HAPPY? MAKE UP YOUR MIND!
SO IT TURNS OUT DARIUS WAS CONNECTED TO STEVE, AFTER ALL...
BUT WHO WOULD HAVE GUESSED THEY WERE FATHER AND SON?
NHS

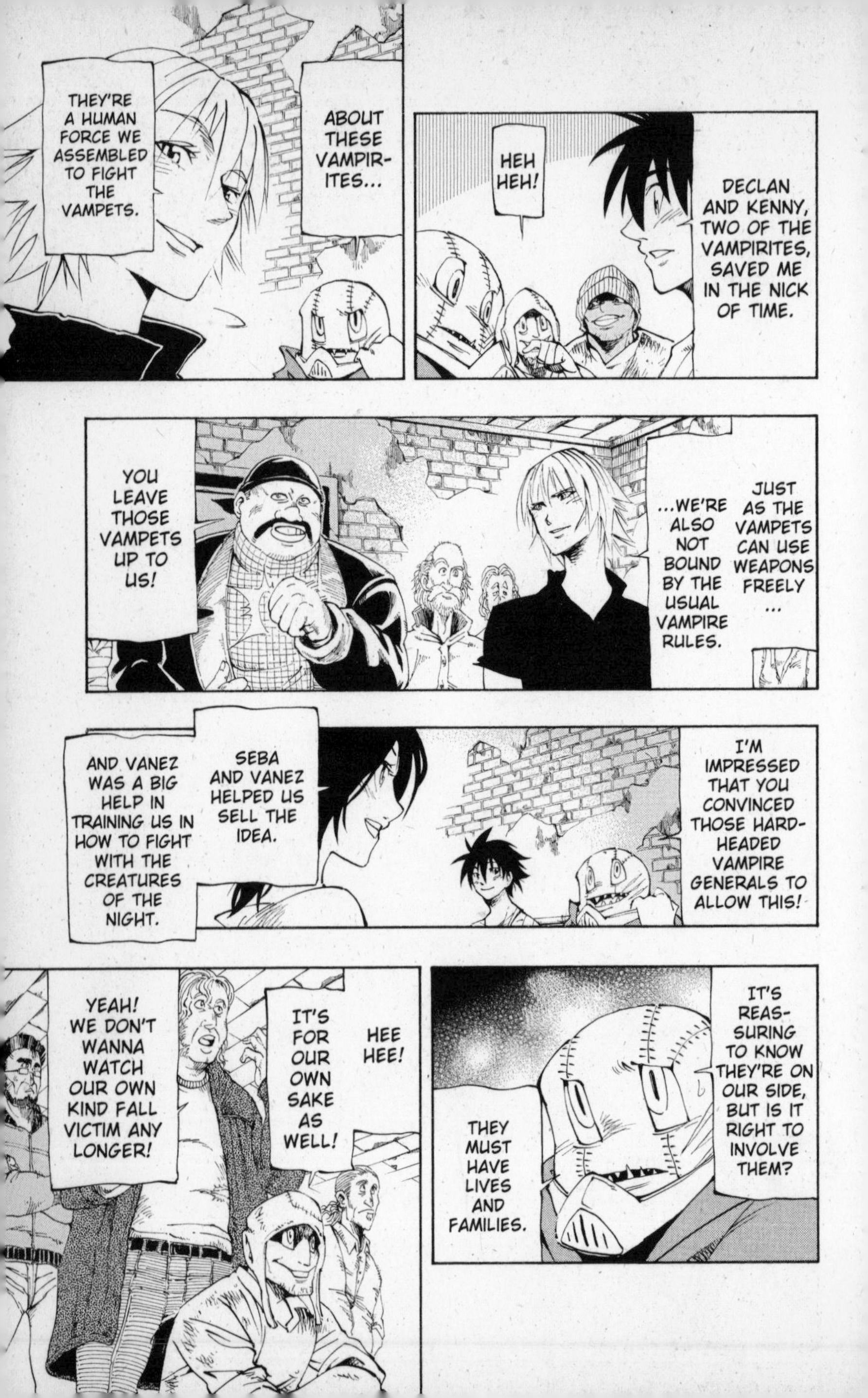
DECLAN AND KENNY, TWO OF THE VAMPIRITES, SAVED ME IN THE NICK OF TIME.
HEH HEH!
ABOUT THESE VAMPIRITES...
THEY'RE A HUMAN FORCE WE ASSEMBLED TO FIGHT THE VAMPETS.
JUST AS THE VAMPETS CAN USE WEAPONS FREELY...
...WE'RE ALSO NOT BOUND BY THE USUAL VAMPIRE RULES.
YOU LEAVE THOSE VAMPETS UP TO US!
I'M IMPRESSED THAT YOU CONVINCED THOSE HARDHEADED VAMPIRE GENERALS TO ALLOW THIS!
SEBA AND VANEZ HELPED US SELL THE IDEA.
AND VANEZ WAS A BIG HELP IN TRAINING US IN HOW TO FIGHT WITH THE CREATURES OF THE NIGHT.
IT'S REASSURING TO KNOW THEY'RE ON OUR SIDE, BUT IS IT RIGHT TO INVOLVE THEM?
THEY MUST HAVE LIVES AND FAMILIES.
HEE HEE!
IT'S FOR OUR OWN SAKE AS WELL!
YEAH! WE DON'T WANNA WATCH OUR OWN KIND FALL VICTIM ANY LONGER!

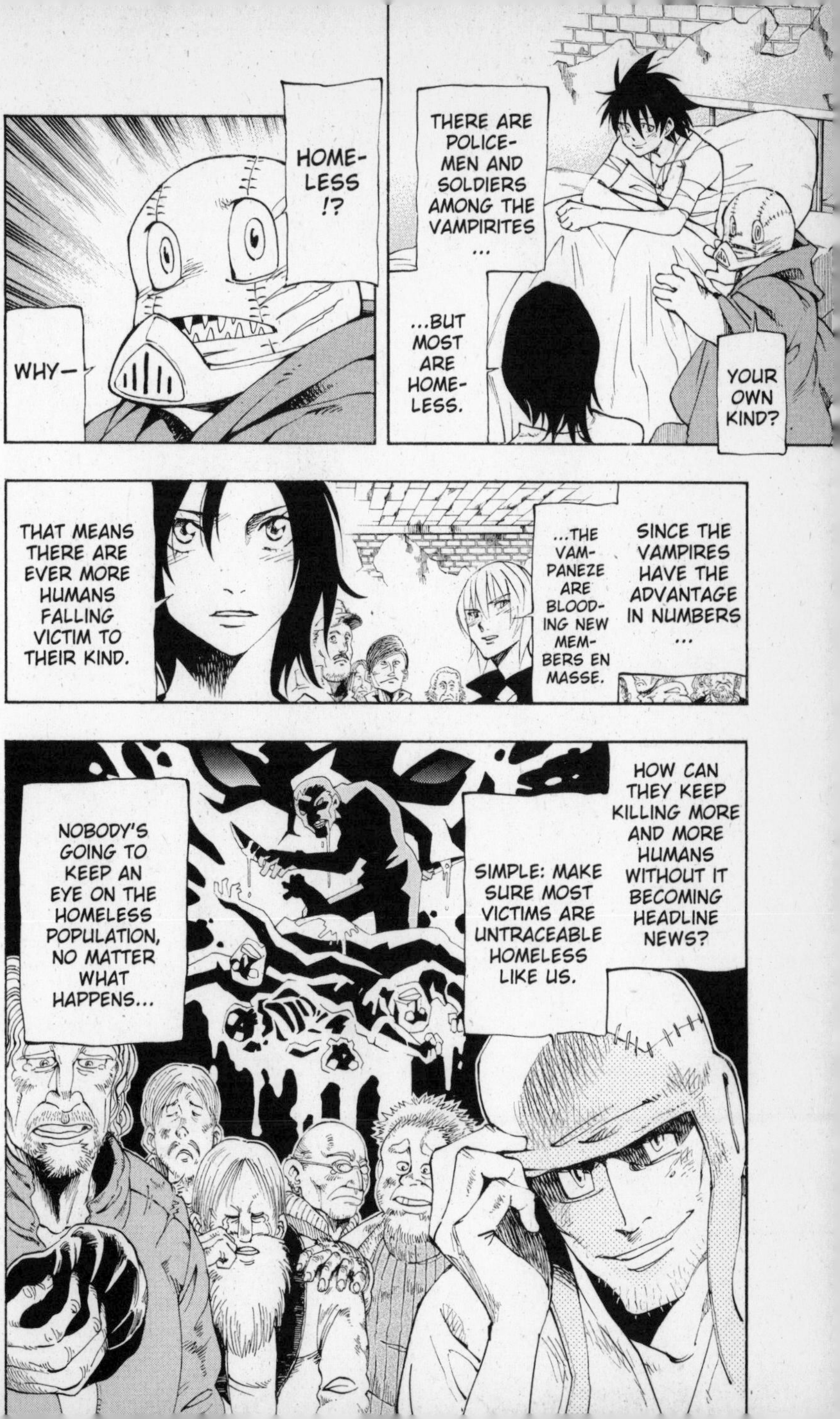
THERE ARE POLICEMEN AND SOLDIERS AMONG THE VAMPIRITES...
...BUT MOST ARE HOMELESS.
YOUR OWN KIND?
HOMELESS!?
WHY—
SINCE THE VAMPIRES HAVE THE ADVANTAGE IN NUMBERS...
...THE VAMPANEZE ARE BLOODING NEW MEMBERS EN MASSE.
THAT MEANS THERE ARE EVER MORE HUMANS FALLING VICTIM TO THEIR KIND.
HOW CAN THEY KEEP KILLING MORE AND MORE HUMANS WITHOUT IT BECOMING HEADLINE NEWS?
SIMPLE: MAKE SURE MOST VICTIMS ARE UNTRACEABLE HOMELESS LIKE US.
NOBODY'S GOING TO KEEP AN EYE ON THE HOMELESS POPULATION, NO MATTER WHAT HAPPENS...

SO THEY'RE FIGHTING NOT FOR JUSTICE OR THE VAMPIRE CAUSE, BUT THEIR OWN LIVES.

IT ALL MAKES SENSE.

AND WHO SHOULD ARRIVE BLOODY AND BRUISED BUT YOU, DARREN!

WE ARRIVED IN THIS TOWN TWO WEEKS AGO.

OUR VAMPIRITES WERE REPORTING A STRONG VAMPANEZE PRESENCE IN THE AREA.

WE'RE ALL IN THIS TOGETHER NOW.

WE FIGHT TO SURVIVE.

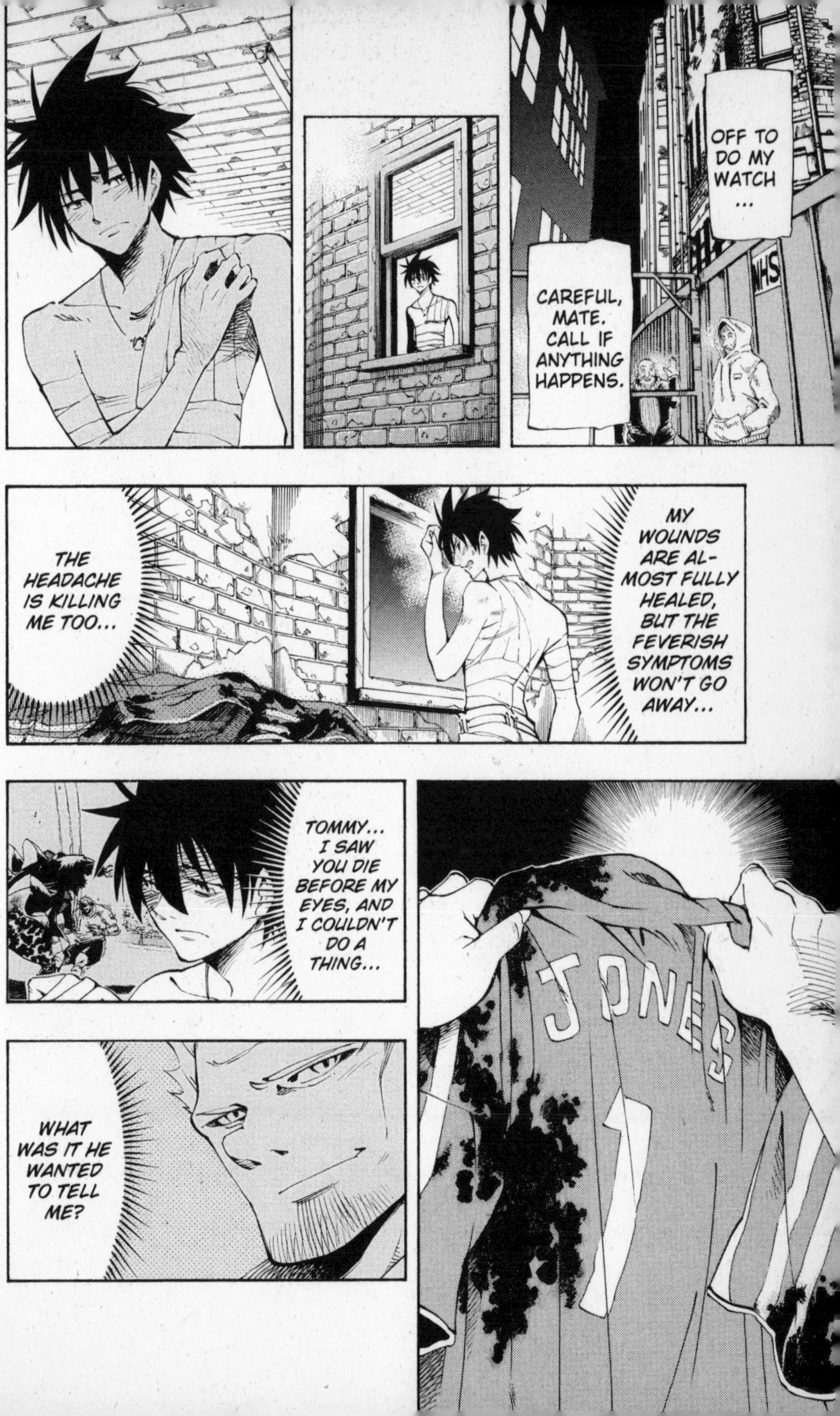
OFF TO DO MY WATCH ...
NHS
CAREFUL, MATE. CALL IF ANYTHING HAPPENS.
MY WOUNDS ARE AL-MOST FULLY HEALED, BUT THE FEVERISH SYMPTOMS WON'T GO AWAY...
THE HEADACHE IS KILLING ME TOO...
JONES
TOMMY... I SAW YOU DIE BEFORE MY EYES, AND I COULDN'T DO A THING...
WHAT WAS IT HE WANTED TO TELL ME?

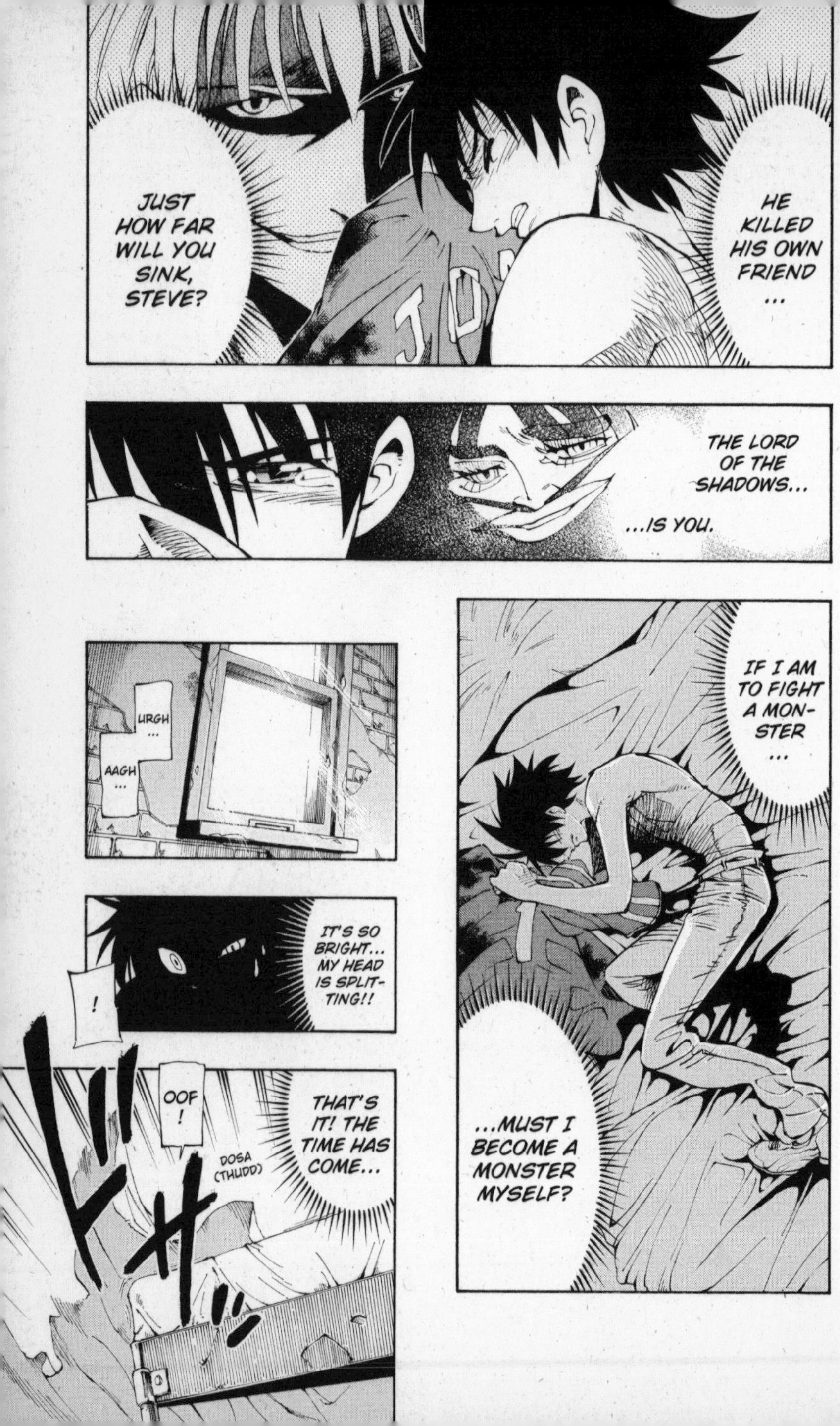
HE KILLED HIS OWN FRIEND...
JUST HOW FAR WILL YOU SINK, STEVE?
THE LORD OF THE SHADOWS...
...IS YOU.
IF I AM TO FIGHT A MON-STER...
...MUST I BECOME A MONSTER MYSELF?
URGH...
AAGH...
IT'S SO BRIGHT... MY HEAD IS SPLIT-TING!!
!
THAT'S IT! THE TIME HAS COME...
OOF!
DOSA (THUDD)

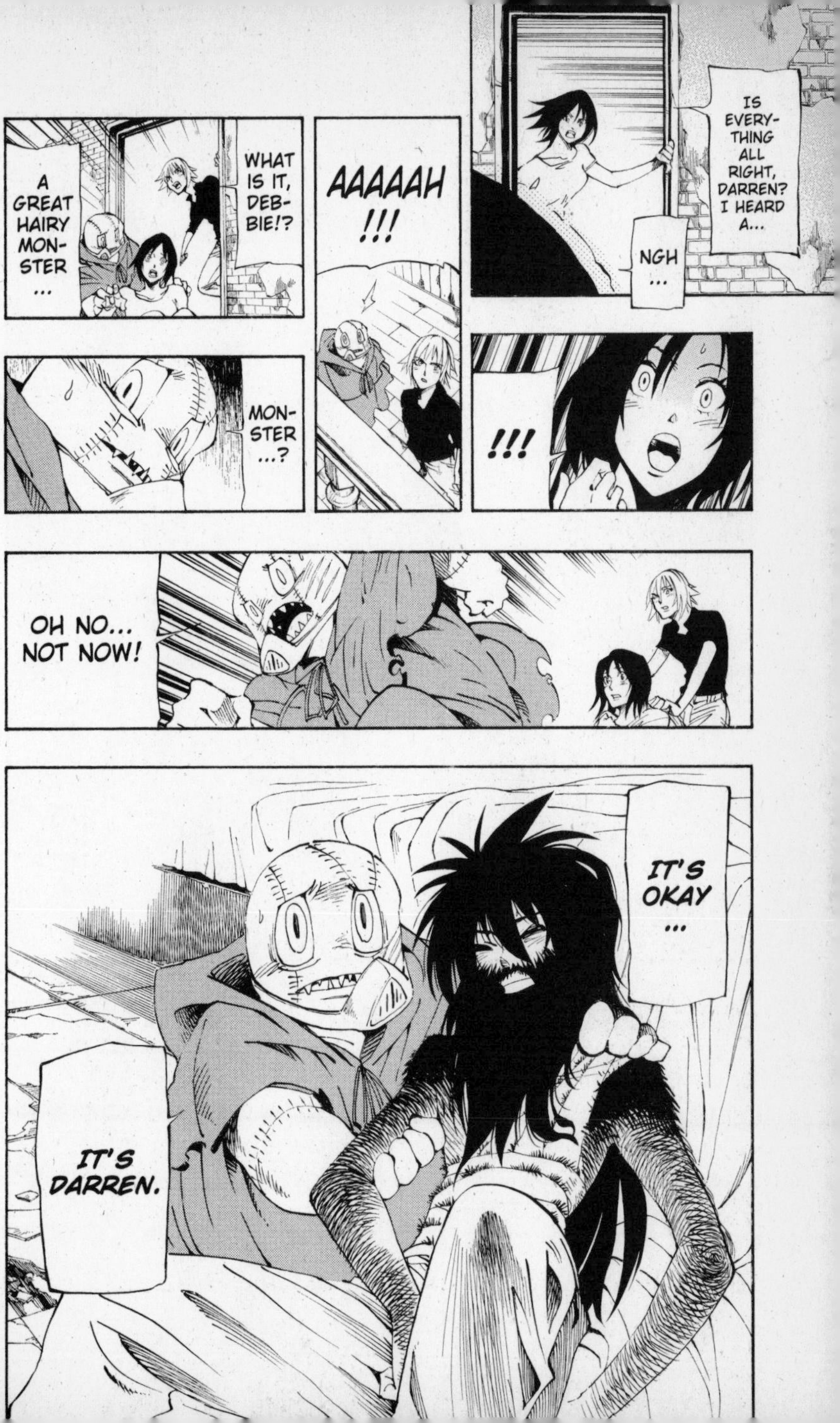
IS EVERY-THING ALL RIGHT, DARREN? I HEARD A...
NGH ...
!!!
AAAAAH !!!
WHAT IS IT, DEB-BIE!?
A GREAT HAIRY MON-STER ...
MON-STER ...?
OH NO... NOT NOW!
IT'S OKAY ...
IT'S DARREN.

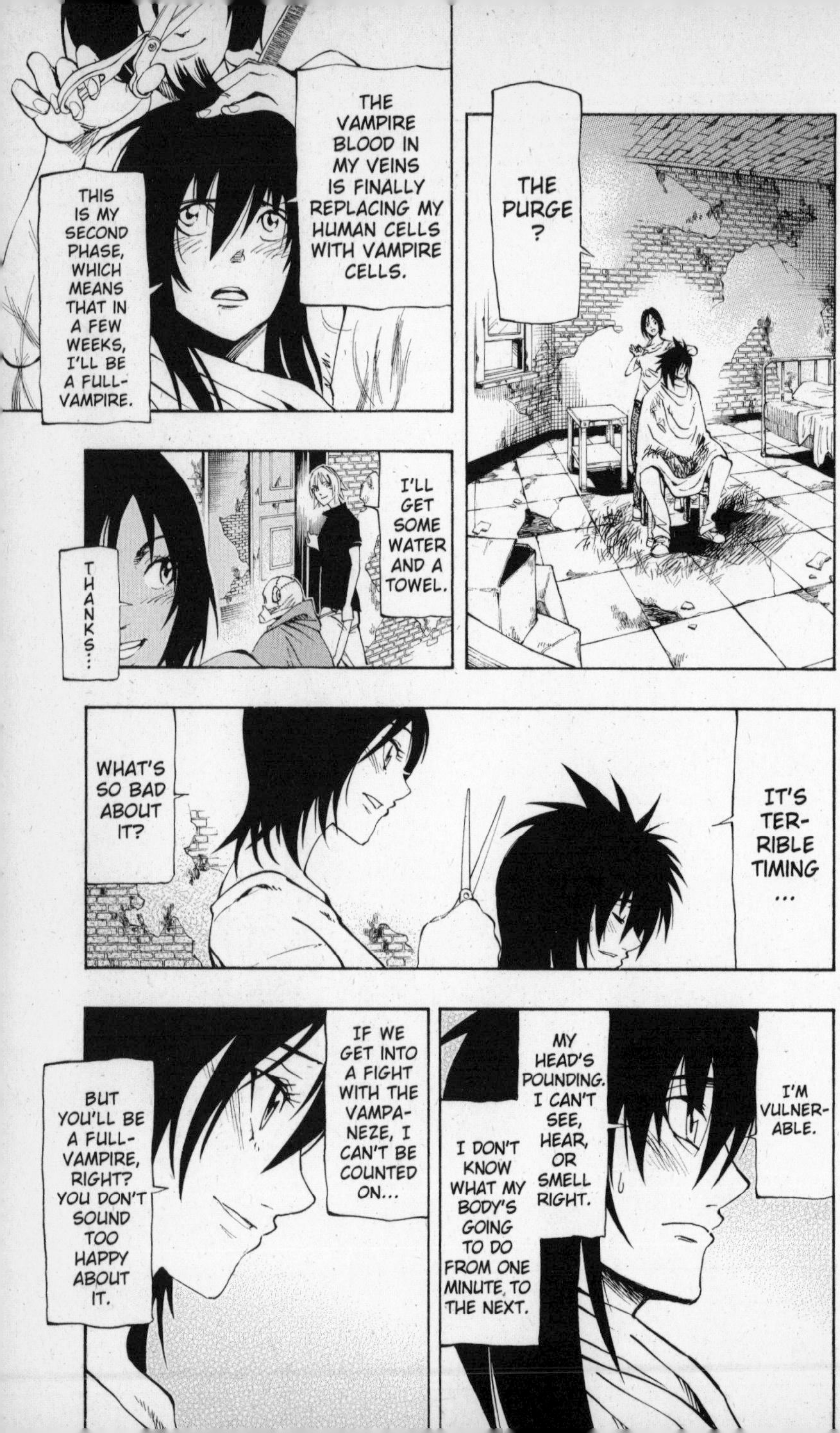
THE PURGE?
THE VAMPIRE BLOOD IN MY VEINS IS FINALLY REPLACING MY HUMAN CELLS WITH VAMPIRE CELLS.
THIS IS MY SECOND PHASE, WHICH MEANS THAT IN A FEW WEEKS, I'LL BE A FULL-VAMPIRE.
I'LL GET SOME WATER AND A TOWEL.
THANKS...
IT'S TERRIBLE TIMING...
WHAT'S SO BAD ABOUT IT?
I'M VULNERABLE.
MY HEAD'S POUNDING. I CAN'T SEE, HEAR, OR SMELL RIGHT.
I DON'T KNOW WHAT MY BODY'S GOING TO DO FROM ONE MINUTE TO THE NEXT.
IF WE GET INTO A FIGHT WITH THE VAMPANEZE, I CAN'T BE COUNTED ON...
BUT YOU'LL BE A FULL-VAMPIRE, RIGHT? YOU DON'T SOUND TOO HAPPY ABOUT IT.

IT NEVER FELT RIGHT TO BE A HALF-VAMPIRE PRINCE.

IT'S BEEN EIGHTEEN YEARS SINCE MR. CREPSLEY BLOODED ME...

IN MANY WAYS I'M GLAD—I'LL FINALLY BE A TRUE VAMPIRE.

ON THE OTHER HAND, I'M FACING THE END OF A WAY OF LIFE.

NOW I HAVE TO LEAVE THE WORLD OF LIGHT BEHIND FOREVER, SKULKING IN THE DARKNESS FOR THE REST OF MY DAYS.

NO MORE SUNLIGHT OR BEING ABLE TO PASS FOR HUMAN.

ALL DONE!

BASA
(FLAP)

THANKS, THAT'S MUCH BETTER.

106

HEE!

STILL GOT WHISKERS?

NOPE.

LOOK...

YOU'RE ALREADY GROWING.

HA HA HA.

YOU'RE RIGHT...

JUST YESTERDAY, I WAS TALLER THAN YOU!

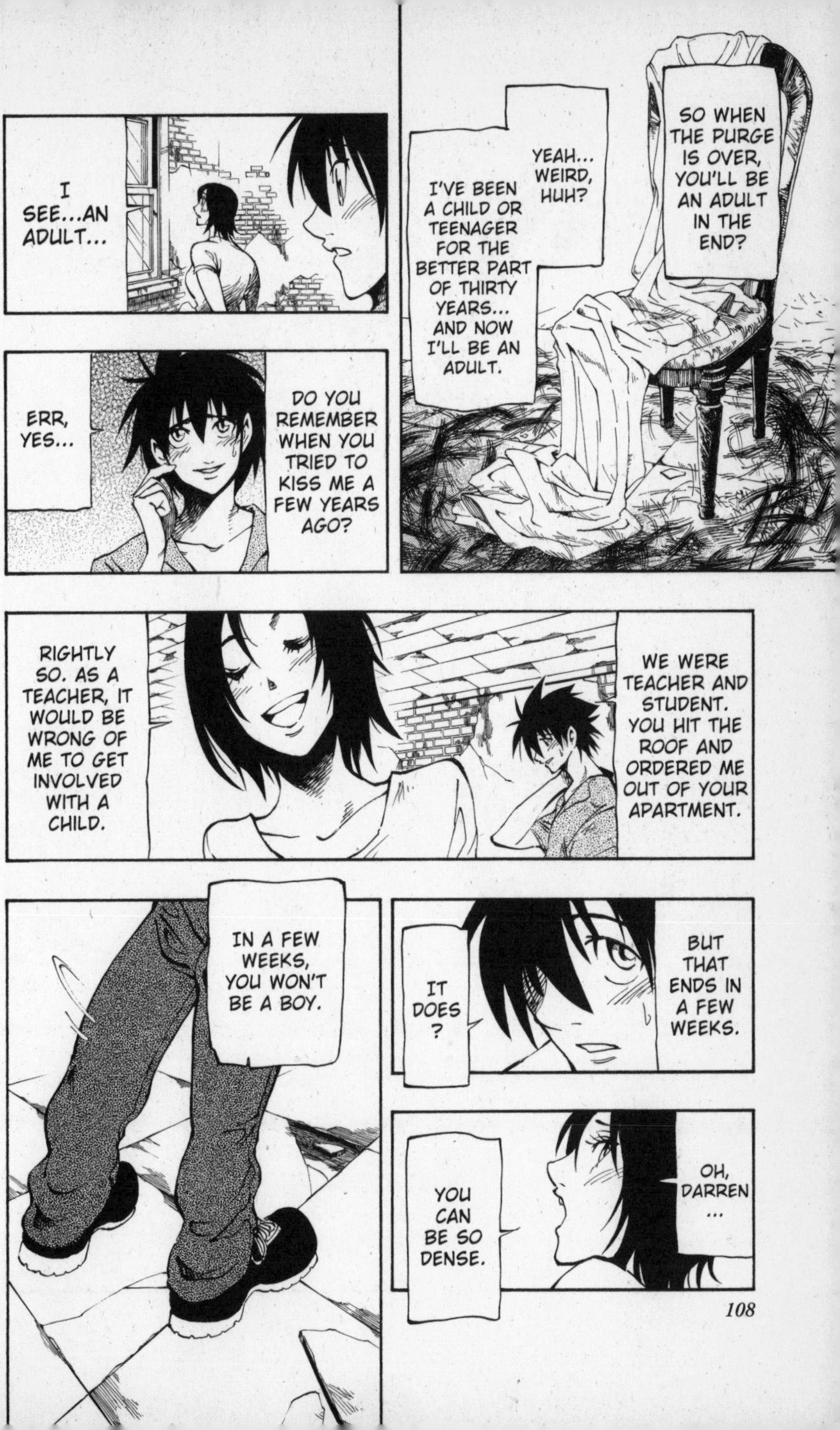
SO WHEN THE PURGE IS OVER, YOU'LL BE AN ADULT IN THE END?
YEAH... WEIRD, HUH?
I'VE BEEN A CHILD OR TEENAGER FOR THE BETTER PART OF THIRTY YEARS... AND NOW I'LL BE AN ADULT.
I SEE...AN ADULT...
DO YOU REMEMBER WHEN YOU TRIED TO KISS ME A FEW YEARS AGO?
ERR, YES...
WE WERE TEACHER AND STUDENT. YOU HIT THE ROOF AND ORDERED ME OUT OF YOUR APARTMENT.
RIGHTLY SO. AS A TEACHER, IT WOULD BE WRONG OF ME TO GET INVOLVED WITH A CHILD.
BUT THAT ENDS IN A FEW WEEKS.
IT DOES?
IN A FEW WEEKS, YOU WON'T BE A BOY.
OH, DARREN...
YOU CAN BE SO DENSE.

YOU'LL
BE A
MAN.

OH...

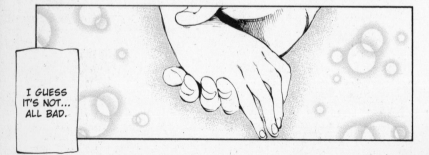

I GUESS
IT'S NOT...
ALL BAD.

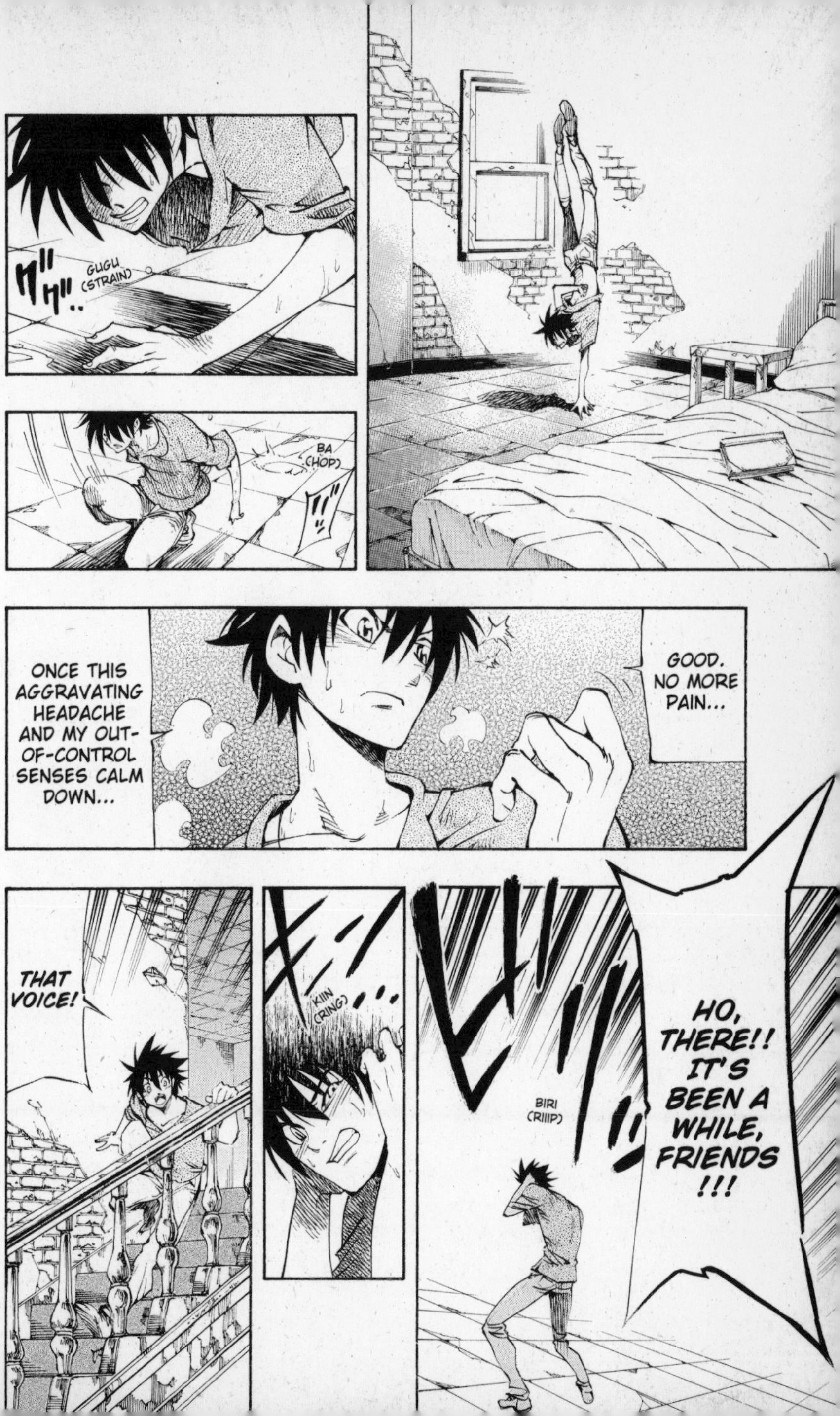
GUGU (STRAIN)
BA (HOP)
GOOD. NO MORE PAIN...
ONCE THIS AGGRAVATING HEADACHE AND MY OUT-OF-CONTROL SENSES CALM DOWN...
HO, THERE!! IT'S BEEN A WHILE, FRIENDS!!!
BIRI (RIIIP)
KIIN (RING)
THAT VOICE!

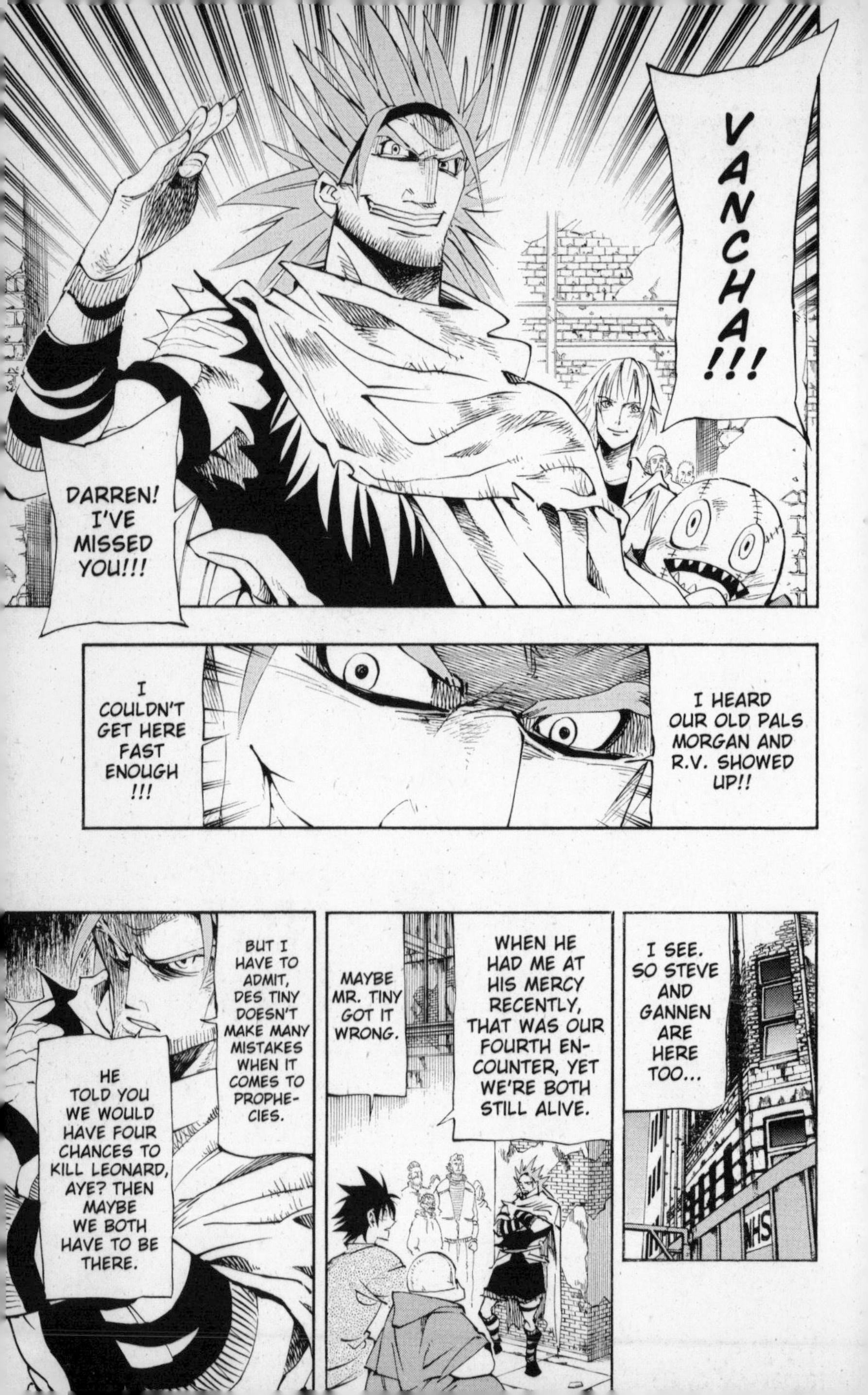
VANCHA!!!
DARREN! I'VE MISSED YOU!!!
I HEARD OUR OLD PALS MORGAN AND R.V. SHOWED UP!!
I COULDN'T GET HERE FAST ENOUGH!!!
I SEE. SO STEVE AND GANNEN ARE HERE TOO...
NHS
WHEN HE HAD ME AT HIS MERCY RECENTLY, THAT WAS OUR FOURTH EN-COUNTER, YET WE'RE BOTH STILL ALIVE.
MAYBE MR. TINY GOT IT WRONG.
BUT I HAVE TO ADMIT, DES TINY DOESN'T MAKE MANY MISTAKES WHEN IT COMES TO PROPHE-CIES.
HE TOLD YOU WE WOULD HAVE FOUR CHANCES TO KILL LEONARD, AYE? THEN MAYBE WE BOTH HAVE TO BE THERE.

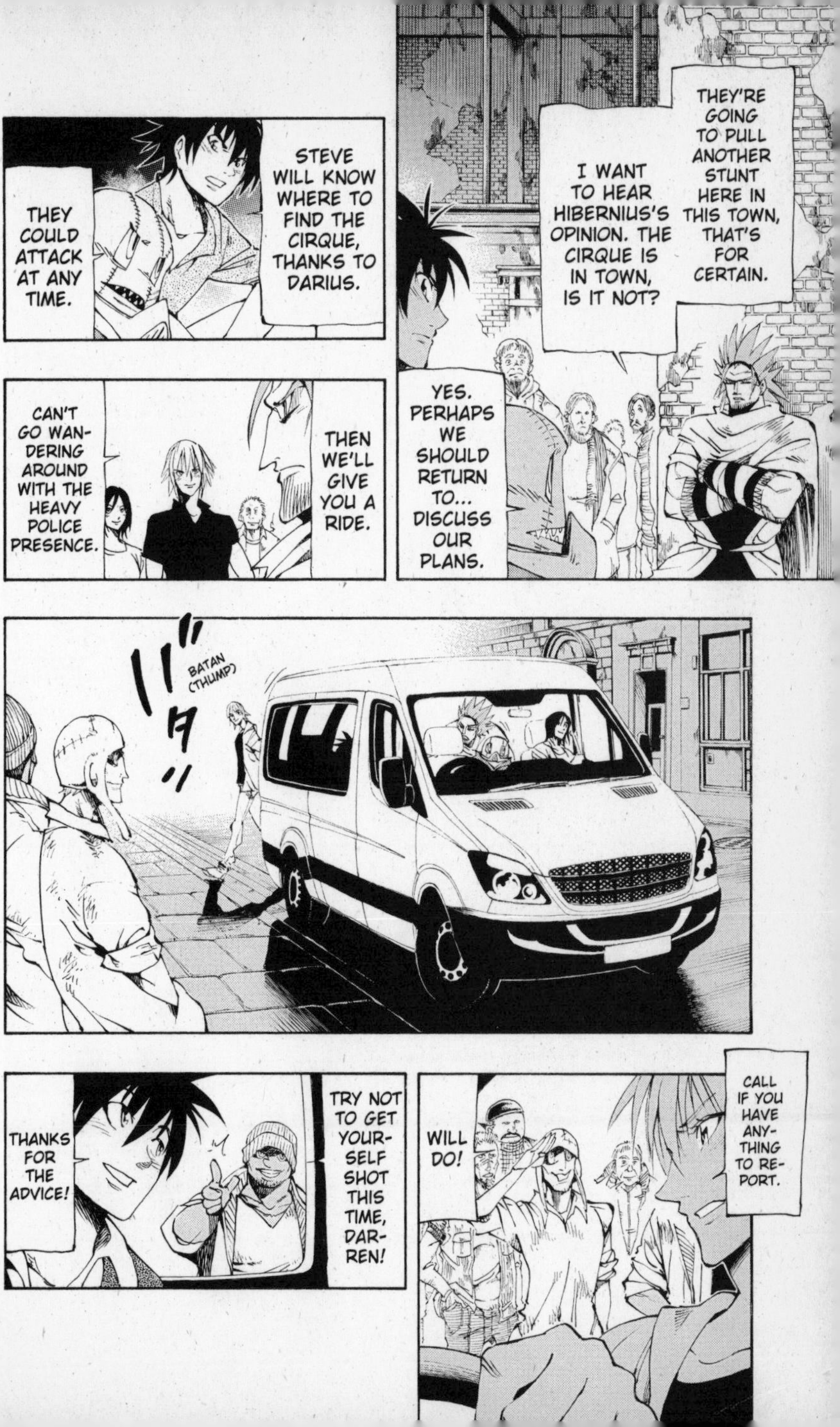
THEY'RE GOING TO PULL ANOTHER STUNT HERE IN THIS TOWN, THAT'S FOR CERTAIN.
I WANT TO HEAR HIBERNIUS'S OPINION. THE CIRQUE IS IN TOWN, IS IT NOT?
STEVE WILL KNOW WHERE TO FIND THE CIRQUE, THANKS TO DARIUS.
THEY COULD ATTACK AT ANY TIME.
YES. PERHAPS WE SHOULD RETURN TO... DISCUSS OUR PLANS.
THEN WE'LL GIVE YOU A RIDE.
CAN'T GO WANDERING AROUND WITH THE HEAVY POLICE PRESENCE.
バタッ
BATAN (THUMP)
CALL IF YOU HAVE ANYTHING TO REPORT.
WILL DO!
TRY NOT TO GET YOURSELF SHOT THIS TIME, DARREN!
THANKS FOR THE ADVICE!

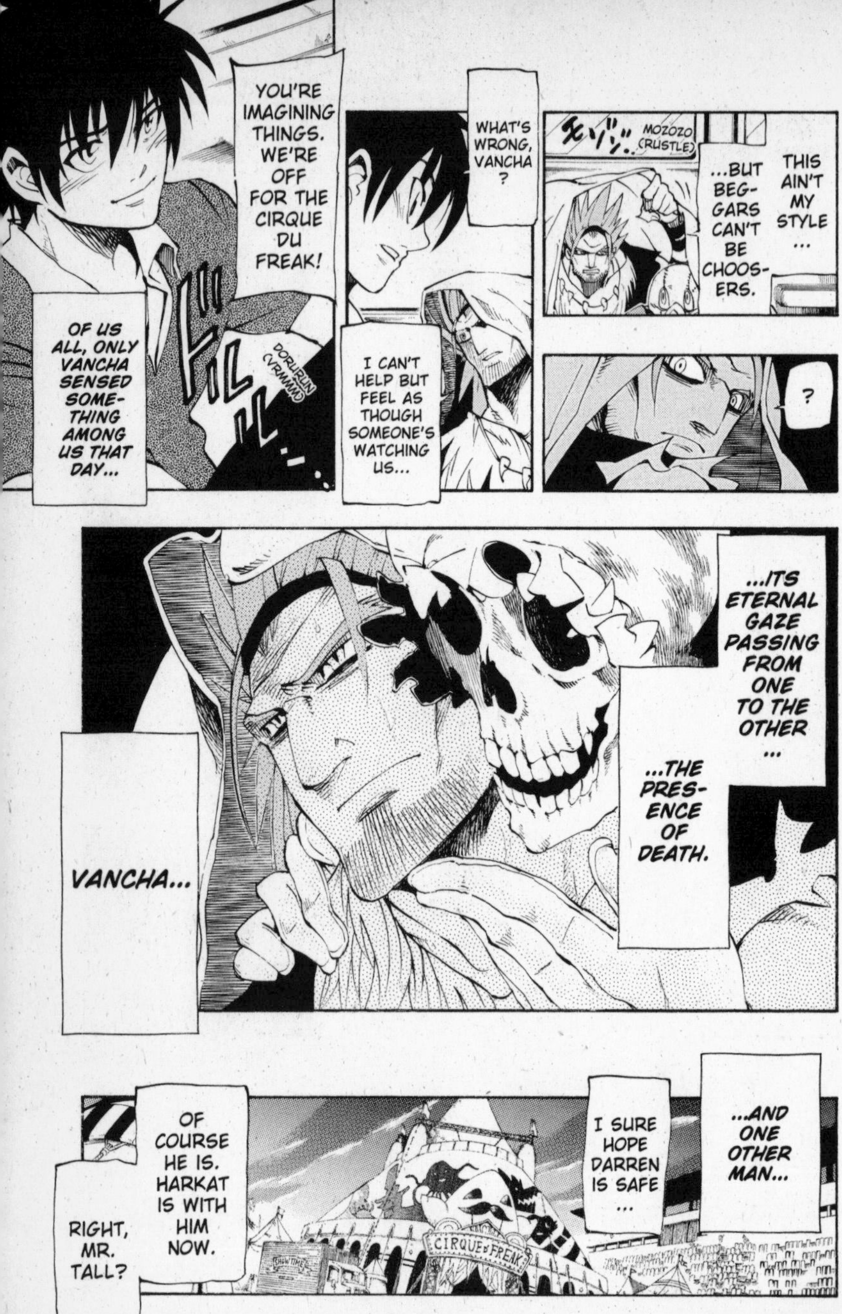
MOZOZO (RUSTLE)
THIS AIN'T MY STYLE...
...BUT BEGGARS CAN'T BE CHOOSERS.
?
WHAT'S WRONG, VANCHA?
I CAN'T HELP BUT FEEL AS THOUGH SOMEONE'S WATCHING US...
YOU'RE IMAGINING THINGS. WE'RE OFF FOR THE CIRQUE DU FREAK!
DORURUN (VRMMM)
OF US ALL, ONLY VANCHA SENSED SOMETHING AMONG US THAT DAY...
...ITS ETERNAL GAZE PASSING FROM ONE TO THE OTHER...
...THE PRESENCE OF DEATH.
VANCHA...
...AND ONE OTHER MAN...
I SURE HOPE DARREN IS SAFE...
CIRQUE DU FREAK
SHOWTIME
OF COURSE HE IS. HARKAT IS WITH HIM NOW.
RIGHT, MR. TALL?

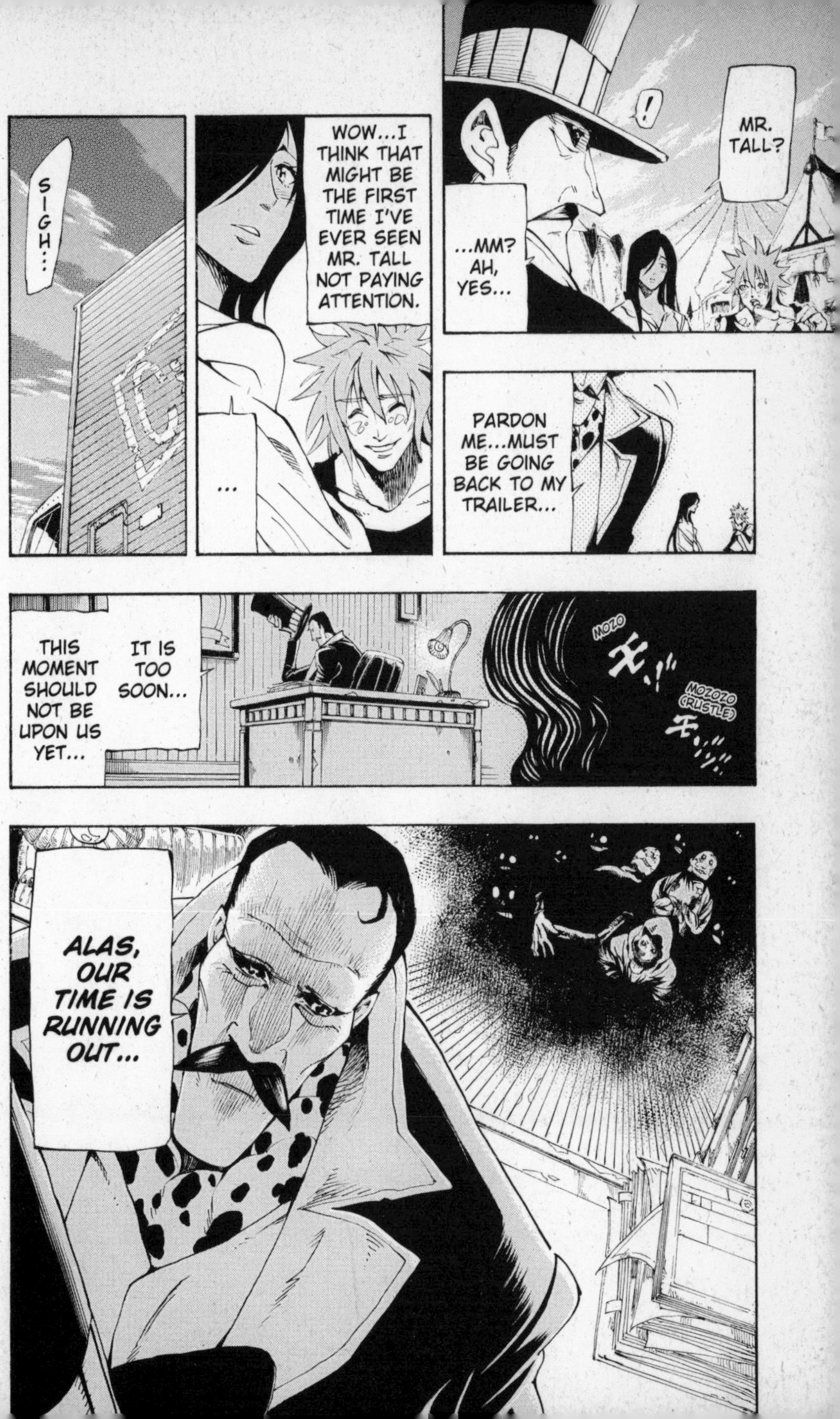
MR. TALL?
!
...MM? AH, YES...
PARDON ME...MUST BE GOING BACK TO MY TRAILER...
WOW...I THINK THAT MIGHT BE THE FIRST TIME I'VE EVER SEEN MR. TALL NOT PAYING ATTENTION.
...
SIGH...
MOZO
MOZOZO (RUSTLE)
IT IS TOO SOON...
THIS MOMENT SHOULD NOT BE UPON US YET...
ALAS, OUR TIME IS RUNNING OUT...

## CHAPTER 101:

# MR. TALL'S PROPHECY

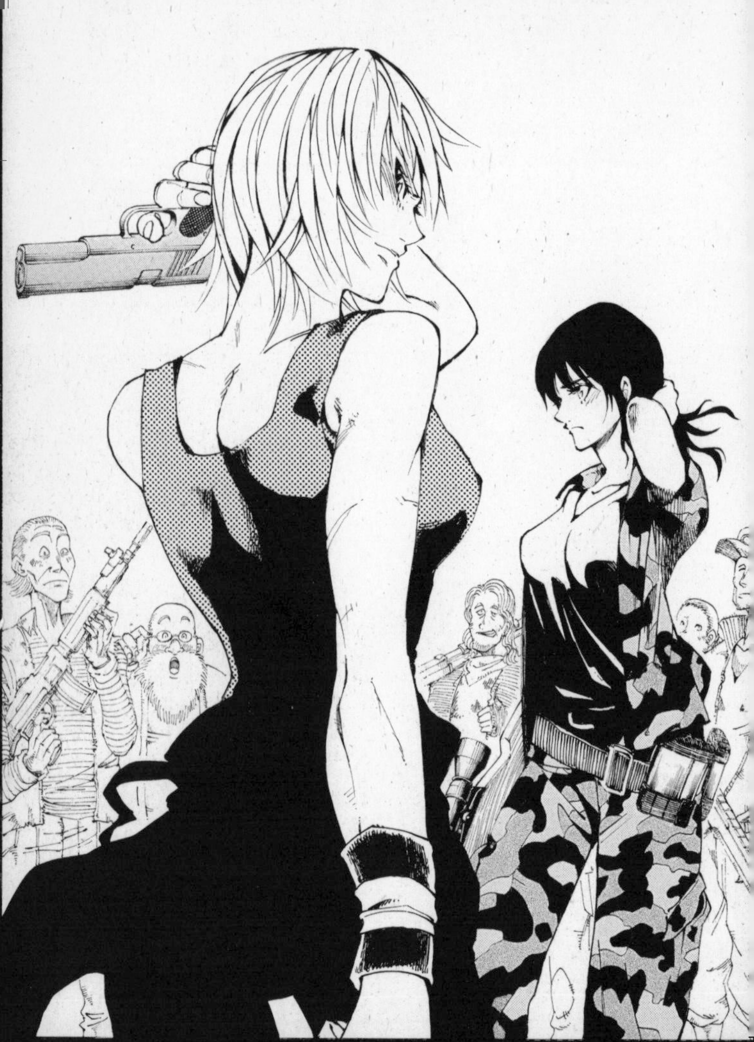

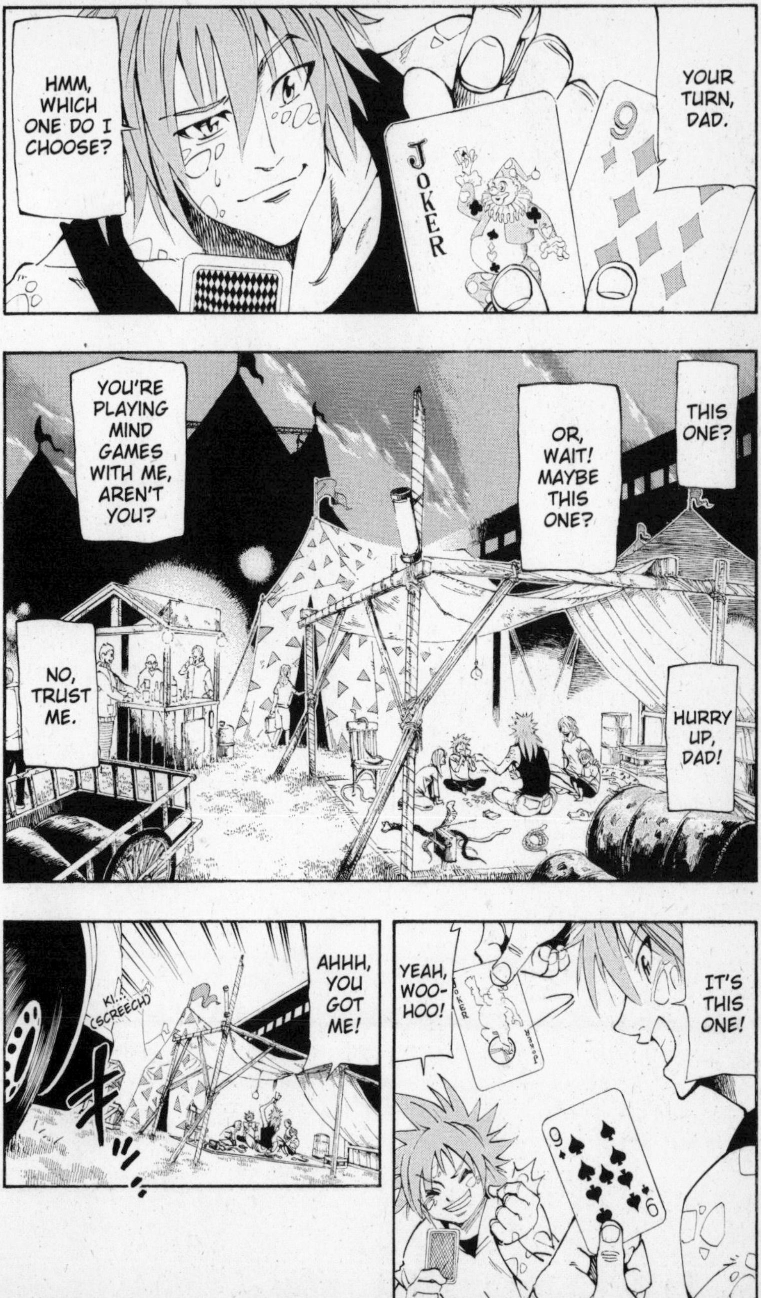
YOUR TURN, DAD.
HMM, WHICH ONE DO I CHOOSE?
JOKER
THIS ONE?
OR, WAIT! MAYBE THIS ONE?
YOU'RE PLAYING MIND GAMES WITH ME, AREN'T YOU?
HURRY UP, DAD!
NO, TRUST ME.
IT'S THIS ONE!
YEAH, WOO-HOO!
AHHH, YOU GOT ME!
KI... (SCREECH)

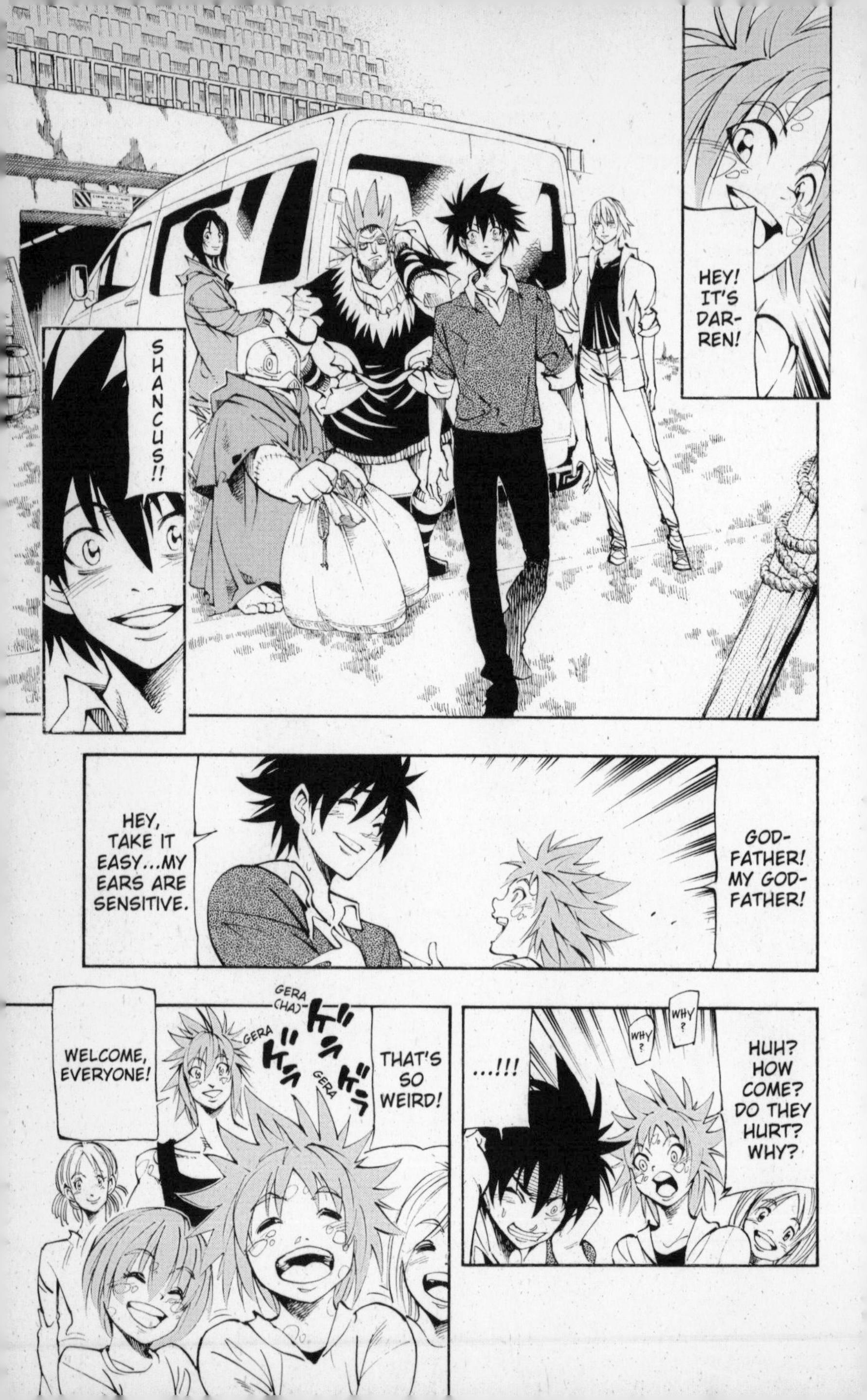
HEY! IT'S DAR-REN!
SHANCUS!!
GOD-FATHER! MY GOD-FATHER!
HEY, TAKE IT EASY...MY EARS ARE SENSITIVE.
HUH? HOW COME? DO THEY HURT? WHY?
WHY?
WHY?
...!!!
THAT'S SO WEIRD!
GERA (HA)-
GERA
GERA
WELCOME, EVERYONE!

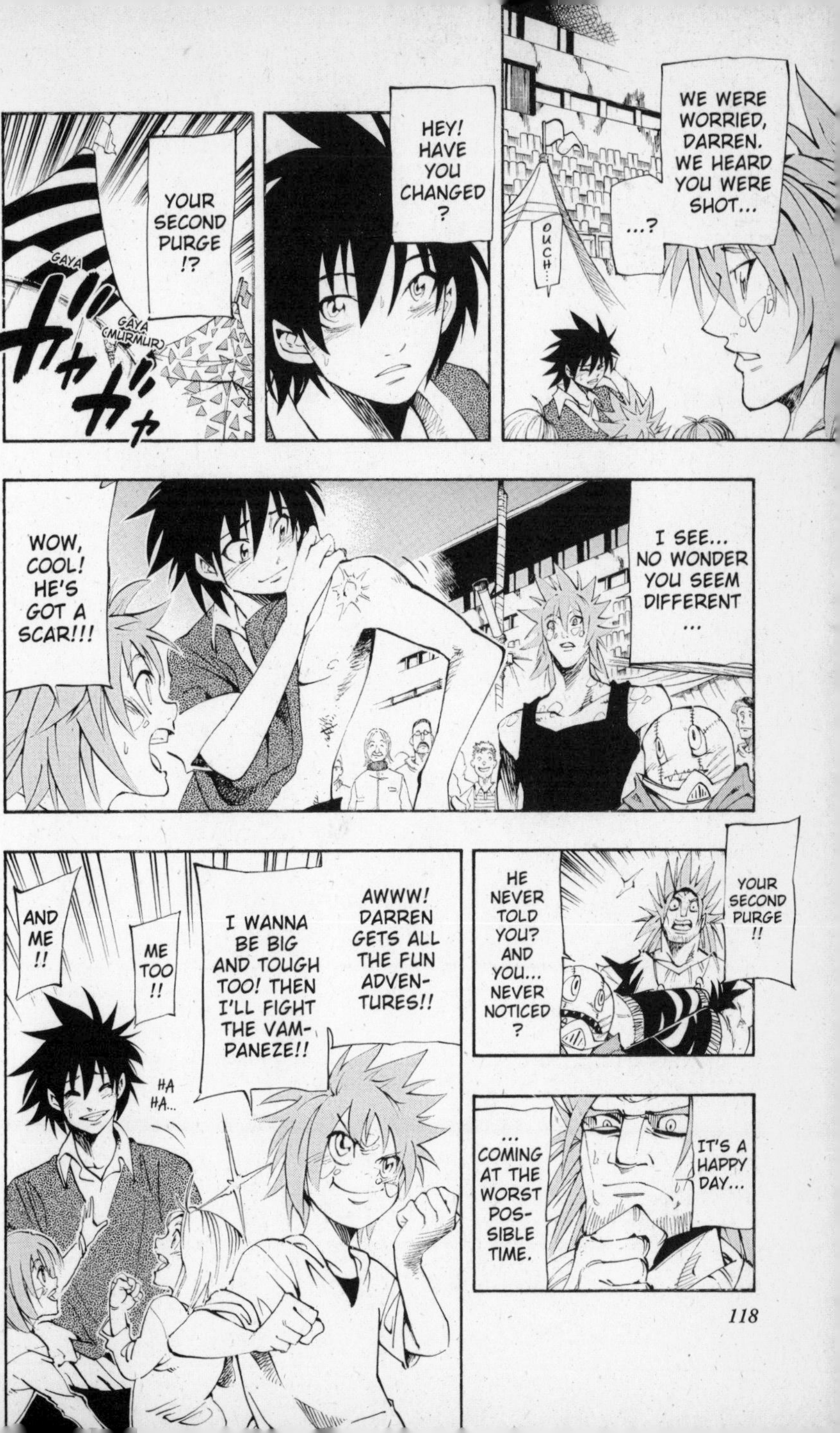
WE WERE WORRIED, DARREN. WE HEARD YOU WERE SHOT...
...?
OUCH...
HEY! HAVE YOU CHANGED?
YOUR SECOND PURGE!?
GAYA
GAYA (MURMUR)
I SEE... NO WONDER YOU SEEM DIFFERENT...
WOW, COOL! HE'S GOT A SCAR!!!
YOUR SECOND PURGE!!
HE NEVER TOLD YOU? AND YOU... NEVER NOTICED?
IT'S A HAPPY DAY...
...COMING AT THE WORST POS-SIBLE TIME.
AWWW! DARREN GETS ALL THE FUN ADVEN-TURES!!
I WANNA BE BIG AND TOUGH TOO! THEN I'LL FIGHT THE VAM-PANEZE!!
ME TOO!!
AND ME!!
HA HA...

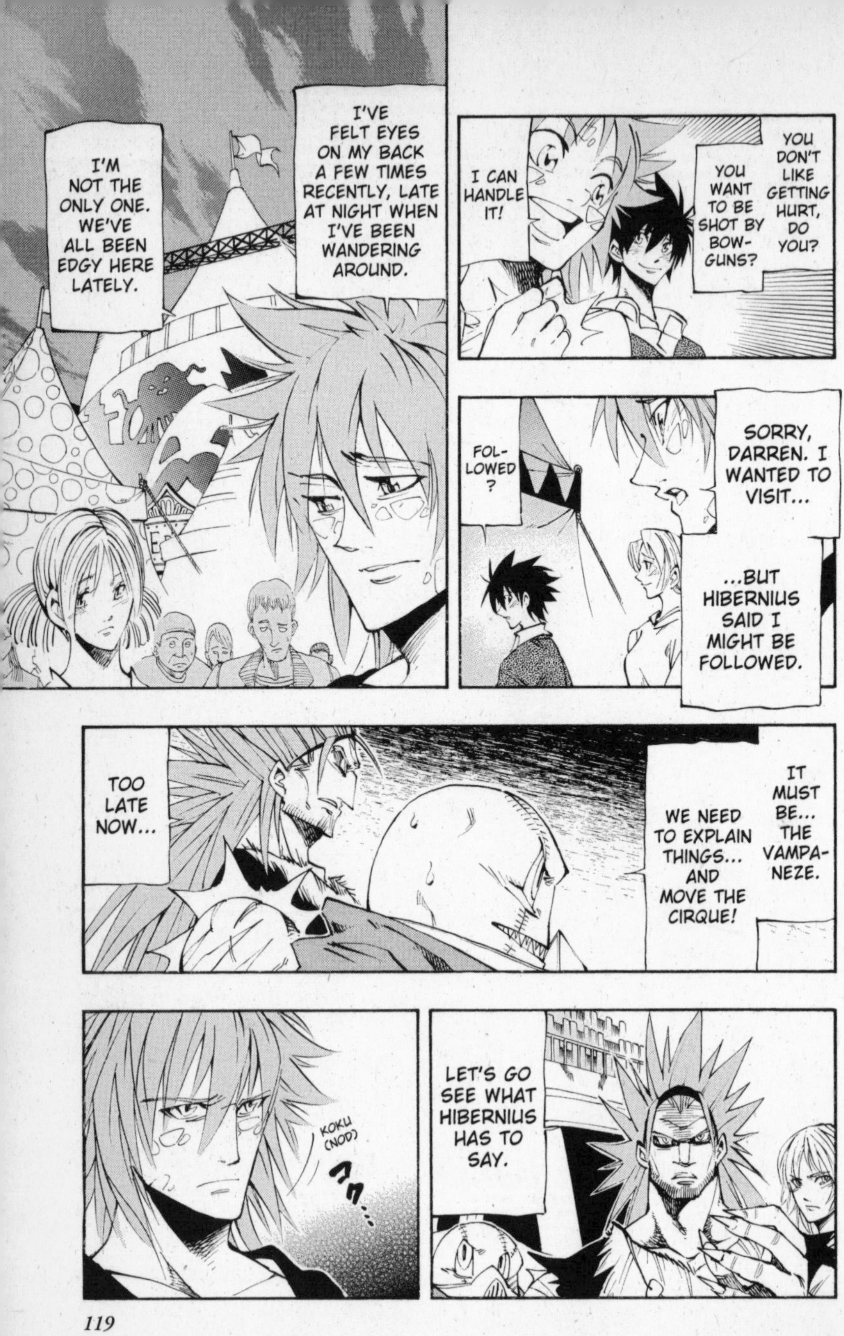
YOU DON'T LIKE GETTING HURT, DO YOU?
YOU WANT TO BE SHOT BY BOW-GUNS?
I CAN HANDLE IT!
SORRY, DARREN. I WANTED TO VISIT...
...BUT HIBERNIUS SAID I MIGHT BE FOLLOWED.
FOL-LOWED?
I'VE FELT EYES ON MY BACK A FEW TIMES RECENTLY, LATE AT NIGHT WHEN I'VE BEEN WANDERING AROUND.
I'M NOT THE ONLY ONE. WE'VE ALL BEEN EDGY HERE LATELY.
IT MUST BE... THE VAMPA-NEZE.
WE NEED TO EXPLAIN THINGS... AND MOVE THE CIRQUE!
TOO LATE NOW...
LET'S GO SEE WHAT HIBERNIUS HAS TO SAY.
KOKU (NOD)

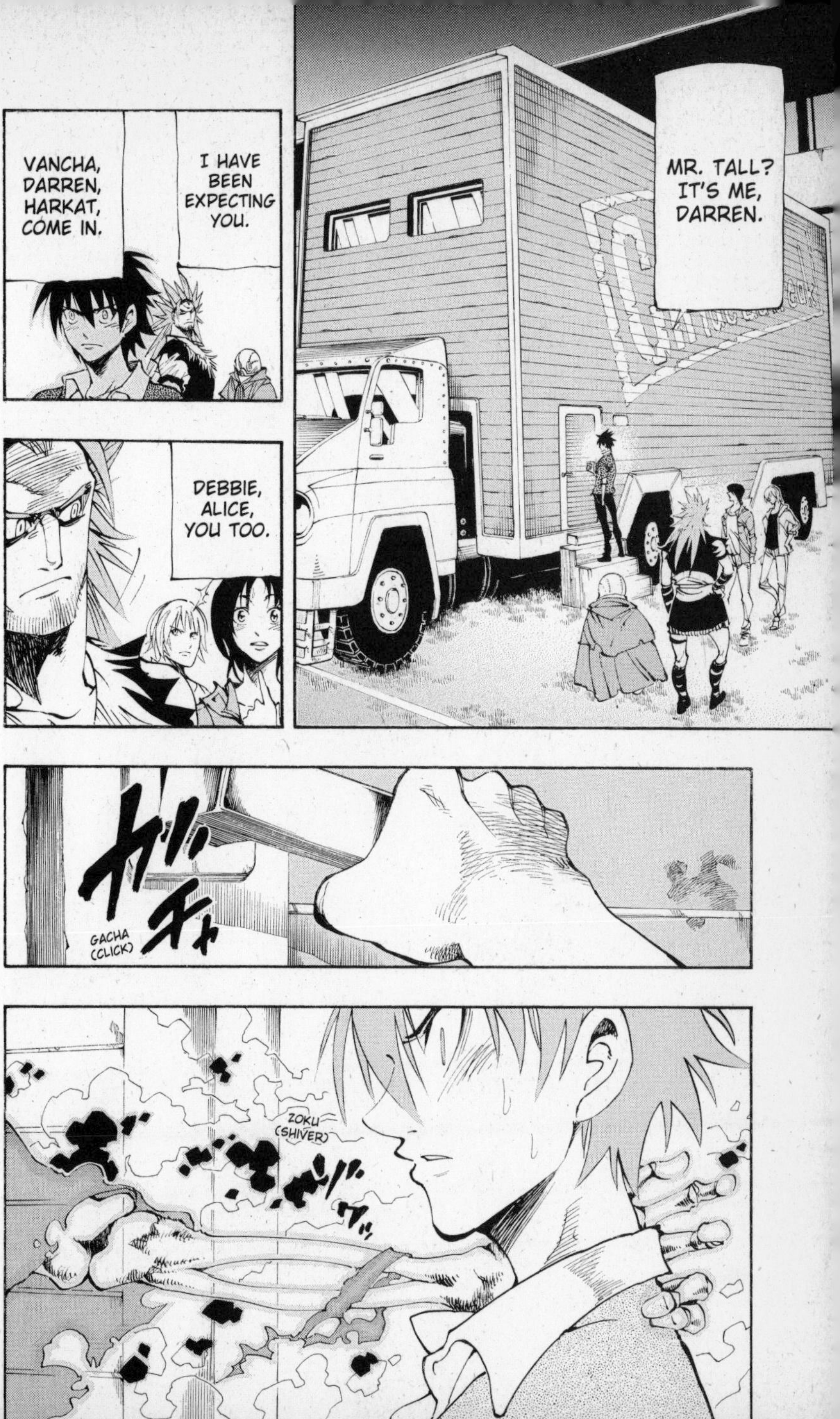
MR. TALL? IT'S ME, DARREN.
I HAVE BEEN EXPECTING YOU.
VANCHA, DARREN, HARKAT, COME IN.
DEBBIE, ALICE, YOU TOO.
GACHA (CLICK)
ZOKU (SHIVER)

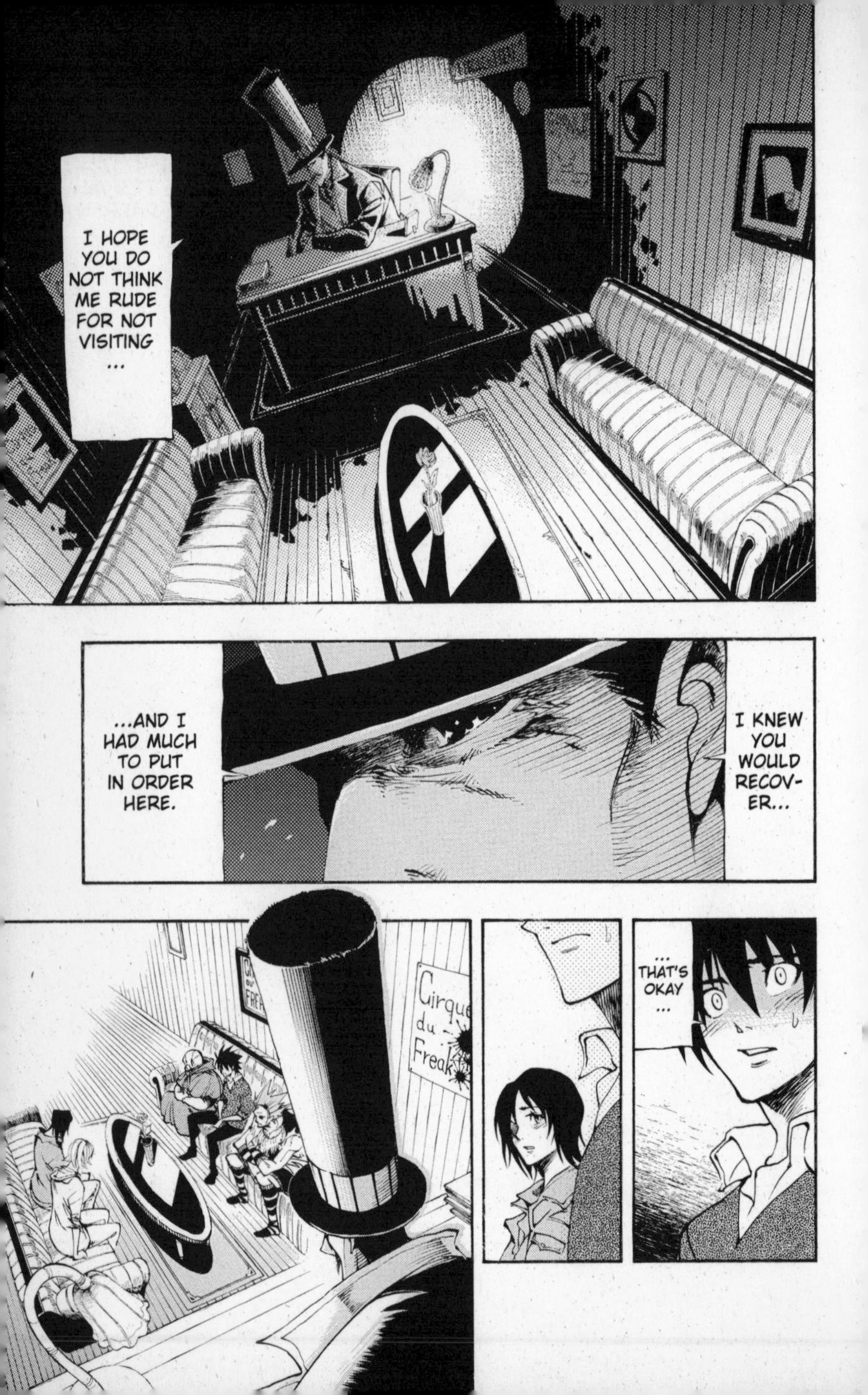
I HOPE YOU DO NOT THINK ME RUDE FOR NOT VISITING ...
I KNEW YOU WOULD RECOV-ER...
...AND I HAD MUCH TO PUT IN ORDER HERE.
... THAT'S OKAY ...
Cirque du Freak

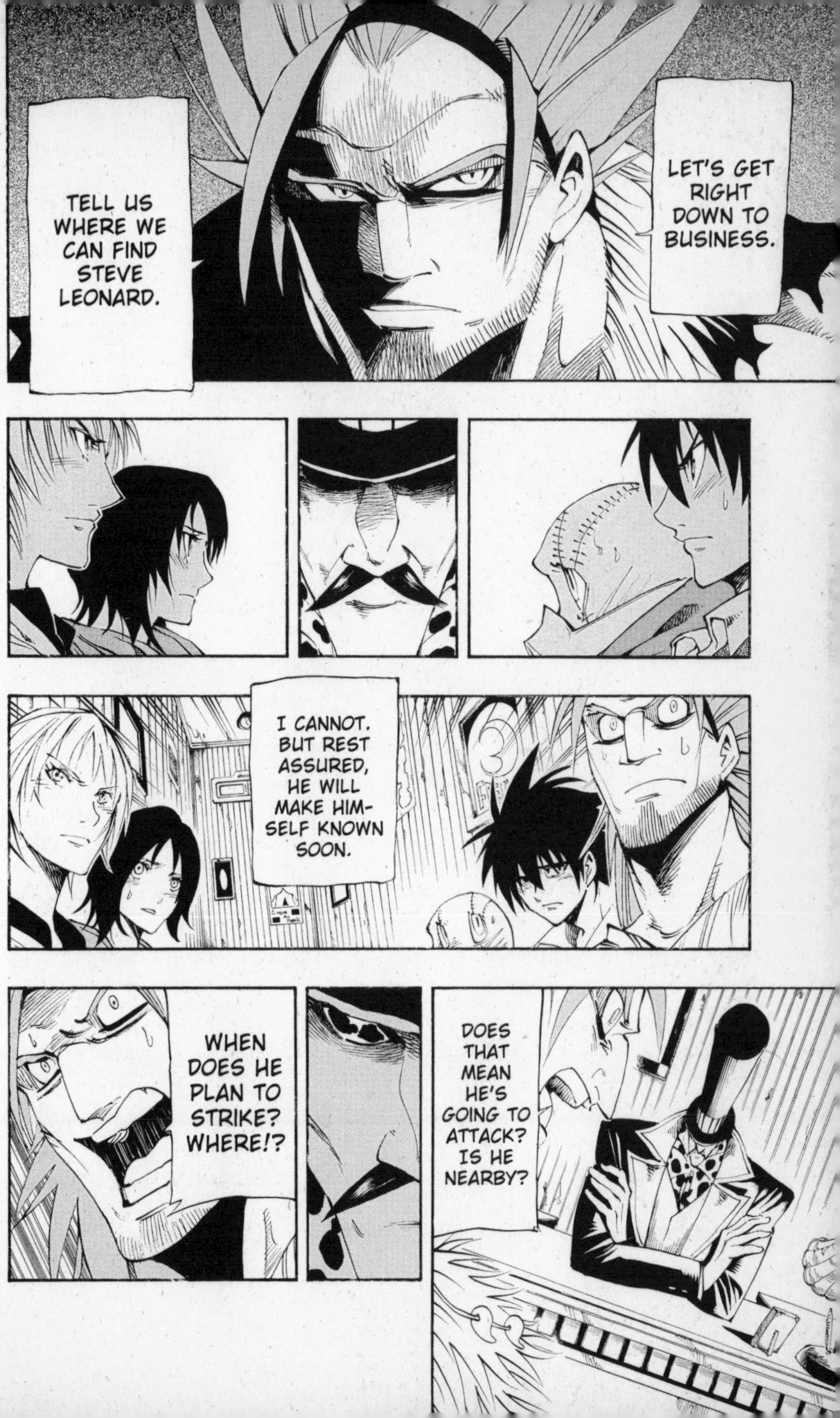
LET'S GET RIGHT DOWN TO BUSINESS.
TELL US WHERE WE CAN FIND STEVE LEONARD.
I CANNOT. BUT REST ASSURED, HE WILL MAKE HIM-SELF KNOWN SOON.
DOES THAT MEAN HE'S GOING TO ATTACK? IS HE NEARBY?
WHEN DOES HE PLAN TO STRIKE? WHERE!?

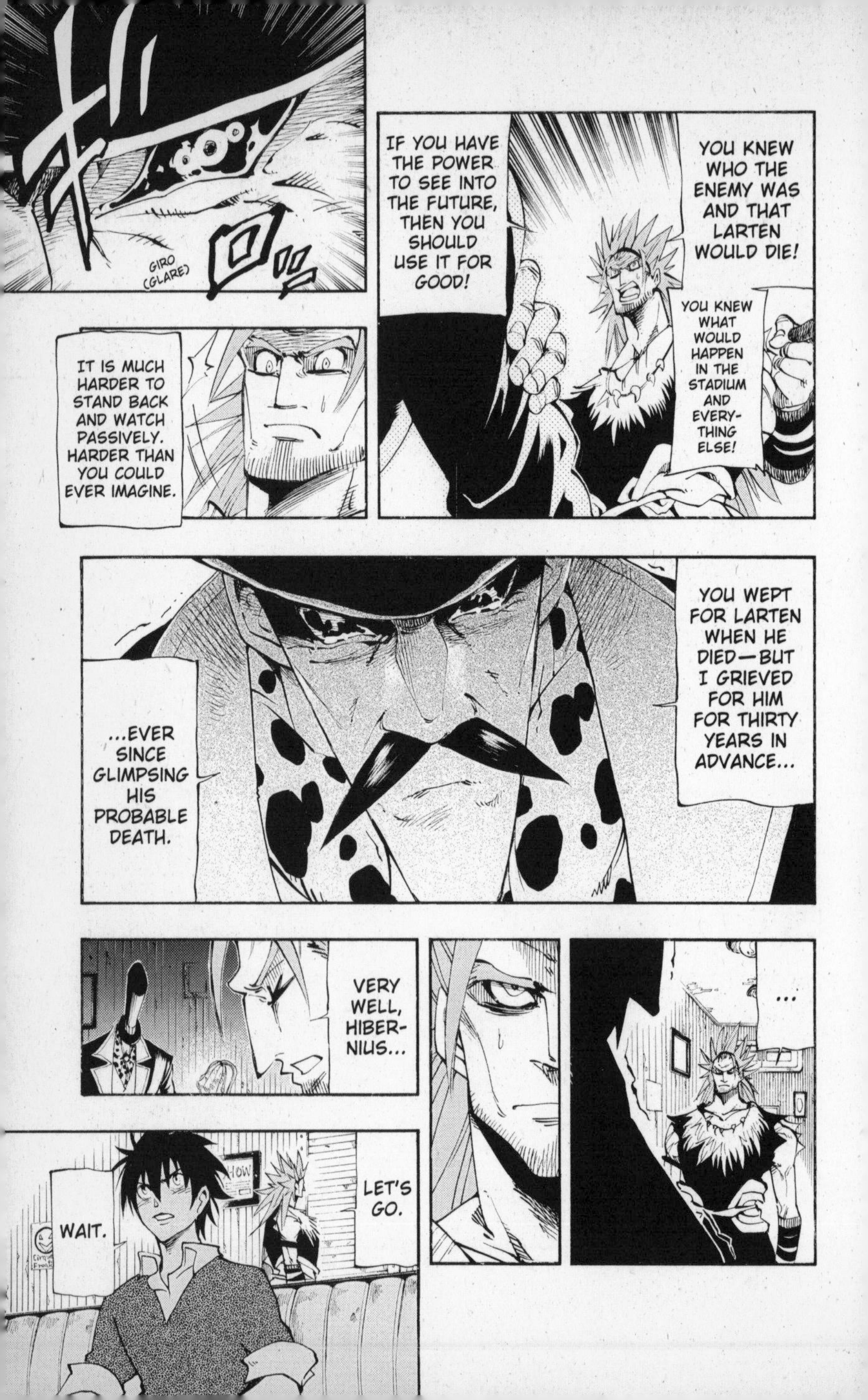
YOU KNEW WHO THE ENEMY WAS AND THAT LARTEN WOULD DIE!
YOU KNEW WHAT WOULD HAPPEN IN THE STADIUM AND EVERY-THING ELSE!
IF YOU HAVE THE POWER TO SEE INTO THE FUTURE, THEN YOU SHOULD USE IT FOR GOOD!
GIRO (GLARE)
IT IS MUCH HARDER TO STAND BACK AND WATCH PASSIVELY. HARDER THAN YOU COULD EVER IMAGINE.
YOU WEPT FOR LARTEN WHEN HE DIED—BUT I GRIEVED FOR HIM FOR THIRTY YEARS IN ADVANCE...
...EVER SINCE GLIMPSING HIS PROBABLE DEATH.
...
VERY WELL, HIBER-NIUS...
LET'S GO.
WAIT.

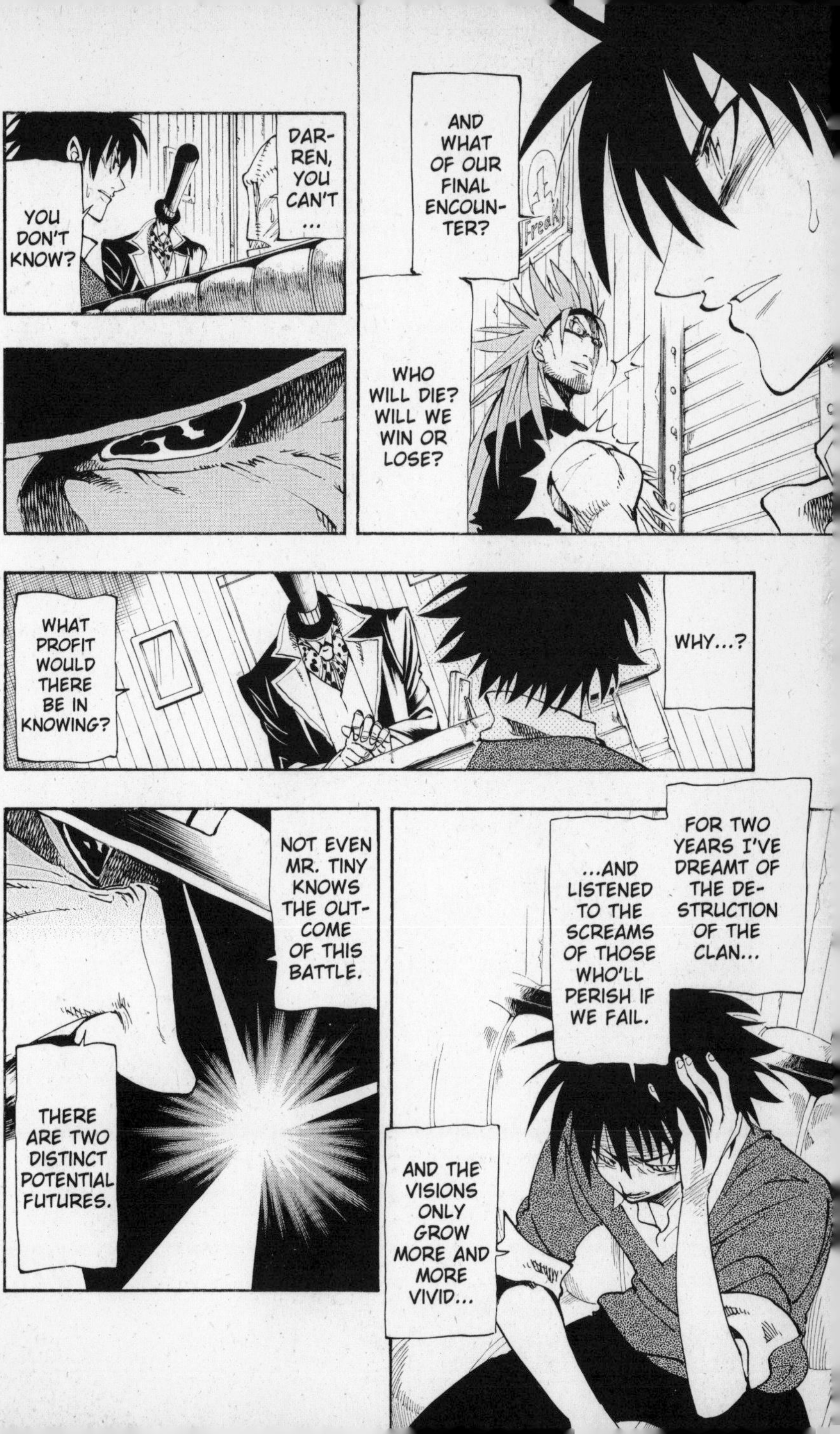
AND WHAT OF OUR FINAL ENCOUN-TER?
WHO WILL DIE? WILL WE WIN OR LOSE?
DAR-REN, YOU CAN'T ...
YOU DON'T KNOW?
WHY...?
WHAT PROFIT WOULD THERE BE IN KNOWING?
FOR TWO YEARS I'VE DREAMT OF THE DE-STRUCTION OF THE CLAN...
...AND LISTENED TO THE SCREAMS OF THOSE WHO'LL PERISH IF WE FAIL.
AND THE VISIONS ONLY GROW MORE AND MORE VIVID...
NOT EVEN MR. TINY KNOWS THE OUT-COME OF THIS BATTLE.
THERE ARE TWO DISTINCT POTENTIAL FUTURES.

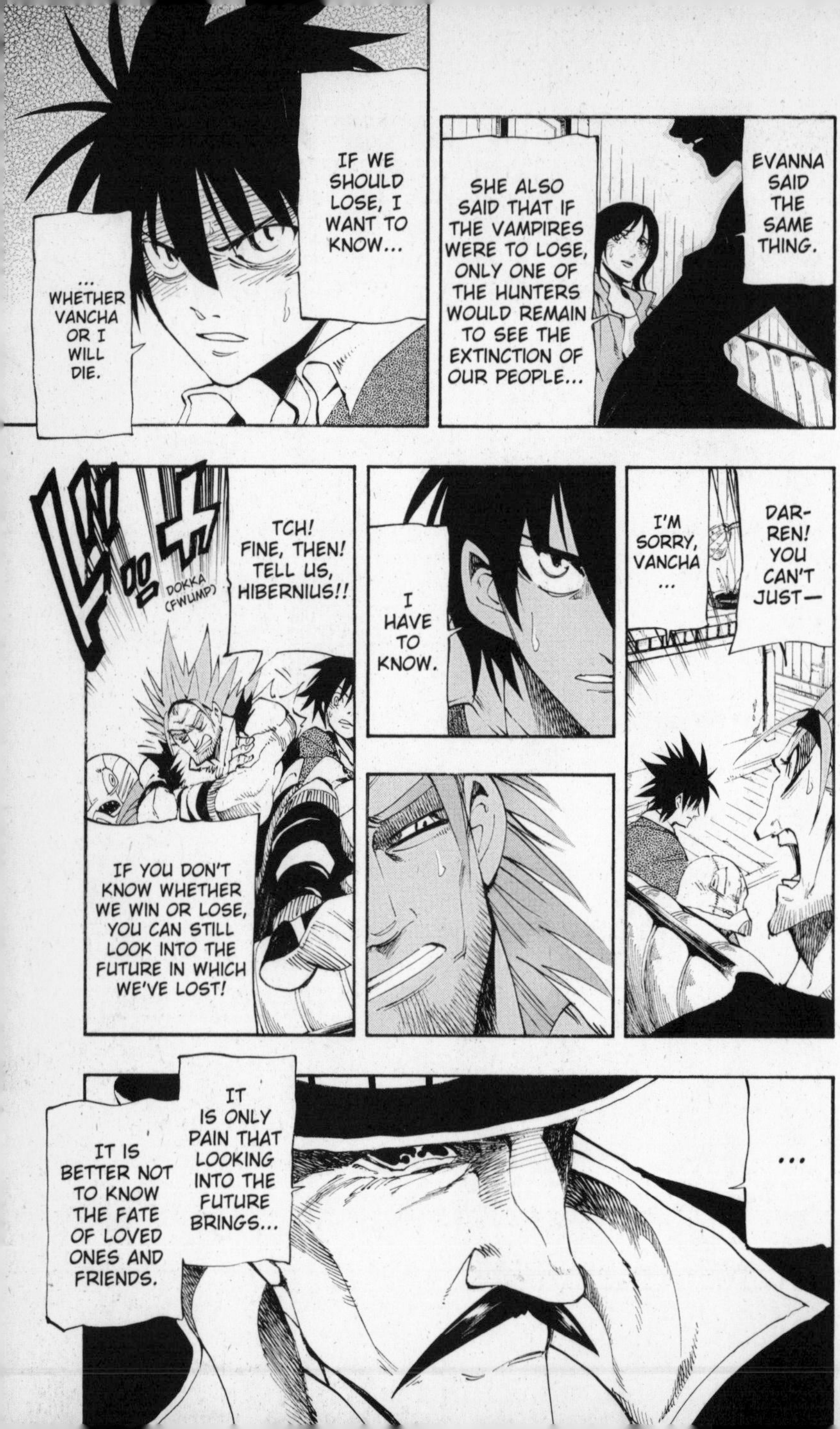
EVANNA SAID THE SAME THING.
SHE ALSO SAID THAT IF THE VAMPIRES WERE TO LOSE, ONLY ONE OF THE HUNTERS WOULD REMAIN TO SEE THE EXTINCTION OF OUR PEOPLE...
IF WE SHOULD LOSE, I WANT TO KNOW...
...WHETHER VANCHA OR I WILL DIE.
DAR-REN! YOU CAN'T JUST—
I'M SORRY, VANCHA ...
I HAVE TO KNOW.
DOKKA (FWUMP)
TCH! FINE, THEN! TELL US, HIBERNIUS!!
IF YOU DON'T KNOW WHETHER WE WIN OR LOSE, YOU CAN STILL LOOK INTO THE FUTURE IN WHICH WE'VE LOST!
...
IT IS ONLY PAIN THAT LOOKING INTO THE FUTURE BRINGS...
IT IS BETTER NOT TO KNOW THE FATE OF LOVED ONES AND FRIENDS.

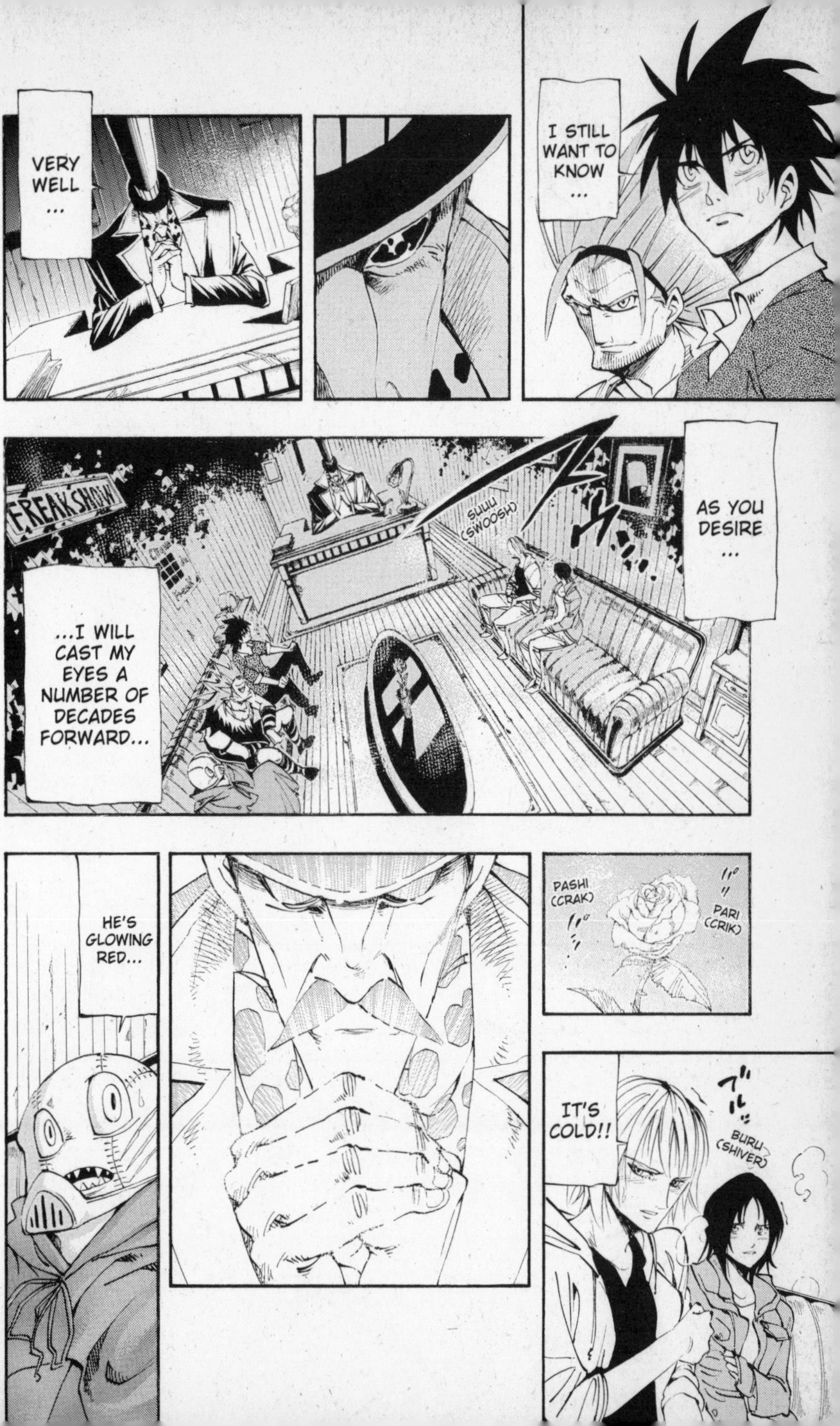
I STILL WANT TO KNOW ...
VERY WELL ...
AS YOU DESIRE ...
SUUU (SWOOSH)
FREAKSHOW
...I WILL CAST MY EYES A NUMBER OF DECADES FORWARD...
PARI (CRIK)
PASHI (CRAK)
IT'S COLD!!
BURU (SHIVER)
HE'S GLOWING RED...

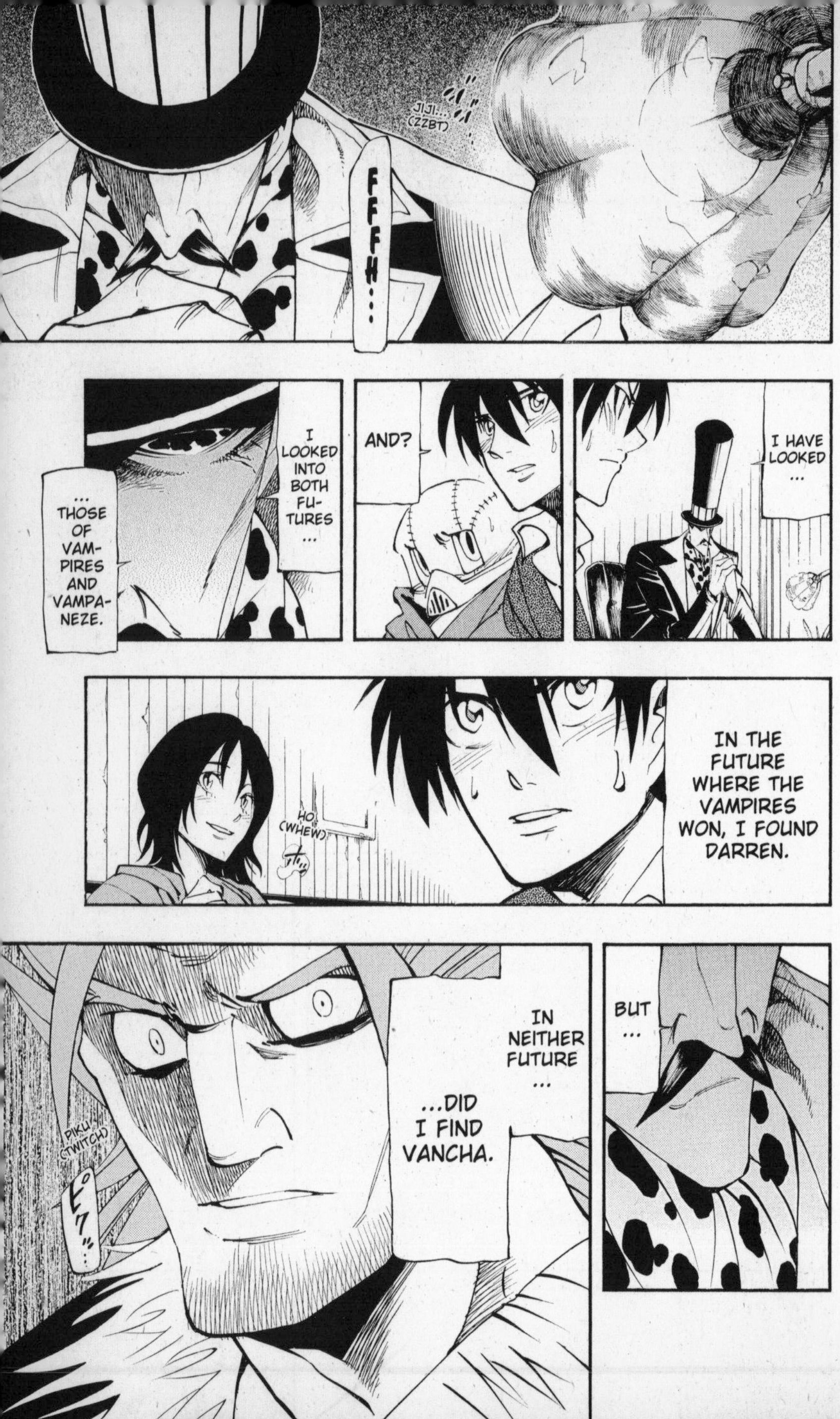
JIJI... (ZZBT)
FFFH...
I HAVE LOOKED ...
AND?
I LOOKED INTO BOTH FUTURES ...
... THOSE OF VAMPIRES AND VAMPANEZE.
IN THE FUTURE WHERE THE VAMPIRES WON, I FOUND DARREN.
HO (WHEW)
BUT ...
IN NEITHER FUTURE ...
...DID I FIND VANCHA.
PIKU (TWITCH)

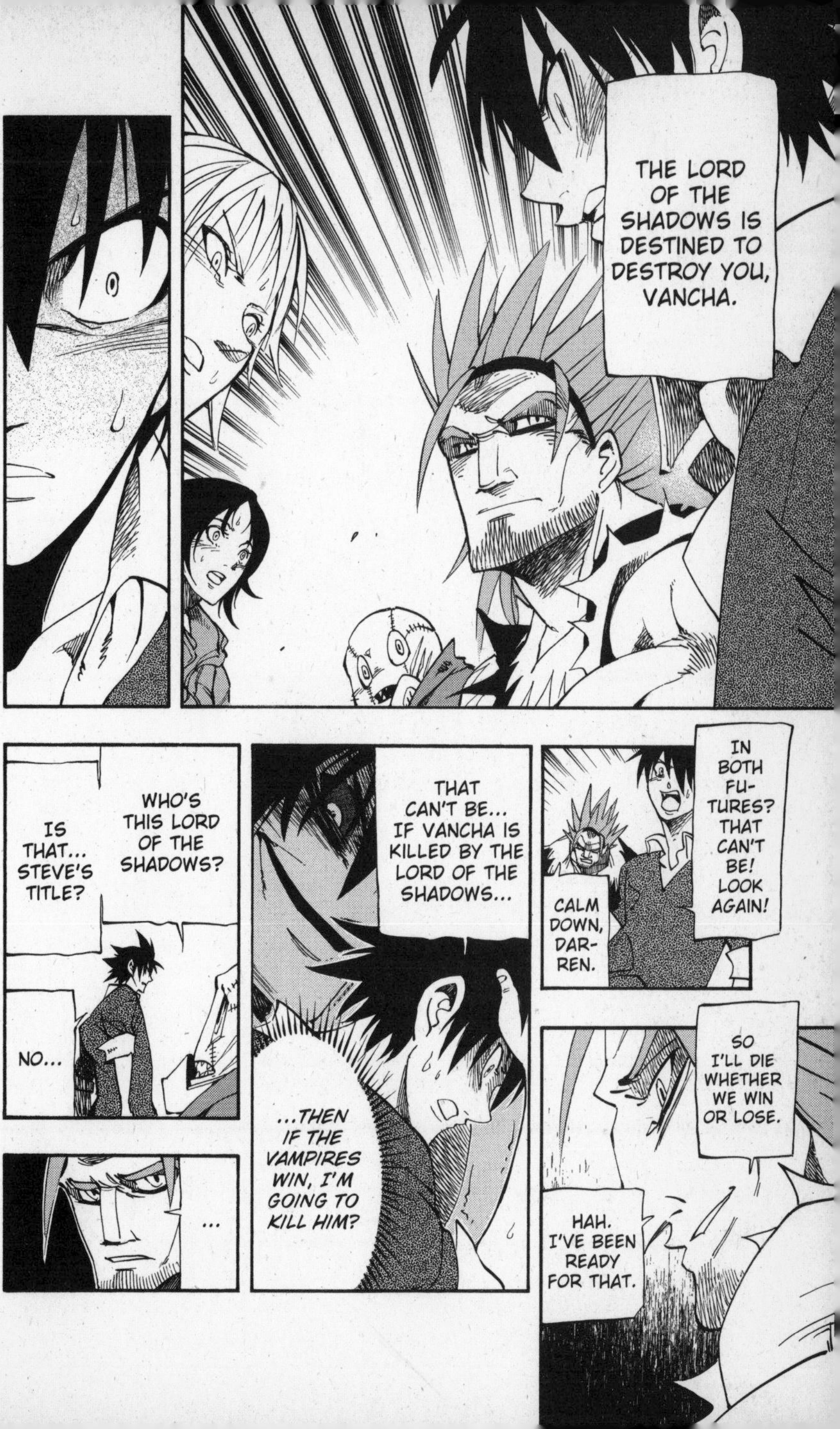
THE LORD OF THE SHADOWS IS DESTINED TO DESTROY YOU, VANCHA.
IN BOTH FU-TURES? THAT CAN'T BE! LOOK AGAIN!
CALM DOWN, DAR-REN.
SO I'LL DIE WHETHER WE WIN OR LOSE.
HAH. I'VE BEEN READY FOR THAT.
THAT CAN'T BE... IF VANCHA IS KILLED BY THE LORD OF THE SHADOWS...
...THEN IF THE VAMPIRES WIN, I'M GOING TO KILL HIM?
WHO'S THIS LORD OF THE SHADOWS?
IS THAT... STEVE'S TITLE?
NO...
...

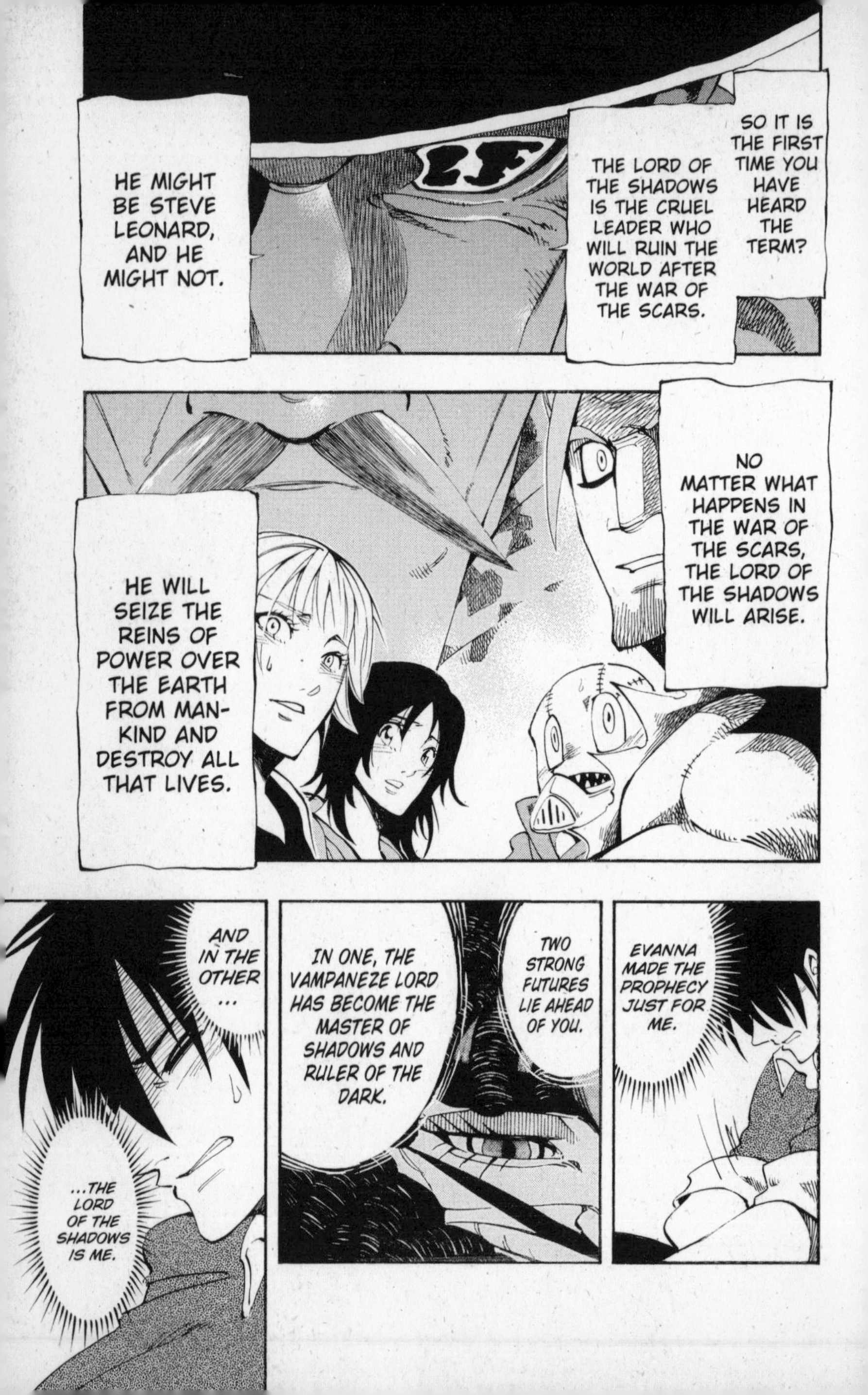
SO IT IS THE FIRST TIME YOU HAVE HEARD THE TERM?
THE LORD OF THE SHADOWS IS THE CRUEL LEADER WHO WILL RUIN THE WORLD AFTER THE WAR OF THE SCARS.
HE MIGHT BE STEVE LEONARD, AND HE MIGHT NOT.
NO MATTER WHAT HAPPENS IN THE WAR OF THE SCARS, THE LORD OF THE SHADOWS WILL ARISE.
HE WILL SEIZE THE REINS OF POWER OVER THE EARTH FROM MAN-KIND AND DESTROY ALL THAT LIVES.
EVANNA MADE THE PROPHECY JUST FOR ME.
TWO STRONG FUTURES LIE AHEAD OF YOU.
IN ONE, THE VAMPANEZE LORD HAS BECOME THE MASTER OF SHADOWS AND RULER OF THE DARK.
AND IN THE OTHER ...
...THE LORD OF THE SHADOWS IS ME.

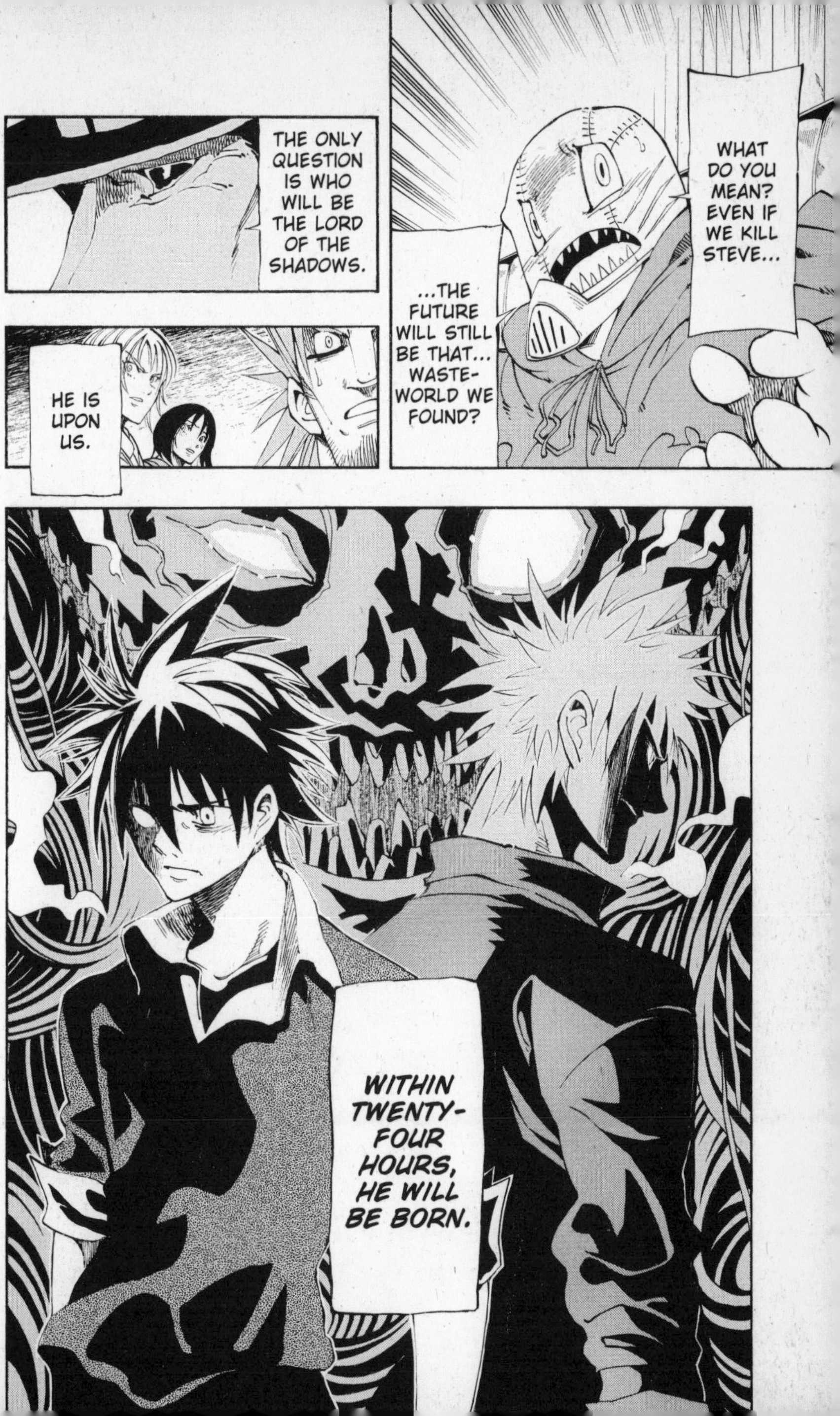
WHAT DO YOU MEAN? EVEN IF WE KILL STEVE...
...THE FUTURE WILL STILL BE THAT... WASTE-WORLD WE FOUND?
THE ONLY QUESTION IS WHO WILL BE THE LORD OF THE SHADOWS.
HE IS UPON US.
WITHIN TWENTY-FOUR HOURS, HE WILL BE BORN.

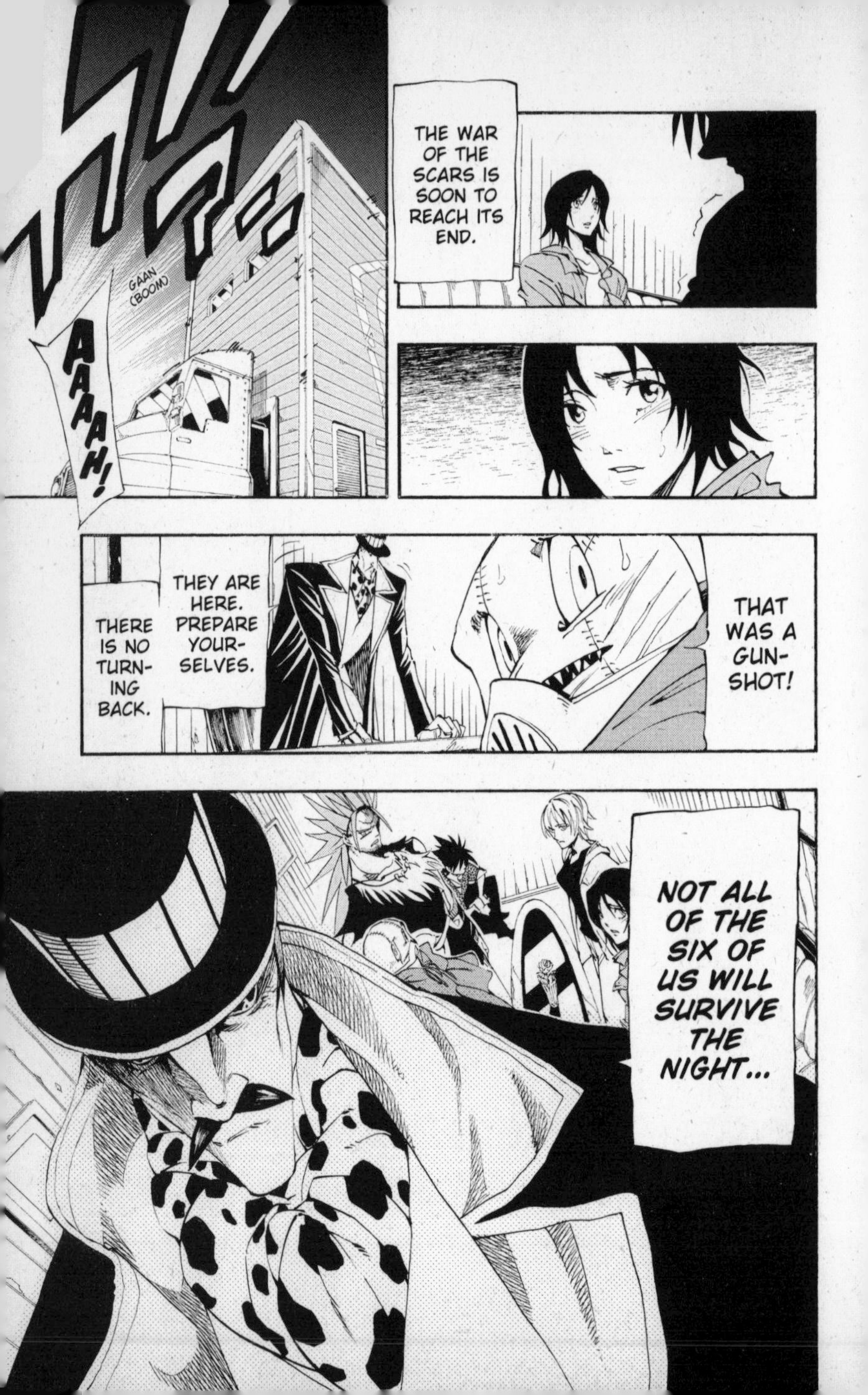
THE WAR OF THE SCARS IS SOON TO REACH ITS END.
GAAN (BOOM)
AAAAH!
THAT WAS A GUN-SHOT!
THEY ARE HERE. PREPARE YOUR-SELVES.
THERE IS NO TURN-ING BACK.
NOT ALL OF THE SIX OF US WILL SURVIVE THE NIGHT...

GA
(THWAK)

EVRA!!

NO! DON'T YOU DARE TOUCH SHANCUS!!

BACK OFF! THAT'S MY SNAKE!

STOP IT!! LET ME GO!!!

I'D SHTAY NISHE AHN QUIEH UHF I WHUUH YOU...

HEH-HEH-HEH! CAUGHT ME A SNAKE-BOY!

I WONDER WHAT KINDA SOUNDS HE'LL MAKE IF I START PEELING OFF THOSE SCALES?

SHANCUS!!!

CHAPTER 102:
FATHER
AND SON

DAR-
REN
!!

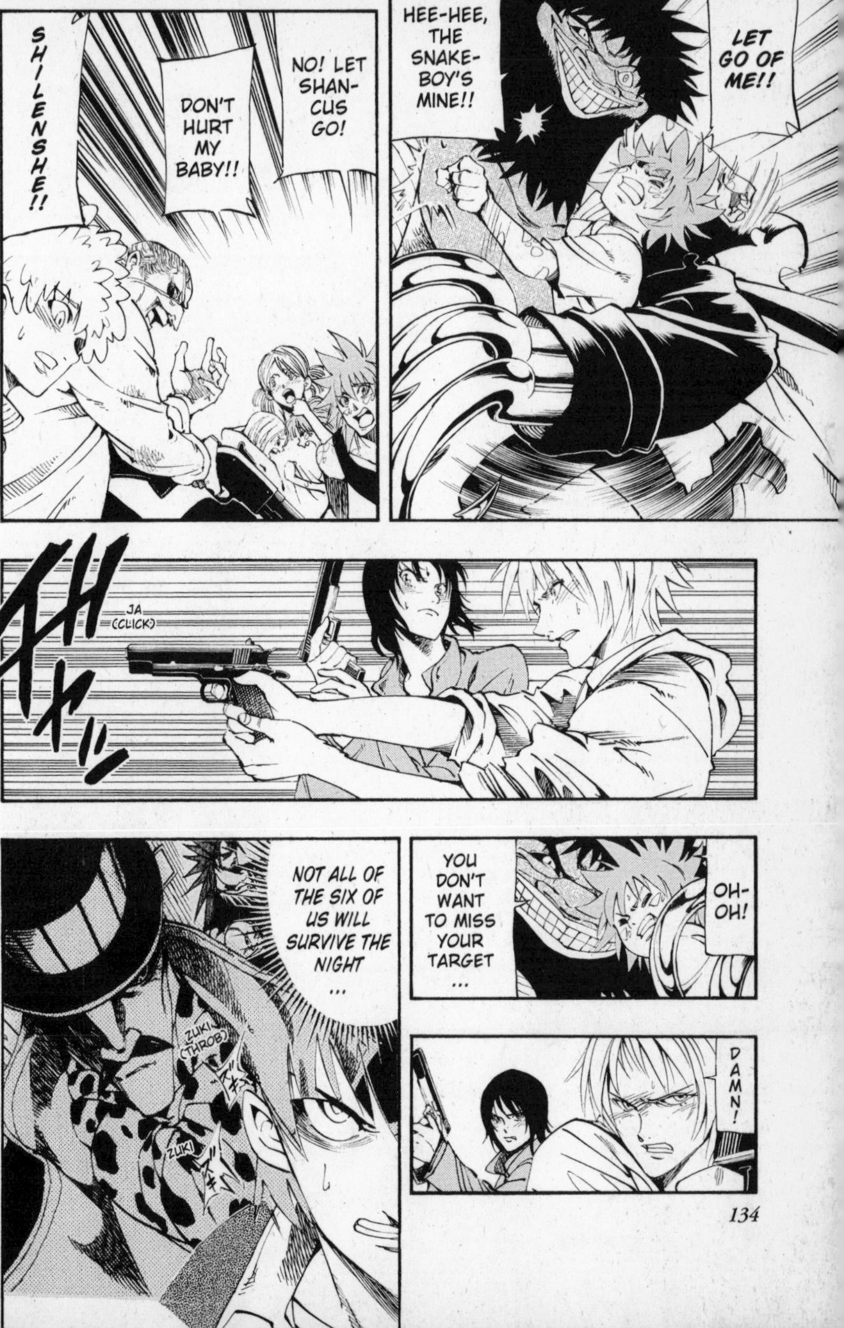
LET GO OF ME!!
HEE-HEE, THE SNAKE-BOY'S MINE!!
NO! LET SHAN-CUS GO!
DON'T HURT MY BABY!!
SHILENSHE!!
JA (CLICK)
OH-OH!
YOU DON'T WANT TO MISS YOUR TARGET ...
DAMN!
NOT ALL OF THE SIX OF US WILL SURVIVE THE NIGHT ...
ZUKI (THROB)
ZUKI

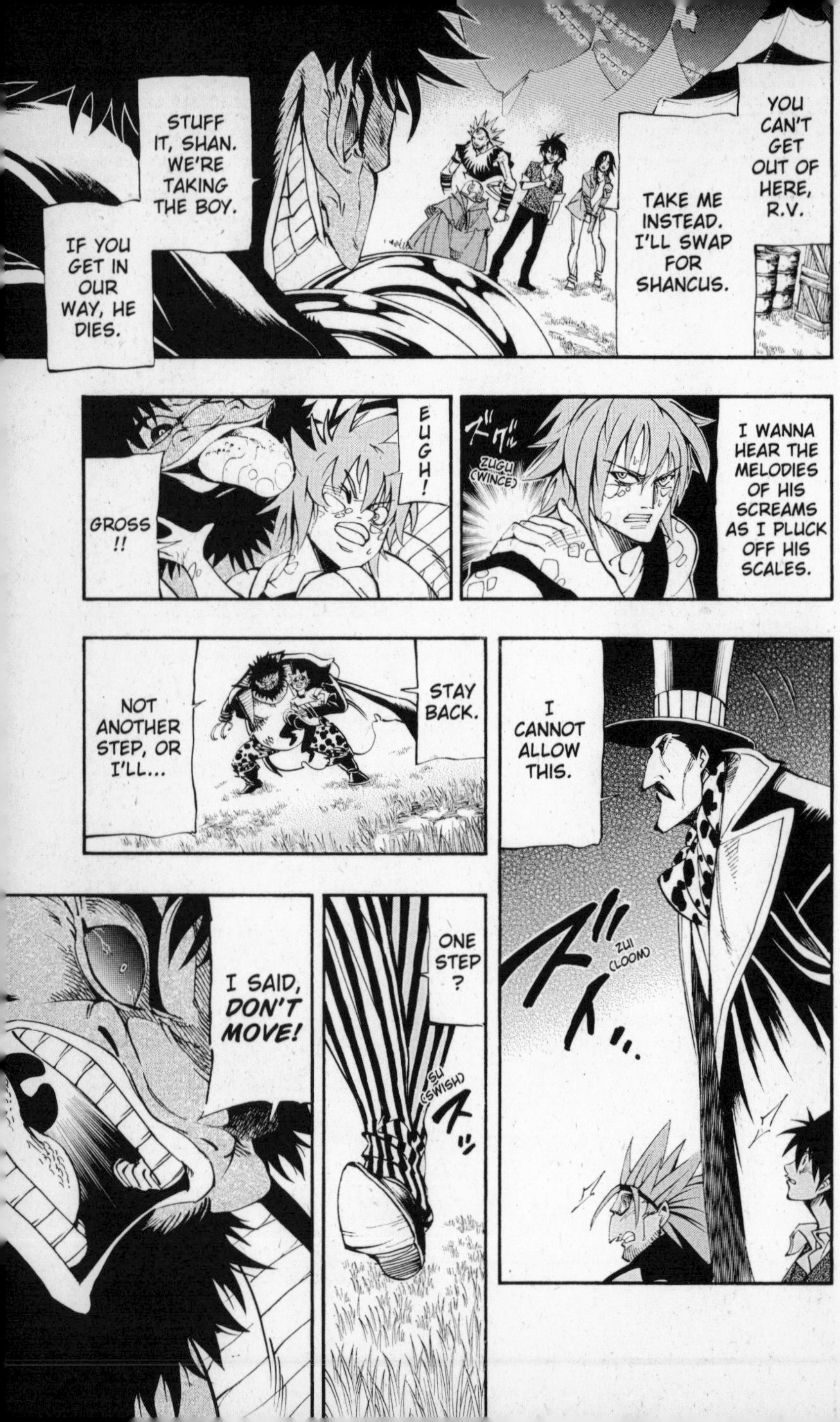
YOU CAN'T GET OUT OF HERE, R.V.
TAKE ME INSTEAD. I'LL SWAP FOR SHANCUS.
STUFF IT, SHAN. WE'RE TAKING THE BOY.
IF YOU GET IN OUR WAY, HE DIES.
I WANNA HEAR THE MELODIES OF HIS SCREAMS AS I PLUCK OFF HIS SCALES.
ZUGU (WINCE)
EUGH!
GROSS!!
I CANNOT ALLOW THIS.
ZUI (LOOM)
STAY BACK.
NOT ANOTHER STEP, OR I'LL...
ONE STEP?
SU (SWISH)
I SAID, *DON'T MOVE!*

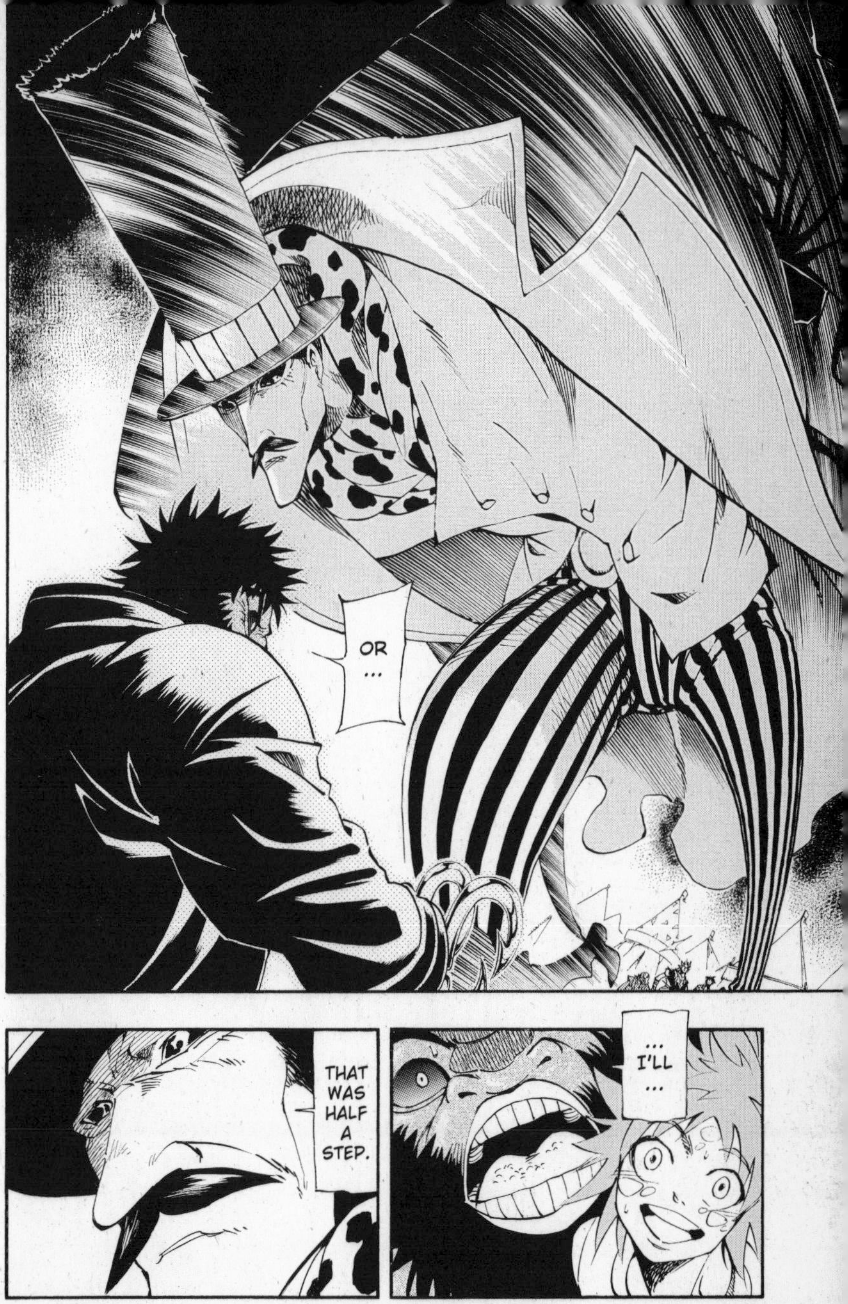
OR ...
... I'LL ...
THAT WAS HALF A STEP.

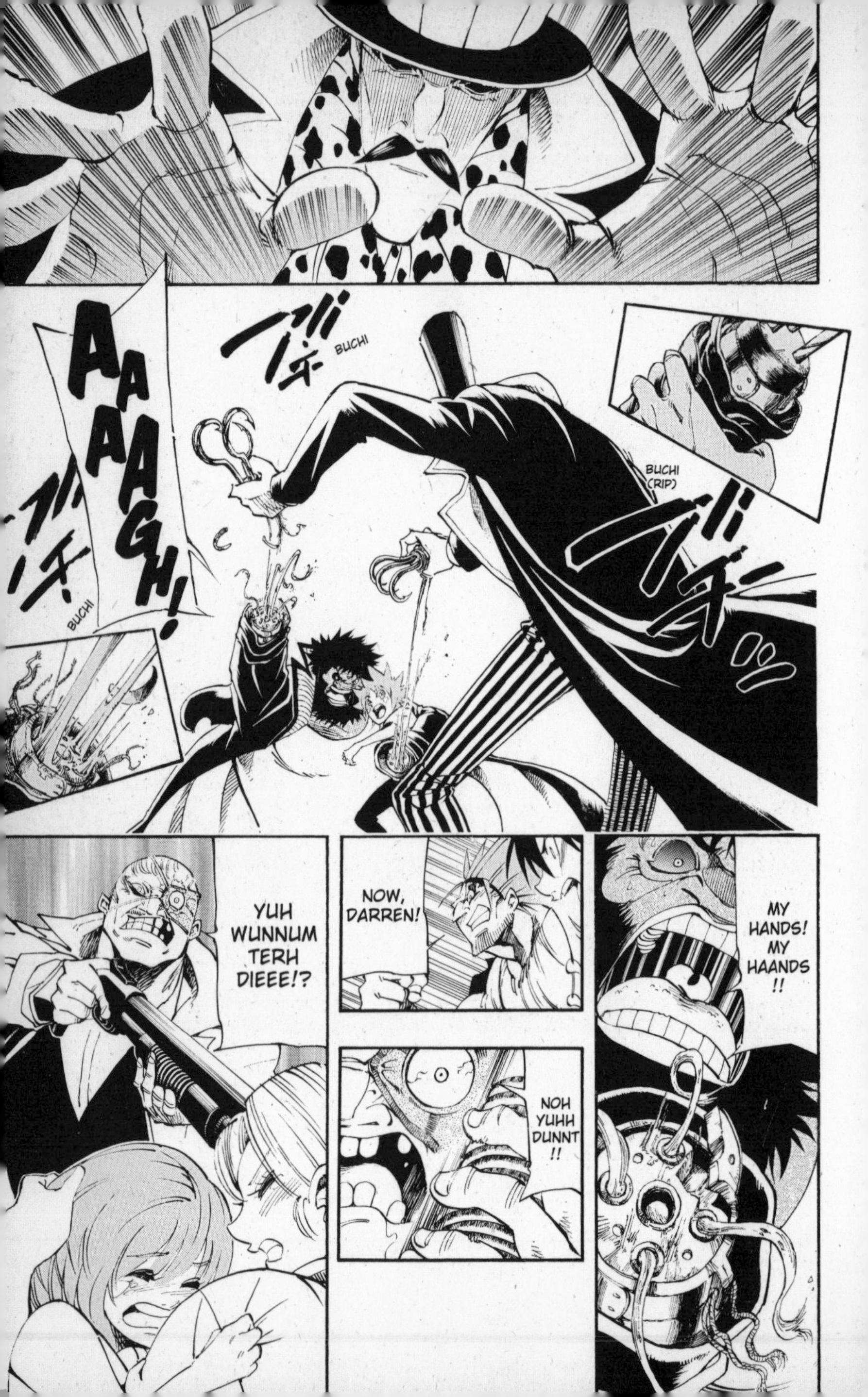
BUCHI (RIP)
BUCHI
AAAAGH!
BUCHI
MY HANDS! MY HAANDS !!
NOW, DARREN!
NOH YUHH DUNNT !!
YUH WUNNUM TERH DIEEE!?

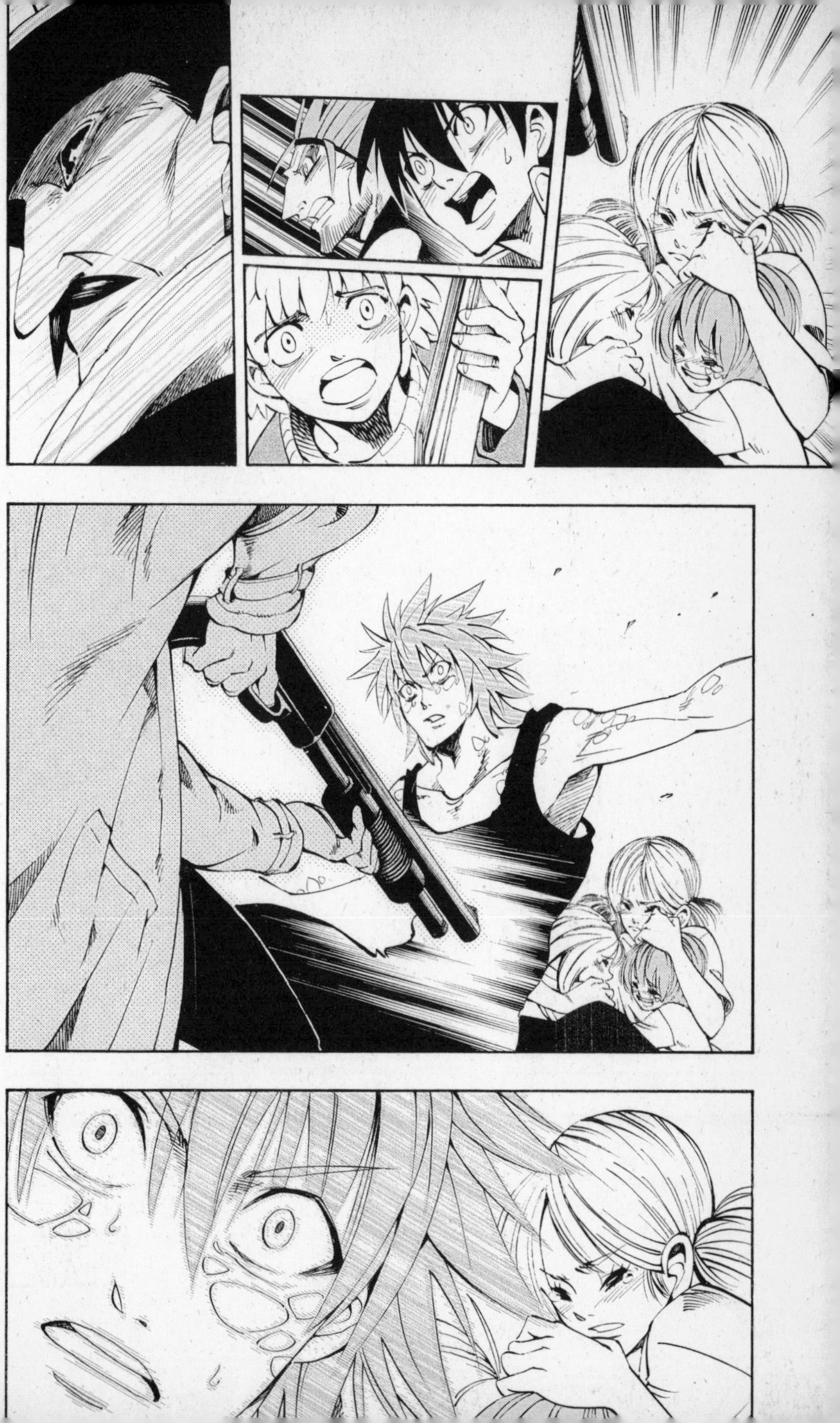

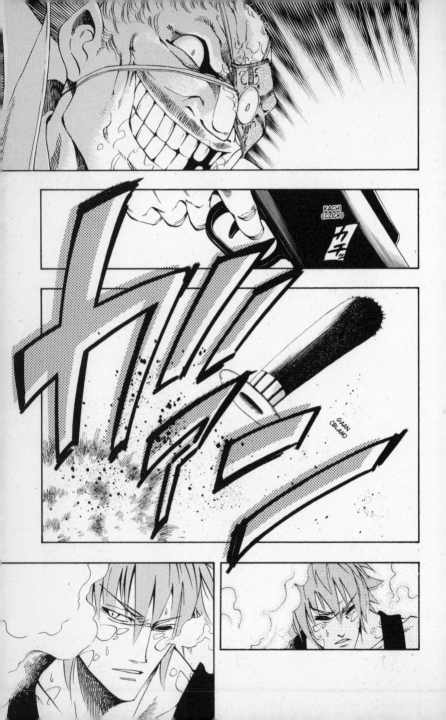

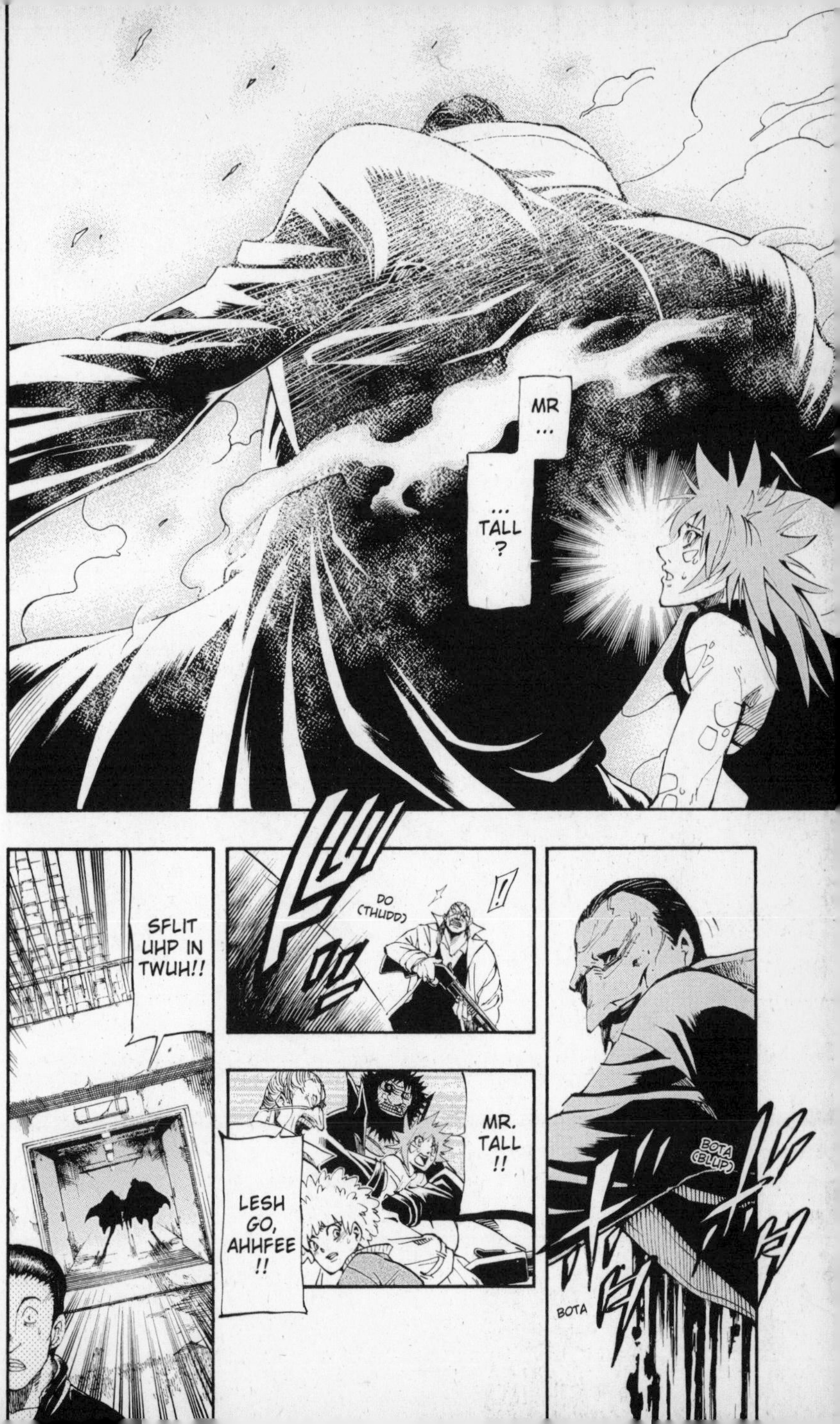
MR ...
... TALL ?
BOTA (BLUP)
BOTA
DO (THUDD)
!
MR. TALL !!
LESH GO, AHHFEE !!
SFLIT UHP IN TWUH!!

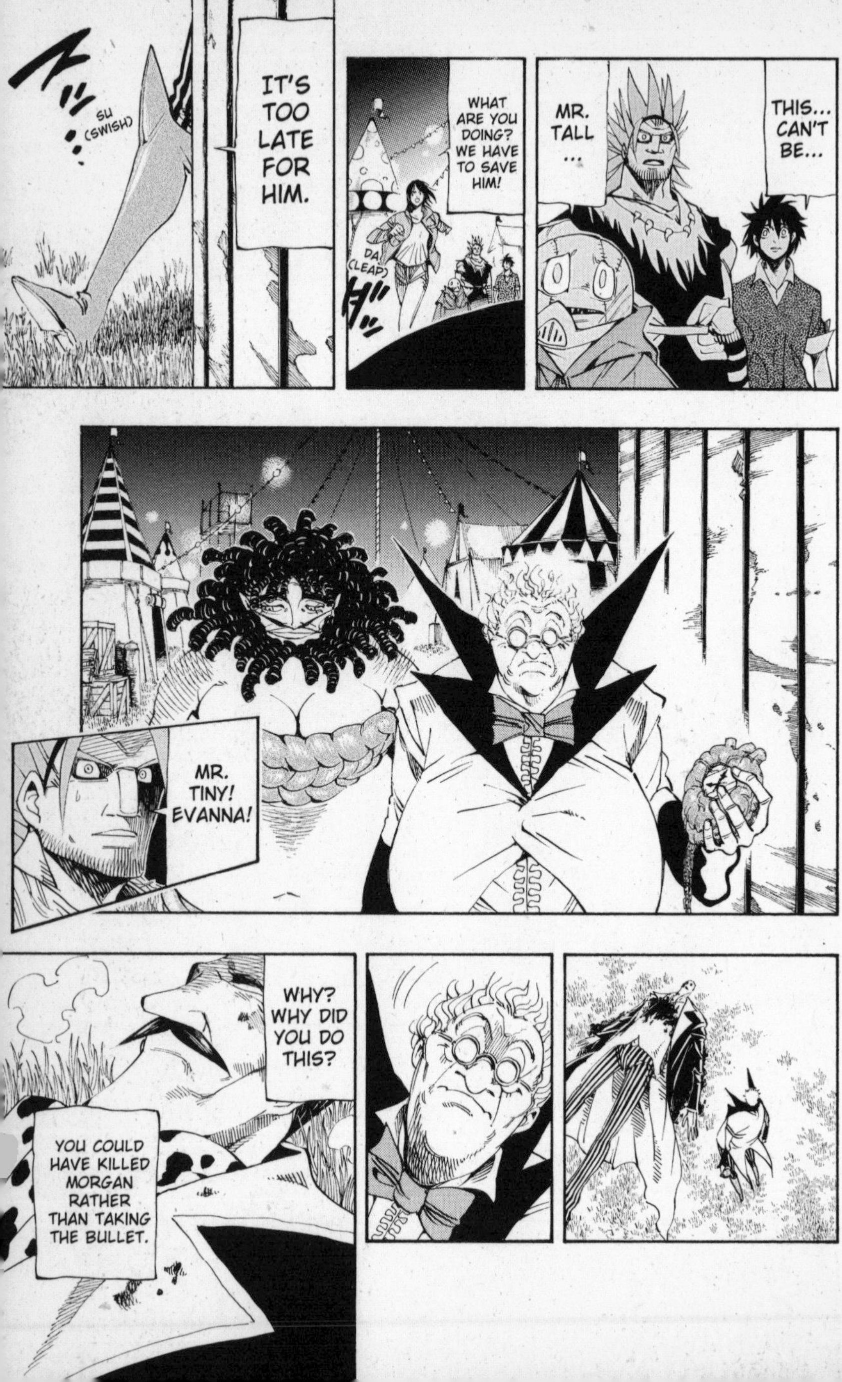
THIS... CAN'T BE...
MR. TALL ...
WHAT ARE YOU DOING? WE HAVE TO SAVE HIM!
DA (LEAP)
IT'S TOO LATE FOR HIM.
SU (SWISH)
MR. TINY! EVANNA!
WHY? WHY DID YOU DO THIS?
YOU COULD HAVE KILLED MORGAN RATHER THAN TAKING THE BULLET.

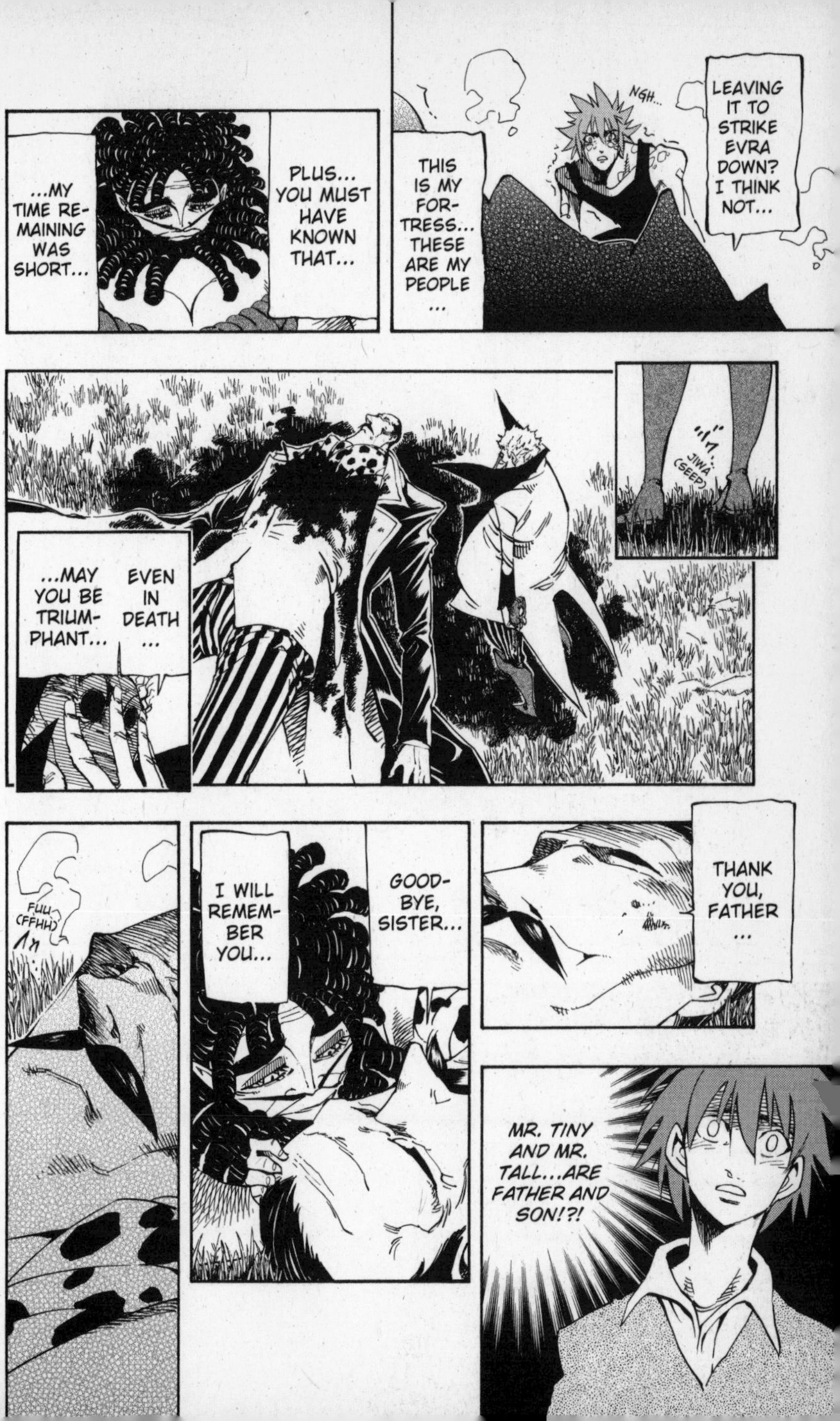
NGH...
LEAVING IT TO STRIKE EVRA DOWN? I THINK NOT...
THIS IS MY FORTRESS... THESE ARE MY PEOPLE ...
PLUS... YOU MUST HAVE KNOWN THAT...
...MY TIME REMAINING WAS SHORT...
JIWA (SEEP)
EVEN IN DEATH ...
...MAY YOU BE TRIUMPHANT...
THANK YOU, FATHER ...
MR. TINY AND MR. TALL...ARE FATHER AND SON!?!
GOOD-BYE, SISTER...
I WILL REMEMBER YOU...
FUU (CFFHH)

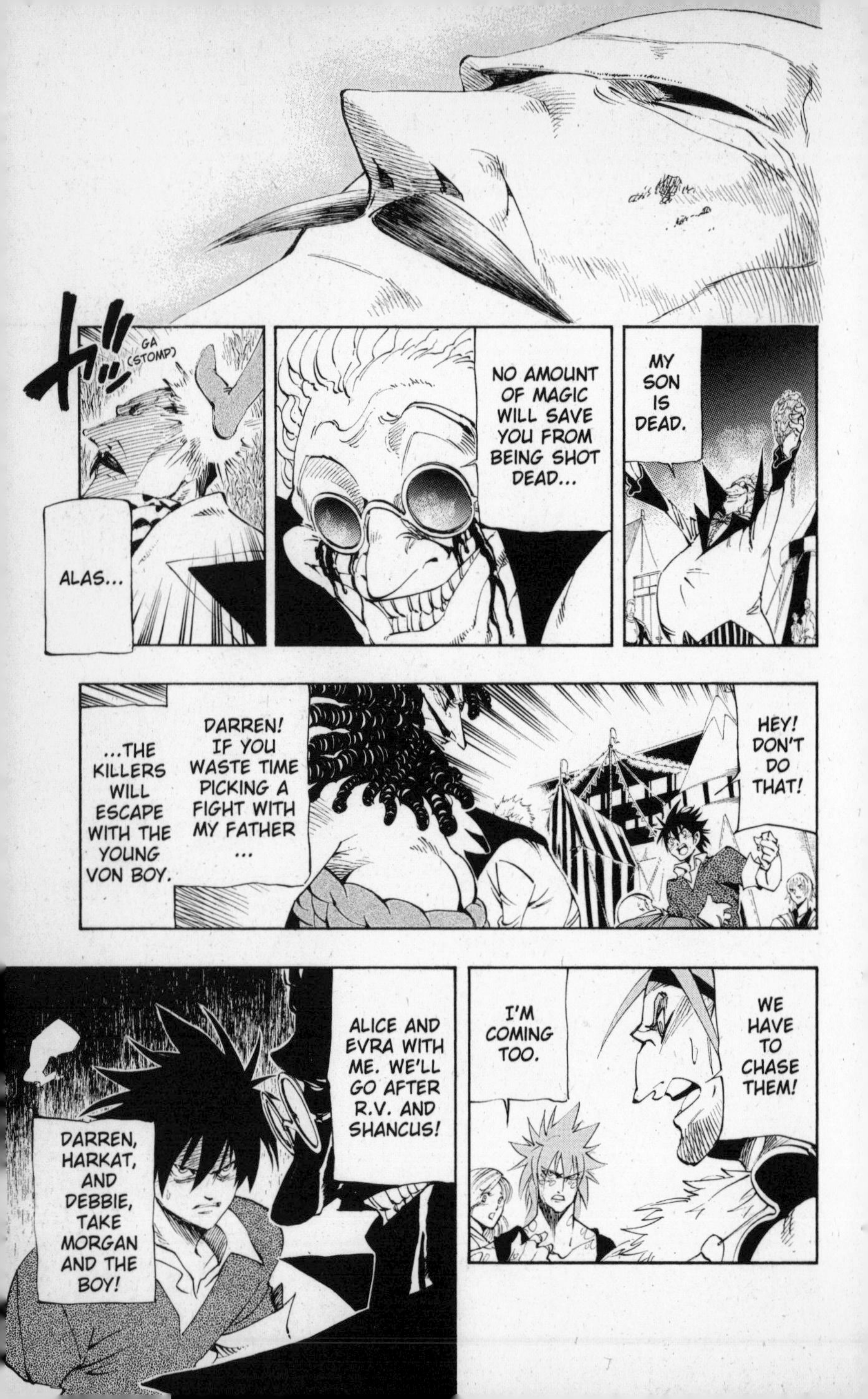
MY SON IS DEAD.
NO AMOUNT OF MAGIC WILL SAVE YOU FROM BEING SHOT DEAD...
GA (STOMP)
ALAS...
HEY! DON'T DO THAT!
DARREN! IF YOU WASTE TIME PICKING A FIGHT WITH MY FATHER ...
...THE KILLERS WILL ESCAPE WITH THE YOUNG VON BOY.
WE HAVE TO CHASE THEM!
I'M COMING TOO.
ALICE AND EVRA WITH ME. WE'LL GO AFTER R.V. AND SHANCUS!
DARREN, HARKAT, AND DEBBIE, TAKE MORGAN AND THE BOY!

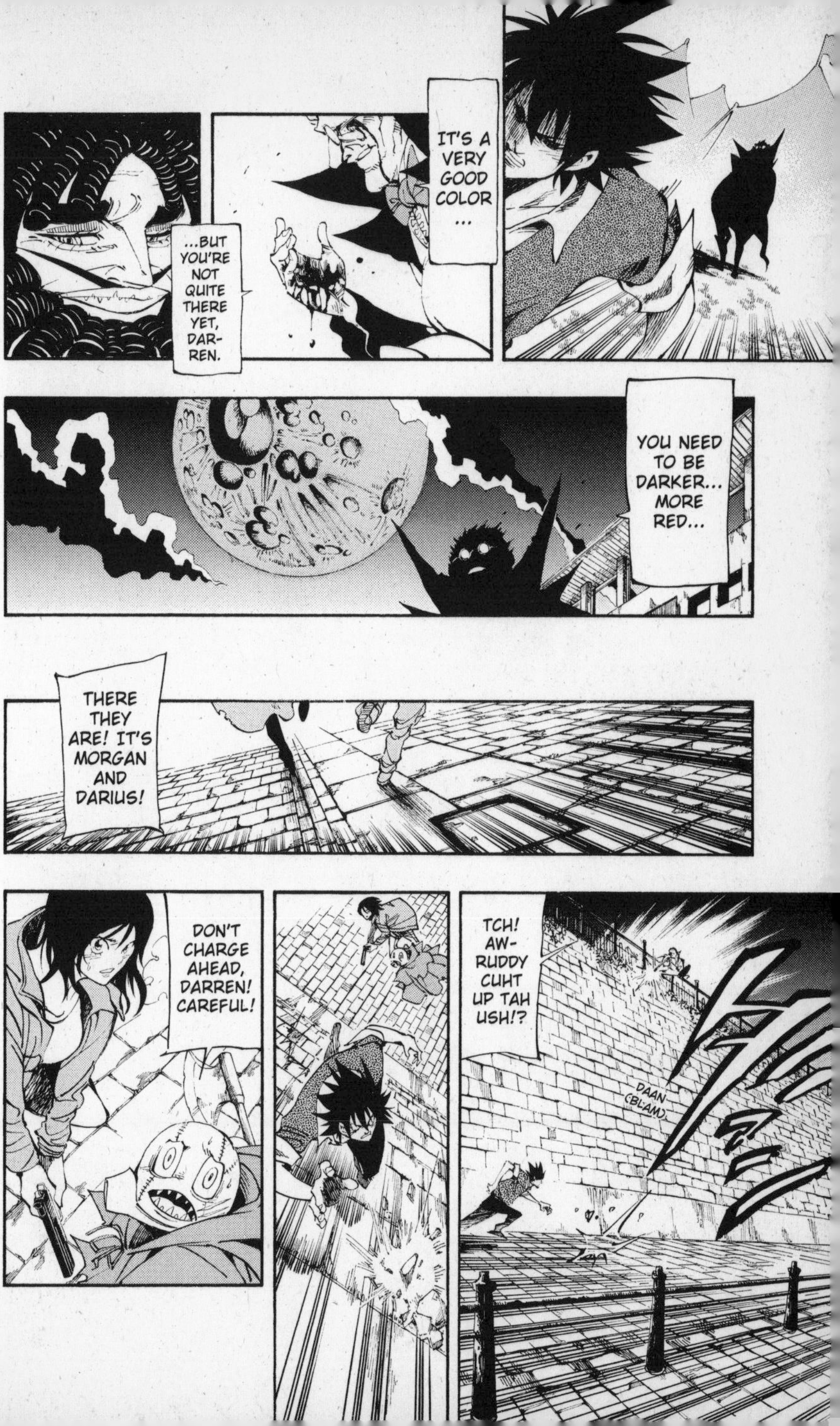
IT'S A VERY GOOD COLOR ...
...BUT YOU'RE NOT QUITE THERE YET, DARREN.
YOU NEED TO BE DARKER... MORE RED...
THERE THEY ARE! IT'S MORGAN AND DARIUS!
TCH! AW-RUDDY CUHT UP TAH USH!?
DAAN (BLAM)
DON'T CHARGE AHEAD, DARREN! CAREFUL!

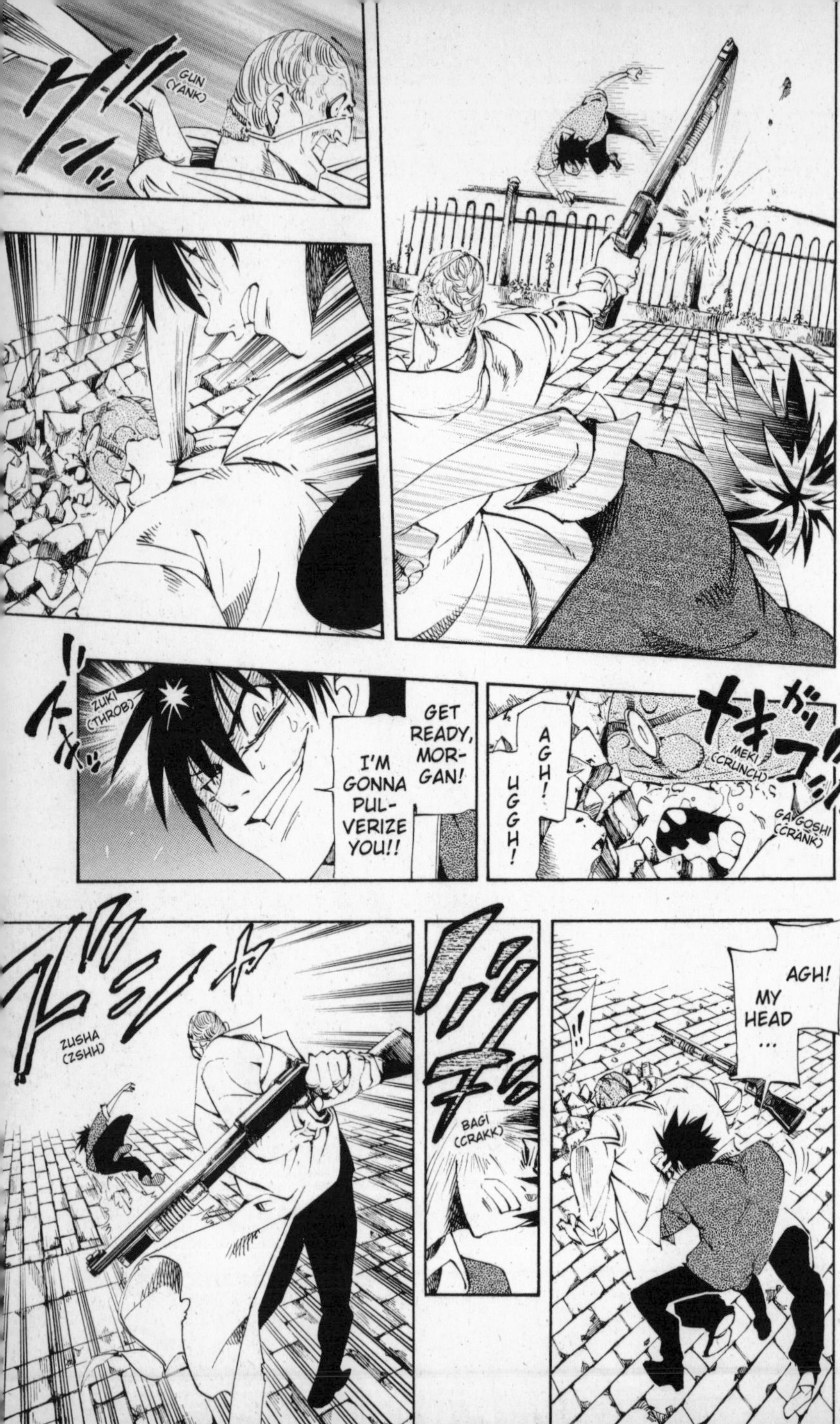
GUN (YANK)
AGH! UGGH!
MEKI (CRUNCH)
GAGOSHI (CRANK)
GET READY, MORGAN!
I'M GONNA PULVERIZE YOU!!
ZUKI (THROB)
!!
AGH! MY HEAD ...
BAGI (CRAKK)
ZUSHA (ZSHH)

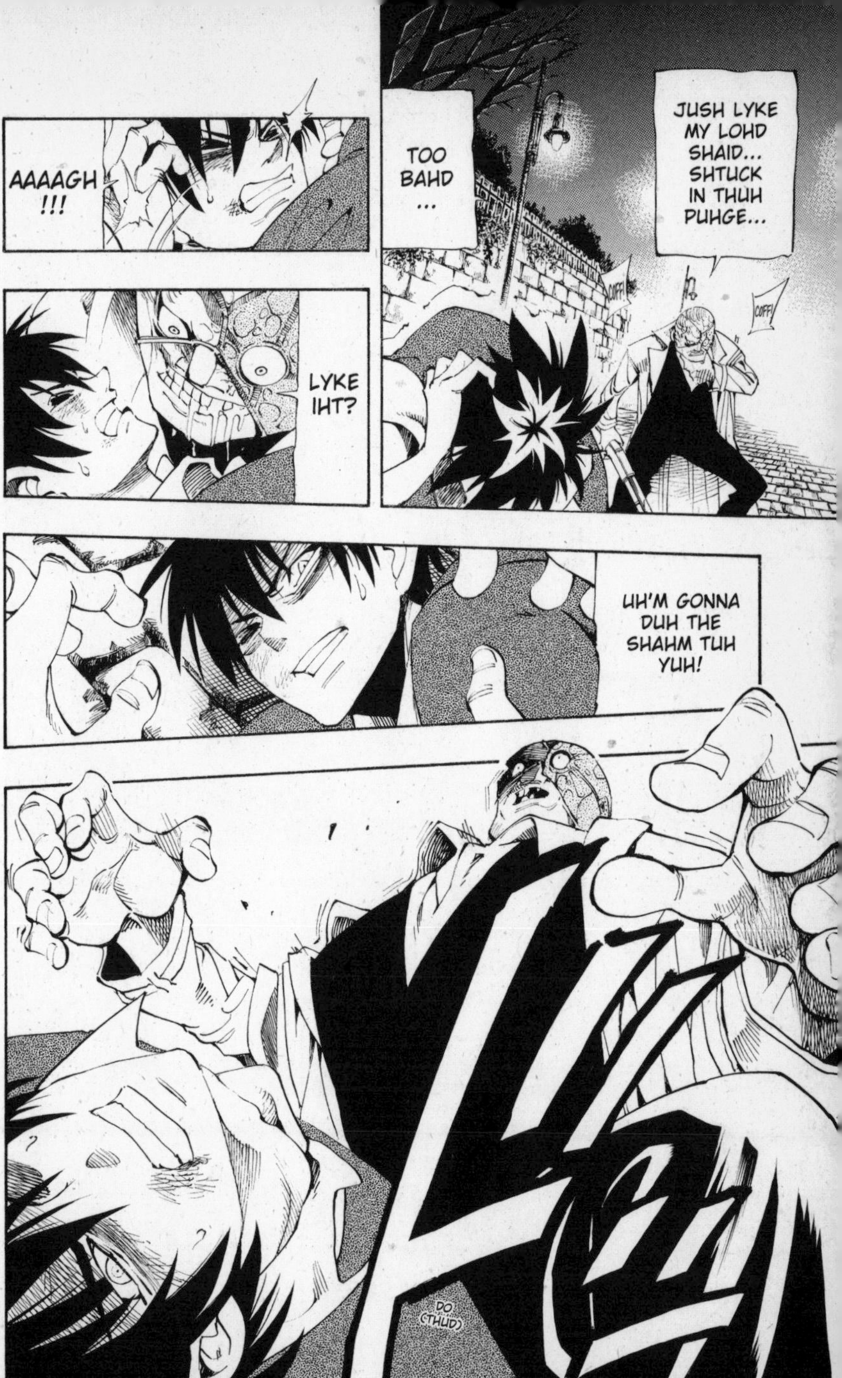
JUSH LYKE MY LOHD SHAID... SHTUCK IN THUH PUHGE...
TOO BAHD ...
COFF!
COFF!
AAAAGH !!!
LYKE IHT?
UH'M GONNA DUH THE SHAHM TUH YUH!
DO (THUD)

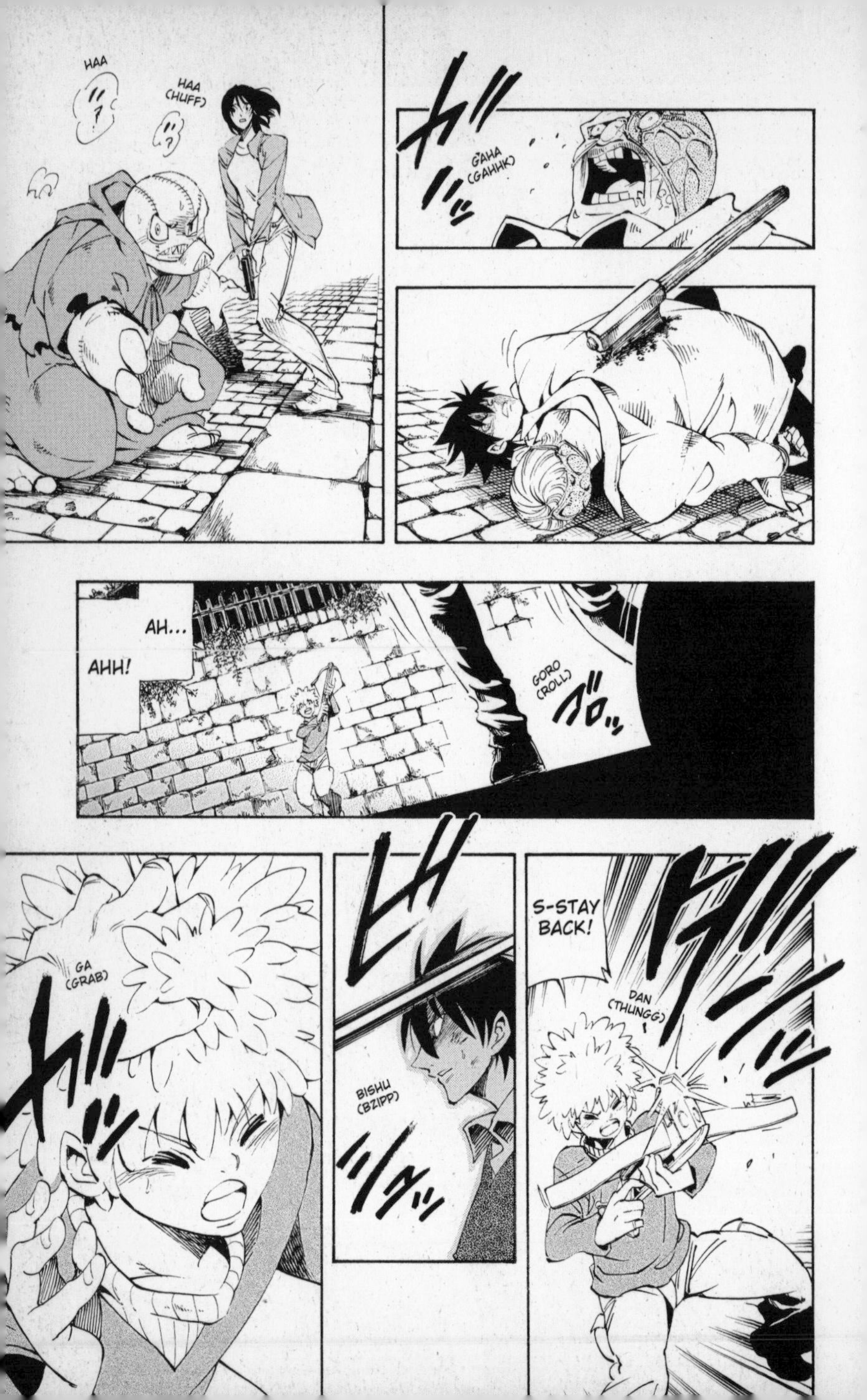
GAHA (GAHHK)
HAA
HAA (HUFF)
GORO (ROLL)
AH...
AHH!
S-STAY BACK!
DAN (THUNGG)
BISHU (BZIPP)
GA (GRAB)

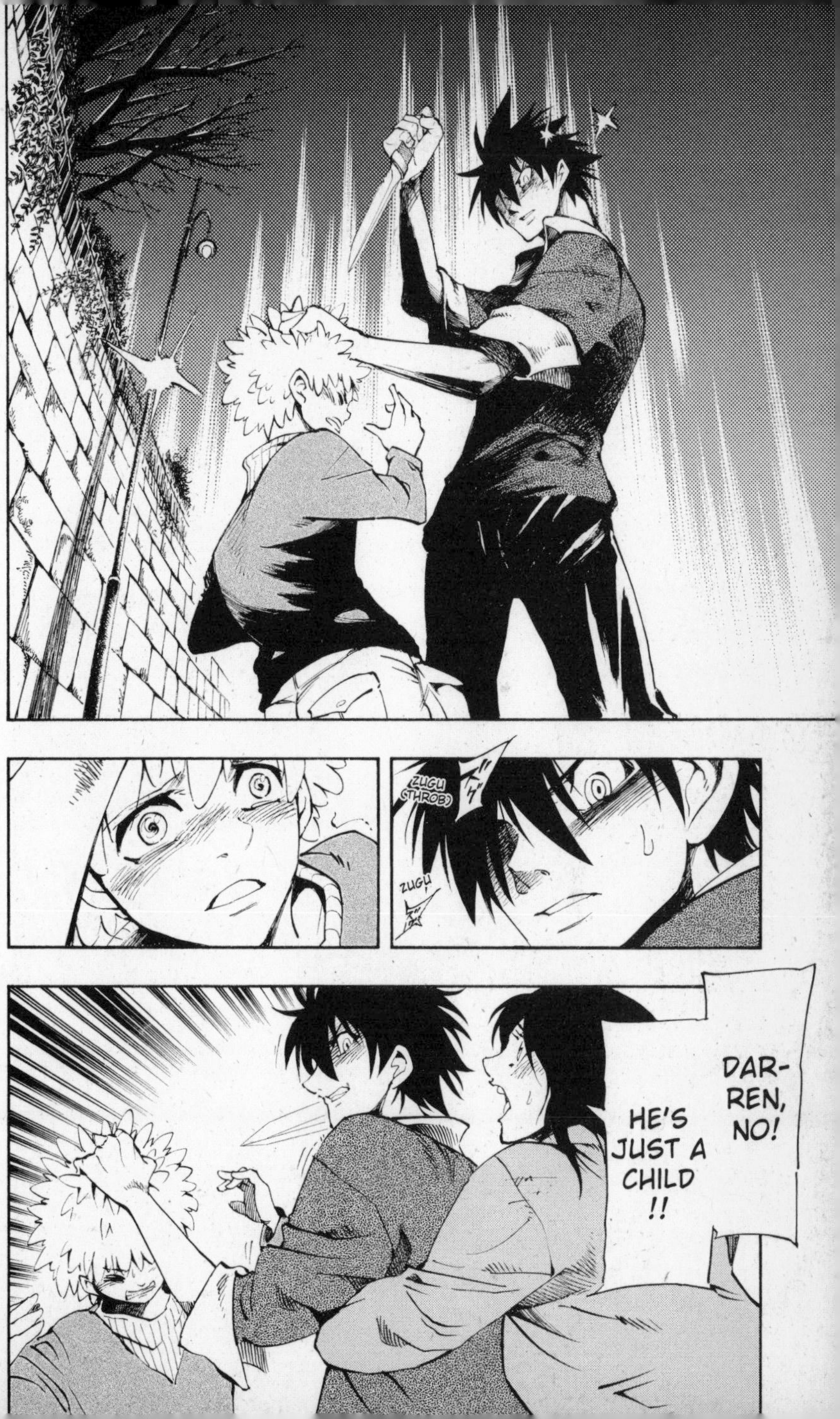
ZUGU (THROB)
ZUGU
DAR-REN, NO!
HE'S JUST A CHILD !!

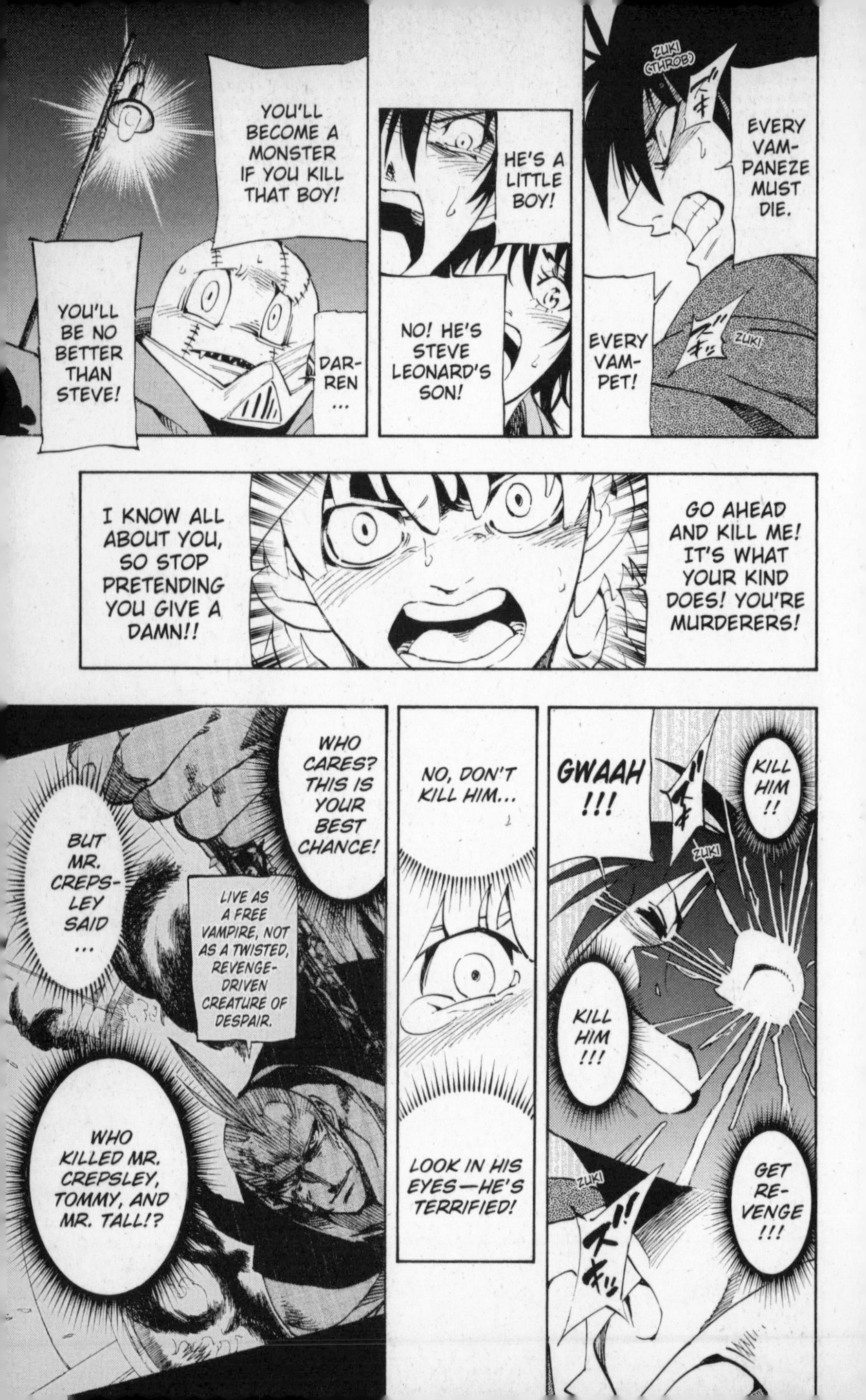
ZUKI (THROB)
EVERY VAMPANEZE MUST DIE.
EVERY VAMPET!
ZUKI
HE'S A LITTLE BOY!
NO! HE'S STEVE LEONARD'S SON!
YOU'LL BECOME A MONSTER IF YOU KILL THAT BOY!
DARREN ...
YOU'LL BE NO BETTER THAN STEVE!
GO AHEAD AND KILL ME! IT'S WHAT YOUR KIND DOES! YOU'RE MURDERERS!
I KNOW ALL ABOUT YOU, SO STOP PRETENDING YOU GIVE A DAMN!!
KILL HIM !!
GWAAH !!!
ZUKI
KILL HIM !!!
GET REVENGE !!!
ZUKI
NO, DON'T KILL HIM...
LOOK IN HIS EYES—HE'S TERRIFIED!
WHO CARES? THIS IS YOUR BEST CHANCE!
BUT MR. CREPSLEY SAID ...
LIVE AS A FREE VAMPIRE, NOT AS A TWISTED, REVENGE-DRIVEN CREATURE OF DESPAIR.
WHO KILLED MR. CREPSLEY, TOMMY, AND MR. TALL!?

# CHAPTER 103: THE PATH OF FATE

NOW YOU'LL KNOW...

...THE PAIN I FELT!!!

DARREN!!!

STEVE NEEDS TO UNDERSTAND THE FEELING OF THE DEATH OF HIS LOVED ONES!

WHAT BETTER WAY THAN TO KILL HIS OWN SON!?

POTA
(DRIP)

HEFF!

HEFF!

HEFF!

## CHAPTER 103:
# THE PATH OF FATE

HAA!?

HAA
CHUFF!

YOU'RE BETTER THAN HIM...

STOPPING STEVE SHOULDN'T TAKE YOU DOWN TO HIS LEVEL...

I-I'LL SUR-VIVE...

URGH...

D-DEBBIE! WHAT HAVE I DONE...

DEBBIE...

DO YOU UNDERSTAND ME, DARREN?

YOU NEED TO BEAT STEVE IN THE WAY ONLY YOU CAN.

IF DEBBIE HADN'T STOPPED ME...

...I'D HAVE...

HENA ^+^

HENA (SHIVER) ^+^

THANKS, HARKAT.

HERE, WE SHOULD STOP... THE BLEEDING.

...

ALICE?

I'LL ANSWER IT.

THANK YOU.

v v v...

VANCHA SAYS HE THINKS... HE CAN KILL R.V. NOW, IF NEED BE...

THEY'VE FOUND R.V. AND SHANCUS... AND ARE IN PURSUIT.

OKAY, I SEE...

...

...

YES, MORGAN'S DEAD.

...

...

...BUT HE THINKS R.V... MIGHT BE LEADING US TO STEVE.

SHOULD WE KILL R.V. NOW, OR FOLLOW HIM?

VANCHA WANTS DARREN... TO DECIDE.

WHAT DOES EVRA SAY?

NO! IF ANYTHING, WE SHOULD BE TRYING TO SAVE SHANCUS!

su...
(SSK)

BUT WE HAVE TO CONSIDER MORE THAN THAT.

EVRA IS ONLY THINKING...OF SHANCUS.

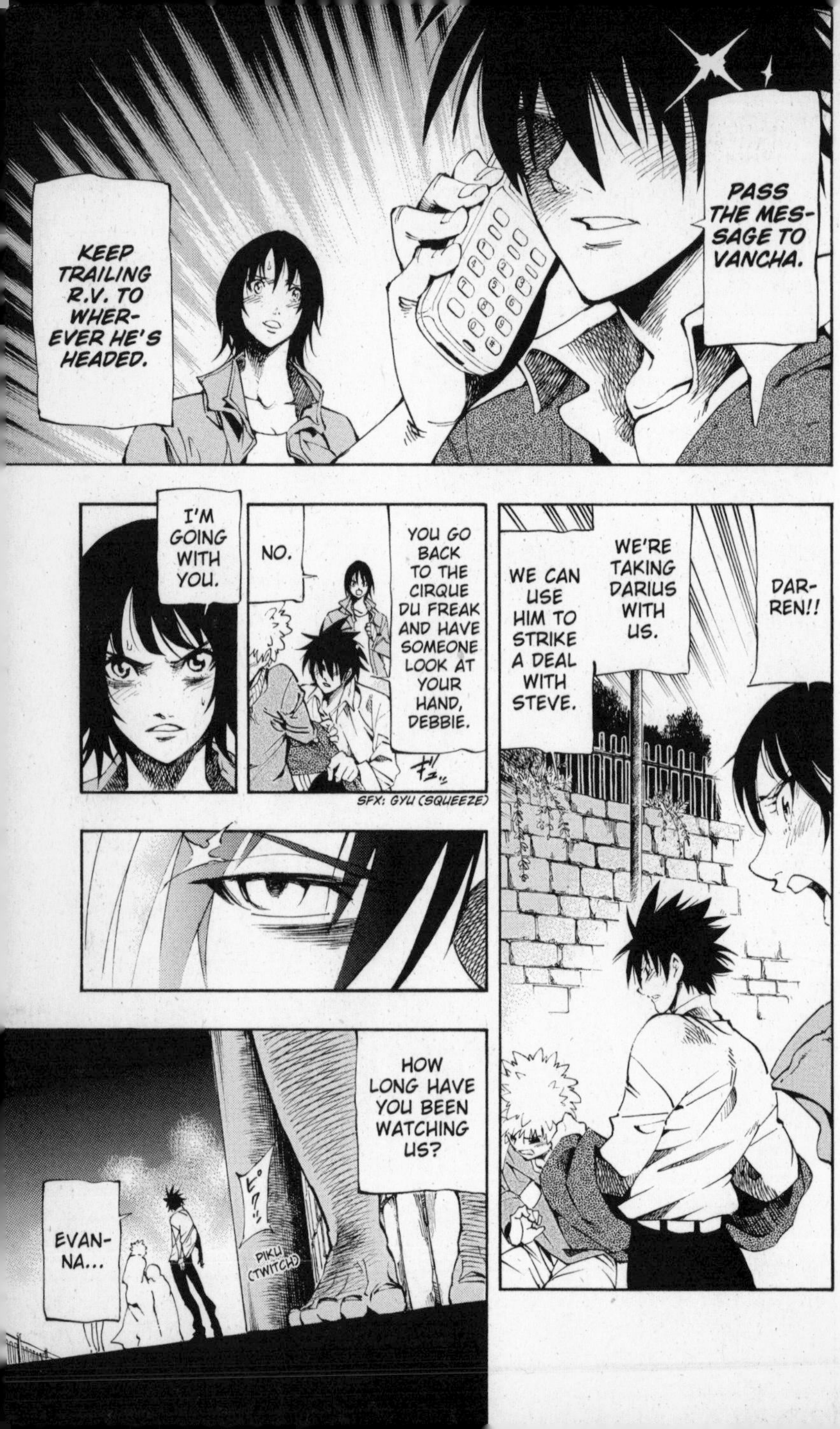
PASS THE MES-SAGE TO VANCHA.
KEEP TRAILING R.V. TO WHER-EVER HE'S HEADED.
DAR-REN!!
WE'RE TAKING DARIUS WITH US.
WE CAN USE HIM TO STRIKE A DEAL WITH STEVE.
YOU GO BACK TO THE CIRQUE DU FREAK AND HAVE SOMEONE LOOK AT YOUR HAND, DEBBIE.
NO.
SFX: GYU (SQUEEZE)
I'M GOING WITH YOU.
HOW LONG HAVE YOU BEEN WATCHING US?
PIKU (TWITCH)
EVAN-NA...

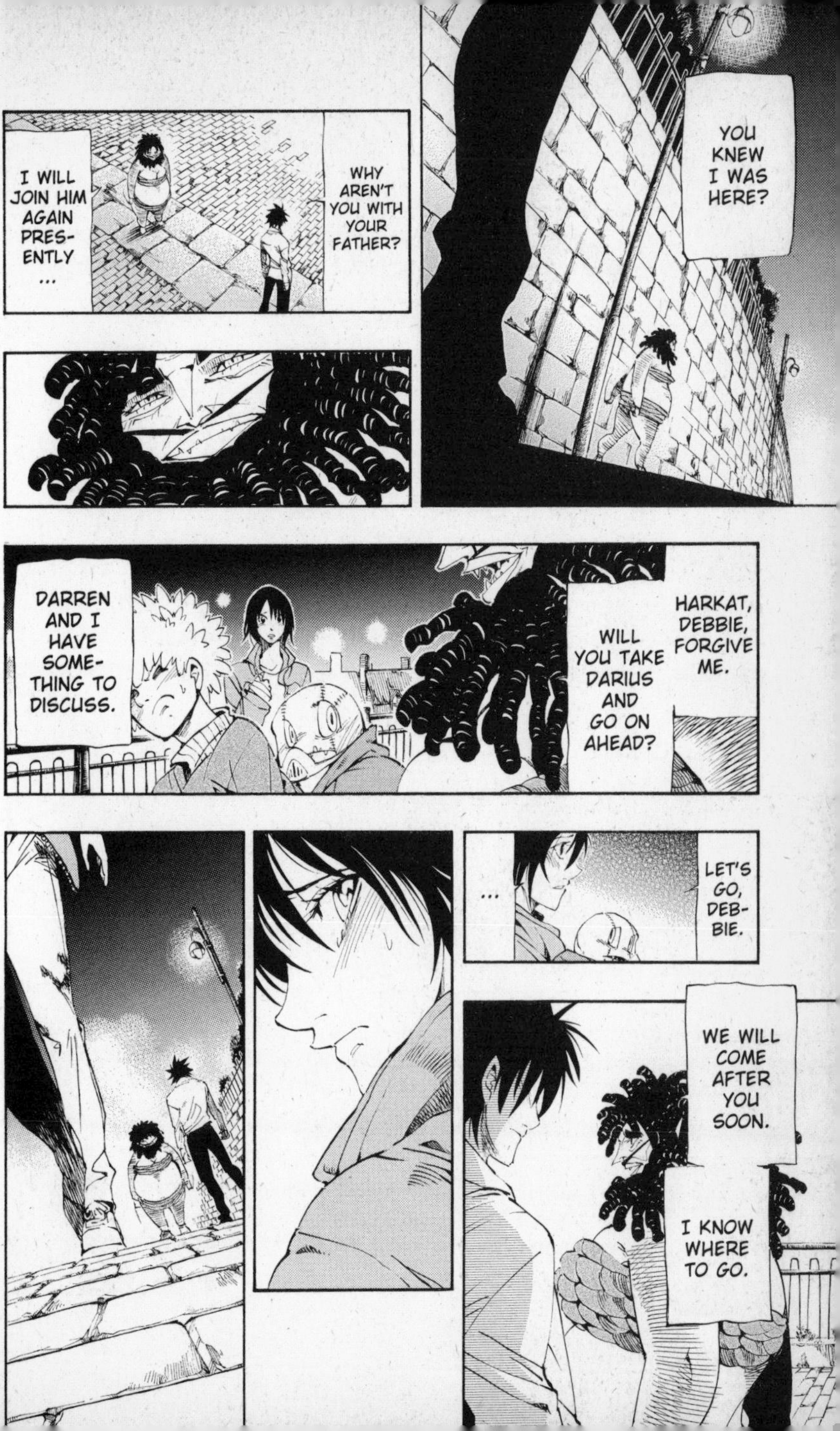
YOU KNEW I WAS HERE?
WHY AREN'T YOU WITH YOUR FATHER?
I WILL JOIN HIM AGAIN PRES-ENTLY ...
HARKAT, DEBBIE, FORGIVE ME.
WILL YOU TAKE DARIUS AND GO ON AHEAD?
DARREN AND I HAVE SOME-THING TO DISCUSS.
LET'S GO, DEB-BIE.
...
WE WILL COME AFTER YOU SOON.
I KNOW WHERE TO GO.

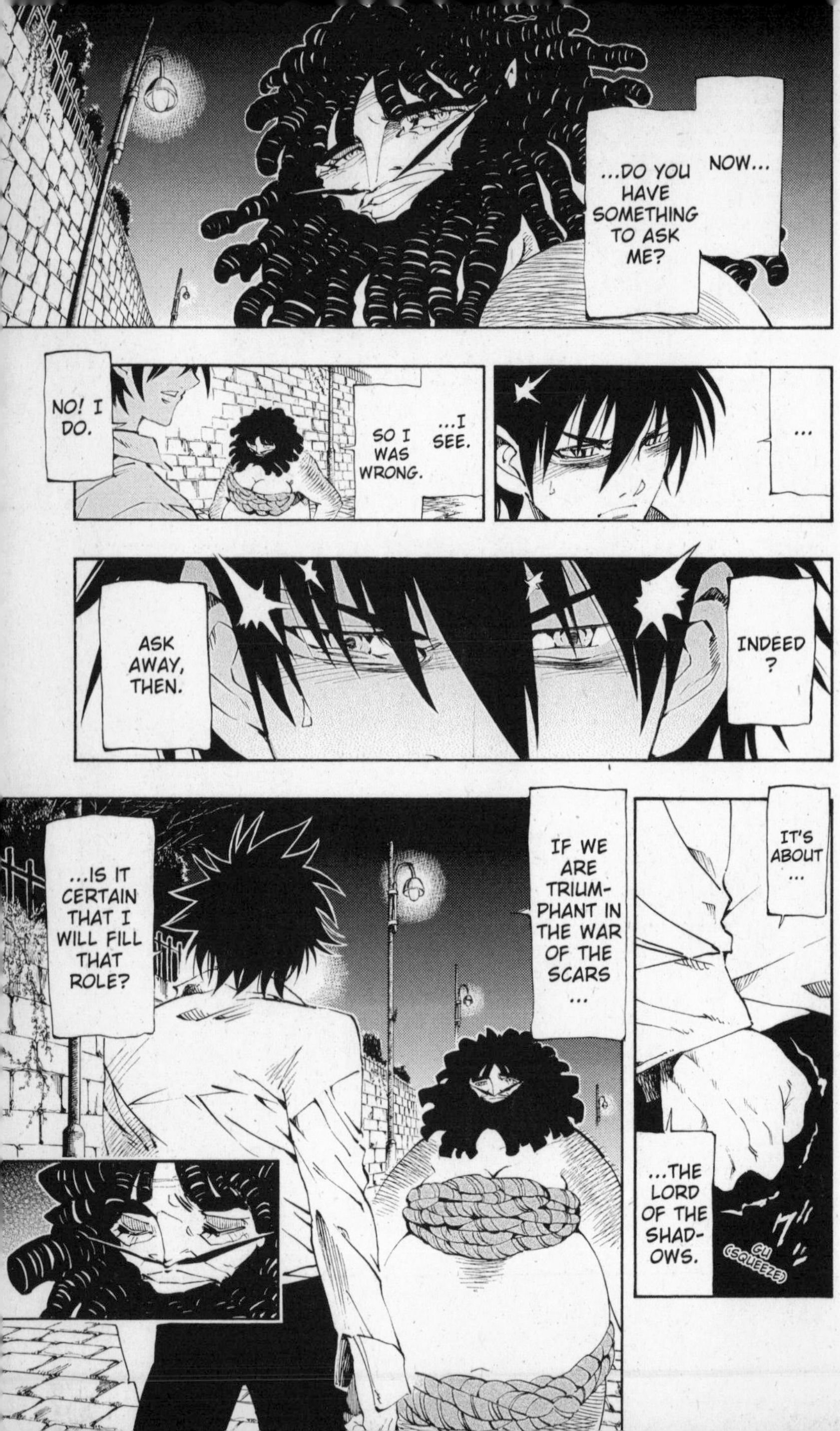
NOW...
...DO YOU HAVE SOMETHING TO ASK ME?
...
...I SEE.
SO I WAS WRONG.
NO! I DO.
INDEED?
ASK AWAY, THEN.
IT'S ABOUT ...
...THE LORD OF THE SHADOWS.
GU (SQUEEZE)
IF WE ARE TRIUMPHANT IN THE WAR OF THE SCARS ...
...IS IT CERTAIN THAT I WILL FILL THAT ROLE?

AND IT WILL HAPPEN WITHIN THE NEXT TWENTY-FOUR HOURS.

IT IS.

IT'S IMPOS-SIBLE...

IT CAN'T HAPPEN...

AGH...

IT WAS NOT LIKE HIM TO BE SO RE-VEALING...

DID HIBER-NIUS TELL YOU THIS?

NO! YOU'RE WRONG! YOU AND MR. TALL!

I WOULDN'T HURT VANCHA... OR MY FRIENDS!!!

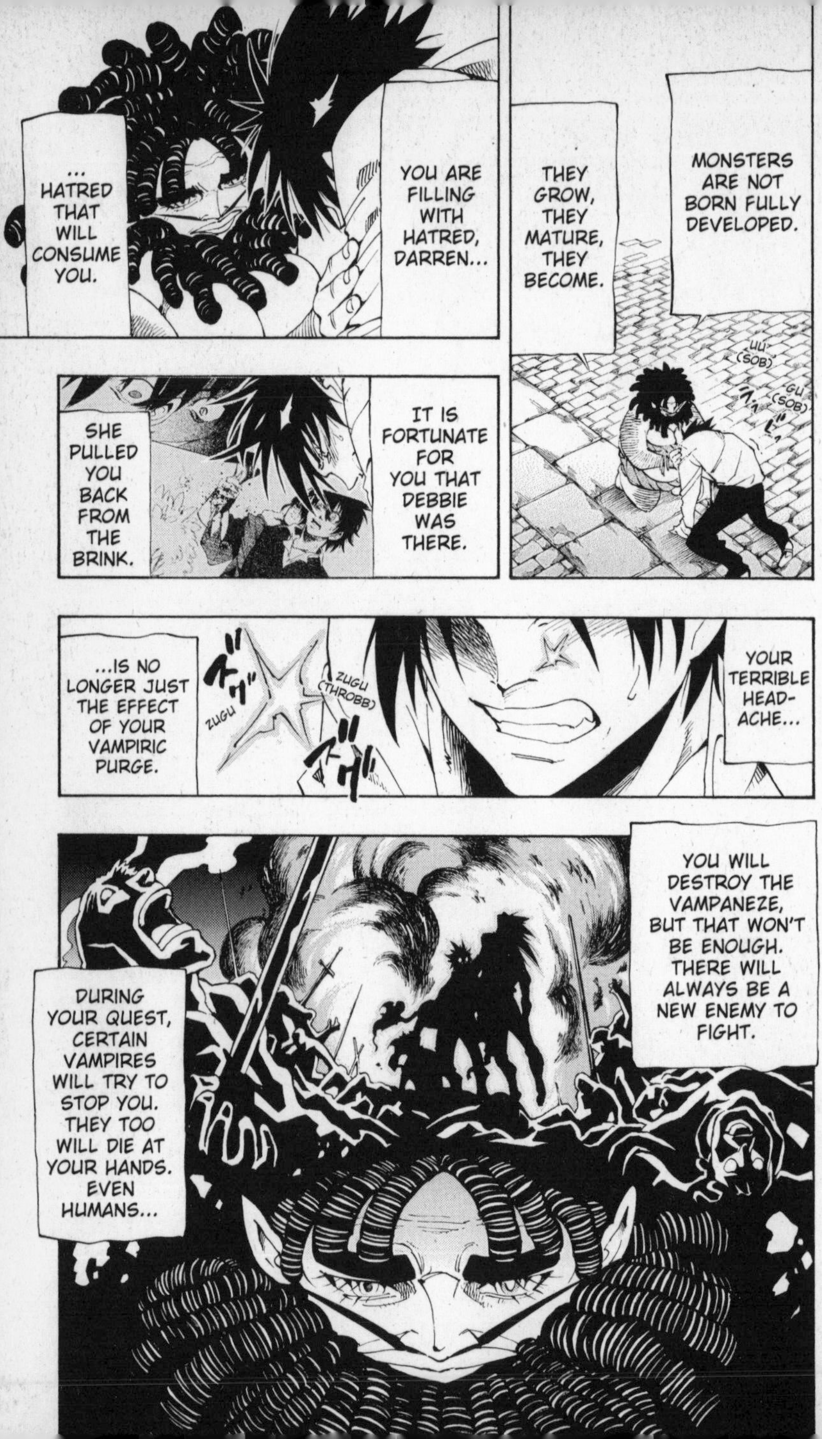
MONSTERS ARE NOT BORN FULLY DEVELOPED.
THEY GROW, THEY MATURE, THEY BECOME.
UU (SOB)
GU (SOB)
YOU ARE FILLING WITH HATRED, DARREN...
...HATRED THAT WILL CONSUME YOU.
IT IS FORTUNATE FOR YOU THAT DEBBIE WAS THERE.
SHE PULLED YOU BACK FROM THE BRINK.
YOUR TERRIBLE HEAD-ACHE...
ZUGU (THROBB)
ZUGU
...IS NO LONGER JUST THE EFFECT OF YOUR VAMPIRIC PURGE.
YOU WILL DESTROY THE VAMPANEZE, BUT THAT WON'T BE ENOUGH. THERE WILL ALWAYS BE A NEW ENEMY TO FIGHT.
DURING YOUR QUEST, CERTAIN VAMPIRES WILL TRY TO STOP YOU. THEY TOO WILL DIE AT YOUR HANDS. EVEN HUMANS...

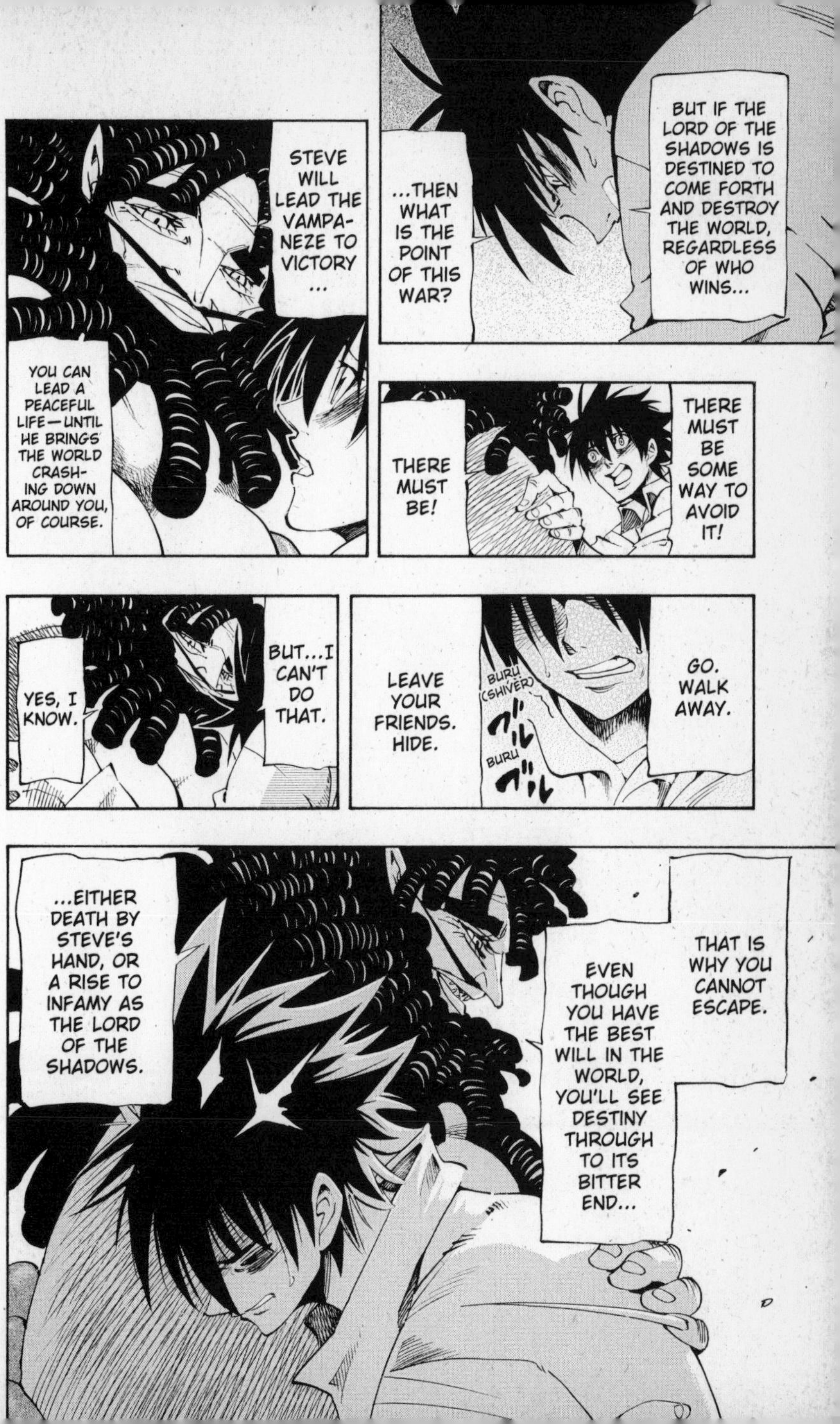

BUT IF THE LORD OF THE SHADOWS IS DESTINED TO COME FORTH AND DESTROY THE WORLD, REGARDLESS OF WHO WINS...
...THEN WHAT IS THE POINT OF THIS WAR?
THERE MUST BE SOME WAY TO AVOID IT!
THERE MUST BE!
STEVE WILL LEAD THE VAMPANEZE TO VICTORY...
YOU CAN LEAD A PEACEFUL LIFE—UNTIL HE BRINGS THE WORLD CRASHING DOWN AROUND YOU, OF COURSE.
GO. WALK AWAY.
BURU (SHIVER)
ブル
BURU
ブル
LEAVE YOUR FRIENDS. HIDE.
BUT...I CAN'T DO THAT.
YES, I KNOW.
THAT IS WHY YOU CANNOT ESCAPE.
EVEN THOUGH YOU HAVE THE BEST WILL IN THE WORLD, YOU'LL SEE DESTINY THROUGH TO ITS BITTER END...
...EITHER DEATH BY STEVE'S HAND, OR A RISE TO INFAMY AS THE LORD OF THE SHADOWS.

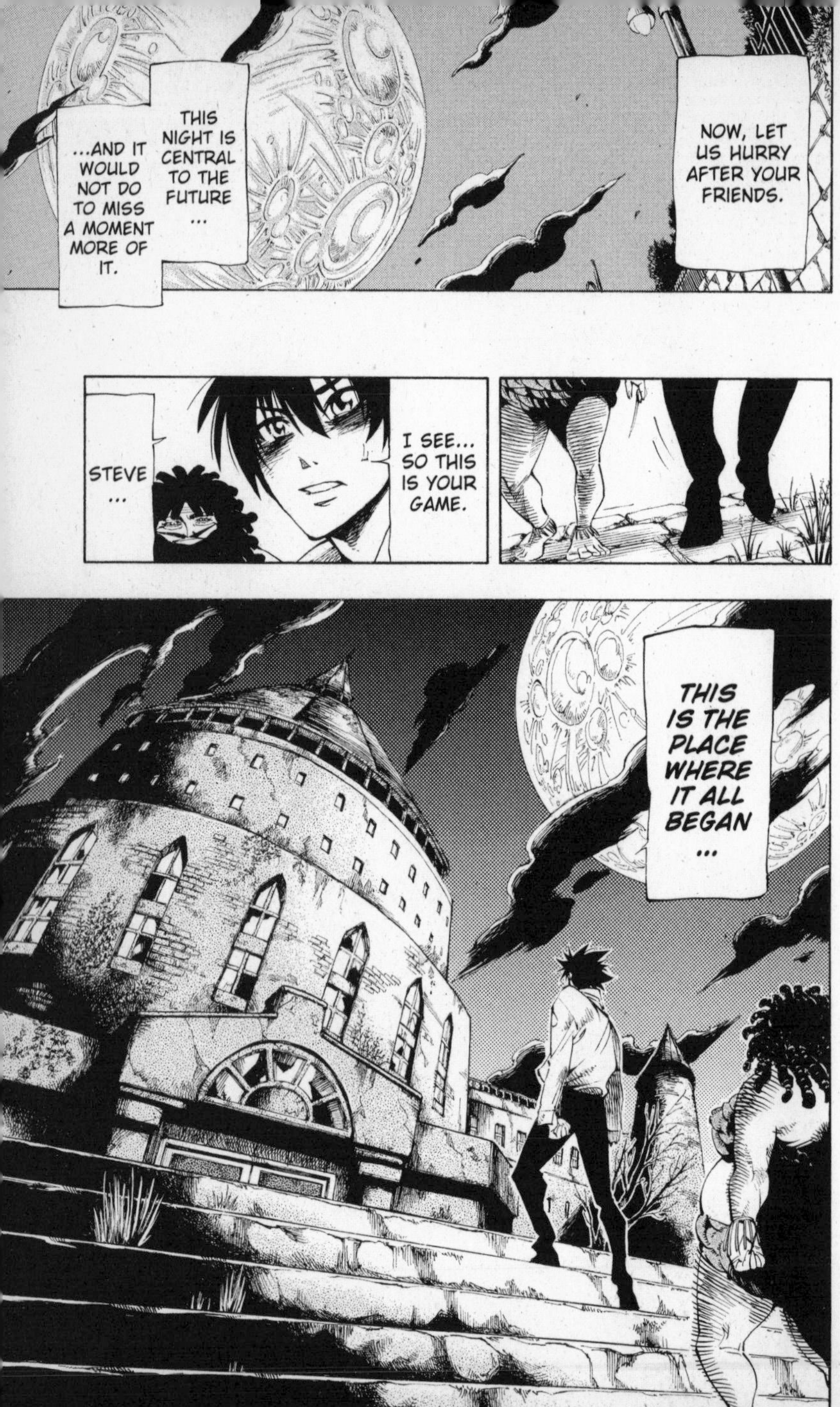
NOW, LET US HURRY AFTER YOUR FRIENDS.
THIS NIGHT IS CENTRAL TO THE FUTURE...
...AND IT WOULD NOT DO TO MISS A MOMENT MORE OF IT.
I SEE... SO THIS IS YOUR GAME.
STEVE...
THIS IS THE PLACE WHERE IT ALL BEGAN...

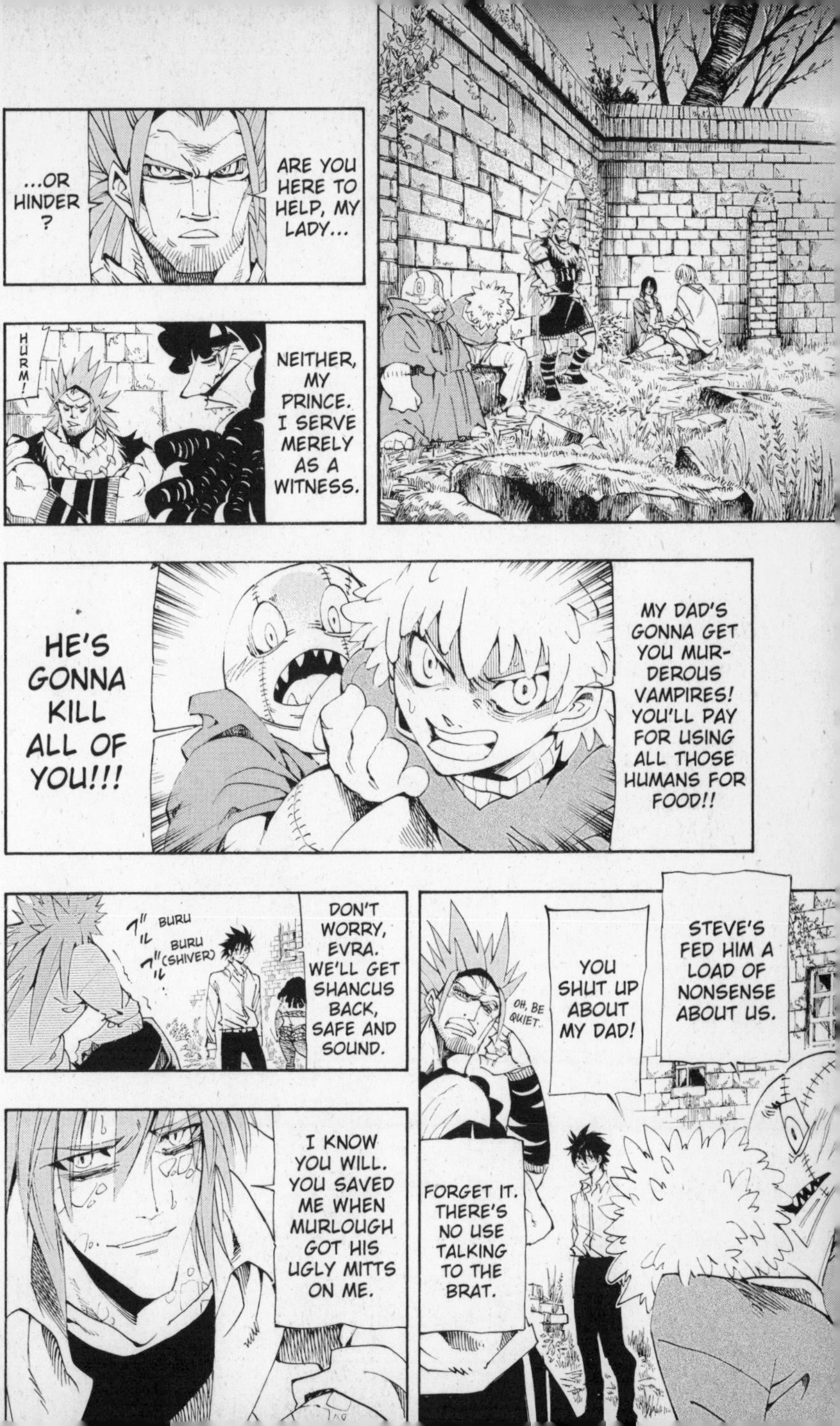

ARE YOU HERE TO HELP, MY LADY...
...OR HINDER ?
NEITHER, MY PRINCE. I SERVE MERELY AS A WITNESS.
HURM!
MY DAD'S GONNA GET YOU MUR-DEROUS VAMPIRES! YOU'LL PAY FOR USING ALL THOSE HUMANS FOR FOOD!!
HE'S GONNA KILL ALL OF YOU!!!
STEVE'S FED HIM A LOAD OF NONSENSE ABOUT US.
YOU SHUT UP ABOUT MY DAD!
OH, BE QUIET.
FORGET IT. THERE'S NO USE TALKING TO THE BRAT.
DON'T WORRY, EVRA. WE'LL GET SHANCUS BACK, SAFE AND SOUND.
BURU
BURU (SHIVER)
I KNOW YOU WILL. YOU SAVED ME WHEN MURLOUGH GOT HIS UGLY MITTS ON ME.

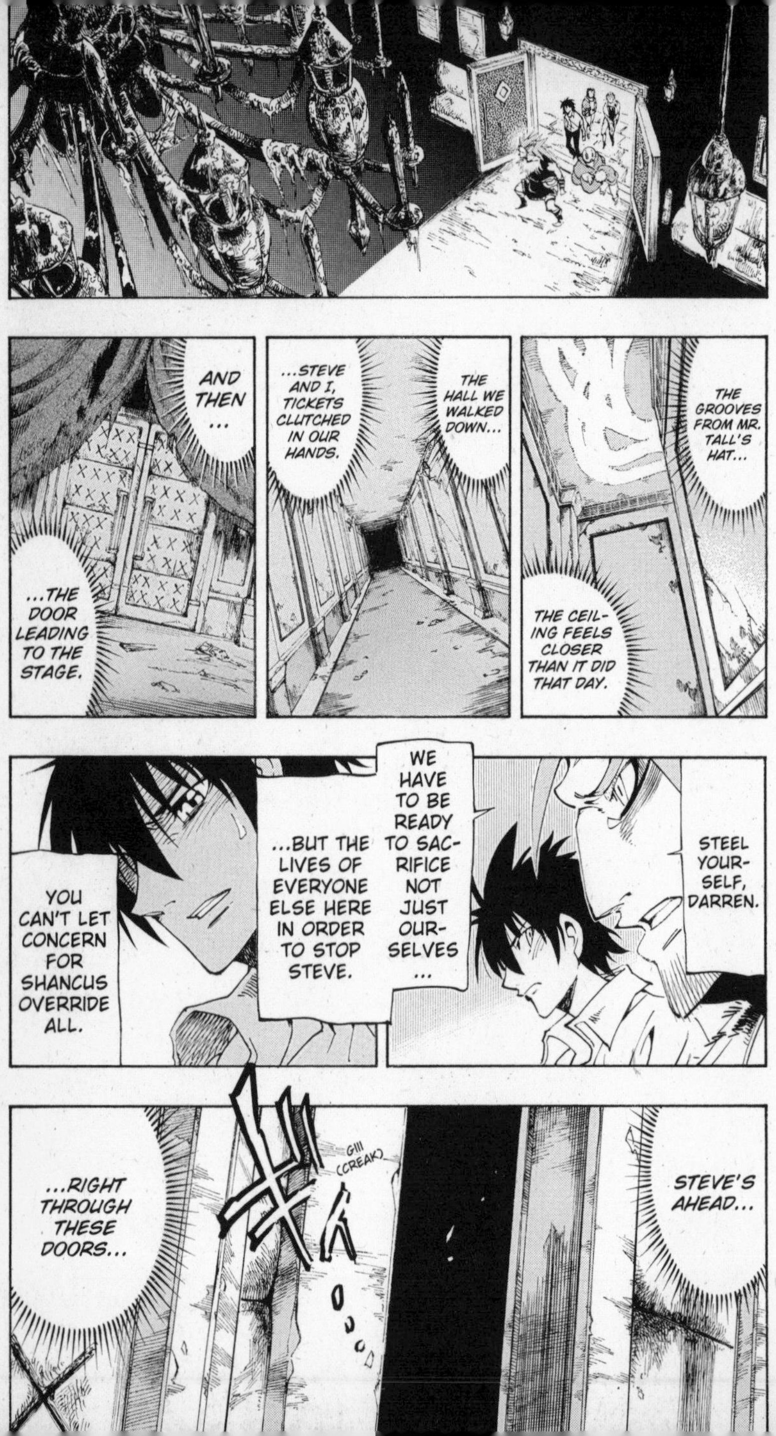
THE GROOVES FROM MR. TALL'S HAT...
THE CEILING FEELS CLOSER THAN IT DID THAT DAY.
THE HALL WE WALKED DOWN...
...STEVE AND I, TICKETS CLUTCHED IN OUR HANDS.
AND THEN...
...THE DOOR LEADING TO THE STAGE.
STEEL YOURSELF, DARREN.
WE HAVE TO BE READY TO SACRIFICE NOT JUST OURSELVES...
...BUT THE LIVES OF EVERYONE ELSE HERE IN ORDER TO STOP STEVE.
YOU CAN'T LET CONCERN FOR SHANCUS OVERRIDE ALL.
STEVE'S AHEAD...
GIII (CREAK)
...RIGHT THROUGH THESE DOORS...

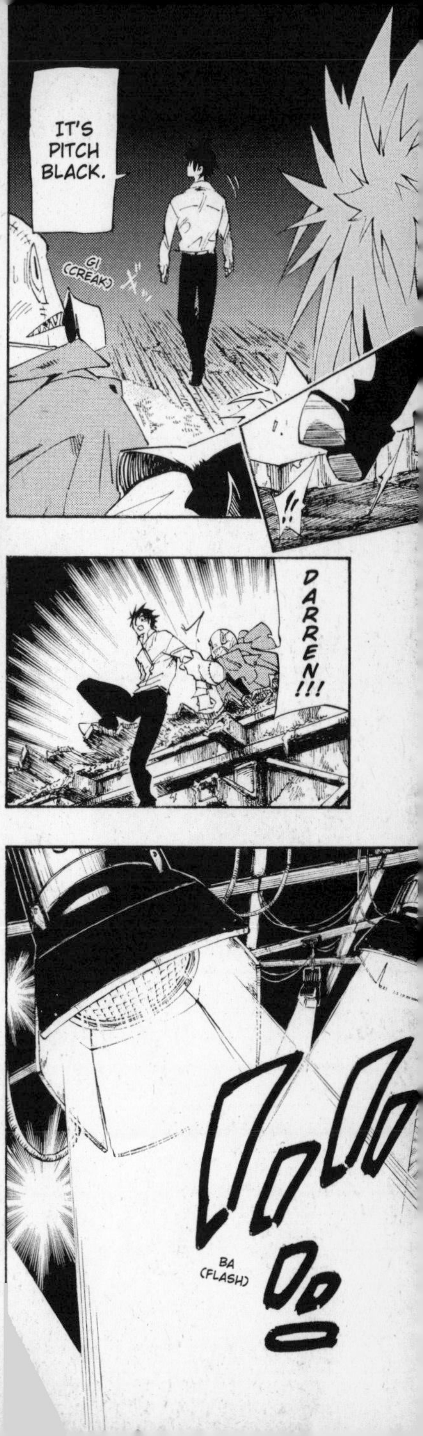
IT'S PITCH BLACK.
GI (CREAK)
!!
DARREN!!!
BA (FLASH)
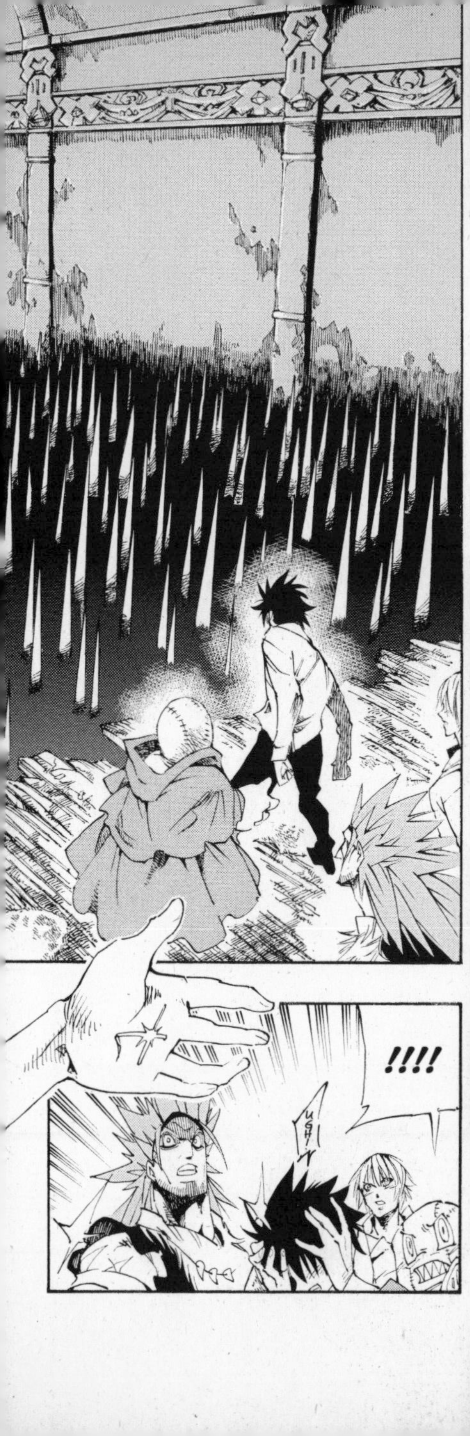
!!!!
UGH!

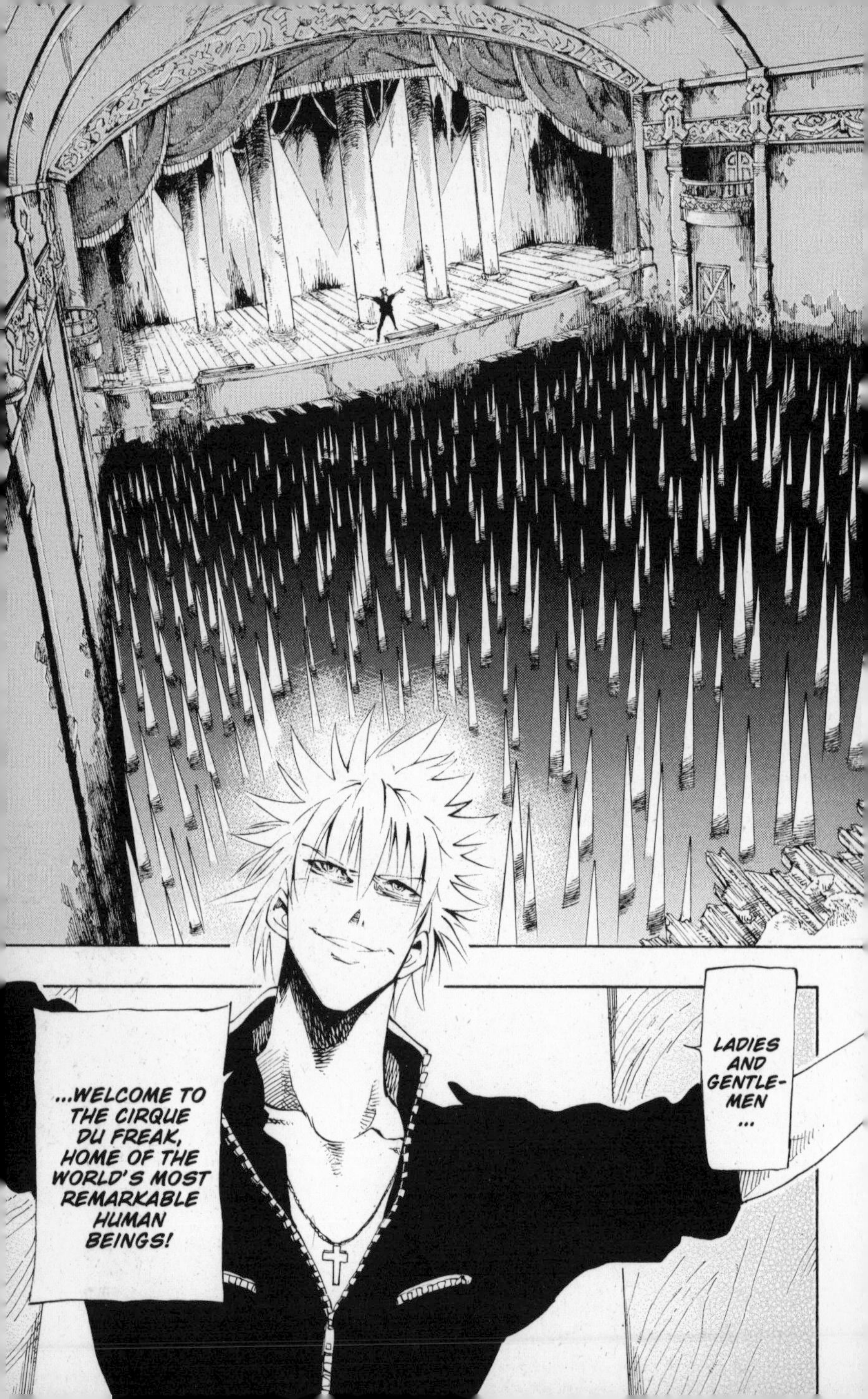
LADIES AND GENTLE-MEN ...
...WELCOME TO THE CIRQUE DU FREAK, HOME OF THE WORLD'S MOST REMARKABLE HUMAN BEINGS!

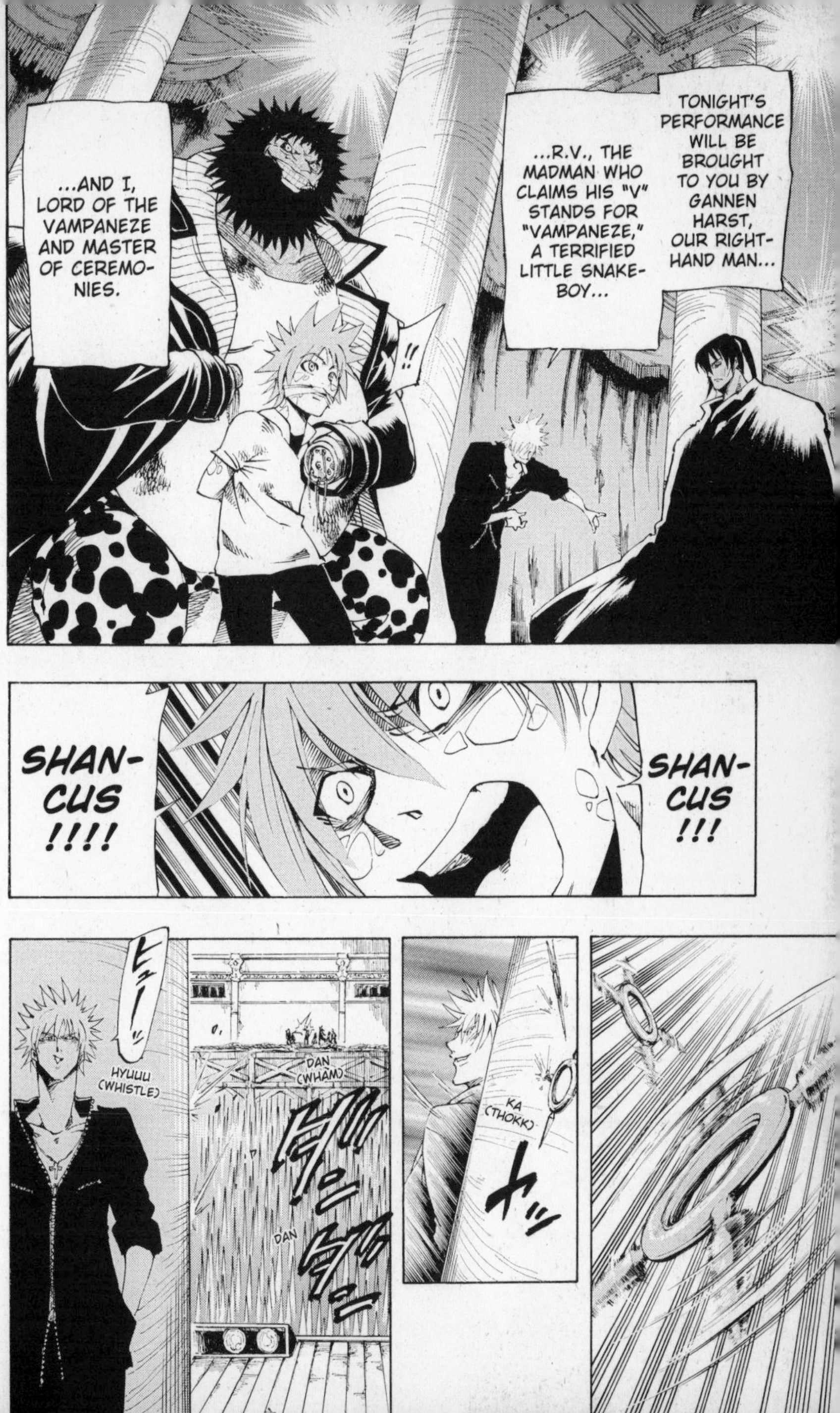
TONIGHT'S PERFORMANCE WILL BE BROUGHT TO YOU BY GANNEN HARST, OUR RIGHT-HAND MAN...
...R.V., THE MADMAN WHO CLAIMS HIS "V" STANDS FOR "VAMPANEZE," A TERRIFIED LITTLE SNAKE-BOY...
!!
...AND I, LORD OF THE VAMPANEZE AND MASTER OF CEREMONIES.
SHAN-CUS!!!
SHAN-CUS!!!!
KA (THOKK)
DAN (WHAM)
DAN
HYUUU (WHISTLE)

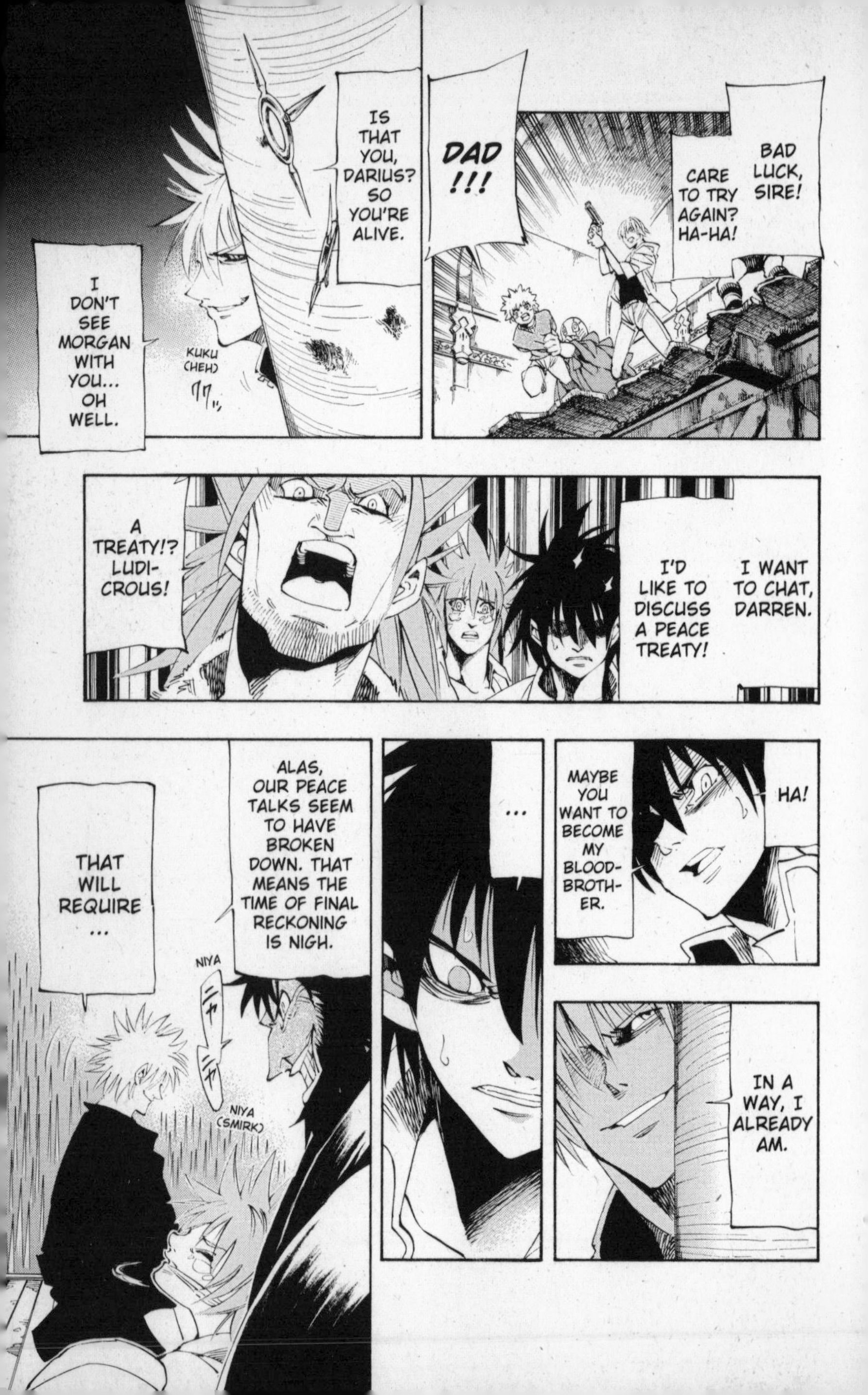
BAD LUCK, SIRE!
CARE TO TRY AGAIN? HA-HA!
DAD !!!
IS THAT YOU, DARIUS? SO YOU'RE ALIVE.
KUKU (HEH)
I DON'T SEE MORGAN WITH YOU... OH WELL.
I WANT TO CHAT, DARREN.
I'D LIKE TO DISCUSS A PEACE TREATY!
A TREATY!? LUDI-CROUS!
HA!
MAYBE YOU WANT TO BECOME MY BLOOD-BROTH-ER.
IN A WAY, I ALREADY AM.
...
ALAS, OUR PEACE TALKS SEEM TO HAVE BROKEN DOWN. THAT MEANS THE TIME OF FINAL RECKONING IS NIGH.
NIYA
NIYA (SMIRK)
THAT WILL REQUIRE ...

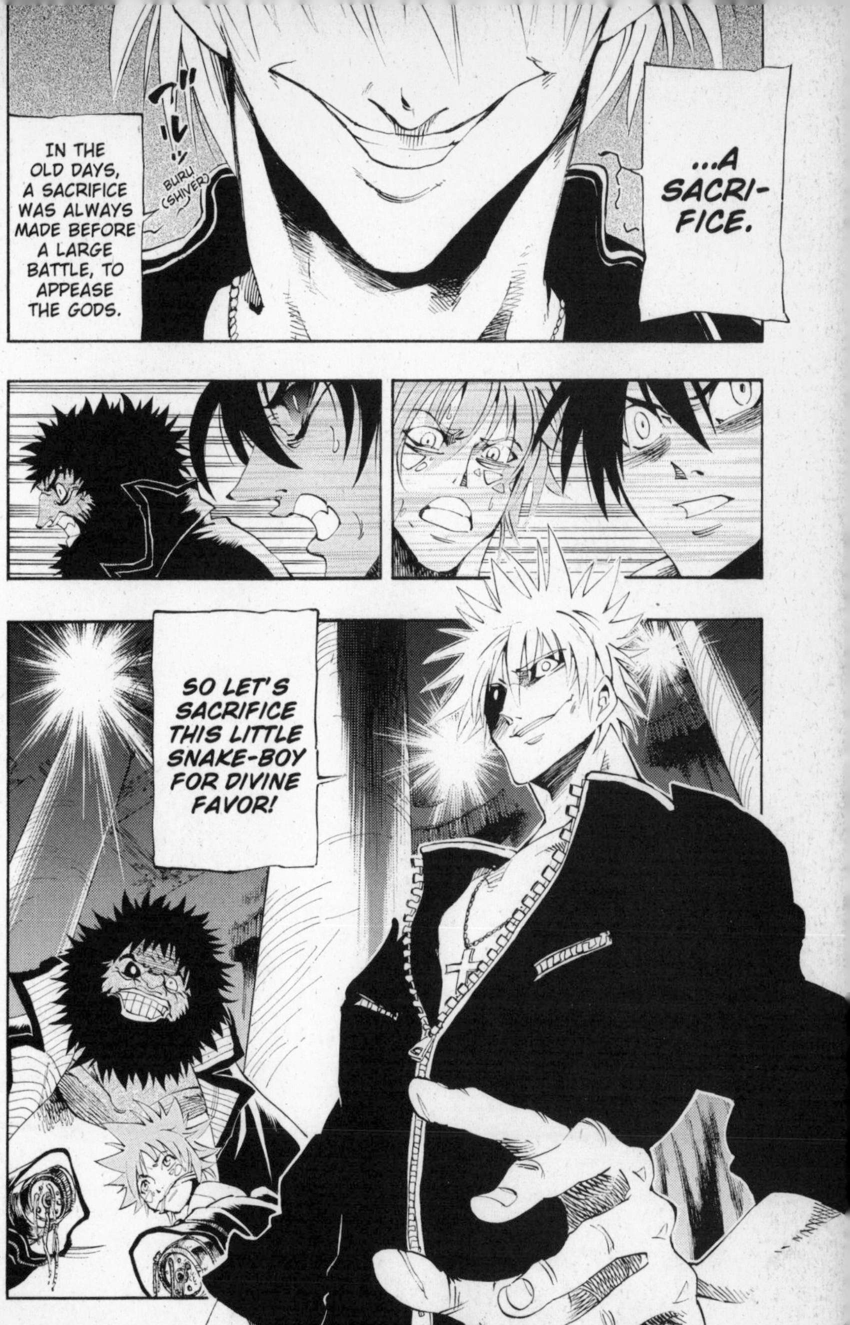
...A SACRI-FICE.
BURU (SHIVER)
IN THE OLD DAYS, A SACRIFICE WAS ALWAYS MADE BEFORE A LARGE BATTLE, TO APPEASE THE GODS.
SO LET'S SACRIFICE THIS LITTLE SNAKE-BOY FOR DIVINE FAVOR!

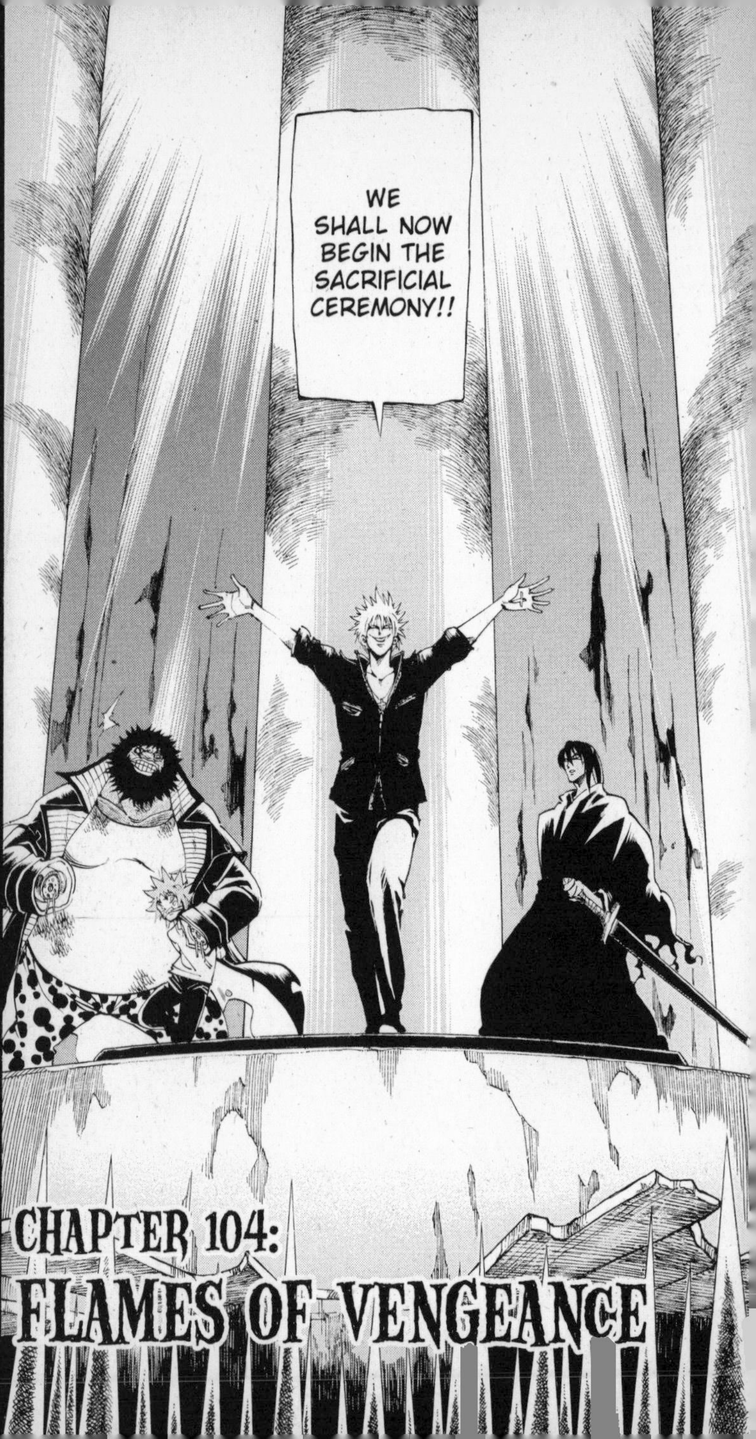
WE SHALL NOW BEGIN THE SACRIFICIAL CEREMONY!!
CHAPTER 104:
FLAMES OF VENGEANCE

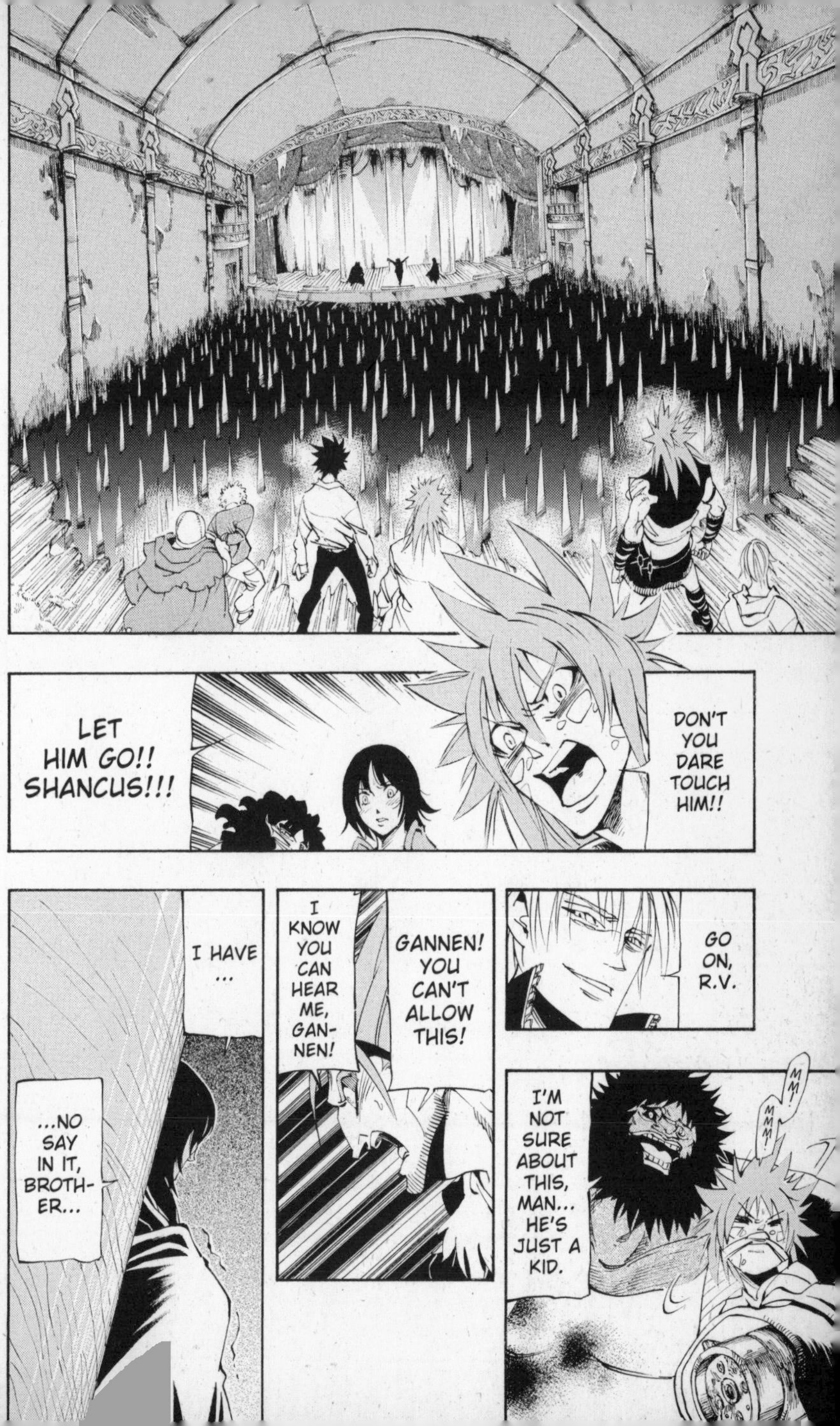
DON'T YOU DARE TOUCH HIM!!
LET HIM GO!! SHANCUS!!!
GO ON, R.V.
MM!
MMM!
I'M NOT SURE ABOUT THIS, MAN... HE'S JUST A KID.
GANNEN! YOU CAN'T ALLOW THIS!
I KNOW YOU CAN HEAR ME, GANNEN!
I HAVE ...
...NO SAY IN IT, BROTHER...

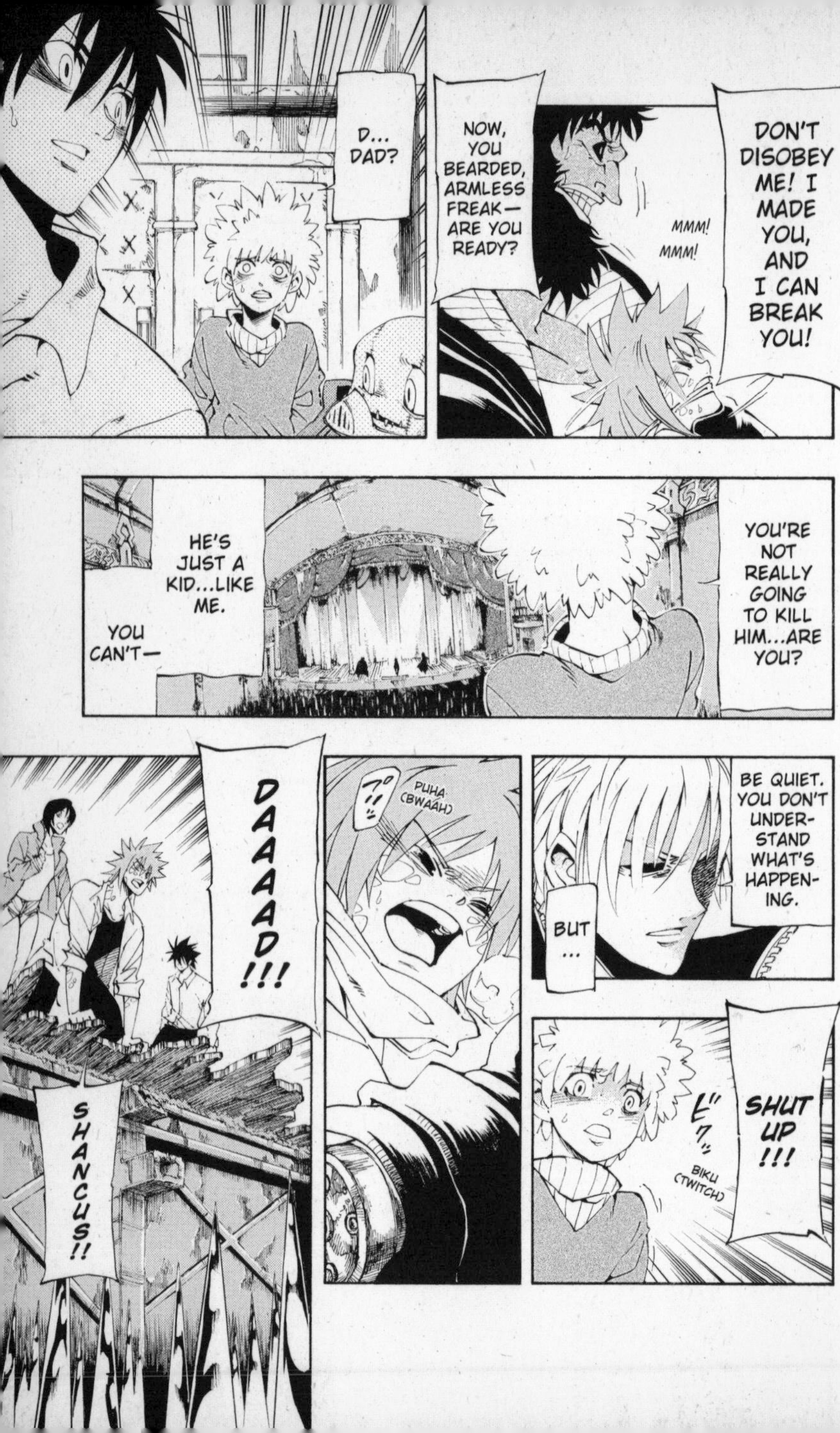
DON'T DISOBEY ME! I MADE YOU, AND I CAN BREAK YOU!
MMM! MMM!
NOW, YOU BEARDED, ARMLESS FREAK—ARE YOU READY?
D... DAD?
YOU'RE NOT REALLY GOING TO KILL HIM...ARE YOU?
HE'S JUST A KID...LIKE ME.
YOU CAN'T—
BE QUIET. YOU DON'T UNDER-STAND WHAT'S HAPPEN-ING.
BUT ...
SHUT UP!!!
BIKU (TWITCH)
PUHA (BWAAH)
DAAAAAD!!!
SHANCUS!!

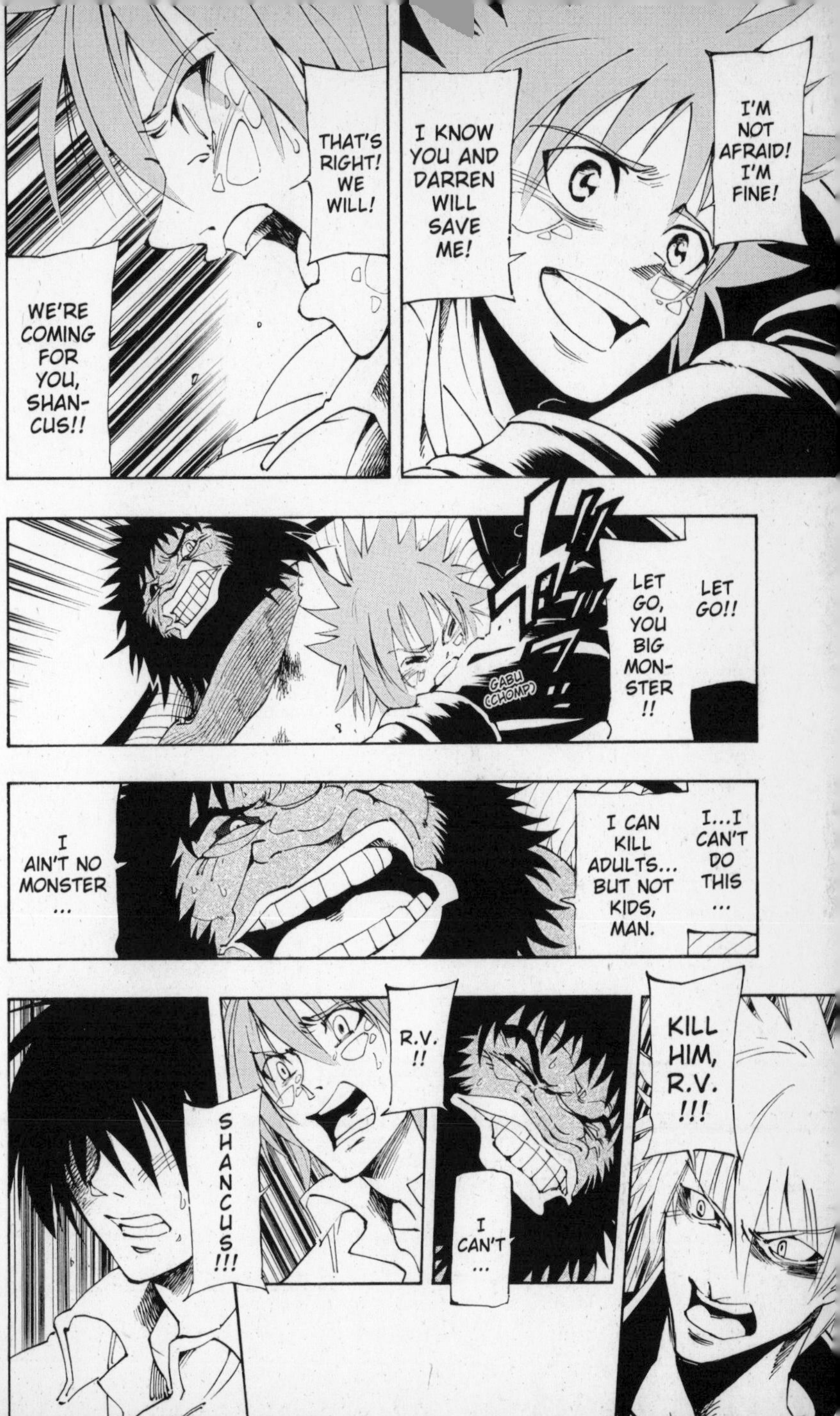
I'M NOT AFRAID! I'M FINE!
I KNOW YOU AND DARREN WILL SAVE ME!
THAT'S RIGHT! WE WILL!
WE'RE COMING FOR YOU, SHANCUS!!
LET GO!!
LET GO, YOU BIG MONSTER!!
GABU (CHOMP)
I...I CAN'T DO THIS...
I CAN KILL ADULTS... BUT NOT KIDS, MAN.
I AIN'T NO MONSTER...
KILL HIM, R.V.!!!
I CAN'T...
R.V.!!
SHANCUS!!!

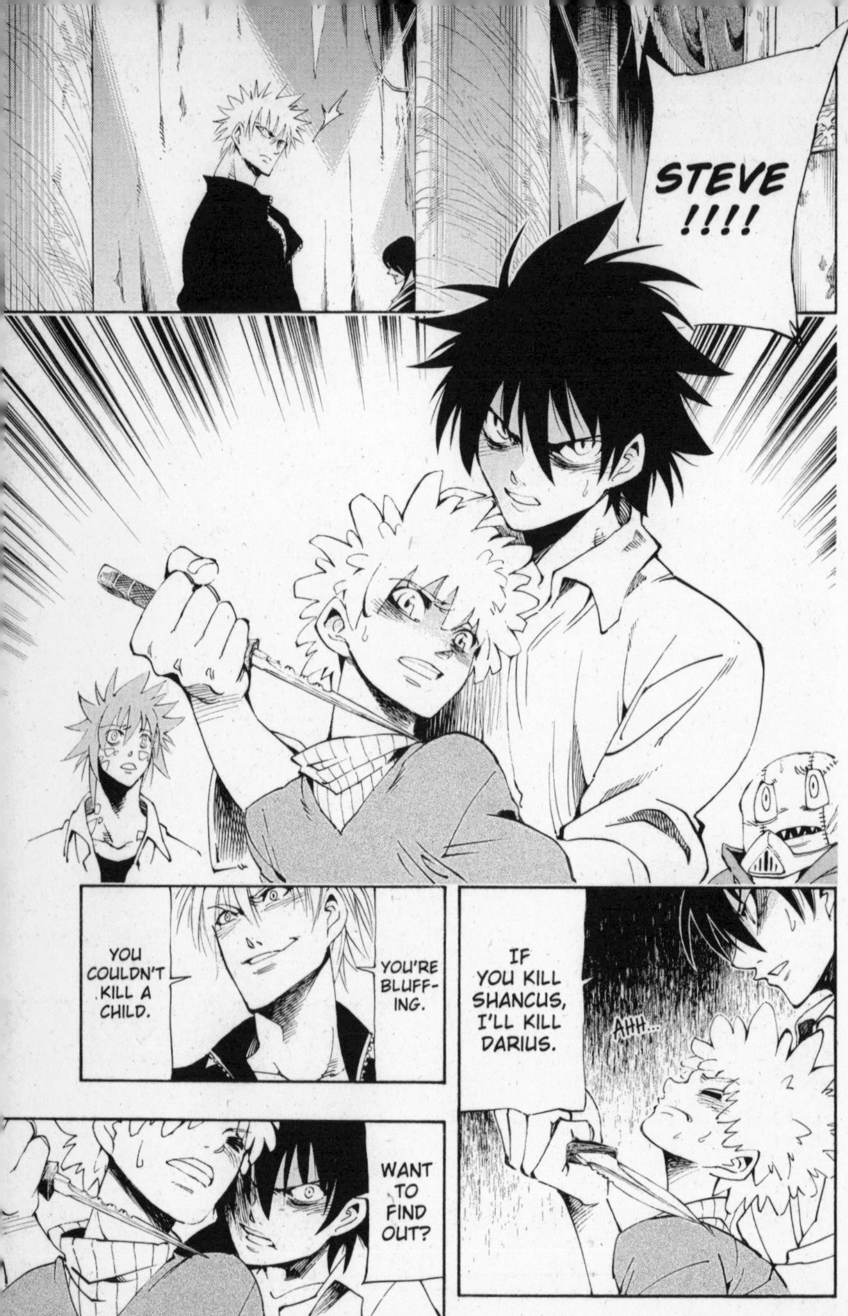
STEVE !!!!
IF YOU KILL SHANCUS, I'LL KILL DARIUS.
AHH...
YOU'RE BLUFF-ING.
YOU COULDN'T KILL A CHILD.
WANT TO FIND OUT?

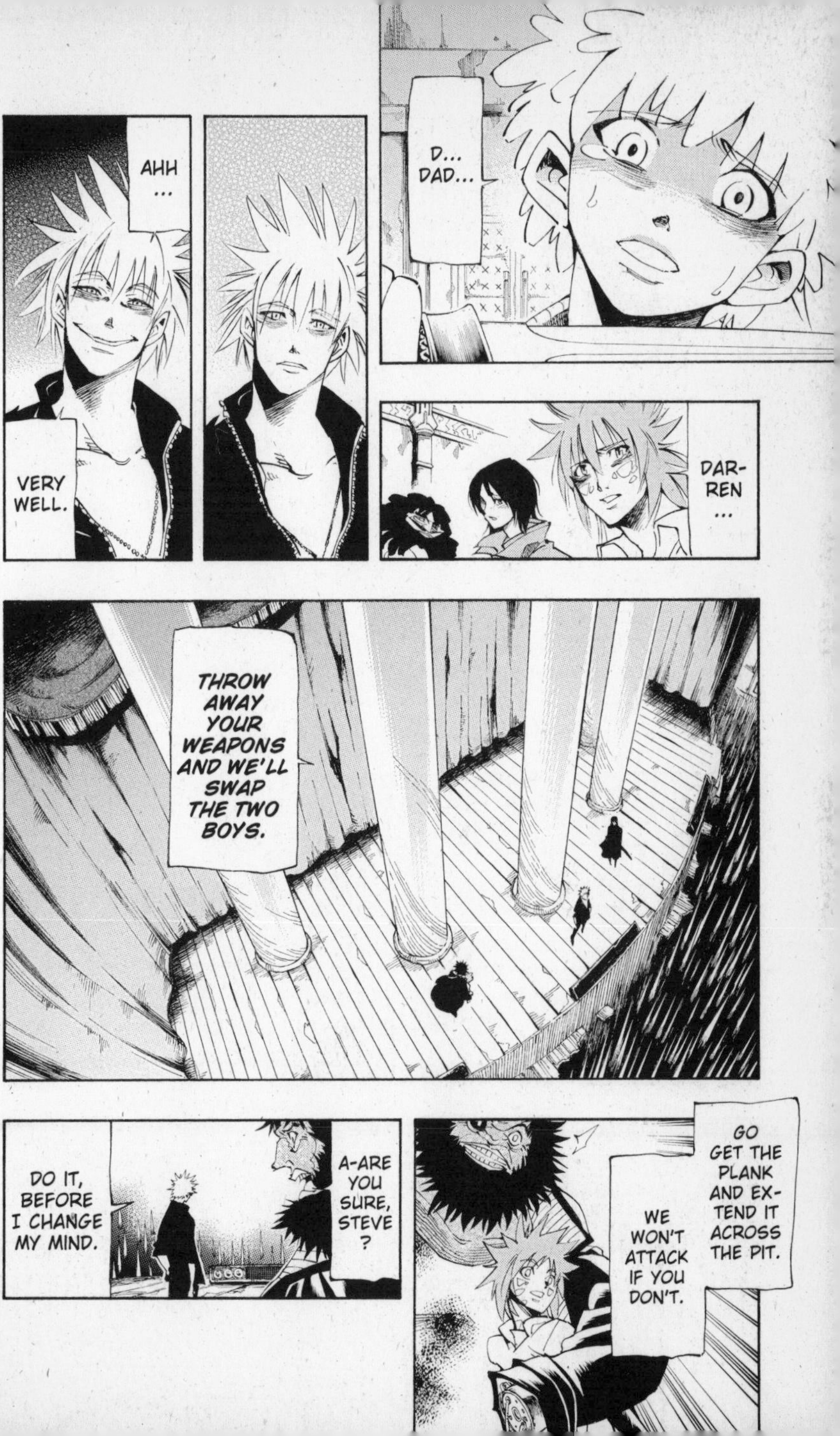
D... DAD...
DAR-REN ...
AHH ...
VERY WELL.
THROW AWAY YOUR WEAPONS AND WE'LL SWAP THE TWO BOYS.
GO GET THE PLANK AND EXTEND IT ACROSS THE PIT.
WE WON'T ATTACK IF YOU DON'T.
A-ARE YOU SURE, STEVE?
DO IT, BEFORE I CHANGE MY MIND.

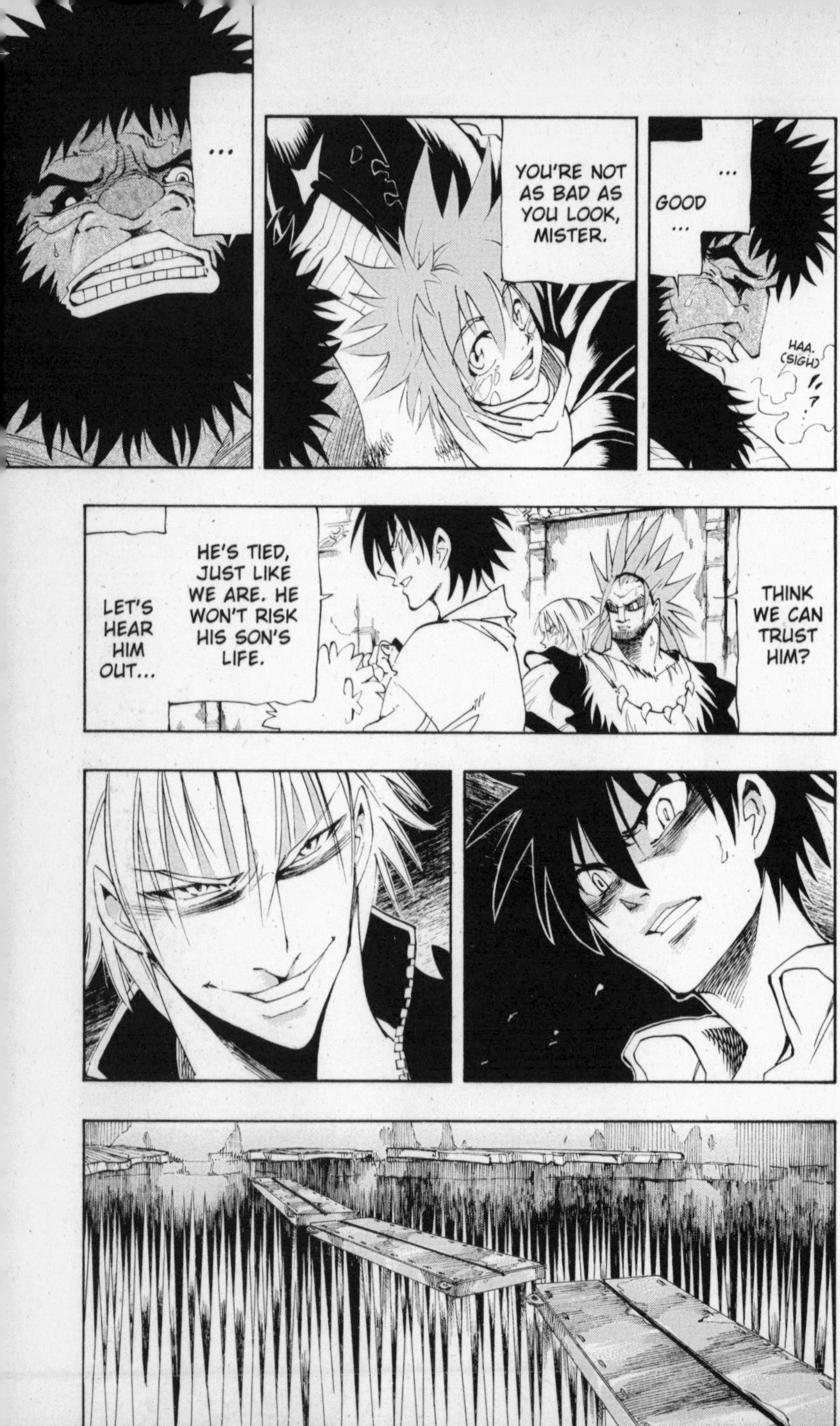
... GOOD ...
HAA. (SIGH)
YOU'RE NOT AS BAD AS YOU LOOK, MISTER.
...
THINK WE CAN TRUST HIM?
HE'S TIED, JUST LIKE WE ARE. HE WON'T RISK HIS SON'S LIFE.
LET'S HEAR HIM OUT...

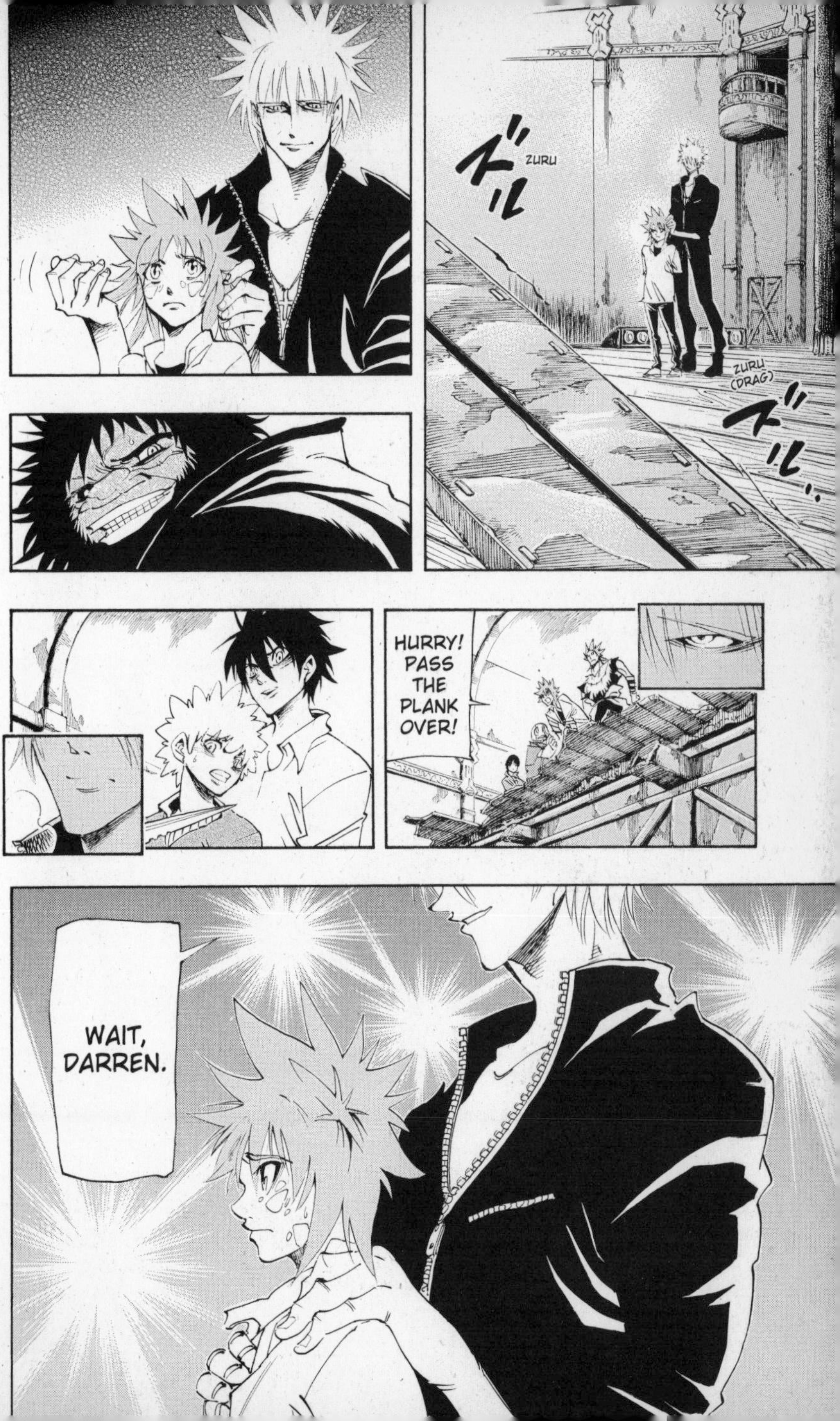
ZURU
ZURU (DRAG)
HURRY! PASS THE PLANK OVER!
WAIT, DARREN.

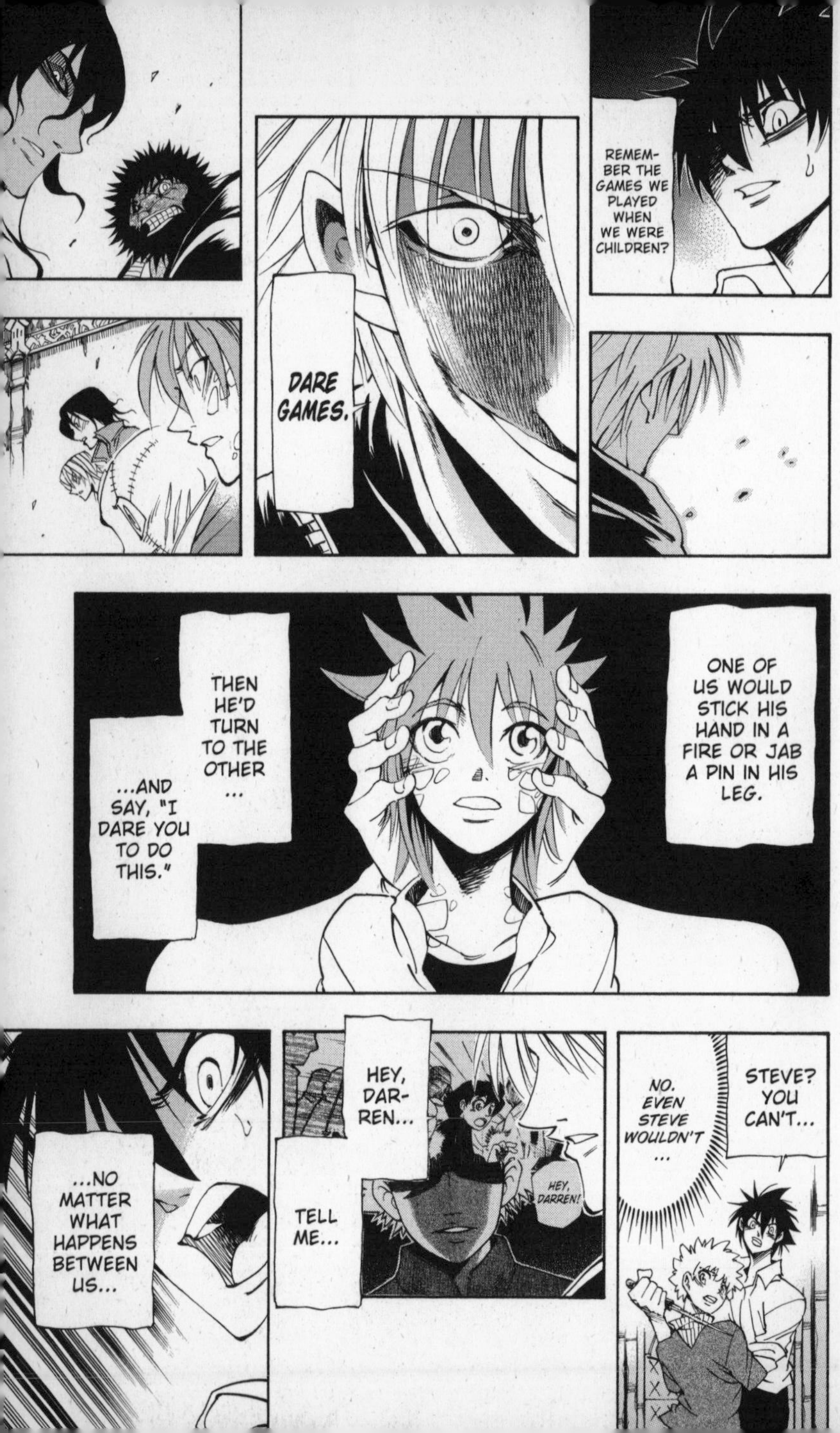
REMEMBER THE GAMES WE PLAYED WHEN WE WERE CHILDREN?
DARE GAMES.
ONE OF US WOULD STICK HIS HAND IN A FIRE OR JAB A PIN IN HIS LEG.
THEN HE'D TURN TO THE OTHER ...
...AND SAY, "I DARE YOU TO DO THIS."
STEVE? YOU CAN'T...
NO. EVEN STEVE WOULDN'T ...
HEY, DARREN...
HEY, DARREN!
TELL ME...
...NO MATTER WHAT HAPPENS BETWEEN US...

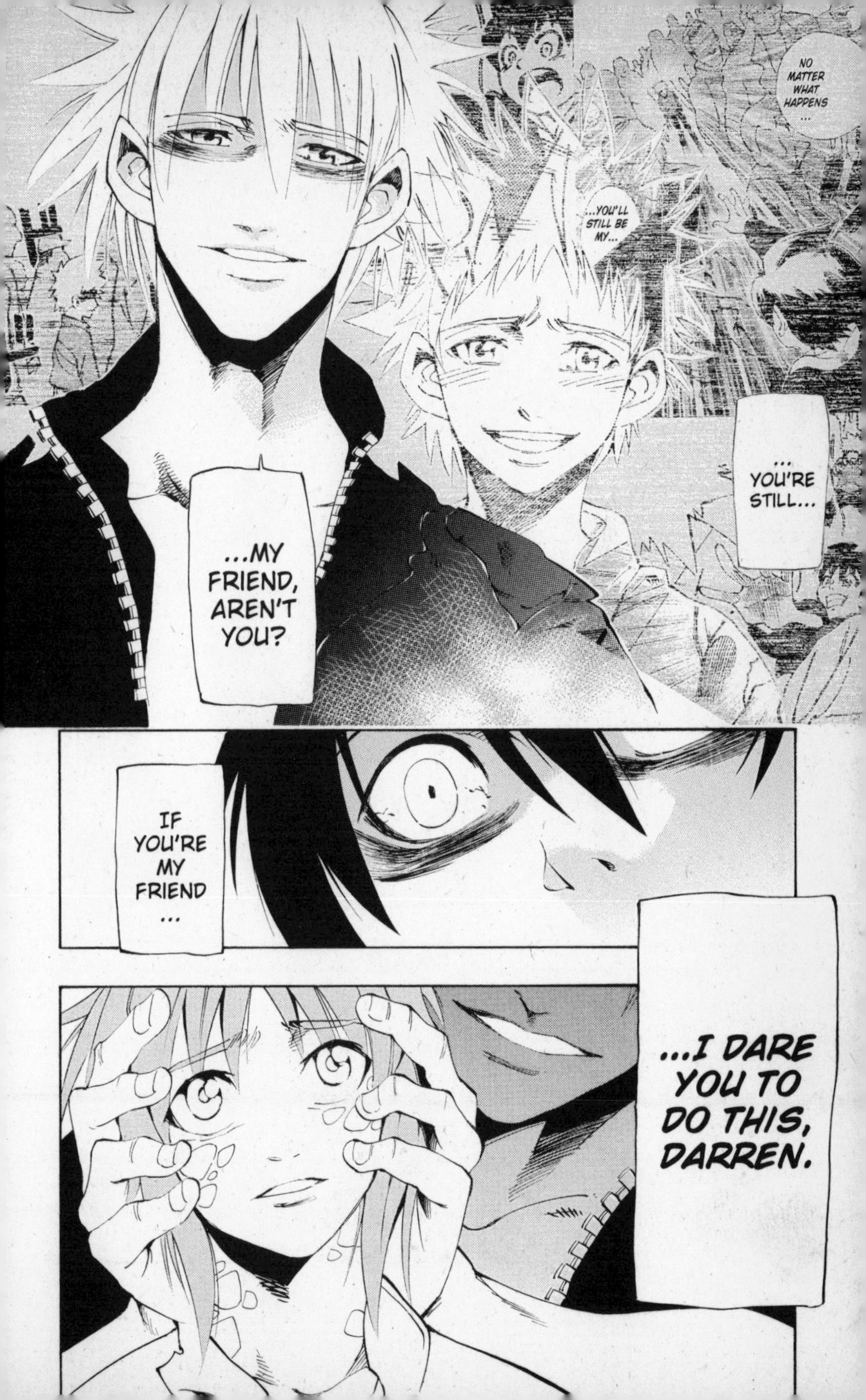
NO MATTER WHAT HAPPENS ...
...YOU'LL STILL BE MY...
... YOU'RE STILL...
...MY FRIEND, AREN'T YOU?
IF YOU'RE MY FRIEND ...
...I DARE YOU TO DO THIS, DARREN.

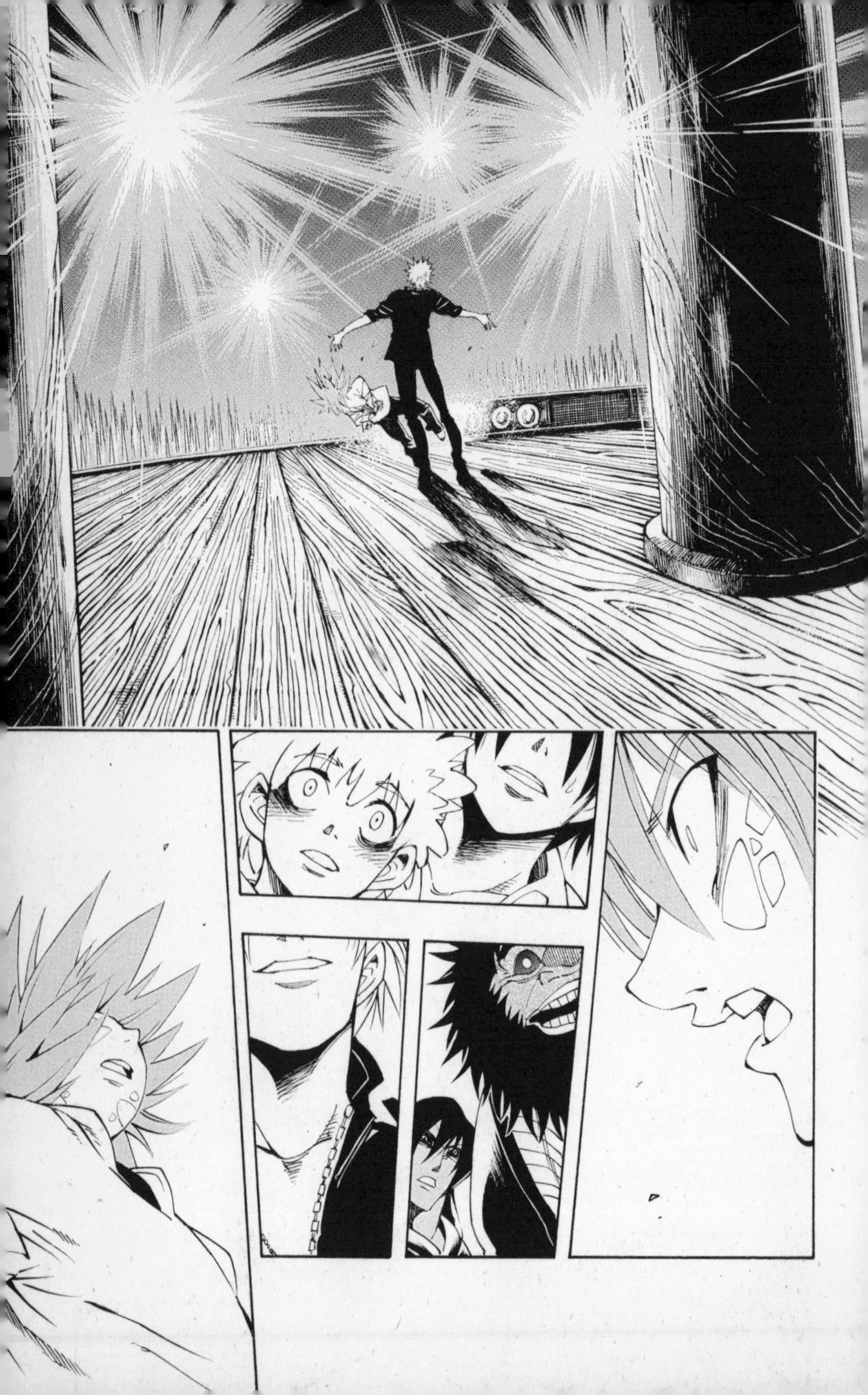

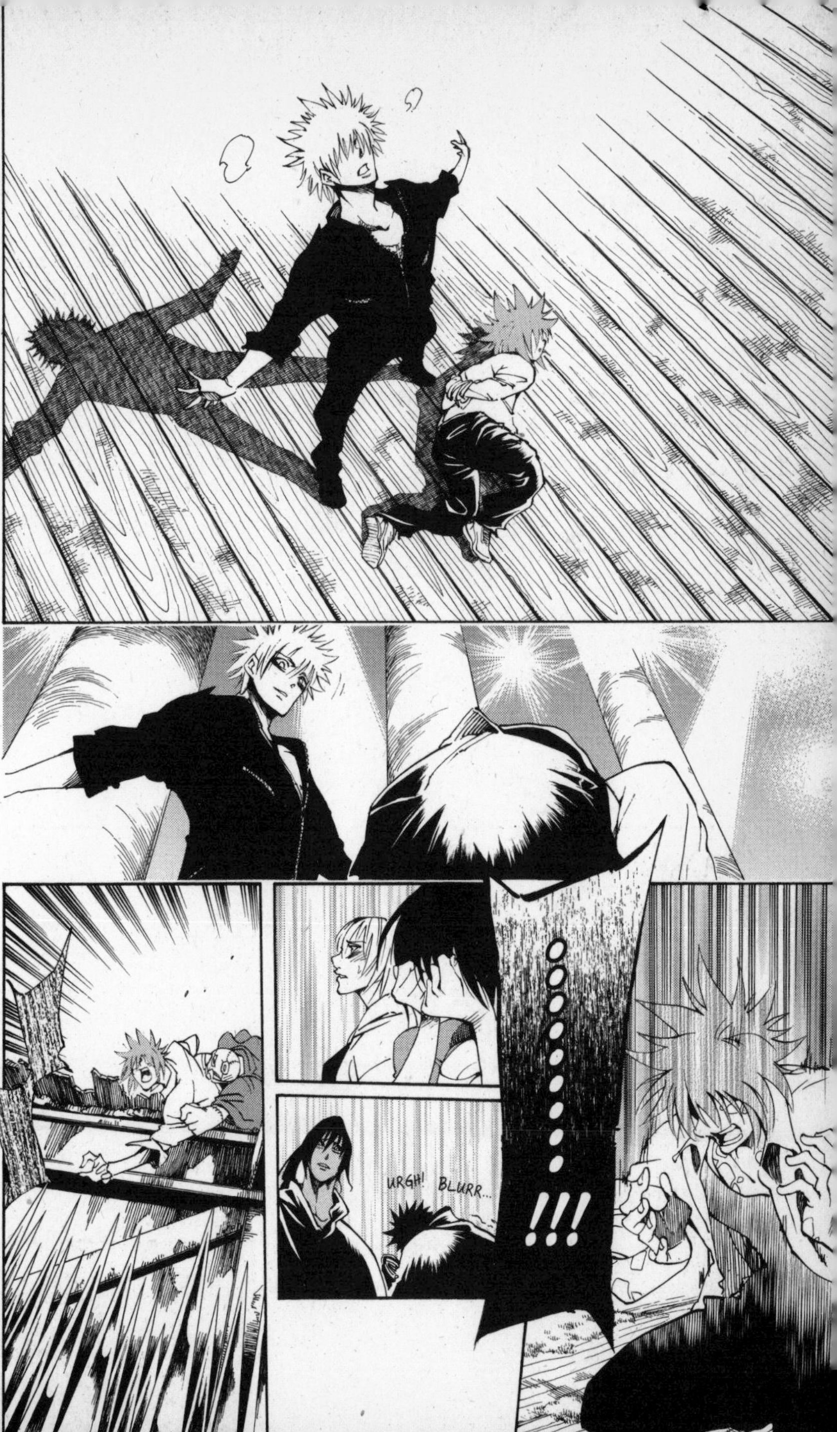
!!!
URGH! BLURR...

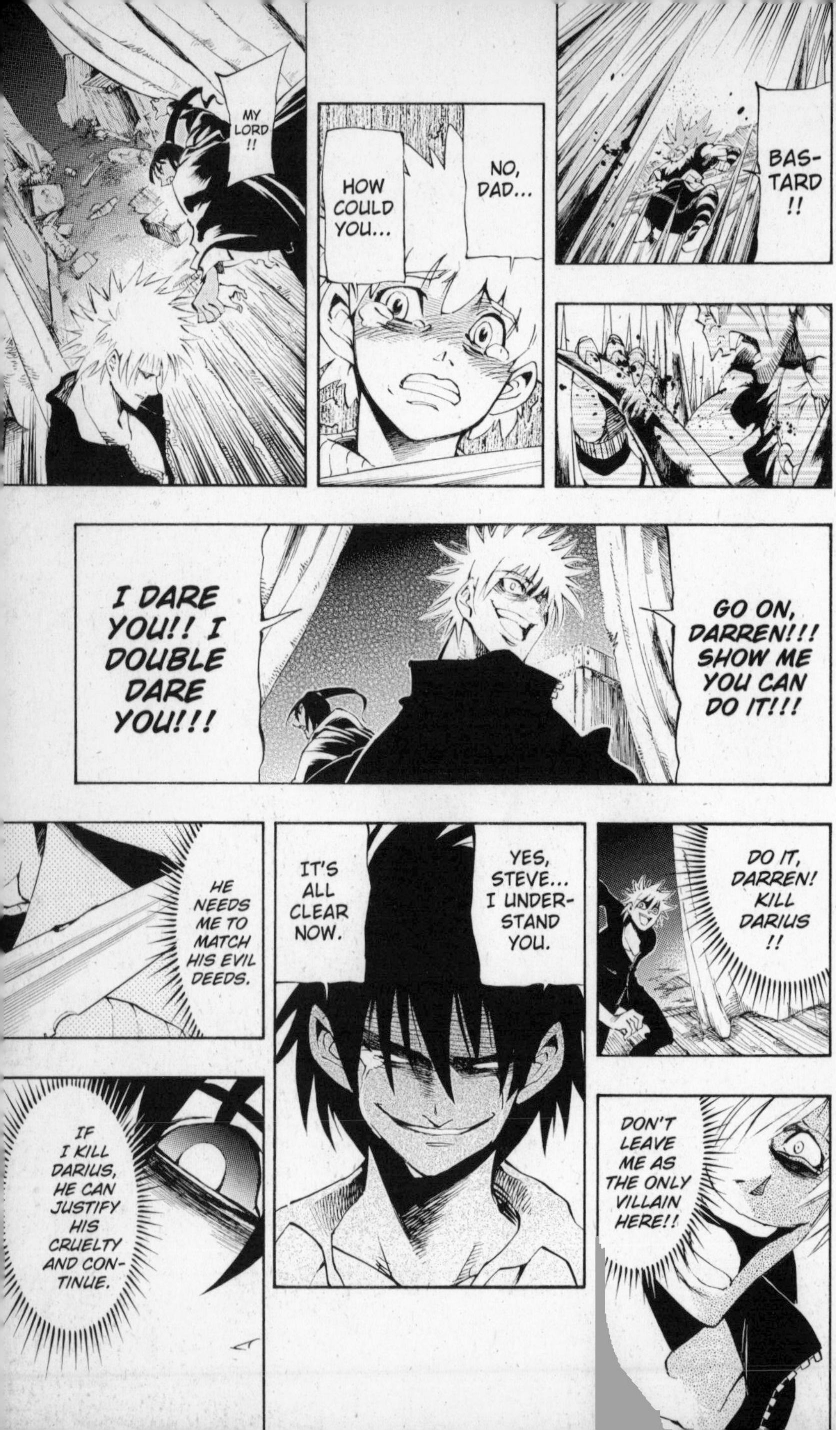
BASTARD!!
NO, DAD...
HOW COULD YOU...
MY LORD!!
GO ON, DARREN!!! SHOW ME YOU CAN DO IT!!!
I DARE YOU!! I DOUBLE DARE YOU!!!
DO IT, DARREN! KILL DARIUS!!
DON'T LEAVE ME AS THE ONLY VILLAIN HERE!!
YES, STEVE... I UNDERSTAND YOU.
IT'S ALL CLEAR NOW.
HE NEEDS ME TO MATCH HIS EVIL DEEDS.
IF I KILL DARIUS, HE CAN JUSTIFY HIS CRUELTY AND CONTINUE.

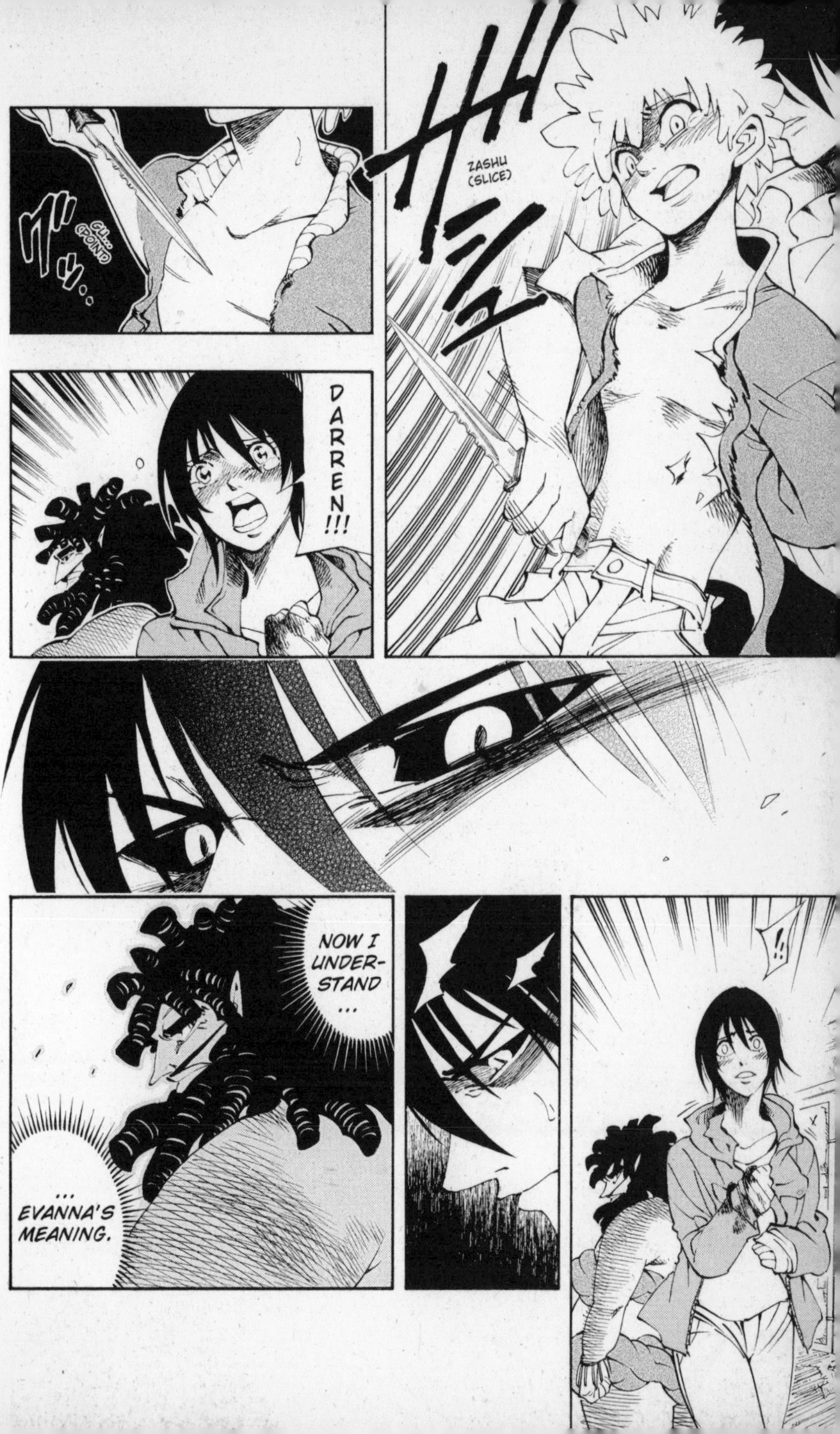
ZASHU (SLICE)
GU... (POING)
DARREN!!!
!!
NOW I UNDERSTAND...
... EVANNA'S MEANING.

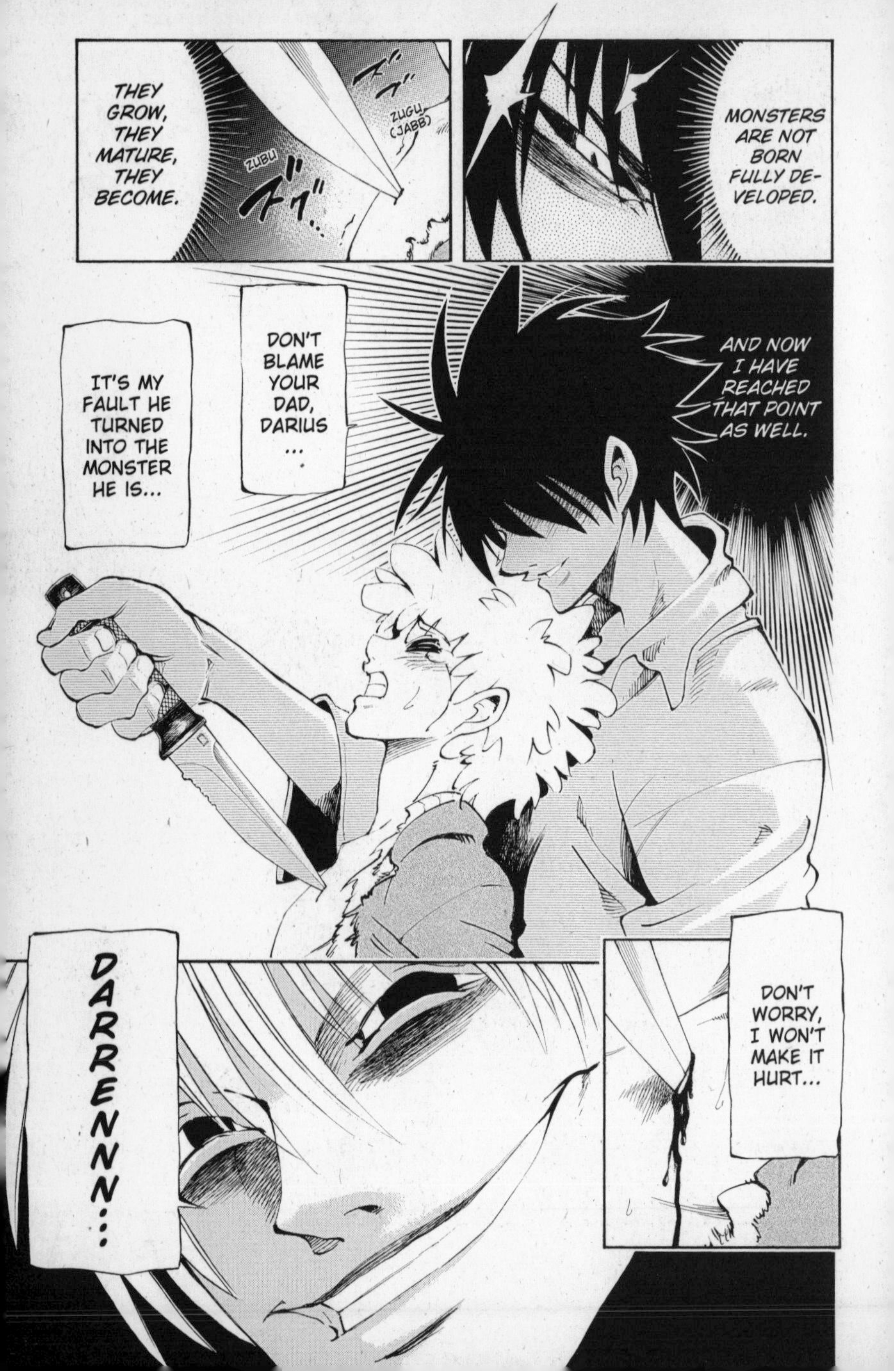
MONSTERS ARE NOT BORN FULLY DE-VELOPED.
ZUGU (JABB)
ZUBU
THEY GROW, THEY MATURE, THEY BECOME.
AND NOW I HAVE REACHED THAT POINT AS WELL.
DON'T BLAME YOUR DAD, DARIUS...
IT'S MY FAULT HE TURNED INTO THE MONSTER HE IS...
DON'T WORRY, I WON'T MAKE IT HURT...
DARRENNN...

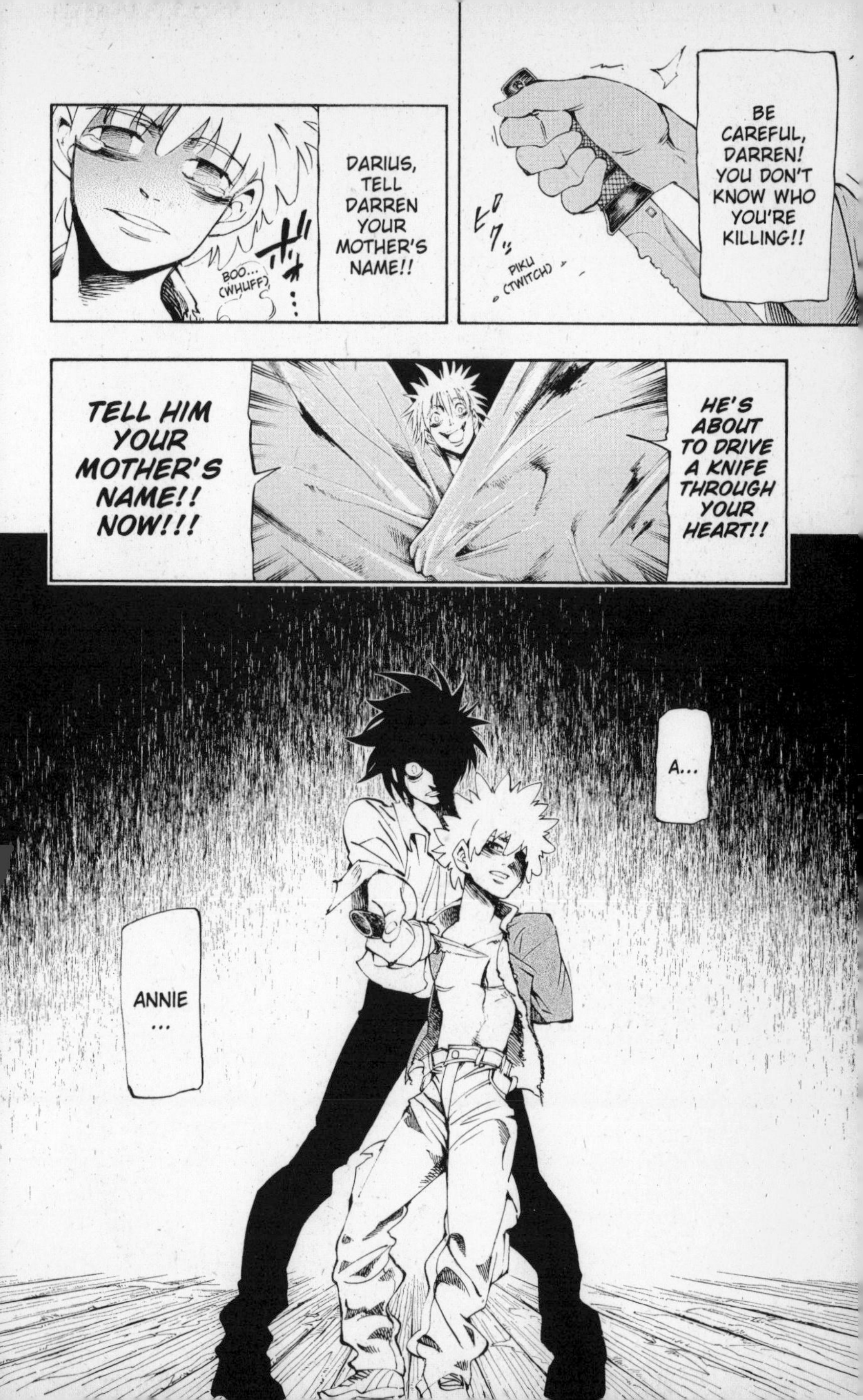
BE CAREFUL, DARREN! YOU DON'T KNOW WHO YOU'RE KILLING!!
PIKU (TWITCH)
DARIUS, TELL DARREN YOUR MOTHER'S NAME!!
BOO... (WHUFF)
HE'S ABOUT TO DRIVE A KNIFE THROUGH YOUR HEART!!
TELL HIM YOUR MOTHER'S NAME!! NOW!!!
A...
ANNIE ...

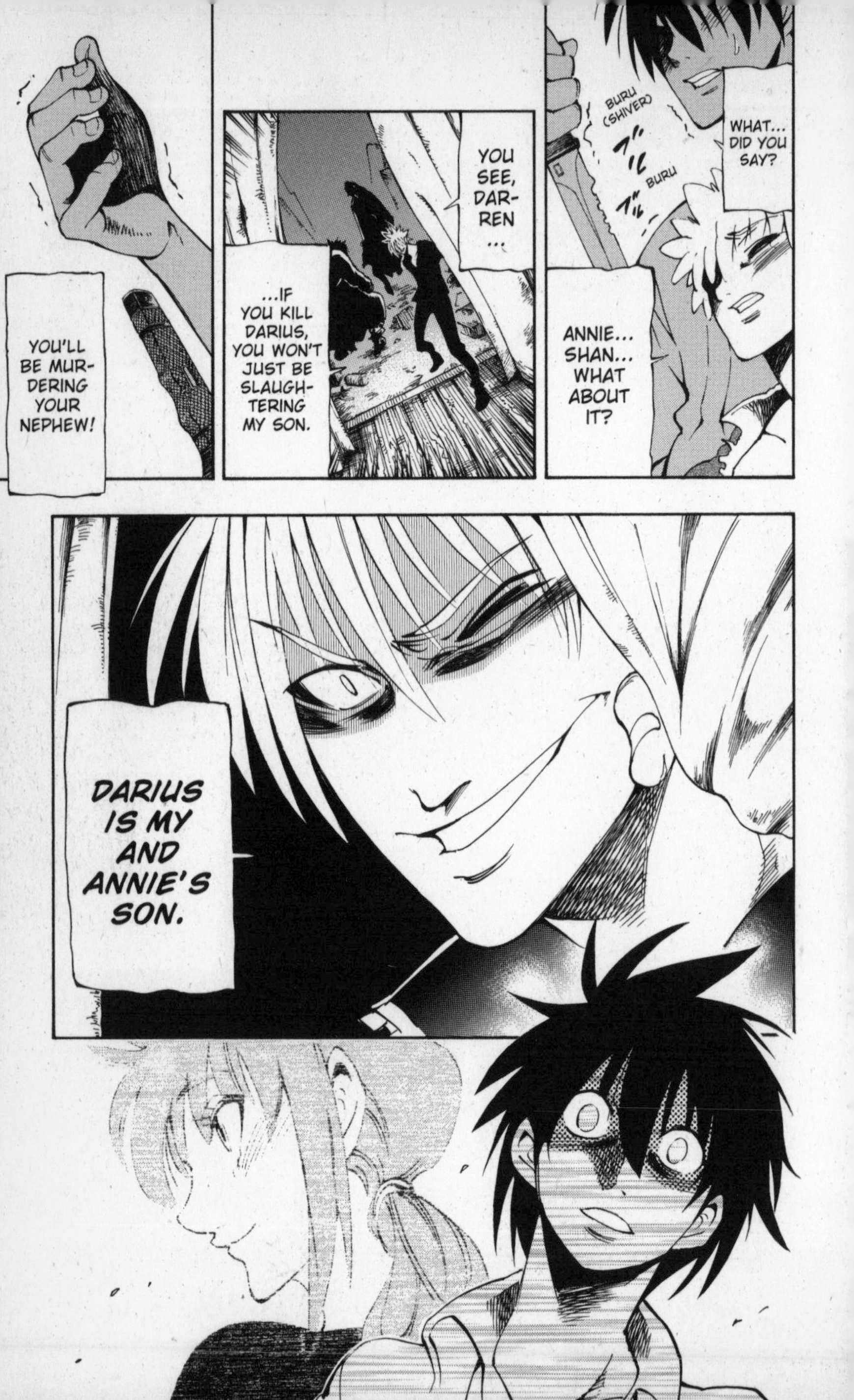
WHAT... DID YOU SAY?
BURU (SHIVER)
ブル
BURU
ブル
ANNIE... SHAN... WHAT ABOUT IT?
YOU SEE, DARREN...
...IF YOU KILL DARIUS, YOU WON'T JUST BE SLAUGHTERING MY SON.
YOU'LL BE MURDERING YOUR NEPHEW!
DARIUS IS MY AND ANNIE'S SON.

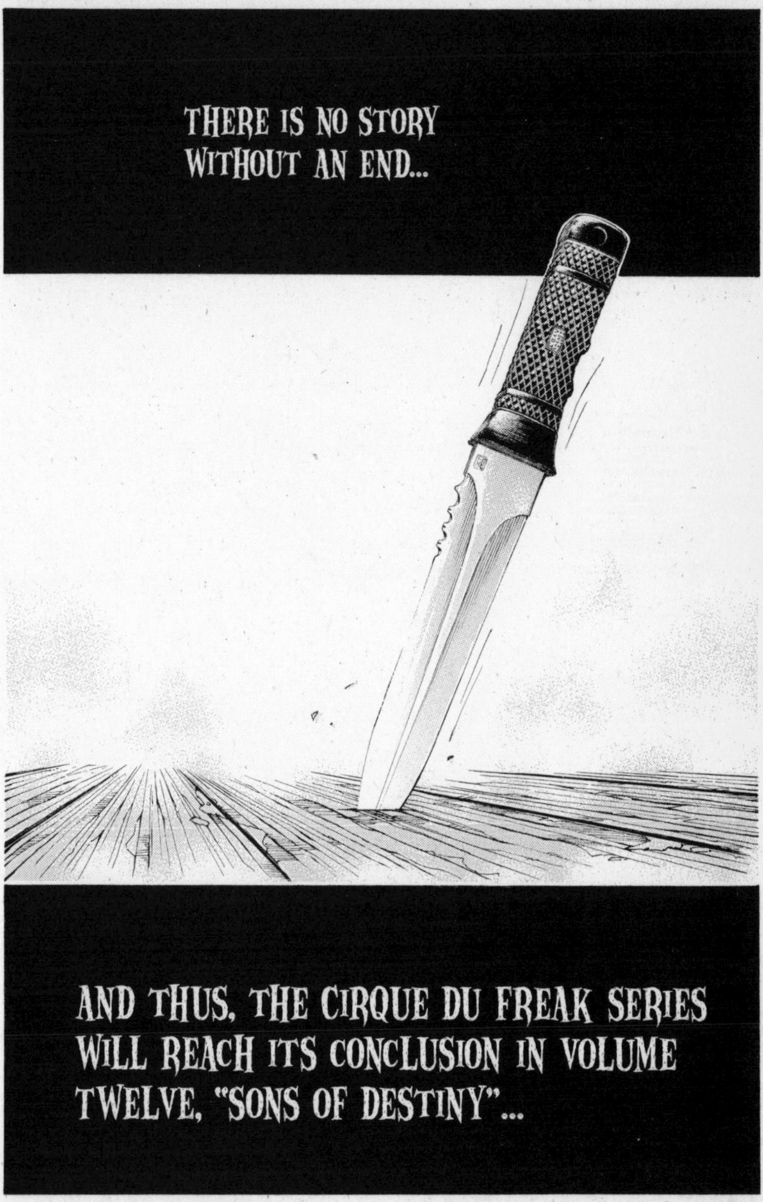
THERE IS NO STORY WITHOUT AN END...
AND THUS, THE CIRQUE DU FREAK SERIES WILL REACH ITS CONCLUSION IN VOLUME TWELVE, "SONS OF DESTINY"...

CIRQUE DU FREAK 11 · END

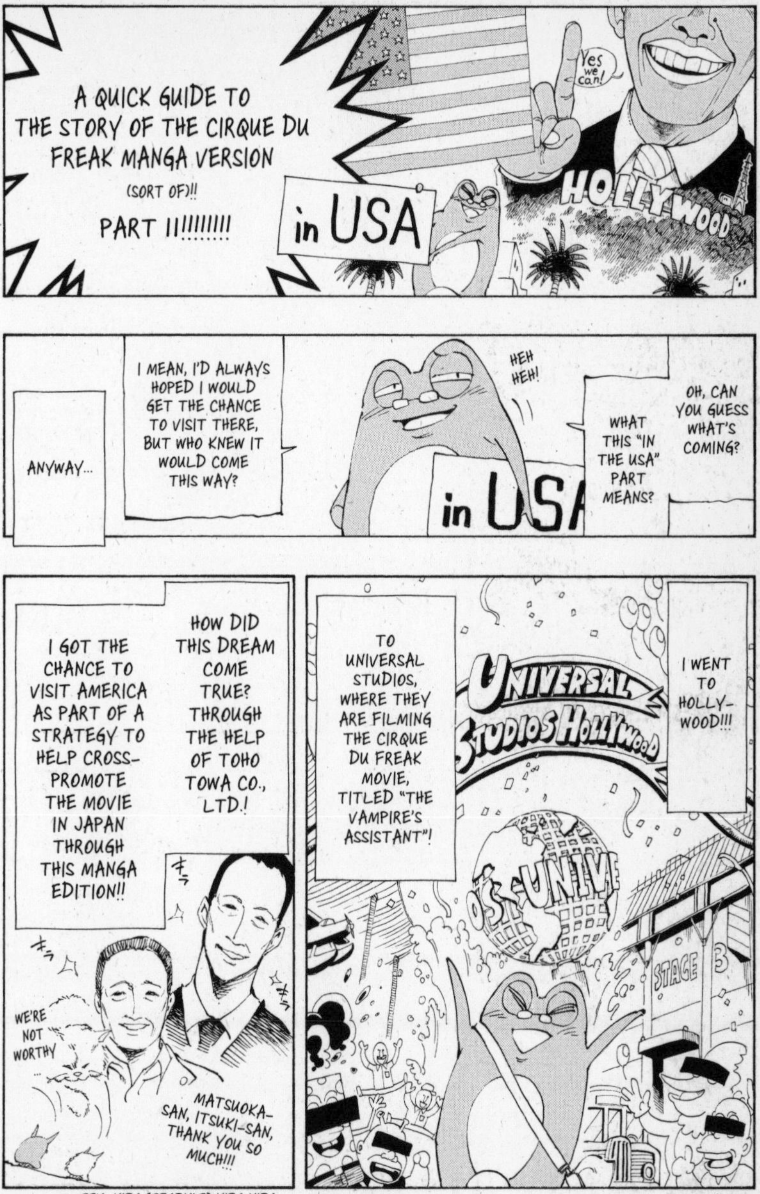
Yes we can!
HOLLYWOOD
A QUICK GUIDE TO THE STORY OF THE CIRQUE DU FREAK MANGA VERSION
(SORT OF)!!
PART II!!!!!!!!!
in USA
OH, CAN YOU GUESS WHAT'S COMING?
WHAT THIS "IN THE USA" PART MEANS?
HEH HEH!
in USA
I MEAN, I'D ALWAYS HOPED I WOULD GET THE CHANCE TO VISIT THERE, BUT WHO KNEW IT WOULD COME THIS WAY?
ANYWAY...
I WENT TO HOLLY-WOOD!!!
UNIVERSAL STUDIOS HOLLYWOOD
TO UNIVERSAL STUDIOS, WHERE THEY ARE FILMING THE CIRQUE DU FREAK MOVIE, TITLED "THE VAMPIRE'S ASSISTANT"!
STAGE 3
HOW DID THIS DREAM COME TRUE? THROUGH THE HELP OF TOHO TOWA CO., LTD.!
I GOT THE CHANCE TO VISIT AMERICA AS PART OF A STRATEGY TO HELP CROSS-PROMOTE THE MOVIE IN JAPAN THROUGH THIS MANGA EDITION!!
WE'RE NOT WORTHY ...
MATSUOKA-SAN, ITSUKI-SAN, THANK YOU SO MUCH!!!

SFX: KIRA (SPARKLE) KIRA KIRA

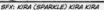

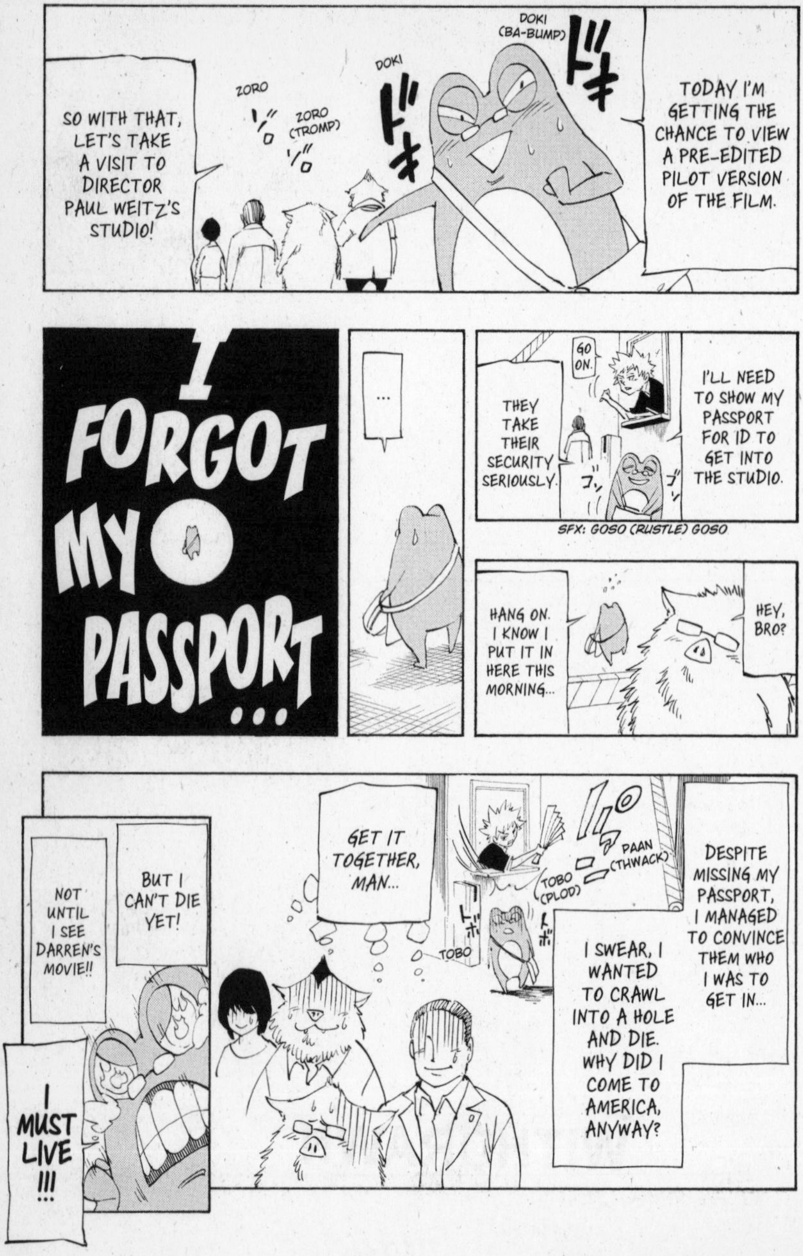
TODAY I'M GETTING THE CHANCE TO VIEW A PRE-EDITED PILOT VERSION OF THE FILM.
DOKI (BA-BUMP)
DOKI
ZORO (TROMP)
ZORO
SO WITH THAT, LET'S TAKE A VISIT TO DIRECTOR PAUL WEITZ'S STUDIO!
I'LL NEED TO SHOW MY PASSPORT FOR ID TO GET INTO THE STUDIO.
GO ON.
THEY TAKE THEIR SECURITY SERIOUSLY.
SFX: GOSO (RUSTLE) GOSO
HEY, BRO?
HANG ON. I KNOW I PUT IT IN HERE THIS MORNING...
...
I FORGOT MY PASSPORT...
DESPITE MISSING MY PASSPORT, I MANAGED TO CONVINCE THEM WHO I WAS TO GET IN...
PAAN (THWACK)
TOBO (PLOD)
TOBO
I SWEAR, I WANTED TO CRAWL INTO A HOLE AND DIE. WHY DID I COME TO AMERICA, ANYWAY?
GET IT TOGETHER, MAN...
BUT I CAN'T DIE YET!
NOT UNTIL I SEE DARREN'S MOVIE!!
I MUST LIVE!!!...

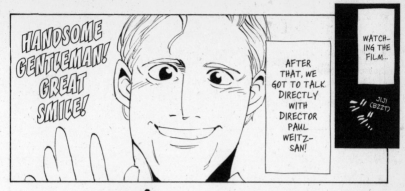

WATCHING THE FILM...
JIJI (BZZT)
AFTER THAT, WE GOT TO TALK DIRECTLY WITH DIRECTOR PAUL WEITZ-SAN!
HANDSOME GENTLEMAN! GREAT SMILE!
AND IN KEEPING WITH MY DUTY TO THE READERS!
ゴォッ
GOOO (WHOOSH)
I MADE SURE TO ASK PLENTY OF QUESTIONS!!!
THE MOVIE'S BASED ON THE FIRST THREE VOLUMES OF THE STORY.
WHEN I READ THE BOOKS, I THOUGHT MR. TALL JUST HAD TO BE KEN WATANABE!
DID YOU LIKE THE WAY WE DEPICTED FLITTING? HA HA! I LIKED THE ARTISTIC STYLING OF IT.
WE SHOT THE FILM NOT IN ENGLAND, BUT NEW ORLEANS IN AMERICA.
WE HAD THE PERFECT THEATER TO SHOOT IN THERE. THE MOLD AND DUST WAS JUST RIGHT FOR THE LOOK OF THE SCENE.
THE BOYS WHO PLAYED DARREN AND STEVE ARE SUPPOSED TO BE RIVALS, BUT THEY WERE BEST OF FRIENDS ON SET!
WILLEM DAFOE'S GAVNER WAS INCLUDED AS A TEASER FOR THE NEXT MOVIE! I HOPE I GET TO MAKE IT!

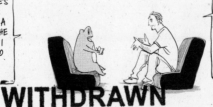

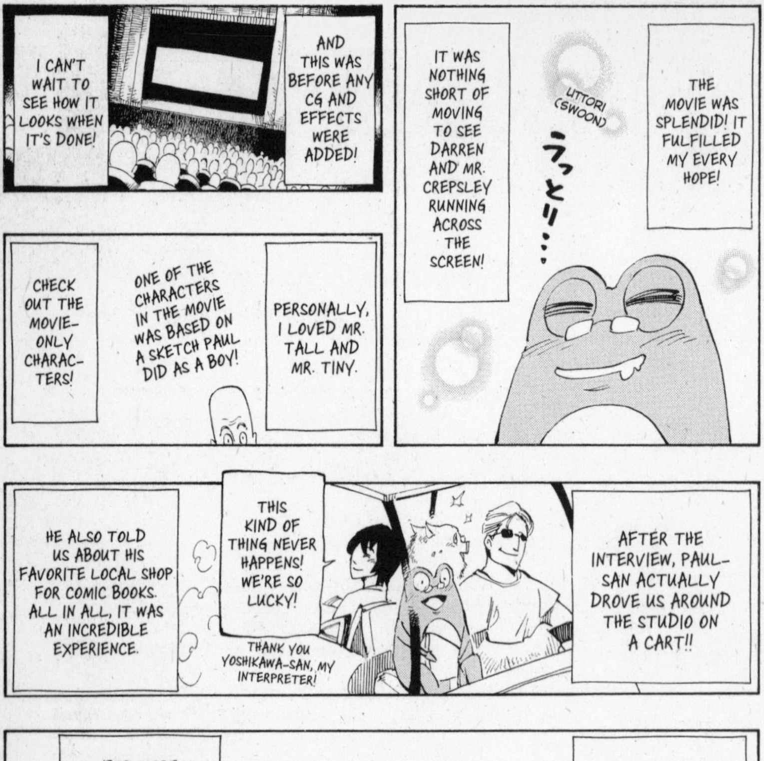

THE MOVIE WAS SPLENDID! IT FULFILLED MY EVERY HOPE!
UTTORI (SWOON)
うっとり…
IT WAS NOTHING SHORT OF MOVING TO SEE DARREN AND MR. CREPSLEY RUNNING ACROSS THE SCREEN!
AND THIS WAS BEFORE ANY CG AND EFFECTS WERE ADDED!
I CAN'T WAIT TO SEE HOW IT LOOKS WHEN IT'S DONE!
PERSONALLY, I LOVED MR. TALL AND MR. TINY.
ONE OF THE CHARACTERS IN THE MOVIE WAS BASED ON A SKETCH PAUL DID AS A BOY!
CHECK OUT THE MOVIE-ONLY CHARACTERS!
AFTER THE INTERVIEW, PAUL-SAN ACTUALLY DROVE US AROUND THE STUDIO ON A CART!!
THIS KIND OF THING NEVER HAPPENS! WE'RE SO LUCKY!
THANK YOU YOSHIKAWA-SAN, MY INTERPRETER!
HE ALSO TOLD US ABOUT HIS FAVORITE LOCAL SHOP FOR COMIC BOOKS. ALL IN ALL, IT WAS AN INCREDIBLE EXPERIENCE.
THE CIRQUE DU FREAK MOVIE HIT JAPAN IN 2009! BUT YOU CAN CHECK OUT THE DVD IN STORES NOW!!
CIRQUE DU FREAK
FOR MORE DETAILS ON THE MOVIE, CHECK OUT RECENT ISSUES OF SHONEN SUNDAY, WHERE YOU'LL FIND SOME MINI TRIP REPORT CARTOONS FROM ME. (JAPAN ONLY)
SEE YOU NEXT TIME!!!

THE END

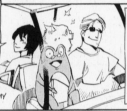

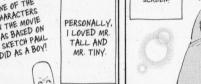

# CIRQUE DU FREAK ⑪

## DARREN SHAN
### TAKAHIRO ARAI

Translation: Stephen Paul　　•　　Lettering: AndWorld Design
Art Direction: Hitoshi SHIRAYAMA
Original Cover Design: Shigeru ANZAI + Bay Bridge Studio

---

DARREN SHAN Vol. 11 © 2009 by Darren Shan, Takahiro ARAI. All rights reserved. Original Japanese edition published in Japan in 2009 by Shogakukan Inc., Tokyo. Artworks reproduction rights in U.S.A. and Canada arranged with Shogakukan Inc. through Tuttle-Mori Agency, Inc., Tokyo.

English translation © 2011 Darren Shan

Yen Press
Hachette Book Group
237 Park Avenue, New York, NY 10017

www.HachetteBookGroup.com
www.YenPress.com

Yen Press is an imprint of Hachette Book Group, Inc. The Yen Press name and logo are trademarks of Hachette Book Group, Inc.

First Yen Press Edition: October 2011

ISBN: 978-0-316-18284-3

10  9  8  7  6  5  4  3  2  1

BVG

Printed in the United States of America